The Husband Tree

MARY CONNEALY

The
Husband
Tree

BARBOUR
PUBLISHING

OTHER BOOKS BY MARY CONNEALY

Montana Marriages series:
Montana Rose

Lassoed in Texas series:
Petticoat Ranch
Calico Canyon
Gingham Mountain

Alaska Brides (a romance collection)
Cowboy Christmas

DEDICATION

My sister-in-law Patricia Crouch Connealy was as much fun to talk books with as anyone I've known. And she was such an encouragement to me when I'd talk writing with her.

We lost her very suddenly last year and I'm still shocked that she's gone. A funny, sweet, kind, brilliant, knitting, reading friend. Our whole family is less because she's gone. I miss you, Pat.

CHAPTER 1

Montana Territory, 1876

Belle Tanner pitched dirt right on Anthony's handsome, worthless face.

It was spitefulness that made her enjoy doing that. But she was sorely afraid Anthony Santoni's square jaw and curly, dark hair had tricked her into agreeing to marry him.

Which made her as big an idiot as Anthony.

Now he was dead and she was left to dig the grave. Why, oh why didn't she just skip marrying him and save herself all this shoveling?

She probably should have wrapped him in a blanket, but blankets were hard to come by in Montana. . .unlike husbands.

She labored on with her filling, not bothering to look down again at the man who had shared her cabin and her bed for the last two years. She only hoped when she finished she didn't forget where she'd buried Anthony's no-account hide. She regretted not marking William's and Gerald's graves now for fear she'd dig in the same spot and uncover their bones. As she recalled, she'd planted William on the side nearest the house, thinking it had a nice view down the hill over their property. She wasn't so sure about Gerald, but she'd most likely picked right, for she'd dug the hole and hadn't hit bones. Unless critters had dug Gerald up and dragged him away.

Belle had to admit she didn't dig one inch deeper than was absolutely necessary. Maybe a little *less* than was necessary. This was rocky ground. It was quite a chore. Her husbands had made too many chores for her over the years. Digging their graves was the least of it.

She'd risked her own life to drag her first husband, William, out of the cattle pen. The pen any fool would know was too dangerous to go into—which Belle always did, not being a fool. Rudolph, their longhorn bull, was a mite cantankerous and given to using his eight-foot spread of horns to prove himself in charge of any situation.

Then Gerald had gotten himself thrown from his horse. His boot had slipped through the stirrup, and judging by his condition, Belle figured he'd been dragged for the better part of the three-hour ride home from the Golden Butte Saloon in Divide by a horse whose instincts told him to head for the barn.

Anthony's only good quality was he'd managed to get himself killed quick. They'd been married less than two years. For a while there, Belle feared he'd last through pure luck. But stupid outweighed luck. Stupid'll kill a man in the West. It wasn't a forgiving place. And Anthony was purely stupid, so he didn't last all that long.

Between William and Gerald—that is between being married to 'em—Belle had changed the brand to the T Bar. Known as the Tanner Ranch from then on, it never changed, regardless of whatever Belle's last name happened to be at the time. She'd also had a real smart lawyer in Helena draw up papers for Anthony to sign so the ranch would always belong to Belle, and if something happened to her instead of a worthless husband, Belle's wishes would be carried out.

She tamped the dirt down good and solid. About the fifth tamp, she admitted she was using more energy than was strictly necessary. She'd whacked it down especially tight over Anthony's pretty-boy face.

Three sides of the Husband Tree used up. She wasn't up to puttin' up with a live one or buryin' another dead one. The tree roots wouldn't appreciate it.

And neither would the children.

She said a quick prayer for Anthony, reflecting silently as she spoke, that knowing Anthony as she did, it was doubtful there were enough prayers in the world to save his warped soul. Never had it been necessary for God to perform a greater miracle, and Belle asked for just that, though she didn't hold out much hope.

She finished the service in one minute flat, not counting the digging and filling, which had taken considerably longer. It had been early in the day when she'd found Anthony dead beside the house. Planting him had interrupted chores, but there was no help for it. She couldn't leave him lying there. He was blocking the front door.

She nodded to the children, four of 'em, one from each husband, and a spare thanks to William. "We got chores."

"Why'd you marry him anyway, Ma?" Lindsay bounced the baby on her hip. They were a study, those two. Lindsay so blond, the baby so dark.

"Not a lick of sense, that's all." Belle had no desire to fancy this up. She'd been pure stupid to get married, and her girls needed to know that.

"Well, have you learnt your lesson?" Sarah plunked her little fists on her hips and arched her bright red eyebrows at Belle.

"It's a humbling thing just how well I've learned it, Sarah. There will never be another husband on this ranch. You have my word."

"The folks in town'll be out here tryin' to push themselves off onto you." Lindsay probably had a few faint memories of how Belle had ended up hitched to Gerald. The girl had made it clear long before Anthony died that when this one croaked, there'd better not be any more of 'em.

"I'll take the shovel, Ma. I need it to clear out the dam. Dirt's backed up on the canal you built to water the garden." Twelve-year-old Emma pulled her Stetson low over her eyes. She'd removed it for the funeral prayer, though Belle hadn't thought to require it.

Handing over the shovel, Emma grabbed it and headed downhill. The other girls turned from the grave and headed for the house. Fifteen-year-old Lindsay carried the baby, Elizabeth, born this spring not long after branding and not old enough yet to walk.

Thank You, dear Lord God, for letting Betsy be a girl. Thank You for all my girls. What would I have done with a boy child?

Eight-year-old Sarah fell in line next.

Belle watched them walk ahead of her. Each of them the image of her pa.

Lindsay and Emma had wispy, white blond hair, bright blue eyes, and skin that burned to a reddish tan from their long hours in the sun. Lindsay'd grown taller than Belle these days, and Emma now looked Belle straight in the eye. William had been a tall one, and as blond as most Swedes.

Sarah had a shock of unruly red curls, eyes as green as grass, and a sprinkling of freckles across her nose from her Irish pa, Gerald O'Rourke.

The baby, Elizabeth, whom they called Betsy, was a beautiful little girl. Belle almost had a moment of affection for Anthony Santoni. Betsy's cap of midnight black hair fell into soft, natural ringlet curls. The dark brown eyes were rimmed with abundant lashes, and her skin had seemed tanned from birth. The little girl was the image of Anthony.

Belle lifted her own straight brown hair, "the color of chocolate" her pa used to say, and thought of her odd light brown eyes—like it would have killed one of the little tykes to take after her just a smidgen. And she had no nationality to speak of either. Her family had been in the country a hundred years before the Revolution, and they'd all been busy for generations being Americans. Who had the time to study ancestors?

"We've been over this now, Ma!" Lindsay hollered to make sure Belle heard. "No more husbands, never."

"Don't waste time fussing at me, Linds. Those men have caused me a sight more trouble than they've caused you. I'm not gonna tell anyone in town Anthony is dead." They'd notice when he didn't show up at the Golden Butte to visit one of the girls. But missing him didn't mean they knew anything. Maybe they'd think he'd quit being a lying, cheating, lazy, no-account man and he was busy. Running the ranch.

It took all she had not to snort out loud at the very idea.

Belle didn't mention the Golden Butte to the girls. She never took them to town, and she didn't think they knew exactly what Betsy's low-down pa did while he was away from the ranch. Probably figured him for a drinker like Gerald.

The four girls were strung out before her, heading downhill. What a pretty bunch they were. Belle dreaded the trouble that could come to a pretty girl.

Pretty didn't matter anyway. Heaven knew that with her weathered skin and calloused hands and straight-as-a-string hair, she was nothing great to look at. The men who came a-runnin' every time she was widowed said pretty words about her appearance. But women were scarce in Montana. And a fertile mountain valley like the Tanner spread was even scarcer. The two-legged varmints would have been out here trying to turn her head with flattery if she looked like the north end of a southbound mule.

Growing up pretty—and who could judge a thing like that as

there wasn't a mirror for a thousand miles—was only a nuisance in her way of thinking. With all the water rights sewed up for over twenty thousand acres, Belle didn't kid herself that her looks brought the men sniffin' around.

Lindsay reached the bottom of the hill.

Sarah sped up to catch her and snagged Betsy out of Lindsay's arms, then angled toward the house. "I'll watch the baby and get the noon meal on, Ma." Just as she went in the door, Sarah glanced back at Belle and said matter-of-factly, "Now that Anthony fell off the roof, can I toss a couple less taters into the pot?"

Belle nodded. "He ate about three."

"We gonna save money on food now that he's dead." Emma tucked the shovel under one arm while she walked, snagged her buckskin gloves from where she'd tucked them behind her belt buckle, and began tugging them on.

Sarah went into the house.

Without comment, Lindsay and Emma headed for the barn.

Belle smiled with pride at her girls. They did take after her in one important way. The girls knew how to work. Belle hadn't been able to marry any help, but she'd sure as shootin' given birth to it.

By the time Belle quit standing around feeling proud over her girls and relieved over Anthony, Emma already had her horse caught. She rode out to work the dam, the shovel they'd used to plant Anthony strapped onto her saddle. Lindsay had disappeared into the chicken coop to fetch eggs.

Belle went into the barn, snagged her flat-topped black Stetson from a peg, and settled it onto her head. She shrugged into the fringed buckskin jacket she'd made from a mule-deer hide. Then she strapped on a six-gun in case she met any varmints on the trail, or worse yet, men come a-courtin'—those two being equal in her mind.

Rounding up one of her green-broke horses, Belle thought with pride of the well-trained cow ponies she'd been selling for good money the last few years. She let the young horse crow hop the kinks out with its usual good spirits, snagged her shotgun leaning on the fence, and shoved it into the sling on her saddle. Then she set out on the long ride to check her cattle. She had herds scattered near and far in her rugged mountain valley.

Lindsay headed into the barn to do the milking, carrying a bucket of eggs, just as Belle rode out of the corral. "I'm not forgettin' this time, Ma. And neither are you. You promised—no more husbands."

"A promise I intend to keep, daughter. Now quit with your scolding and get to work." Belle had known for some time now that both of her older daughters talked to her almost as if they were equals. She could still make them mind if it came right down to it. But mostly, she valued their opinions and listened when they talked, just as they listened to her. They made a good team, and it was possible her older girls already knew as much about ranching as Belle.

Lindsay held Belle's eyes for a long second. "I reckon you learned your lesson, all right. Anthony Santoni, worthless excuse for a man. What were you thinking to marry him?"

Belle shook her head. "He wasn't a worthless excuse for a man, Lindsay."

Lindsay's white blond brows arched. "He wasn't?"

"Nope, he was just a *man*. Same as any other man, leastways any I've known." Not strictly true. Seth worked hard at the general store. Red Dawson was a decent sort, what little she knew of him. Her pa hadn't been so bad; he was a hard worker, no denying it. But he'd done Belle wrong, and she lumped him in with the other men. "I thought I had to. It was never *shall* I get married. It was *who* shall I marry. Not anymore though. We all know well and good that a man just slows a woman down."

Lindsay gave Belle a firm nod and went on into the barn.

Smiling, enjoying being free of a husband—this time forever—

Belle spurred her horse and smiled as the wind blew the pesky wisps that always escaped from her tightly braided hair.

Thank You, Lord, for making me a widow.

Belle hesitated briefly, pretty sure that God wouldn't exactly welcome such a prayer. But the Lord giveth and the Lord taketh away. And he'd takethed Anthony, praise be. Who was she to complain?

It was great to be a widow.

Now if she could just stay one!

❦

New Mexico Territory

"Silas!" Lulamae Tool came to the door of the livery stable, caterwaulin' and waving her arms like she was being stung to death by bees. "Help me!" Her fearful eyes met his. "Help me please, Silas."

Silas Harden dropped his hand from the saddle horn of the buckskin he was about to mount and turned to the pretty girl with the scared eyes. "What's the matter?" He strode toward her. He'd talked with her a few times, and she was a dim critter. Who knew what little thing had made her kick up this ruckus?

She whirled and nearly ran back toward the livery. "My horse!" She glanced over her shoulder, oozing with gratitude. "Something's wrong with him, and Dutch isn't here."

With Dutch the hostler gone, it was up to Silas to save the day. He felt big and strong and in charge as he picked up his pace. He caught up with Lulamae as she dashed inside.

She grabbed his arm as if she were so upset she needed him to lean on, sweet little thing.

They rounded the row of stalls, and Lulamae skidded to a stop and jumped in front of him. She launched herself into his arms and kissed him.

Silas wasn't thinking straight, or he was caught up in his notion of a damsel in distress maybe, but all he did was enjoy the moment. The woman could kiss like a house afire. In fact, he threw in with the idea and kissed her back with plenty of enthusiasm.

A shotgun blasted.

"You've ruined my daughter!"

Silas turned toward the noise. Lulamae clung like a burr, and he dragged her with him as he whirled to face the gunfire.

Hank Tool charged inside. Lulamae's father'd been yelling before he'd even seen them. Behind him came the banker along with Dutch, who owned this livery.

Hank snapped more shells into his shotgun and aimed straight at Silas's heart.

Shrieking and crying, Lulamae said, "But you promised to marry me, Silas!" Lulamae dropped to the ground, crying and clinging to his ankles.

It didn't escape Silas's notice that now Hank had a clear shot right at his heart. Silas raised his hands skyward; his head was spinning too hard for any clear thought, with the crying and primed gun and Hank's steady, deadly threats.

Things came clear when he heard Hank Tool say, "March yourself right on over to the preacher. You're doing right by my girl."

Silas figured it out then. "Hank, I just walked in here to help Lulamae with her horse. She grabbed me. We've been in here less than a minute. Nothing happened."

"You're not gonna shame Lulamae and my family and live."

Then Silas figured out two more things: Hank knew exactly what Lulamae had done, and the look on Hank's face was determined and killing mean.

Well, Silas knew he was stupid, and no mistake. He'd gotten himself good and trapped, and now he could marry Lulamae or die, because whatever kind of lying, sneaking polecat Hank Tool was, his hand was steady on that trigger and his eyes meant business.

Silas shook his head.

Hank leveled his shotgun. Dutch and the banker bought into the game with their sidearms.

"Looks like we're having ourselves a wedding." Silas marched forward.

Lulamae sprang to her feet and latched onto Silas's arm and gave him such a smug, satisfied smile, it was all Silas could do not to shake her off. Not such a sweet little thing after all. And Silas would be switched if he'd marry the little sneak. But right now he didn't have a notion of a way out as they headed for the church.

"Put your hands down, you coyote. You're only adding to the shame you've caused my daughter by walking through town, letting all and sundry know you aren't marrying her willingly."

"I think the shotgun is enough of a clue, Hank." But Silas lowered his hands even as he knew that was the *last* order he planned to obey from Hank Tool.

Dutch ran for the preacher, and by the time they got to the church, both men were standing out front, frowning at Silas. The version of the story Dutch had told had put the holy man firmly on the Tools' side.

The gun nearly jabbed through Silas's buckskin coat as they went inside and up to the front of the church. He expected to look later and find a hole worn into the leather and on past his shirt from the prodding of Hank Tool's fire iron.

"Dearly beloved. . ."

Silas ignored the preacher and looked sideways at Lulamae and knew, even if he ended up with his backside full of buckshot, he'd be glad for the scars to remind him of what a fool a man can be over a pretty gal. Outwardly, Lulamae was everything a man could want—pretty as a rising sun on a cool spring morning, sweet-talking as a meadowlark perched in a willow tree, fair-smelling as the first rose of summer.

"We're gonna be so happy, Silas." Lulamae smiled. "Aren't we?"

Silas's skin crawled. He didn't answer.

Hank jabbed Silas with the gun and answered for him. "Sure you will be, honey."

The preacher arched an eyebrow at the interruption and looked back at his prayer book.

Silas was glad the preacher glared them into silence, because "Yes sirree, we sure are gonna be happy" weren't words that were capable of escaping from Silas's lips.

Because, besides being a pretty little thing, the woman was also a sneak and a liar. Add to that, Silas had talked to her once or twice on a rare trip to town, and he'd been struck by the woman's pure stupidity. She was dumb as a post, no offense to posts, which at least did what they were put on this earth to do without any surprises.

Silas thought it over a second and reconsidered the dumb part. After all, who was standing here in front of the preacher with posies in her hand, smiling and eager to say, "I do," to one of the area's up-and-coming ranchers, and who was standing here with an angry pa poking him with his shotgun muzzle until he said, "I do," or died saying, "I don't"?

"We are gathered here today. . ."

Silas decided to pick dying over marrying Lulamae. He was going to die before he married *any* woman, no matter how fetching her sweet little hide was. He'd learned that from his ma and all her man troubles well enough. Then, when he'd decided there was a woman who would suit him and he'd proposed, she hadn't stuck when times got tough.

But he was hoping to come up with a third choice. Some middle ground between "get married or die." Which, as far as Silas was concerned, were the same thing.

"To join this man and woman in holy matrimony." The preacher closed his prayer book, and Silas's stomach took a dive. They hadn't been married while he'd been daydreaming, had they? He was more than sure he'd never said the words, "I do," but the way this day was going, maybe Hank had said them for him.

To Silas's relief, the parson droned on. An unlikely time for a sermon, but it appeared that the man dearly loved the sound of his own voice.

Lulamae smiled and batted her eyes and clung to her posies and Silas's arm. And her pa jabbed him with the long gun from time to time so Silas wouldn't forget he'd been found in a compromising position with a decent girl.

Silas much preferred the attitudes of dance-hall girls, who'd pull guns *after* they'd collected their money to make men go away.

Not that Silas had any kind of woman he was particularly fond of, and he avoided dance-hall girls out of respect for his faith. But any kind of woman was pure trouble when getting right down to it and best to be avoided. But they smelled good, and a man lost his head from time to time, as Silas had in the livery.

Silas thought of the way Lulamae had smiled and made him feel like she needed rescuing. Now Silas wasn't a man to dodge the truth when he'd made a mistake, and when Lulamae had gotten so generous with her affections, Silas hadn't gone running, screaming for the hills like he'd oughta. So everything that was happening to him right now was his own fault.

"Do you Lulamae Tool, take this man. . ."

The preacher quit with his preachifying and started asking for promises, and Silas knew the time had come to root hog or die. Honestly, he deserved this. He knew better than to let some calf-eyed woman near him. Silas had a normal man's weakness when sweet-talking women were involved.

Hank jabbed him again, and this time Silas wondered if his coat had been torn away and Hank had broken Silas's hide.

"Will you quit stabbing me? You might as well have a bayonet on that fire iron."

"Shut up and pay attention, Harden."

The preacher cleared his throat, glared at them both as if threatening them with eternal fire, turned aside from his vows, and did a bit more scolding, all aimed at Silas, which stung. But Silas wasn't in any position to clear things up.

"I do." Lulamae fluttered her lashes, and Silas's stomach fluttered even faster.

"Do you, Silas Harden, take this woman to be your lawfully wedded wife. . ."

Letting her kiss him like that was such a stupid thing to do, he almost deserved to end up hitched to the empty-headed little sneak.

"In sickness and in health. . ."

But no amount of guilt or prodding was going to shake "I do" loose from Silas. If he belted Hank and jilted Lulamae, he'd have to quit the country, and that rankled something fierce, because he'd just started up a nice little herd on some rugged desert grazing land that he bought for next to nothing because no one could grow a cow on that wasteland.

"For richer or poorer. . ."

He was going to be a sight poorer all right, because what Silas knew that no one else did was that back up-country, just a couple long, rugged miles on the higher slopes of the San Juan Mountains, was a beautiful valley, lush with belly-high grass and year-round water. This would be the second ranch he'd lost, and leaving it burned him bad.

"As long as you both shall live?"

He might not live all that long, considering his plans for the next few seconds.

Hank jabbed him, which Silas figured was a hint that it was time for him to say his vows.

"If so, say, 'I do.'"

The honorable thing to do would be to marry Lulamae. He'd

had the first few steps of his hoedown, and now the fiddler wanted to be paid. Except Silas'd been set up. His jaw got all tight like it did when someone pushed him hard—like Hank and Lulamae were doing.

Silas looked at the nice glass window straight ahead of him and knew he was going through with it. Or, if he wasn't as quick as he hoped, he might be leaving feet first out the main door. But before either of those things happened, he'd feed that shotgun to Hank Tool.

Silas turned to face Lulamae. He got nudged right sharp as he moved, but Hank thought he'd bagged himself a son-in-law, so he didn't pull the trigger when he should've.

Silas grabbed the shotgun and shoved the muzzle up. It went off, proving Hank was serious. Silas jerked it out of Hank's hand and dropped him with a butt stroke to his skull. Silas took two long running steps and dived through that window, knowing Hank had friends in that church and he had none.

Lulamae screamed, a sound so high-pitched it might have broken the window for him if he hadn't gotten a head start. It liked to have made his ears bleed, but mostly it just made him proud to have done the right thing.

He ran straight for the livery where his horse stood saddled and bridled outside—he'd been on his way home when Lulamae struck.

He tore the reins loose of the hitching post, grabbed the mane of his horse, vaulted onboard, and lit out, ignoring the shouts and whizzing bullets from behind, because his horse was the fastest critter in the area.

Shaking shards of glass off his shirt and trying to stop some stubborn bleeding—all at a full gallop—he hit the high country north of town and decided he'd had enough of New Mexico anyway. He left like he'd come into this miserable state fifteen years ago—with nothing.

Except he did have something. He had the sense to never get near a woman again.

He kicked his buckskin, and he got the feeling that the horse felt the same way about Lulamae that Silas did, because that horse settled into a ground-eating gallop and didn't stop until they were swallowed up into the sky-high belly of the San Juans.

CHAPTER 2

Anthony being dead changed his body temperature, but otherwise, as far as how it affected Belle, he hadn't changed much. Her summer had been the same as usual.

Until now.

She swung down off her horse, just back from a brutal two-day ride into a valley at the far end of her property that had led her to a disaster.

Betsy pulled on Belle's hair and kicked her legs, obviously happy to be home.

Striding to the house, knowing supper would be about ready to hit the table, Belle studied her tally book. Looking at it again didn't change those numbers one bit.

She had to thin the herd. And she had to do it now.

Snapping the book shut with as much violence as a woman could inflict on a pad of paper, she slid it into the breast pocket of her gingham blouse that was only slightly still tucked into her riding skirt. She'd pushed hard all day to get home.

The news she had couldn't wait. She fretted as she went to talk to the girls.

The weather was still nice, though the nights were getting sharp. Winter came early up here, but they still had time. Barely.

That part didn't worry her so much. The disaster wasn't about running out of time.

Pushing open her sagging door, she didn't waste time prettying up the bad news. "I've got trouble."

Emma and Lindsay were inside setting the table. Sarah usually kept Betsy in the house and cared for her and did all the cooking while the older girls did chores. But this time Belle had taken Betsy with her. The baby was still nursing, and Belle knew she'd be gone two full days. So Sarah'd planned to work outside more, and she must have, because her big sisters were helping inside.

All three girls turned, giving her their full attention. From their grim expressions, she knew they recognized her tone. Something bad.

"I found a whole herd of cattle I didn't know I had in that high valley."

"You knew there were some up there, Ma," Emma said.

"I thought maybe a hundred head, two hundred, three even. But I must have had cattle sneaking up there all last year. You know I didn't get up there to check in the spring or the fall before that."

"Because you were fat with Betsy last fall and feeling poorly. Then she was so little this spring you decided to skip that long trip." Lindsay's hands fisted. "I should have made the trip. I should never have let you talk me out of it."

"A young girl's got no business out on a long trail like that alone."

"Emma and I could have gone together. The two of us together are as tough as you, Ma."

Probably tougher, but Belle hadn't wanted them in danger. That valley was too close to the low pass toward Divide. If intruders came, they'd come from that direction.

23

"I'd say now that I should have let you go. I'd have had the whole summer to get this drive arranged. It's gonna be hard to find hands this late in the year."

"How many are up there?" Emma lived and breathed cattle and horses even more than Belle. The girl was already figuring.

"There were over six hundred head."

Lindsay's blond brows arched.

A hard breath escaped from Emma. "Our grass is stretched thin with the herd we've got. We were pushing our luck to make do until spring. . .and we were hoping we could use that high range."

"Well, there's no grass up there. They've eaten it to the nub and started heading down closer to the ranch. There's a healthy crop of calves that I've never branded—good, sturdy, fat stock that are over a year old, plus a nice bunch of spring calves. But they won't be fat for long."

"We don't have enough hay to fill in." Lindsay frowned. "We can't begin to sell that many head in Divide."

"We're going to have to take 'em to Helena." Belle jerked off her buckskin gloves and gripped them to keep from strangling herself. They'd lose the whole herd by spring if they didn't thin it. She'd been lazy, and now her daughters were in danger because they could lose everything. She'd let having a baby slow her down. She deserved *all* of this mess. But her girls didn't deserve it.

"Helena's the closest place with cattle buyers looking for a whole herd." Belle still hadn't told them the really awful part.

Sarah's green eyes formed perfect circles. "I've been with you up and down that trail, Ma. Can we punch five hundred head of cattle over those narrow passes?"

Up and down was right. And side to side and over rock slides and alongside cliffs. A more treacherous trail hardly existed in the whole country.

"More like a thousand, Sarah. We've got to thin this herd down here, too, because we don't have the grass we thought we had. I've got three thousand head of cattle, and we need to run a third of them to market."

Lindsay squared her shoulders. "We can manage that, Ma."

"We've got a hard week of work to do to cut out the cattle we want to drive and brand them. Some of those year-old animals in the highlands are thousand-pound longhorn bulls," Belle warned. "We'll take as many as possible from down here, just to skip as much branding as we can."

Emma gave a shrug. "We've had hard weeks before."

Belle liked the calm way her girls were reacting. She'd have done the same, except for the worst of it. That was making her edgy. "We need to get the cattle we want to sell penned into that canyon with the low pass toward Helena."

Slapping her gloves in one hand, Belle thought of that long stretch that needed fencing. Hours of backbreaking work, and Belle was no carpenter. She'd be lucky to build a fence that would hold cows. But the grass was still good in that canyon and the water plentiful. She'd kept the cattle out of there so she could move them in come winter. The cattle wouldn't take much persuading to stay put in there.

Sarah turned back to her stew. "We cleared the rocks off the pass a few years back. That's not so hard to drive the cattle that way."

It was a razor-sharp climb and twisted as a Rocky Mountain rattlesnake. But yes, they could do that.

"It's a big job, Ma." Lindsay started setting the tin plates around the table. "And the drive will be tough, but there's nothing you've told us to get worked up about. You seem pretty upset."

"I've waited till last to give you the worst of it."

All three girls turned back to face her. Even Betsy, still strapped on Belle's back, seemed to tense.

"We can't handle this drive alone, girls."

"We can do anything, Ma," Emma said defensively.

Belle shook her head. "Not this time."

"So we just give up? We let our cattle starve?"

"Nope. Worse that that."

"Worse than starving our herd, Ma? What could be worse than that? Unless. . .you think *we're* gonna starve?" Sarah's lip trembled.

"No, we'll live. But there is something worse than all of that."

"What is it, Ma?" Lindsay asked, her eyes frightened.

Well, good. She should be afraid. Very afraid. "I'm going to have to bring home. . ." Belle shuddered, but she forced herself to go on. "Men."

The rest of the dinner was sadder than the day they'd buried Anthony.

By a Rocky Mountain mile.

"Before I fetch them, I want to tell you one more time what low-down, worthless skunks men are. You can't trust nothin' a man makes you feel, especially if the men are good-lookin' and too ready with a smile."

Her girls listened closely while they ate.

Belle had said it all before. But she'd never say it enough.

She wished she knew a way to thin the herd of men.

Silas was so hungry for a meal not fixed by his own hand that he couldn't think of much else.

When he saw LIBBY'S DINER scrawled on the side of a clapboard building in Divide, Montana, he practically ran in, following his nose. He sank down on a bench at one of only two long, roughly built tables.

A bustling woman with a pleasant smile brought him coffee and a plate of stew without asking him what he wanted.

That was exactly what he wanted. Besides, it was most likely all Libby had. So a lot of time was spared.

Libby laid down the food, and Silas waved at the bench across from him. "I haven't heard another voice in an age. I'd be right pleased if you'd set a spell and talk to me while I eat."

Libby was agreeable and fetched her own cup of coffee and settled in on the bench across from Silas. They'd only covered half the town when a woman walked in, ringing the bell that hung over the door.

Now, Silas knew two kinds of women. In fact, to his knowledge until this moment, he'd've told anyone that there were only two kinds.

There were the dance-hall girls, all frilled up and doused with cheap perfume, with come-hither smiles that didn't cover the hardness behind their eyes. Their conversations were heated and direct, and their hands were always reaching for men's wallets.

And there were good girls, sorta like Libby here, though Libby was old enough to be Silas's mother, so she hardly qualified as a girl. Good girls wore calico and bonnets. They kept their eyes down—only glancing up once in a blue moon with their own version of come-hither—versions that were just as potent if a man wasn't careful. Their dresses were carefully loose to conceal their curves, although that didn't work well, a man's imagination being a powerful thing. Their conversations were discreet and shy. The funny thing about good girls was, just like the dance-hall girls, the good girls were also reaching for men's wallets. It was a longer reach, though, because a good girl got to a man's wallet with a side trip past a preacher.

The woman who strode into Libby's Diner was neither kind.

Her skin was tanned until she almost looked part Indian, but her light brown eyes made Silas believe she wasn't. She wore a fringed buckskin jacket with some of the fringe missing, the way a working-man's jacket was, because one of the points of having the fringe was to have a piggin' string available at all times. She had on a split riding skirt made of softly tanned doeskin that hugged her hips and flared loose around her ankles, and chaps over the skirt. None of it concealed her curves, even though every inch of her was covered.

She had on worn-out boots with spurs that jingled when she walked. A faded blue calico blouse showed under her jacket, with several buttons open that kept it from covering her throat as a decent dress ought. It looked like it was done for comfort, not for come-hither. A kerchief was tied at her neck the way a cowboy wore one, so it could be jerked up to filter dirt on a cattle drive. She wore leather gloves and a wide-brimmed, flat-topped black hat, and a six-gun in a holster on her neat little hip.

More unusual than that, she walked with a strong stride and looked Libby directly in the eye, even as she sat herself down next to Silas on the bench. She glanced at him with eyes that were neither hard nor demure, and no come-hither to be seen anywhere.

Even more interesting, Libby looked at her and spoke as she had to Silas, no giggles and hugs, none of the frilly manners one woman had with another. "Howdy, Belle. Eatin' today?"

"Anything you got is fine. I've had a hard ride in and got another one ahead of me to get home."

Libby got up and gave Belle the same service she'd given Silas.

Belle looked Silas straight in the eye but didn't linger over looking. Still, he had the sense that she'd taken in everything there was to see about him. There was nothing flirtatious in her glance, and it occurred to Silas that a woman often looked twice at him. He'd gotten used to women being interested.

Belle wasn't.

She turned back to Libby and took the coffee. "Obliged, Lib." She drank it two-fisted, like a man did who had gotten used to savoring the heat on cold nights on the range.

After she'd gotten some of the boiling hot, ink black coffee into her, she turned to Libby. "I'm huntin' hands. Anybody in town need work?" Her voice was deep for a woman. Businesslike. Somber. It tugged on something deep inside of Silas like sometimes beautiful music did.

Libby shook her head. "Cain't think of no one right off hand, Belle, but I can ask around. Most everyone huntin' work signed on with a herd heading for Oregon a month ago. My boys are off hauling freight, or they might help you out. It's late in the season."

"I hadn't heard about the other drive. I haven't been to town in a long time."

Although she kept her voice steady, Silas heard her underlying frustration and knew she needed help.

Libby said uncertainly, "I reckon there's a couple of loafers in the Golden Butte Saloon who might need the money bad enough to work for it."

Belle set her tin cup down with a hard *clink* and pulled her plate of stew closer, plunking her elbows on the table and surrounding the food as if afraid someone would take it from her. "I'll go check, but I don't want anyone who needs babysittin'. I'd rather do it alone."

"How many you need?"

"I want six. A month's work driving a thousand head to Helena."

"You're finally culling your herd that deep? Never thought I'd see the day." Libby poured another cup of coffee for Silas and topped off her own cup.

Nodding, Belle chewed thoughtfully. "I haven't sold more'n ten or twenty head in my life. Always trying to build. But I'm using up my range too fast this year. Had a calf crop I can't believe and didn't count close enough until about a week ago."

Libby refilled Belle's cup. "Uh. . .is your husband in charge then?"

Belle sat quiet for so long that Silas couldn't figure what about that question had stumped her so badly.

He sipped his coffee, watching this new kind of woman closely.

Finally, with a quick glance at Silas and an unreadable look, she said, "Anthony won't be makin' the drive. I'll be in charge."

Silas spit coffee across the table and started choking. Lucky Belle was beside him and Libby straight across from Belle.

Libby jumped up and grabbed a cloth.

Belle gave him a couple of thumps on the back, apparently thinking he'd swallowed his coffee wrong.

Mopping the table, Libby glanced at Silas and didn't quite conceal a smile.

Silas wiped his mouth and shirtfront. A woman in charge of a cattle drive? It sounded like Silas's very own worst nightmare!

Libby's reaction shocked him again. "You'll have more luck getting hands if'n they know Anthony's out, Belle."

Silas decided then not to drink any more coffee until Belle left, because he had no idea what she or Libby would say to surprise him next.

Belle quit beating on him and took her hand back to her coffee, nodding silently.

"Name's Silas Harden. I've punched my share of cows, and I could use a month's work." Silas heard the words come out of his mouth, and he had his third shock in the space of a single minute. He couldn't think of a worse fate than taking orders from a female, a particularly male kind of female at that. What had made his tongue slip loose with that offer?

"I'm Belle Tanner. Thanks for the offer." She angled her body a bit to face him then reached her hand out to shake, like a man would have.

Silas took her hand and felt the tough calluses. It made Silas want to punch somebody that this pretty little woman was running a cattle drive and had been doing hard physical labor for years, judging by her leather-tough hand.

Anthony seemed like a good place to start.

She pulled loose from his grip quickly, but not too quickly. Just right. Again like a man.

That irritated Silas for some reason.

"I've never heard of you, Silas. You from around here?"

"No, I just drifted into town today. I'm from New Mexico mainly."

"No offense, but I'll be using folks I know or who can be recommended by folks I know." Belle went to scooping up stew with her fork, brushing aside his offer as if he were crumbs she'd found on her shirt.

Silas should have breathed a sigh of relief at his lucky escape. Instead, her rejection bit a fair-sized chunk out of his pride. "It figures a crew run by a woman would be afraid of strangers." Again Silas should have just kept his mouth shut. And challenging her. . . what kind of stupid way was that to talk to a woman? "I've hired on to a dozen outfits in my day with nothing but my word and an understanding that if I couldn't pull my weight I'd be sent down the road. A man's used to proving himself in the West. When you're dealing with women, I suppose it's all about whatever fancy notion she takes in her pretty little head."

Belle looked up from her stew and stared directly into his eyes. No quick, dismissive glance this time.

Silas thought, if he checked later, there'd be singe marks on his skin where her eyes burned a hole through him.

Finally, without taking her eyes off of him, she asked, "Libby, whatta ya think? Has he got the stuff to go with that mouth?"

Silas's eyes shifted to Libby, and she studied him, too. He sat still, being judged by two women, and not for what a woman usually judged him for. He fought the urge to squirm like a schoolboy caught hiding a garter snake in the teacher's desk.

"I think he'd do to ride the river with, Belle." Libby sipped at her coffee. "He's right. You can always show him the trail."

Silas looked back at Belle to tell her he wouldn't work for her even if she decided he measured up.

Before he could cut her down to size, she was talking again.

"Well, I reckon I should take your word for it, Lib. Whatever else I am, I am the worst judge of men who ever walked the earth."

Libby started laughing. For a few seconds Silas wondered if the woman would topple off her chair, she was so caught in her laughing fit. Finally, Libby got herself under control. "No one can say that ain't true, Belle. Not knowing Anthony the way we do." Libby started in laughing again.

Belle quit trying to stare Silas to death and looked at the laughing woman and grinned.

Something twisted hard and sweet inside of Silas when he saw that serious face light up with a smile. She was younger than he'd first thought. And although he'd known from the first moment he saw her she was uncommonly beautiful, when she smiled like that, she seemed innocent and approachable. He wondered what kind of fool Anthony was to let his wife go off on a cattle drive with a half dozen men while he stayed home.

He was struck again by the idea that this was a kind of woman he never knew existed. He had no use for women, and he shuddered at the idea of working for one. When he opened his mouth to say he'd rather spend the next month being danced on by a herd of longhorns than work for her, he said instead, "So, am I hired, boss lady?"

Silas gave up any hope of controlling his mouth. It seemed to have struck out on its own for good. He shook his head and wondered at his willingness—no, his eagerness—to do this.

Belle tilted her head to study him. "You're too good-looking and you're too blasted smart—I can see that already. I'll probably have to shoot you down like a foam-at-the-mouth, rabid skunk before we're two days down the trail."

Silas froze. He had no idea how to react to that.

He'd shoot a man for less than calling him a "rabid skunk.'"

He'd kiss a woman for less than saying he was smart and good-looking.

Their eyes met and the moment stretched. Her shining brown eyes widened, and he felt his own narrow. They were locked together until something almost visible vibrated between them.

Into the dead silence, Libby spoke. "That means you're hired."

CHAPTER 3

"Are you in town for long?" Silas stood from the table, pushing his chair back with a scrape.

"A couple of hours, more'n likely." Belle wished she'd never shaken his hand. The feel of it more than anything else had made her refuse his offer to work. Libby had spoken up in time to keep Belle from foolishly turning down a willing drover. "I'm laying in supplies for the drive, and the general store will be awhile filling the order and packing my horse string."

He nodded and offered her his hand again to seal the deal. "I'll be sleeping at the Golden Butte. Wake me up, and I'll ride out with you."

At mention of the Golden Butte, Belle frowned. She looked at that hand and was tempted to slap it aside. But some people might really sleep at the Golden Butte, and it didn't matter to her what he did. Swatting her new cowhand would have too much to do with Anthony and nothing to do with him. Good manners overcame her reluctance, and she gave him another quick handshake.

He tossed some coins on the table and left her sitting by Libby.

She rubbed her hand on her chaps to get the feeling of him off. She watched him walk away before she turned back to her coffee. "What do you know about him, Lib?"

"He came in huntin' a meal about an hour ago." Libby shrugged. "He's been ridin' the mountain country for a while. He didn't say much. But he saw to his horse before he ate. His outfit looked good and his gun was clean and loaded."

"It ain't much to go on." Belle studied her coffee.

"I liked the look of him. He'll do to ride the river with."

Somehow, Belle was sorely afraid he wouldn't do at all, but not for lack of practice at cowboying. "Keep kickin' over rocks to see if any hands crawl out. We're lightin' out at sunup, but they could catch us if you find anyone who's of a mind to."

"I'll do that." Libby fetched the pot and poured.

While she listened to Libby talk, Belle considered her options. Six hands. She needed that many cowpunchers to make this crossing. Seth had told her the same as Libby, a cattle drive had taken all the men available. But Seth had thought Libby's sons might be in town and they might set aside their mule skinning for a month to make solid cash money.

Belle knew how much help Lindsay and Emma were. And Sarah, though she wasn't big enough yet to bulldog or rope, could haze cattle and stick a saddle like a little burr. But Belle hadn't really counted the girls as hands. She'd more considered them as extra and just thought to bring them along because she couldn't leave them home alone. Now she was going to have to count them. So, she had those three and Silas. That was four hands. She wanted six men besides herself. With a sigh, Belle knew they could make the trip, but it would be as tough as anything any of them would ever endure.

It made her twitchy to sit drinking coffee, but listening to Libby talk was nice. A few more minutes wouldn't hurt, because it wasn't time to head back for a while. She'd left a list with Seth and Muriel at the general store, and it was a long one. She'd pulled a string of packhorses to town rather than bring her buckboard. After nearly giving birth to Betsy on the trail while driving her slow-moving buckboard home, she'd come to prefer the faster pace of the packhorses.

Libby went for the coffeepot again.

While she was gone into the kitchen, the bell tinkled over the door. Belle looked up expecting to see Silas Harden coming—wanting to shake her hand again. Instead, in traipsed a mystery.

Cassie Dawson. A woman forced into marriage who was happy. Impossible.

And yet the woman glowed. She had one hand resting on her stomach, obviously expecting a baby. Her husband swung the door inward then stepped back to let Cassie go first as if she were made out of the most fragile china. Red then followed his wife in.

Then bringing up the rear—of all people—Wade Sawyer. Belle decided she was improving as a judge of men, because she knew Wade Sawyer was bad news. Except he was carrying a little girl with a head full of short black curls, and dark brown eyes, who looked about a year old. Wade smiled down at the child with more pleasure and pride in his eyes than Belle had ever seen from her husbands toward their own children.

The last time she'd seen Wade, he'd had bloodshot eyes and a bad attitude and smelled like a mangy coyote. Now his eyes were clear, and a smile wiped all the cruelty from his face.

"Belle?" Cassie hurried over to the table, her eyes lit up, an excited smile on her face. This young woman had awakened a mother's instinct in Belle from the first. Cassie would have benefited from some of Belle's teachings. But Red got her first, and he'd done right by the little woman.

Belle also noticed that the baby looked the image of Cassie. Belle frowned, wondering how a woman managed such a thing.

Libby came out of the kitchen with her pot.

"I'm just dropping Cass and Susannah off." Red took the baby from Wade and hugged her till she giggled and grabbed at his nose.

"Papa." Susannah squealed and squirmed, and Belle couldn't take her eyes off the little girl surrounded by love. She'd done her best by her girls, but she'd never been able to provide them with a father's love.

"Bye-bye, Suzie." Red settled the baby on Cassie's lap. "I've got work to do. Libby, we'll haul your supplies over as soon as we can. Wade's going to help."

"Thanks, Red. I'll leave the door open. I planned on abandoning the place and having coffee with Cassie and Muriel and Leota over at Muriel's."

"Seth told us Muriel's out doctoring one of Leota's young'uns." Cassie ran her hand over her baby's curls.

Libby gasped. "Is it serious?"

"I think the little boy is running a fever from a cold. Leota hadn't slept all night, so Muriel went to give her a chance to rest." Cassie bounced her little girl on her knee. "They're going to try and get over here before Red comes back from his chores."

Belle looked to be on the verge of getting pulled into a hen party. She hadn't done such a thing in her adult life. Of course, with four daughters, her whole *life* was something of a hen party. But they were a hardworking flock.

Just as she was ready to stand up and walk out, Libby poured coffee and slipped a piece of cake in front of Belle. She knew this dessert wasn't for anyone but Libby's women friends—it was too pretty, with crumbled brown sugar and speckles of sweet-smelling cinnamon.

"That's perfect then." Libby nodded, clearly glad her party was going to grow.

Ruefully, Belle wondered what it would feel like to be welcomed like that. Libby was polite to her, but no friendlier than she'd been with Silas.

Red looked at Belle a long time, a serious expression on his face. "You had your baby, then? Everyone's okay?"

Belle nodded. "We named her Elizabeth. We call her Betsy." Anthony had insisted they name the baby Caterina, of all outlandish names. To keep him happy, they'd tried to call the tyke Caterina, or more often The Baby, when Anthony was within earshot. She and the girls privately called the child Betsy, and since Anthony had been gone more than home, that was pretty much all the time.

Figuring Anthony wasn't long for the world, considering the foolish way he conducted his life, they bided their time and watched their tongues, and now that the man had faced his inevitable death, they were free to call Betsy by her real name all the time.

"Glad to hear it. You were too far out to send to town for Muriel. Cassie, Wade, and I worried some."

Belle's eyes shifted to Wade's. "You're. . .living at Red's place?"

Wade nodded. "When I'm around. I've been doing some scouting for the army, some trapping. Hired on to a couple of cattle drives. I quit working on my dad's ranch. Got sick of living under his thumb." Wade's calm, clear eyes brightened. "Red and Cassie have helped me learn more about God. I'm a believer now."

Libby patted Wade on the arm. "It's been a pleasure having you attend our church. Your pa was in here kicking up a fuss about you living out at the Dawsons'."

Wade shrugged and smiled. "My pa's good at that."

He seemed to be completely at ease with his father's wrath, neither afraid nor angry. Belle had spent most of her married life being one or the other or both.

Belle lived far enough from everyone not to have come up against Mort Sawyer and his legendary temper, but she'd met the man a time or two. He expected everyone to stand aside or be crushed under his boot. Now she realized she had a skilled hand standing right in front of her.

"You're not hunting work, are you?" Belle felt foolish to hire on the son of the area's more powerful ranchers and offer him a dollar a day and campfire meals.

Wade seemed to focus on her for the first time. "Doing what?"

"I'm taking my cattle to market. I could use more hands."

Wade rubbed his thumb over his chin as if considering. "I've got a run to make first, promised to deliver some supplies to a line shack for Linscott. When are you heading out?"

"First light."

"Tomorrow?" Wade asked.

Belle nodded.

"I'll be a few days, but tell me your trail. I can catch up."

Belle would have told anyone who asked that she'd rather do this drive alone than let Wade Sawyer with his coyote eyes help her. But he'd said he was a Christian. More than that—because a man's word didn't mean much to Belle—he looked calm and settled. Much like Silas Harden.

She sighed. She didn't have the luxury of being picky. At least Wade, with his vast holdings, even if he'd walked away from them for now, wouldn't want to marry her to gain Tanner Ranch.

"Fine, we're taking the high trail out of the north side of my ranch."

Wade flinched. "Tough passage. You won't be hard to find. There's not a way off that trail once you start it."

Belle nodded. "I'd welcome the help."

Wade and Red left, jangling the bell behind them.

Belle found herself pulled into talk of babies and husbands and making a home. Three things Belle knew a lot about. And she'd tried to avoid all three with no success.

"So how old is your baby, Belle? I haven't seen. . ." Cassie faltered. "Did you have a boy or a girl?"

"A girl, thank goodness."

Cassie's eyes sharpened, and she held her squirming daughter. "Didn't you want a son?"

Obviously itching to get her hands on the tyke, Libby relieved Cassie of the little girl.

Belle snorted. "I haven't had much luck with men. I'd probably raise 'em up to be as worthless as their pas."

"Pas?" Libby asked. "More than one?"

"Yep, Anthony was my third husband. Uh. . .*is* my third husband."

"Was?" Libby plunked down on the bench next to Cassie. "What happened? Did Anthony die, too?"

Belle felt her neck start to heat. She had no talent for lying. She could skip a subject well enough and not feel the need to blurt out her every thought. But pure, straight-from-the-shoulder lies just didn't sit on her tongue nor her conscience. "I don't want to talk about Anthony."

Libby leaned closer and whispered, "You can tell us, Belle. I knew Anthony. It was only a matter of time until he turned up his toes."

Belle rubbed the back of her neck. "I don't want anyone knowing he's dead, okay?"

"Of course you're not ready." Cassie's eyes shone with compassion. "If he just died, you're still grieving."

"Grieving?" Belle snorted in a way that reminded her of her horse and shook her head. "Not hardly. I just don't want the no-accounts around here to know I'm widowed. They'll be out there pestering me to marry up with them. I'd probably finally just marry one to keep the others away." Belle glared at both women. "And I *don't want another husband*. If you breathe a word, it'll all be ruined."

Libby nodded.

"Why don't you want a husband, Belle?" Cassie's huge eyes were as warm and brown as her coffee.

"I just have a knack for picking a poor lot. It's something wrong with me. I know that. But I can't seem to get it right." Belle didn't like admitting that, but it was her only hope for keeping her secret. "So, I'm quitting."

"Quitting the ranch?" Cassie asked, pure innocence.

Belle should have taken her home and toughened her up, no matter that she was already married. "No!" Instead, Belle had stepped aside and let Red have her, and now look at the little woman, wide-eyed, innocent, sweet, cheerful. Not a brain in her head.

"Quitting men." Belle hadn't meant to shout, but the idea of giving up her ranch startled a yell out of her. "Three times a widow is enough. Now promise me you won't say a word."

Cassie nodded solemnly.

"I'll keep your secret, Belle. But word will get out soon enough," Libby predicted.

"If I can get through this cattle drive then get snowed in for the winter, I'll have a long stretch of peace and quiet. I'll spend my time whipping up a backbone to turn men away." Belle stood, sorry she'd stayed this long. Hoping these women could keep a secret. "I don't have time for jawing. I've got to buy supplies, pick up the hand I hired, and get back to my young'uns. Thanks for the coffee, Lib." Belle tossed a coin onto the table and left before they could ask any more personal questions.

She stalked out of the diner, spurs clinking, the bell over the door tinkling, and her ears ringing from the gossiping she knew the women would do about her. It served her right. She should have brought hardtack and biscuits instead of being so weak as to eat her meal in the diner.

She headed for the general store, determined to hurry Seth up and get out of Divide even if it meant packing her horses herself.

❧

"Sawyer, why haven't you hit the trail yet?" Tom Linscott was already snarling as he rode up to the general store on his thoroughbred black stallion and dismounted.

There'd been plenty in and around Divide who believed Wade

had changed, but some still had their doubts. The difference was Linscott took the time to do it right.

"I've just come from Bates'." Wade jerked his thumb at the general store he'd just exited. "Belle Tanner rode in with a long order, and Seth's gotta finish that up first."

"Well, I want you on the trail today." Linscott wrapped his reins around the hitching post in front of the general store. His black stallion snorted and fought with the rope and tried to take a bite out of Tom's shoulder, but Linscott dodged; he'd reinforced all the hitching posts in Divide long ago, for this very reason. The stallion was as cranky as his owner.

Wade looked straight into Linscott's cold blue eyes and went on as always, being the best he could be and not worrying about anyone else. Linscott had let him do some work here lately. But even that was the tall Swede rubbing in his contempt. It was a big improvement over the days Wade hadn't been able to keep from goading Linscott until Wade ended up bleeding, sprawled on his backside in the dirt. What Tom felt or believed wasn't Wade's problem. He had enough of his own. "I'll be moving as soon as Seth gets time."

"Then I want you back here. I've got some more work, if you're willing." Linscott said it like he was sure Wade *wouldn't* be willing.

Smiling, enjoying the moment, Wade said, "Belle's driving a herd to Helena, and I signed on with her. Once I'm back from the drive, I'll stop out to the ranch. But it'll be a month or more."

"She's taking a herd to Helena this late in the year?"

"So she said."

Linscott settled his gloved hand on top of his Stetson and adjusted it so it rode low over his eyes. "Who's she finding to work for her? If she's askin' you, she must be scraping the bottom of the barrel."

Wade knew better than to even clench a fist. He was a believer now. A man of faith. Getting into a fistfight on Main Street wasn't part of the way he conducted himself. "Lucky for me she is. I need the work."

With a snort that probably charmed the black stallion, Linscott showed clearly that by *not* defending himself, Wade had just proved he was a weakling.

That didn't upset Wade much either. Much. He had so many weaknesses he couldn't count 'em all. That's why he needed God. Trouble was everyone needed God. Linscott included. And since the man didn't believe himself one bit weak, he'd be hard pressed to ever figure it out. That reminded Wade of his father—a man who thought he didn't need anything and had never admitted to a weakness in his life.

"Just get the supplies out to that line shack." Linscott stripped his gloves off his hands and tucked them in the pocket of his fringed buckskin coat. My men're running out of food by now." Linscott brushed past Wade and stomped into the store.

The horse snorted, speaking Linscott's language.

Wade stared at the beautiful beast for a few long seconds. "What do you think, boy? You like takin' orders from that grouch?"

The thoroughbred's midnight black eyes flashed, almost like an answer, and Wade knew the horse didn't take orders from anyone. He lived on his own terms, and he'd judged Tom Linscott to be worthy, or the horse would have stomped the man to death by now.

It occurred to Wade that the horse had the same temperament as Wade's father. Then Wade mentally apologized to the stallion.

CHAPTER 4

Belle conducted her business, doing half of Seth's work for him to move things along. Then she headed over to the saloon where Silas would be sleeping above stairs.

Belle strode into the Golden Butte, a place two of her husbands—one a drunk, the other a cheat—had taught her to hate. Two flouncy-dressed women sat playing poker with a couple of no-accounts. She had no idea how many women worked here, but since there was no sign of Silas down here, he might have been telling the truth about wanting to sleep.

"I'm heading out, Harden!" she hollered up the stairs. "You awake?"

Silas was only a few seconds coming out. He must have been sleeping with his boots on.

"What are you doing in here?" Silas clumped down the steps, scowling at her. No woman followed after him. Belle didn't care, but she noticed. "This is no place for a respectable woman." He glanced at the scantily clad female. "No offense."

One of them raised her glass. The other crossed her legs and hooked her arm over the back of her chair. "None taken, cowboy."

"I'm in her to get you. How'd you think I was supposed to get you without coming in?" Belle supposed her behavior was shocking. She didn't care much, but she could see he did. She took a long look at the two women and was tempted to take them with her, get them away from these men, teach them to work, to grow up, to have some shame.

He clapped his hat on his head. "You should have sent someone up for me."

"I reckon you're right." She didn't respond beyond that. Instead, she gave up on the women, turned on her heels, and led the way out of the saloon. She had her string of pack horses lined up out front.

Silas had a buckskin standing at the hitching post. He swung up, and the feisty little horse perked up its head like it was rested and rarin' to be on the move.

The buckskin had the look of a mustang that'd run wild for a time, and Belle knew the sure-footed mare would make the treacherous cattle drive with ease. The horse also looked well fed, and it had no ugly scars where a cruel man might work his mount with a whip or spurs. It raised Belle's opinion of Silas. She did a quick check of the ropes tying her four heavily laden horses to her roan and tested that her supplies were well secured.

Silas rode up beside her. "Did you find any more drovers?"

"Nope. Well one, maybe, who might come along later." It grated on Belle to think she might have to settle for help from that low-down Wade Sawyer. "I found a few no-accounts here and there. None of 'em needed work." She wondered angrily if she'd told them she was widowed would they come slithering out from under rocks and come along out to the place. She probably could have had those two bums from the saloon.

She glanced at Silas, knowing he might figure out Anthony was dead sooner or later. His well-groomed horse stretched out to a brisk walk beside her.

Silas had brown hair and eyes and was just under six feet tall. Belle had the strange thought that if she had a baby with this man and it looked like *him*, at least some of the time she could convince herself it looked like her, too.

Then she realized what she was thinking and almost spurred her horse into a gallop. The string of ponies she was dragging along kept her from running.

"Okay, what about the trail we're taking?"

The question thankfully took Belle's mind off nonsense. "It's a killer. There's a canyon near my cabin that has a high pass out of the north side. We're going in on the south—that's the only other trail in, and it's a few hundred feet lower in altitude than the one we'll take tomorrow. I've got the cattle settled in that grassy pasture, and they'll fight us leaving it and climbing up the side of a cliff to get out."

A thin whistle escaped Silas's lips as he listened.

"Then is when it gets really bad."

Silas shook his head. "Sounds like a killer all right."

"Yep, we've got a hundred miles of treacherous turns, flanked by steep cliffs a good part of the time and going up and down one mountain after another. The trails are blocked in places with talus slides. The landslide areas seem like they're looking for a horse's leg to break."

"A hundred miles isn't much as cattle drives go."

"Nope, we'll make it. But where there aren't cliffs, there are heavily wooded mountainsides that will have to be constantly combed for bunch quitters. This trail is part of the backbone of the Rockies. The herd will be strung out over miles. The—" Belle faltered. She'd almost said "the girls," but she'd let him find out about the girls when they were well away from Divide. "The drovers will be forced to move constantly, circling, pushing."

"And we're heading out tomorrow?"

"Yep. I already have the cattle cut out. Old stuff and almost all my steers, plus a few head of heifers just to cull the herd down to a level that won't ruin my pasture. The cattle have been getting fat and lazy for the last week. I've also scouted the trail a bit, and the start's not so bad. I've cleared the first couple of slides and found some likely pastureland. We should be able to keep the herd well fed and content for the first couple of days. By then they'll be trail broke, and hopefully, when they have to scale the rugged pass along Mount Jack, the cows and my. . .my cowhands will come through."

"How many hands did you find? You wanted six."

"There'll be five of us. And I talked to one man who had a couple of days' work to finish, but he might catch up to us along the drive."

"That's still a short-handed drive. But we should manage since it's so short." Silas settled his hat more firmly on his head as if he were ready to shoulder the work.

Belle doubted he'd be one that came though—he was a man after all—but she could hope. Right at this moment she was worried enough that she almost wished for all three of her husbands back just because she could make them come along at least and add their body count to the number. In the end she knew they'd just be extra, ornery bulls to deal with, so all in all, she decided their being dead was for the best.

"Now tell me details about this trail. Tell me everything." Silas looked back, as if checking on the horse string was his job. The man had knowing eyes, studying the ropes and packs. Then, apparently satisfied, he turned back to her.

As they made the trek home, she did more talking than she'd ever done with a man, and that certainly included her husbands.

As she talked, he asked questions and impressed her with his knowledge of cattle. By the time they rode up to the ranch, they were talking like old friends.

Silas swung off his horse and paused for a moment to look at her house.

It was a ramshackle, leaking wreck, and Belle knew it. But she didn't know how to fix it. Mostly she was used to it, but having Silas stare at her house made her cheeks warm. When was the last time she'd given a whit what anyone else thought of her? Then she remembered that she'd blushed in front of Cassie and Libby today and hoped her tanned skin didn't show red.

"Let me unload the supplies. Then I'll put the horses up."

Belle glanced up, startled. She'd never expected help. When Lindsay and Emma came out and started hauling, Silas was helpful and respectful—two traits Belle didn't know existed in a man.

Silas picked up the reins of two horses then reached for a third, obviously to lead the horses toward her crumbling barn and makeshift corral. Belle and the older girls each grabbed a horse before he could collect them all. Then there were horses to rub down, hay to pitch, a cow to milk, and eggs to gather. With Silas helping, evening chores were done in quick time.

"Supper!" Sarah's little voice called.

All four went toward that homey call.

Belle stepped into the house through the sagging door.

"I put the same amount of potatoes in the pot I did afore Anthony turned up his toes," Sarah spoke from the stove.

Belle gasped and glanced at Silas who was visibly surprised by the news.

He arched one brow at her in an unasked question.

She resolutely looked away. She had learned a long time ago not to give too much away about what she was thinking and feeling. She'd discovered that a husband often made himself feel more like a man by battering on a woman's feelings, and men not used to doing business with women dealt better when there was no feminine behavior on the woman's part.

She scoffed inwardly at her foolishness. She had assumed that whoever she hired would know that Anthony was dead—probably before they got on the trail. Word would eventually get back to town. But since the only man who'd come with her wasn't from around here, she'd been sifting ideas in her head about claiming Anthony was just away.

Not a complete lie. God had definitely come and taken Anthony away. Chances were she could pull off Anthony being somewhere just for overnight. Then the drive would start and there was no reason Silas would have to know anything more about the missing husband.

She'd never considered it before she left for town, so she hadn't had a chance to mention it to the girls, and for all her mental gyrations, she'd known there was a good chance Anthony being dead would come out. So why did she feel her face heat up? This was the second time it had happened since she'd gotten home and the third time today.

Also the third time in her adult life.

To conceal her overly warm cheeks, she headed for the washbasin to stand in line behind Emma.

Lindsay was already washed up and putting bowls of food on the table.

Sarah had contrived fried chicken, mashed potatoes, a baking of bread, and the last of the green beans from their kitchen garden. A custard stood cooling by the window, rich with their own eggs and cream and honey.

They were seated at the table, and Belle said grace quickly but from the heart, because she considered being spared a husband's company the act of a loving God.

When the food had been passed and everyone was settled in to eat, Silas asked casually, "So what exactly did Anthony die of?"

Belle thought he was looking at his food rather suspiciously, like maybe it was poisoned.

She almost smiled. Then he caught her eye and did smile, and she knew he was teasing her. She looked back at her plate. That moment of mutual amusement might well constitute the nicest exchange she'd ever had with a man. And that definitely included the four times she'd gotten pregnant.

Sarah, always helpful, piped up. "He claimed to be looking for leaks, but he were hiding out from work like always. He fell off the roof."

Silas quirked the corner of his mouth but managed not to smile. "That's terrible."

Without looking up from her food, Sarah responded, "Not really."

Silas pressed his hand to his mouth for a second. "How long has he been gone?"

"A couple months, I reckon." Emma was, as a rule, shy around strangers. Not today, more's the pity. But then Anthony's worthlessness was one of her favorite subjects. "Didn't rightly notice what day it was. We planted him by the Husband Tree with the other husbands. Lost nearly a quarter of a day of work, but we made it up soon enough."

Sarah said with overly solemn dignity, "They was a worthless lot. Anthony Santoni was Betsy's pa." Sarah pointed her fork at the dark-haired, dark-eyed toddler.

Sarah shook her head of red curls and yanked on one of the corkscrews, pulling it down past her eyes before letting it spring back. "My pa, Gerald O'Roarke, was drunk when he died, as usual. He fell off his horse on his way home from the Golden Butte and let hisself get dragged for nigh onto twenty miles. Ma says he was no great loss 'ceptin' it was right hard on the poor horse."

Silas coughed into his napkin for far too long. "Husband Tree?"

Somehow Belle had never heard her words echoed back at her in quite this way before. Her neck was getting warm again, and she thought desperately of something to say to change the subject. The best she could come up with was, *Let's talk about something else.* She opened her mouth to say it, but before she could. . .

"My and Emma's pa was William Svendsen." Lindsay, who had been mercifully silent until now, smoothed her white blond hair, pulled back in a single, waist-length braid, and spoke. "He got hisself gored by Rudolph."

"And Rudolph is. . ." Silas waited.

"Our bull. Maybe a ten-foot spread of horns. Getting old now, but he's been a good bull. Wasn't his fault William went right into his pen." Lindsay rolled her eyes.

Emma arched her blond brows over her crystal blue eyes. "Any idiot knew better than to climb in that pen with Rudolph."

Silas covered his mouth with his napkin and seemed to be having a problem breathing.

Belle was pretty sure he was choking to death, and she wished he'd get on with it.

"Any other husbands planted around here?"

Sarah mulled it over for a moment. "Umm. . .no, I think that's the lot of 'em. . .so far. Likely another one'll come sniffin' around now that ma's a widow lady again."

"They always do," Emma said with heavy resignation.

"We've learned our lesson." Very sternly, Lindsey added, "Haven't we, Ma?"

Belle rubbed her forehead and stared at her plate as she nodded without saying a word.

"Yep, don't care how many of the mangy varmints come a-courtin'," Sarah said blithely. "We finally got shut of husbands for good. Now we can settle down and run this ranch right."

"We always did run it right," Emma added. "The husbands just slowed us down some."

Finally, far too late, Belle said weakly, "Let's talk about something else."

Betsy chose that moment to whack her spoon against the table and splatter mashed potatoes across Silas's face. He was at the foot of the table and Belle at the head, with Betsy beside her, so the man was clear across the table from the baby. Even at that distance, the potatoes hit him square in the eye.

Belle snatched the spoon out of Betsy's hand and began wiping her messy face while Silas cleared his vision.

Betsy grinned straight at the poor man. "Papa!"

Glancing up, Belle saw mute horror in Silas's eyes as his face turned a startling shade of pink under his deep tan. He rose from the table, knocking his chair over backward in his haste.

The girls didn't seem to notice and started cleaning up the supper dishes.

"Thank you for the fine meal." He set the chair back up. "I'll bunk down with the buckskin in the barn." Silas backed toward the door, grabbed the knob, and wrenched the door open. "I'll be ready to move out with the herd an hour before first light." He practically ran out of the house and slammed the door so hard Belle waited to see if it would fall in.

As soon as Belle could get her humiliation under control, it occurred to her that Silas had known she was a widow lady for several minutes now, and instead of proposing to her on the spot, he'd run like a rooster with his tail feathers afire. That man was horrified at the very thought of marrying her.

It was the nicest thing a man had ever done for her.

She cheered right up and even sang with the girls while they cleaned the kitchen.

It looked like, when it came to men, hiring Silas was the smartest thing she'd ever done.

That wasn't saying much.

Taking this job was the dumbest thing he'd ever done!

He hunkered down in the barn and wondered whether Belle had set her cap for him already.

The Husband Tree?

He was tempted to cut and run, and likely he'd've done it if he hadn't given his word.

Papa!

That child had called him Papa, and Silas had nearly turned tail and run out of the cabin.

But wait a minute! He remembered the way Belle got all embarrassed. It was the most womanly thing she'd done so far.

Except she loosened up on the ride home and talked to him intelligently and smiled real regular.

He couldn't recall having a better time talking to anyone, let alone a woman. He caught himself thinking about how pretty she was, and he remembered a couple of times he'd gotten close to her accidental-like and he'd noticed how good she smelled. He considered on that for a while, how a woman could dress like a man, ride a horse like a man, work like a man, and still have something so purely female about her.

Belle Santoni—or was it Belle Tanner? Silas hadn't gotten it all straightened out in his head yet. Belle Whoever. . .worked this place like any man rancher would. And Silas would bet his life the woman didn't even own a drop of perfume or a bar of sweet-smellin' soap. But she still smelled like 100 percent, genuine woman.

Silas sat in the cold barn and remembered how she felt when he shook her hand. Strong and soft and. . . Silas rubbed his hand on his pant leg, trying to put into words what else she was. The best way he could describe her was honest, although the woman had already lied to him at least once about Anthony being dead. But there was honesty in Belle's handshake and in her eyes. Or maybe a better word was *directness*. She didn't have any of the women's wiles that had pitched him such fits in his life.

So, if she was direct, then Silas had to believe she meant what she said. She was foreman of the cattle drive. She'd said she had more hands, but they must be coming in the morning, because there was no one else around. She'd said one of the drovers might be late, meet up with them along the trail. Was she meeting the others that way, too? If so, it might be that he and Belle would have to at least get the drive started alone.

He had no illusions about long, romantic nights by the fire. There would be none of that with a shorthanded cattle drive. He didn't want to think of the brutal month of hard work ahead of them.

He also realized that meant she was leaving the girls home alone. That was the one thing so far about Belle he didn't respect. Even the lying didn't bother him too much, because she hadn't really lied. She just hadn't mentioned a few important details.

But leaving those girls. Silas shook his head. The two older ones were as tall or taller than Belle—but they were still young girls. Rough, dangerous men prowled this wild country, and even an occasional band of Indians. It was no place for a gaggle of little girls to be left alone.

He lay awake, thinking about the drive ahead. He dozed lightly several times and knew the day was coming soon when he'd look back on this night's lost sleep with regret.

Finally, he decided to declare it officially morning. He tossed his blanket aside and went to saddle up in the early hours of the morning. He started with his own. Then he started making packs out of the grub Belle had brought back on her string of ponies.

As he worked around the place in the bright moonlight, he began to really see the Tanner ranch. It was a mess.

He remembered what Lindsay—or was it Sarah?—had said about Anthony falling off the roof checking for leaks. In the glow of the full moon, Silas could see the patched, shoddy job Belle's husbands had done building this place. The fences sagged and were braced haphazardly with tree branches and strips of rawhide. The door to the barn hung from drooping leather thongs, and the logs on the barn and the house were all small ones, as if someone didn't have the gumption to go cut down the big trees a solid house needed.

He started tying a line of horses to the hitching post in front of the barn, and the top rail fell off in his hands. He spent long minutes repairing it, and his fingers itched to set the rest of the property to rights. It was a beautiful site Belle's husband had picked to settle, but the house was set wrong for the winter winds and the warm summer sun. The man who built this had been a poor excuse for a carpenter.

In a brief instant, Silas could see how it was for Belle. He knew how much a woman needed a husband in the West. Someone to lift heavy things. Someone to saddle the broncos. Someone to sign legal documents and deal with the rough characters who were the only kind of men who lived in an area like this.

So, she'd been widowed. The country was hard on people and there were a thousand ways to die that had nothing to do with outlaws or marauding Indians. And once widowed. . .well. . . women were rare out here, especially women as pretty as Belle Tanner. Especially pretty women who owned a valley as rich and fertile as this. The men came calling. And like any wise woman, Belle had said yes. But it sounded like she was no judge of men, because her three husbands, to quote Sarah—or was it Lindsay?— were "a worthless lot."

As Silas moved around the yard feeding the chickens, collecting eggs, and milking the cow, the work helped ease out the snarls in his mind. He remembered Lindsay, he was sure it was the oldest girl, saying, "We've learned our lesson. Haven't we, Ma?"

And one of the other girls had responded, "We can settle down and run this ranch right." A weight lifted off his back as he realized that Belle Tanner had *not* set her cap for him. In fact, it was just the opposite.

That's why she'd hidden the fact that Anthony was dead. That's why she spent the whole mealtime last night blushing like a nun in a dance hall. The last thing Belle wanted was another husband, and she was doing everything she could think of to keep from acquiring one.

Grinning, Silas carried hay and water to the milk cow. He glanced up when a lantern flickered to life in the house. He smiled when he thought about the houseful of womenfolk, everyone of whom agreed that keeping men out of their lives was the only way to run the ranch right.

He picked up the basket of eggs and the bucket of milk and headed in with them and knew he'd finally found a woman he could stand to be around.

At least he thought he could stand it. . .for a month.

CHAPTER 5

Silas showed up at the door with milk and eggs. Belle was dressed and on her way out, and they almost collided.

"The morning chores are done." Silas hoisted the milk bucket a few inches to prove it. "But you'd better check. I may not do things your way."

"You gathered eggs?" Belle stared up at him as if he were speaking Flathead.

"Yeah, and milked the cow. And I've got the packhorses ready to go."

Without another word, Belle dodged around him and darted out the door.

Lindsay came close, acting wary, and snatched the egg bucket almost as if she expected him to fight to hang on to it. Sending him a suspicious look, she relieved him of the milk, too, and took both buckets over to Sarah.

Emma was busy in the corner of the one-room cabin, changing the baby's diaper, but she glanced over her shoulder and arched a brow.

Sarah had a cast-iron skillet on the stove heating, and as soon as Lindsay set the buckets on the wobbly counter next to Sarah, the little redhead began cracking the two dozen or so eggs and dropping them with a homey sizzle into the frying pan.

Emma finished with the baby and pulled some contraption onto her back. Then Lindsay stuck the baby in while Emma adjusted the little pack. Dressed in boots, chaps over a riding skirt, and a fringed jacket just like her ma's, and with the baby strapped on her back in a little leather sling the way an Indian carries a papoose, Emma headed for the door.

Lindsay said, "He done the chores already."

Emma stopped short and stared at Lindsay. Silas had the impression Emma didn't understand, as if *Lindsay* had begun speaking Flathead. Finally, Emma shifted her eyes to Silas. She looked so skeptical he almost grinned.

Sarah flipped open the door on the potbellied stove and stirred the fire with a poker, then went back to breaking eggs. She seemed bent on cooking them all up, and he bit back the urge to tell Sarah to go easy and save some eggs for the rest of the day.

Without looking at him, Sarah said matter-of-factly, "She ain't marryin' you. So don't even think about it."

At Sarah's comment, the two older girls turned on him like starving wolves that'd spotted a three-legged mule deer.

Silas was momentarily speechless. Then he remembered last night and set right out to put their fussy female minds at ease. "I wouldn't marry your ma if you wrapped her up in ribbons and tissue paper and gave her to me as a Christmas present."

"And I wouldn't marry you either, Mr. Harden."

Silas let his eyes drop closed at the belligerent tone of Belle's voice. He collected his thoughts, turned to face her, and went right to setting *her* mind at ease, too. "Good. So we understand each other. Now explain it to your girls so we can get these cattle on the trail."

He saw that reddish tint start crawling up her neck again,

and he wanted to laugh. He didn't think Belle was a woman who blushed very often, but she'd spent most of her time with him all pink and embarrassed.

She looked past him. "Girls, we've finally found a man we can stand to have around. I promise not to marry him. Now don't scare him off until after the drive. Then I'll *help* you scare him off."

Silas turned to see how the girls took the news.

Sarah was still scrambling eggs.

Emma shrugged and set to untangling Betsy's fingers from her braided hair.

Lindsay looked between the two of them, then, with a resigned sigh, she said, "You never learn, Ma." She started setting the table.

Belle came up beside Silas with her arms crossed. The two of them exchanged a look that was in complete accord.

Children!

Then Belle said, "I let the milk cow out with the herd. She's due to calf in about six weeks, so it's the perfect time to dry her up. I penned the chickens up in the barn and gave them plenty of feed. They should spend this time setting chicks. I hope so, because if they don't, they're bound to escape that wreck of a barn and the coyotes will be thinning them out the whole time we're gone. Otherwise everything was done. We're going to get an hour's jump on the sun thanks to you, Mr. Harden."

"Go back to Silas. I had a schoolmarm who used to call me Mr. Harden when she scolded me. I keep half expecting you to take a ruler to my knuckles."

Belle nodded.

Silas grinned.

Sarah fried.

Emma played with Betsy.

Lindsay sighed again.

"Eat up quick, girls," Belle said. "I want you all saddled so we can start punching those cattle up that high pass in fifteen minutes."

Silas was a man who thought things through. Who considered angles before he acted or spoke. He was a man with a temper, but it wasn't explosive. All of a sudden he figured something out he should have known all along. "We aren't taking a baby on a cattle drive!"

The whole gaggle of women froze. Even baby Elizabeth stopped her cheerful torment of Emma and stared at Silas.

Belle stepped away from his side, where just a second before he'd decided it was to be the two of them against the girls and liked that just fine. She lined up with her daughters.

Sarah took the eggs off the stove and, with a towel wrapped around its handle, held the hot pan like it was a weapon. Lindsay set down the tin plates she was laying out with a sharp click.

The five women stood shoulder to shoulder against him.

They didn't look much alike. Lindsay and Emma some, but otherwise they were as different from each other as if they shared not a drop of blood. But their eyes, whatever the color, held the same cold glare.

Belle could have slit his gullet with the sharp look she was giving him. She said quietly, but with a voice that spelled Silas's doom, "There's no question about the girls going on the drive. The only question is, are you going with us?"

Not his doom as in he was fired. His doom as in he was going to have to go on a cattle drive with a passel of women. One of 'em wearing diapers!

"B–but. . .but we have one hundred of the hardest miles of—" Silas sputtered to a stop.

"What kind of person *are* you who would go off and leave children home alone for that long?" Belle spoke with a rage that was deadlier for being quiet.

Silas had thought that about Belle earlier; still he had never considered— "You have. . .I thought you said one thousand steers. . . none trail broke. . .we. . .four cowhands. . ." He couldn't give voice to the impossibility of what Belle was proposing.

"My older girls can ride circles around any man."

Suddenly Silas quit being stunned. He was furious. He stepped forward and grabbed Belle by the arm and dragged her out of the house in a single motion and slammed the door behind them. He dragged her a dozen long strides from the cabin then turned her to face him and leaned down so his nose almost touched hers. "Don't you mean they can ride circles around any man you've ever been so stupid as to let crawl into your bed?"

He saw the cold anger in Belle's eyes switch over, all of a sudden, to blazing hot. "I owe you for your work, Mr. Harden. Thirty a month and found. You've worked one hour. I'll get you your *nickel* and you can be on your way!"

Silas jerked her fully against him. "I can't let you and a bunch of baby girls go off on a cattle drive alone. What kind of man do you think I am?"

"The usual kind, Mr. Harden." Belle jerked against his hold, but he hung on. "Isn't there only one kind?"

The door to the cabin opened, and in the gray light of the approaching dawn, Silas saw Lindsay standing in the door with a rifle. She had it aimed at him, and he had no doubt the girl could pull the trigger. Except for the part where he might end up with a belly full of lead, it made him feel a little better to see the young'un be so salty.

"Get you hands offa my ma and get away from her." Lindsay levered a shell into the chamber with a sharp crack. It was a Winchester .44.

It occurred to Silas that this was the second gun pulled on him in recent months. The first one, bandied by Hank Tool, was to force Silas to stay close to Lulamae. This one was the exact opposite.

Silas let Belle go, raised his hands slowly, and stepped away. But he wasn't done talking, regardless of the feisty young'un with the fire iron. "You can't take them, Belle. You'll have to wait. Find more drovers and send *them* on the drive." Then he got slightly less reasonable as he thought of what the crazy woman was proposing. "You stay home and take care of your children the way a decent woman should!"

Belle took a step closer to him, which was just what Lindsay had been threatening to shoot him for. "Go back inside, girls. Mr. Harden and I are having an argument, but he won't hurt me."

Silas glanced up and saw four girls watching him yell at their mother and manhandle her. It made him feel like the lowest form of life that ever slithered across the face of the earth.

"Men have hurt you before, Ma," Lindsay said evenly.

Silas's stomach twisted at the hardness in Lindsay's voice. He'd heard the girls' hostility toward men last night, but it had all been talk about men being lazy and worthless. None of them had indicated a man had laid his hands on Belle in anger.

"Only Gerald when he was drunk. I took care of it then, and I can take care of this now." Belle added, "Anyway, Silas won't."

Lindsay hesitated, the gun still raised.

"I won't, Lindsay. Your ma and I might fight with words, but I'd never harm a woman."

Lindsay kept the gun up.

"Go, Lindsay. Mind me." Belle had the voice of a mother who'd had a lot of practice ruling the roost.

Lindsay gave them both a long look, then reluctantly she lowered the gun, backed into the cabin, and shut the rickety door.

Belle surprised him because she spoke softly. He assumed it was because she was afraid the girls might be listening, because her expression and the fire in her eyes were pure rage. "I may not be what you think of as a decent woman, Silas Harden, but I wasn't born being what I am. Looking and acting like a man wasn't something that I planned on. I didn't ask to have to do everything alone. And it wasn't my wish to raise up girls who wanted to be just like me. I know I'm doing wrong by my young'uns. I know I'm not a—not a decent woman." Belle's voice broke, and she fell silent.

It was then he realized she was speaking softly because his words had struck home hard.

After a second she continued. "But I have to make this drive. My cattle have to be driven to market. *Now.* Without delay. To avoid the winter. If I don't go, all of them will starve to death by spring. My range will be ruined from overgrazing. My way to provide for my daughters will be destroyed. My girls can go with me and face hardship and danger by my side, or I can abandon them to the hazards of staying here without me to protect them." Her hands clenched at her sides.

Silas imagined some of the peril the girls could face. No, they couldn't stay here alone.

Belle lifted her fists and laid them on his chest without striking him. All she needed to do was to entwine her hands and she would be begging.

He hated himself for reducing this proud woman to that.

"The choices I make aren't ones I'm proud of." She tilted her head back to look up at him, her eyes almost level with his chin. He saw those eyes fill with tears. "They're just the only ones I can live with."

He hated himself for making her say she wasn't a decent woman. So far she was the most decent woman he'd ever met.

"The worst part of all of this is you're right. I can't do it without you. I have my doubts if I can do it *with* you. But *without* you we're beat before we start. I need you to go with me, Silas. To go with me and my girls."

The tears and the pleading in her voice and the softening of the sky and the mourning dove's song were all too much. Without any good reason why he would do such a fool thing, he leaned over and kissed her.

Belle gasped and jerked her head away.

For a long second their eyes met, as if a force stronger than both of them was binding them together.

A rooster crowed in the barn. The sun sent its first rays over the horizon. A lazy cow mooed in the morning breeze.

Silas's hand went around the back of her neck and sunk into her long, chocolate brown braid and pulled her mouth back against his.

Her clenched fists held them apart until her hands opened and lay flat against his shirt. She tilted her head and let her neck drop back under the force of his kiss as she opened her mouth. Her hands slid up his chest to his shoulders and around his neck.

Silas slid one strong arm around her waist.

"Ma! You promised!"

Glowing Sun ducked under the low branches of the outstretched ponderosa pine, covering her mouth to still her laughter. She watched her little sister scamper about hunting. Hide-and-seek. A game Glowing Sun remembered from when her parents were alive. It was much like the one she now played with her new family, the Salish. Her parents had called them the Flathead tribe.

When yellow fever had taken the rest of the family, leaving Glowing Sun, nearly ten years old, alive and alone in the remote mountain cabin, a band of Salish warriors had found her, taken her home, and cared for her as one of their own.

Watching her little sister head in the wrong direction, back toward the village, Glowing Sun snickered. Then she realized she'd run too far away. Fear twinged her belly. Her Flathead mother had warned her often enough about leaving the safety of the village. She'd head back in soon, but not quite yet. She waited, grinning, for her chance to dart into the open and touch the base.

A hard hand clamped over her mouth.

Glowing Sun screamed, but no sound got past those hard fingers.

An arm circled her waist like a vise.

She reached behind her head, clawing. She kicked and twisted her body. Wrenching wildly, she tried to break the iron grasp. Then she thought of her knife.

As she reached for it, the man shifted his grip and trapped both her arms, locking her hands to her sides so she couldn't get to the razor-sharp blade. The man holding her grunted in pain but kept a firm hold. "She's wild. She don't know we're savin' her." Rasping breaths and vague, mostly unknown words sounded from behind her, not far up. The man seemed to be only a little taller than Glowing Sun.

From a foot or so farther behind, someone whispered, "Let's put some distance between us and them Flathead."

She jerked violently and nearly slipped from his grasp, but then his arms tightened. His smothering hand stayed in place, and her arms were bound even more firmly to her sides.

If she could just scream once, her father would come. Wild Eagle, too. They were promised to each other. Even her younger brother, Thunder Light. Her mother and sister would fight for her. The whole village. They had always protected her.

She hadn't heard the white language for nearly eight summers, and few of their words were clear.

"I'll grab her feet. Then we'll make tracks for the nearest settlement."

The second man rounded her, and she saw one of her assailants for the first time. His ugly, heavily furred face, his stinking body covered in crudely cut furs, his filthy hands reaching for her.

She lashed out a foot, and he grabbed it, then caught the other and wrapped his arms around her knee-high moccasins. He caught her deerskin dress, wrapping it around her legs like binding. He sneered. A thick scar glowed red across one eye, down into his beard, and up his forehead into his heavy beaver-skin cap.

The man behind her kept a tight hold, solid as an iron clamp on her waist, never releasing her mouth.

She fought them and saw the beading of her dress snap. The pretty beads she'd sewn so painstakingly along her neckline scattered. She wanted to cry. The beads were so dear. She yanked at the man's arm, substituting rage for sorrow. Rage made her strong, sorrow weak. She'd learned that well, despite the words of the kindly missionaries who told her anger was a sin. Surely it wasn't a sin to hate men such as these. She cried out in her heart for God to send her family, the Salish.

God save me. Save me from whatever these vile men have in store.

She shouted her fury, but the words remained buried behind the suffocating hand.

The men carried her at a near run away from her village.

Oh, why hadn't she listened to her parents and stayed near safety? She clawed at the wrist of the captor behind her, but he began nearly crushing her, and she quit so she could breathe.

They slipped along, dodging trees, sliding more than walking down the steep, heavily wooded mountain that surrounded her village.

A cold wind warned of approaching winter. If they took her far, her family would have to leave for the winter campgrounds. She would never find them again.

Their tepees were set up along the low valley, surrounding the crystal water rushing through this part of the Bitterroots. It was the tribe's favorite fall hunting ground. Trout swam thick in the rushing stream, and elk and bighorn sheep were abundant. They could gather food for the harsh winter months ahead.

She left that safety farther behind with every step. Her muffled shouts did nothing to stop the men. Rescue became more and more distant.

A desperate jerk pulled her foot loose. She drove her heel into the man's belly.

His eyes turned wicked, furious. He snagged her flailing foot and wrapped one arm around her feet so tightly she cried out in pain, but no sound escaped.

The man at her feet swung back a fist.

"Not now." The man gagging her lifted her higher against his chest, her breath nearly cut off. "How're ya gonna hit her without hitting me? Knock my hand away, and she'll get loose hollarin'. We'll be out the reward her family'll pay."

Family. She recognized that word. What were they saying about her family? She couldn't bring in a breath. The men roughly pulled her this way and that as they stumbled and ran and moved, moved, moved ever farther from home.

Emerging from the thickest trees, the men picked up their pace. She'd heard horrid tales of the white man, especially from Wild Eagle and Thunder Light, who delighted in scaring her to death. She was old enough to remember that her real parents were good. She understood the Salish people's fear yet knew the wild tales of evil didn't apply to all whites. But these looked like the kind her white mother would have feared and her white father would have watched with cautious eyes. She had no doubt they meant her ill.

Too long without a deep breath of air. Too long fighting and turning. Too long terrified. Her head began to spin. She wrenched her neck, trying to find even a small bit of air.

The man stifling her breath gripped her face harder.

Her cheeks burned from the fight. Her thoughts slowed until she felt dull and stupid. The edges of her vision grew dark until she was looking down a tunnel.

No, Lord, I have to stay awake. I have to be ready if there is a chance to escape.

But the hand tightened more. The arm around her waist

weighed on her lungs like stone. The eyes of the man at her feet burned evil, as if he only waited for his chance to repay her for that kick.

She shook her head, trying to say no without the ability to speak. Trying to beg for air.

"Horses just ahead. We'll gag her, and I'll carry her on my pack mule. We can be far from her village before they know she's gone."

"Far. . .village. . ."

Those were words she understood. She'd been alone before. She'd lived for weeks in her family's cabin after her parents died. She'd buried them one by one in the hard, rocky ground. Digging those graves nearly killed her, and she'd prayed that the sickness that was taking her mother, father, and two little brothers would take her, too.

She'd stayed healthy in that house of death, with no idea how to exist except one day at a time. The aloneness after her real family's death haunted her. To this day, she often woke up screaming to find she'd been trapped back in that deserted cabin.

Into that monstrous aloneness, her new father had come. Though she remembered her terror of the huge, dark-skinned warrior, she had been given no choice. He'd swung her high on his horse and taken her to a new home. A home with so many people she could never be alone again.

"Far. . .village. . ."

No air. No hope. No family.

No, no, God, please no.

The swirling darkness came closer and faded to only the red eyes of the man who held her legs. The rest of the world faded to black, but those glowing eyes followed her.

Burning in the darkness like the eyes of Satan.

CHAPTER 6

Belle jerked away from Silas as if she'd been burned.

He wasn't sure he wasn't on fire himself.

His eyes went to that doorway and that gun aimed at him. Again.

Lindsay aimed that rifle at his chest as if he were wearing a big fat target that had been pinned on him for the sole purpose of collecting bullets.

Belle wrenched away from Silas, muttered, "What is happening to me?" and practically ran to the house, ignoring Silas and Lindsay. Then, in a slightly throaty voice, she called out, "Breakfast is ready."

Silas could smell the eggs and biscuits. He had a long day ahead of him. He'd barely slept the night before. Now he decided without one split second of hesitation to start the day without eating. There was no force short of God Almighty Himself—coming down from heaven with a big stick—that was powerful enough to get him to go into that house and sit all cozy with the Wild Bunch.

He mumbled something about already having eaten and rode out to the steers without looking back, although his hair tingled

69

with the feel of Lindsay and her fire iron drawing a bead on his backside. He was almost out of the yard when he finally heard the door swinging shut.

Just before it closed, he heard Lindsay say, "Ma! How could you—" The door slammed, and whatever else she said was cut off, which didn't matter, because he was riding away so fast he couldn't have heard anyway.

He rode into a lush canyon full of fat, lazy cattle, mostly lying down like the contented beasts they were. Belle had a knack for tending cattle; there was no denying that this all-girl crew was doing a good job.

Silas began hollering to wake the herd up, and as they rose he hazed the glossy herd of T Bar cattle toward the notch in the high side of the canyon where Belle had said they had to take the trail out. He admired the healthy animals as he stirred them from their sleep.

Belle had contrived a rickety fence and held them in a box canyon that seemed to have only one entrance. But on the far north side, a fissure cut into the looming cliffs surrounding the canyon.

Silas could see the rubble, some stones as big as a man, that had caved off that fissure over the years. He knew the trail up had been cleared by hand, and he knew, after listening to Belle and her girls at supper last night, that none of her husbands had done the backbreaking work.

Emma was the first of the girls to show up. She had the baby strapped on her back, and Silas had his hands full with not starting to scream. She set right to work without speaking to him. Lindsay was close behind. Then Belle came with Sarah.

No one had spoken; they'd just fallen to work, Sarah included, on a wiry little cow pony that she handled like an old puncher. Belle came and took the baby from Emma, but even carrying an infant on her back, she gave herself no quarter that Silas could see. Still, the sight of that baby and what lay ahead of Silas almost set him to screaming and running.

With his jaw tightly clenched, he kept working until he had all the steers on their feet. A good number of them had already finished filling their bellies with water from the pond that had been dammed up behind a creek. They were starting to crunch on the shoulder-high prairie grass. Silas had shooed them toward the back of the canyon.

Sarah rode straight for the high trail, pushing a few cattle along in front of her. That trail was so narrow and steep the cattle had to go up single file. The stretch wasn't long but high and treacherous as anything they'd face. Sarah led the string of pack animals and spare mounts tied together on a long rope. That along with a few cattle she pushed left a marked trail for the herd. They liked none of it, but with Silas and the womenfolk punching, once the lazy things began moving, they were contented enough to go where they were told.

The cattle weren't the only thing being hazed. Silas had been in a haze since Lindsay had broken up whatever madness was going on between him and his boss. He pushed himself harder, hoping to keep himself busy enough to forget those minutes alone with Belle.

With the girls working with him, they had the herd headed in the right direction in minutes. Sarah took the lead with the horses. The cattle trailed after her.

Belle took the drag, and taking his life in his hands, he rode up to her.

"Let me do this." Every drover knew drag was the worst. Dirty, hot, slow, exhausting. It was a man's job, and that was the long and short of it.

"I've got it." Belle didn't look him in the eye.

He wanted to argue. He was all set to argue. Then he saw the stubborn set of her jaw and gave up without a fight. "Fine, you take the first shift."

"The boss rides drag. I don't take shifts. Get back to work, unless you're already tired of the hard labor." She finally lifted that clenched jaw and looked him in the eye.

"Look, there were two people back there. It wasn't only me—"

"You asking for your time already, Mr. Harden? I'd hoped you'd stick with us longer than midmorning the first day, but I can't say I'm surprised."

Narrowing his eyes, he thought maybe there was going to be a fight after all. "I'm staying." He wheeled his horse and rode away before he had to share one more word with the stubborn woman.

Drag wasn't too hard now, but when they got off grassland and the herd kicked up dust, it would be choking, bitter work. Silas let her stay, although his instinct was to take the worst spot himself. He'd relieve her later when the conditions were worse, and maybe she'd accept it as his duty to take a turn. On a normal cattle drive, everyone rode drag for a spell, but Belle and her prickly pride might make it hard for her to give up the job.

Besides, to take over he'd have to stay there and argue, and right now that was beyond him because he didn't know what to say. He couldn't remember ever kissing anyone who made him lose his senses quite so thoroughly.

Silas shifted on the saddle and noticed a feisty longhorn with a rack almost six feet across trying to drop back behind the herd and return to the easy living of that valley. He spurred his horse toward the troublemaker, glad for a chance to keep busy dodging horns and hooves. The drive should have been demanding every ounce of his attention anyway. He got to work and firmly ignored the whole Tanner family.

He probably ought to be grateful he didn't have to take a turn carrying the baby.

❧

Wade pushed to make his trip to the line shack in record time.

He couldn't pull his mind away from Belle Tanner and that cattle drive.

Everyone who knew Belle knew she'd take her little girls along. Wade shuddered at the thought, remembering the times his father had forced him to do things beyond his ability and drive his horse even harder.

It was late in the day, and he wasn't going to make the line shack tonight. First, Seth had been slow getting the supplies packed. Linscott seemed to stay in town for the pure pleasure of goading him. Wade finally got out of Divide, and a horse came up lame five miles down the trail. He had to go back and get a new critter. The sun had been high in the sky before Wade was laying tracks at a good clip.

As he crested a rise, still with many miles of rugged riding ahead into the wooded area that abutted Sawyer and Linscott land, a silhouetted figure came riding out of the setting sun.

Wade didn't have to see a face to know who it was. Nobody sat a horse like his pa.

They rode toward each other on the narrow, heavily wooded mountain trail. Wade had the sense of a showdown. It wasn't on Main Street at high noon, but the tension drummed in Wade's ears at the sound of hoofbeats.

His father pulled to a stop, and Wade did the same. To pass each other on the trail would be a close thing. Wade had seen his father in Divide a time or two since he'd left the ranch, but they'd never been alone. All Wade could think was, if he rode on past, for a few paces, he'd be within striking distance.

Please, Lord, help me be a real man. Help me respond to my father with love and strength. I know only a pure miracle could make Pa love me, but can You somehow make him respect me just a bit? Or at least help me get out of here without a black eye?

Facing his father, he recognized the gunslinger eyes, even though to Wade's knowledge his father had never killed anyone.

Wade nodded a greeting.

"What are you doing out this way, boy?"

Wade thought of several evasive answers. Pa would hate that his son was working for Linscott, another big rancher. He'd hate that Wade was living with Red Dawson, working as a hired hand. He'd hate that Wade had plans to meet Belle Tanner along the trail and throw in as a drover.

The fact wasn't lost on Wade that, no matter what he said right now, his father's reaction would be to hate.

There was freedom in that, knowing that nothing would make his father happy. Happiness had to come from inside, from God. So since no answer was going to please the old goat, Wade told the simple truth. "I'm taking supplies to Linscott's line shack. After that, I'm going to hunt up Belle Tanner's cattle drive. She's culling her herd and driving a bunch to Helena."

Mort's face darkened. His fists clenched on the reins, and his horse shook its head nervously and snorted, rattling the metal in its bridle. "You'll be an errand boy for Linscott and work as a cowhand for a woman boss, but you won't come home to take your place?"

Wade nodded. "That's right, I won't." He had ten excuses, or rather reasons, the main one being he wasn't going to put himself under a tyrant's iron fist ever again. But his father had heard this before.

"I'm cutting you out of my will if you don't come home and mind your responsibilities."

Wade knew the ranch and cattle were worth a fortune, and he was working hard now, earning enough to get by with none to spare. But he couldn't bring himself to give one whit about that fortune his pa dangled in front of him. "It's your ranch to do with as you please." Wade swallowed and forced himself to speak the truth. "You've always said you were ashamed of me. Well, I've finally done the growing up I needed to do. I can't be a man with you ruling over me. And you don't know how to be anything but a tyrant. So forget about me. Forget I'm your son. Cut me out of your will. I won't take that land and those cattle and your money even if you do leave it to me."

Wade had a softening of his heart as he said those words. Not because he was changing his mind, but because somewhere deep inside, buried in fear and even shadows of hatred, he still loved his father, still wanted his father's respect. He cared enough to speak of what was important. "You know I've made my peace with God now. No more drinking, no more cards, no more looking for notches in my gun. I'm a man now that *I* can respect, even if you can't. You're getting older, Pa. You need to start coming in to Red's church. You're long past time preparing for the next life."

Mort spurred his horse and rammed into Wade, nearly unseating him. "I don't want to hear about what a weakling I've raised."

Wade's horse pranced sideways, nearly smashing Wade's leg between the saddle and a stout oak. He had his hands full settling the startled animal.

"I want you back on the ranch." Pa jabbed his finger like a knife aiming for Wade's heart. "I want a son I can be proud of, not ashamed of."

"I *am* a son you can be proud of." Wade fought with his horse until he brought it under control. "If you'd stop and listen to me, you'd know that, but you're too stiff-necked to admit it. If I come home, it'll be more of the same bullying, just like what you're doing now, just like what you've done all your life. I refuse to live like that. No *man* would put up with being knocked down and kicked, yelled at and insulted."

Wade's shoulders squared and he said the awful ugly truth. "You *hate* me for leaving, but you hated me for staying, too. Admit it, Pa. You just plain hate me." A piece of Wade died with that simple statement.

Then Wade thought of a bigger truth. "And it's not just me. You hate everybody. What joy has all your money and land bought you? You're the most miserable man I've ever known."

"Why, you little whelp." Mort guided his horse closer, his fist clenched and raised.

"You're going to hit me, Pa?" Wade got ready to duck. He wasn't having a fistfight with his pa, but he wasn't going to stay still and let himself be beaten either. "Just for refusing to come home? Well, that'll sure convince me I should come, won't it?" Bitterly, Wade laughed at what a stubborn old coot his pa was. And what a fool Wade was for still loving him.

"I don't have to do much to earn a beating from you, do I? I think you oughta know I'm ashamed you're my *father*." Not the loving words Wade had hoped to share with his pa. Not the gentle call to turn to God. "*You're* a poor excuse for a man." The anger poured out of Wade with such venom it surprised even him. "Once I started growing up, once I got to know what being a man really meant, once I found God, I knew *you* were someone to be ashamed of."

Mort froze, his elbow bent, his fist drawn back.

God, I know it's wrong to tell him I'm ashamed of him. I know I'm supposed to reach him with love. Forgive me. Make me wise and kind. Let my boldness be from You and for You.

His father, eyes blazing, lowered his arm. "I'm doing it. I'm changing my will. You'll be penniless."

Wade had already said his piece. He had only one thing left to add. "I love you, Pa. If you ever get to the day when you think you can love me back, I'd be obliged to try and get along. But I'll *never* live on the ranch again, and I'll wish whoever gets it after you die good luck. It'll be broken up, I reckon. It'll make good homes for a whole lotta people."

Mort sneered and jerked the reins, guiding his horse past Wade without swinging a fist.

Wade looked after his father and felt the loss of a parent's love. Even worse, the loss of a man's soul. All of that burned like tears made of brimstone as Pa rode away without looking back.

Silas checked on the girls a thousand times throughout that first relentless day.

They were fine.

He couldn't have helped them if they weren't, because he didn't have a moment to spare beyond seeing that they were still in the saddle and working. By the time they got the last steer driven out of the canyon, the whole herd had spread itself across the rugged, rocky plain, hunting succulent young plants that were a sad comedown from their rich grasslands. Silas didn't think there was a single steer that hadn't tried ten times to go back into that canyon, and he swore the critters were working together at times, one to distract him while ten made a break down the back trail for home.

There was no thought of a noontime meal; the cattle would have been back at the ranch by the time the coffee boiled. Silas ate hardtack and jerked beef that he'd packed in his saddlebag, and he saw the girls and Belle doing the same.

He saw Belle swing the baby around to the front from time to time and drop back slightly at drag to attend to Elizabeth's diaper, or whatever else a baby needed.

Silas had kept a lot of space between him and the rest of the crew, but once in the late afternoon, when Silas was so tired he was beginning to forget why he had to avoid the other cowpunchers, a steer cut from the herd and ran within a few feet of Belle while she held the baby in front of her.

Belle, without hesitation, worked her cow pony to stop the steer.

Silas raced his horse over to her, and with a quick glance and nod at Belle so she knew he had things under control, he hazed it back in the right direction. It was only after he had settled in a couple of hundred yards away from Belle that he thought about the way she'd handled her cow pony with one hand on the reins while she clutched Elizabeth to her chest with the other arm. His stomach dropped all the way down to below his belly when he realized Belle had held the baby just so to feed her.

Silas's logical mind told him that, although he hadn't thought of it, of course a woman fed her baby that way, and really it was more convenient than driving a milk cow along on the trail and taking time to milk her several times a day. But no amount of logic could stop his stomach from tap dancing around inside him. It was just too crazy a situation to grab ahold of. No one would ever believe it.

And with that thought, Silas knew he was a dead man.

Even if they all survived the trip without a scratch—which seemed unlikely—he was going to have to spend the rest of his life on the dodge against the chance that the other hard, lonely men who worked cattle in the West would hear he'd signed on for a drive with a baby, a breast-feeding mother, and three little girls. He was never going to be able to live it down.

As soon as they had the cattle safe in Helena, he'd just go ahead and shoot himself.

Silas watched Belle ride right up despite that kiss this morning and look him square in the eye.

Working like a dog and being ten steps beyond exhausted must help a woman get over things.

"I'll take first watch," she said. "The cattle will hold here because of the water."

Exhaustion hadn't been enough for him. He couldn't look at her without remembering and wondering and wanting. "You go get some supper. I'm fine for a while."

"No." Belle shook her head. The boss, clear as could be. "I need time later seeing to Betsy. You go."

Silas glanced at the camp and saw Lindsay and Sarah. Emma was riding a slow, wide circle around the thirsty cattle lining the narrow mountain stream. Belle had left Elizabeth with Lindsay, who already had a fire going.

Silas thought about what "seeing to Betsy" meant. He wanted to be a hundred yards away from the camp when that event took place. Make that a hundred *miles*. "Fine, I'll eat now and take next watch."

Then as he rode into the roughly made camp, he quit thinking about babies and kissing and remembered this morning and the angry girls he'd faced. Wishing there was another choice but to eat with them, he admitted he was starving. Stiffening up his backbone, he rode in, cool as a Montana winter. Then he went to work making the fire smaller and hotter.

The cattle were drinking out of the creek, so he went upstream a piece and fetched back water. He stripped his saddle off his horse and rubbed him down with a handful of grass then slapped him on the flank to send him off with the horses. He proceeded to do the same with Lindsay's horse.

Lindsay came up beside him, carrying Betsy on her back. With hostility that didn't conceal the girl's fatigue, she said, "I care for my own horse."

Silas glanced over his shoulder at the thin, pretty woman-child with the glowing golden hair coated in dirt and sweat and the too-old eyes. He had a burst of insight as to what might convince the girl to let him help her. "I know you can do it, Linz, but I think Sarah's about all in. Let her see me do your horse, then she'll let me do hers. I'm almost finished here. By the time you get supper on, I can have the rest of the camp set."

Lindsay hesitated. It reminded Silas of the way she'd gone

about taking her rifle off of him this morning. At last she looked over her shoulder at Sarah, her face contorted from the effort, heaving a heavy pot full of cut-up dried beef and water onto the fire. Silas realized he had been right on target about how tired Sarah was.

Lindsay looked back at him with weary eyes rimmed in dark shadows. "Thanks." She turned back to the camp.

Before she stepped away, Silas had to ask, "Did just one of her husbands hurt her once, Linz? Or was it more husbands, and more than once?"

Lindsay didn't turn around, but she quit walking. The baby stared at him from Lindsay's back, and he braced himself to be called Papa again.

Finally, Lindsay looked him in the eye over her shoulder. "Gerald tried it from time to time, but he only laid his hands on her once I ever knew about. Ma. . .well, Ma was sober and tough as a boot and Gerald was just a no-account drunk. The reason they were having a fight to begin with was because she didn't like the way he was cussin' us girls. After he swung on her, Ma picked herself up offa the floor."

Silas wanted to go dig Gerald up and kill him all over again.

"She just laid him out flat with the kitchen skillet. The fat lip he gave her quit bleeding and healed in no time. After that, she just let him drink, and we girls learned to lay low when he came home. He weren't a smart man on his best day. Hiding from him was easy."

Silas's heart ached at her acceptance of that kind of life. "Lindsay, not all men are like the ones who married your ma."

Lindsay shrugged and a sad smile crossed her face. "I know that's true. So I guess it's something wrong with Ma that she picks men who are useless. I think it's easier to think bad of all men than to think bad of my ma."

Silas didn't know what to say to that.

"It ain't all her fault, though," Lindsay continued. "I was seven or so when Gerald come a-courtin'. I know what it was like. There were men all the time. Every day someone else would come, and the ones who'd been by before stopped back. Sometimes they'd fight over her, and I know Ma was scared. She had me and Emma and the ranch to run alone. There were always men coming by, and some of 'em not very nice. I think one day she just snapped. She grabbed at the closest man to get the others to stand off. And that ended up being Gerald.

"With Anthony it was the same only worse. Everyone just assumed she'd marry someone, and they acted like she was a nuisance, making them ride all the way from town over and over. She didn't want another man. She wasn't scared of being alone anymore, but she finally just caved under the pressure, and Anthony was there. 'A good-lookin' devil,' Ma said. Looked a lot like Betsy, and easy to boss around. And Ma just thought she had to. So many people said, 'A woman's got to be married.' Like it was in the United States Constitution or something, and Ma went along."

Silas did his best not to roll his eyes. What was the woman thinking to keep picking bums? Surely good men had come courting.

"This time, when Anthony died, she was gonna hold firm. She promised us." Lindsay scowled at Silas. Then after a long silence, she said, "And now you're here."

Silas didn't know what to say. He had no intention of marrying Belle, but he'd been kissing her this very morning in front of all her girls. He couldn't blame Lindsay for thinking what she did. And a part of him wanted to trot out his virtues as if he were speaking to Belle's father. He wanted to say, *My intentions are honorable. I respect your ma. I don't drink. I'm a hardworking man. I'd never hit a woman or cuss you girls.* But why would he say all that to Lindsay except if he was thinking to marry her ma? Which he wasn't.

Except every time he'd seen Belle today, he'd wanted to ride up next to her, drag her off her horse onto his, and taste her all over again. He couldn't explain that to a young girl when he couldn't even understand it himself. "I'd never hurt your ma, Lindsay."

Lindsay looked away from him. "There's lots of kinds of hurt, Mr. Harden. It ain't all done with fists." She turned her back on him and walked over to the fire.

Silas watched Lindsay urge Sarah down onto the ground so she could lean back against a fallen log. She put Betsy in her little sister's arms and eased the two little girls around until they were practically lying down.

He heard Lindsay say softly, "I need help, Sarah. I need you to sit still and cuddle the baby up, or she'll cry for Ma, and Ma's riding herd. And if Ma comes by on a circuit, she'll have to stop. You know how tired Ma is. You've got to do this to help her."

"Getting grub's my job, Lindsay. And Betsy don't cry none. You take Betsy and sit."

"Please do it for me, sweetie. My back is tired from carrying her."

Sarah subsided with the baby in her arms.

By the time Lindsay began stirring the stew, Sarah was fast asleep, the baby awake in her arms, looking around and kicking. Lindsay came over and lifted the baby away, strapped Betsy on her own back, and went back to the campfire to work.

Silas hurried through the horse chores so he could help her, but by the time he was finished, Lindsay had a plate ready to hand him.

"Eat quick and go spell Emma." The look in her eye told him not to offer any help.

He sat and ate, and finally Lindsay ate beside him, feeding bits to the baby. Silas went to find a fresh horse and another tired little girl.

CHAPTER 7

Wade rode up to the line shack and was surprised at the number of horses: four in the corral behind the little log building, three tied out front.

His hand stayed cautiously near his six-gun and prayed there wasn't trouble. One of the things he'd never managed to hand over to God was the deep sense of his own cowardice.

When he'd been drinking and carousing, he'd wanted to put a notch in his gun to prove himself a man. He'd never been able to pull the trigger though. Now he was glad. Glad he didn't have a death on his conscience.

And now he knew better than to judge his courage against so false a standard as the ability to kill. But his heart still contained a seed of sickness deep inside, calling himself a coward.

What if he needed to defend himself? What if one day he took a wife and had a child and they were in danger and only Wade and his gun stood between his family and death? Seeing these strange horses reminded him that in this rugged land death was just one dumb move away. And a life-and-death decision, like drawing and shooting a gun, was the only thing keeping a man on this side of the pearly gates.

Wade no longer worried about those gates; he knew where he'd spend eternity. But it fretted him like an itch he couldn't scratch to know he was a coward.

He rode his horse to a grassy area back a ways from the shack. He swung down and ground-hitched his mount. That kept the pack animals, which were tied up in a line behind Wade's cow pony, together. The animals went to chomping grass, and Wade walked toward the house, wary. Before he got close, the door swung open and five men sauntered out. Wade knew two of them; Linscott's hands seemed at ease, not worrying about the three strangers.

"You brung vittles." An old drover, one of Linscott's longtime cowpokes, rubbed his hands together like he was eyeing a feast.

Wade smiled. "Yep, oughta be enough supplies in those packs to keep you fat all winter."

"I'm Buck Adams." One of the strangers stepped forward and extended a hand. His eyes were clear and his expression pleasant. Buck was the tallest of the bunch. He looked to be nearing forty. A man at the height of his strength and ability.

"Wade Sawyer." While they shook, Wade wondered if, like so many men, Buck had heard of Wade's pa. Often men would be extra friendly to him, thinking to befriend the son of a wealthy, powerful rancher they'd heard of by reputation. Others would immediately be hostile, and Wade figured they'd been stomped on by his pa or knew someone who had. There were plenty of 'em out there.

Buck nodded but didn't react, which meant Wade didn't have to live up or down to his father with these men.

"This here's Shorty."

Shorty was gray-haired and had a quick laugh and didn't speak a sentence when a syllable would do. But he had eyes that told a hard story of a life in an unsettled land and a toughness no one could earn except by facing a thousand dangers and surviving. Silas saw a lifetime of wisdom in Shorty's watchful eyes.

"And this is my son, Roy." Buck clapped a skinny kid on the back who had a man's height but not a spare ounce of meat on his bones.

Roy seemed to practically buzz with nervous energy. He used that energy to throw himself into the unpacking with a good nature.

The men, all six of them, fell to unpacking and stowing away the food. The tiny shack was lined with cans and bags before long.

"These fellas are just passing through," Linscott's old drover said.

From the look of their well-kept horses and the way they threw in to help work, Wade was impressed with the trio.

When the work was done, Roy twitched and looked around, bouncing his knee as if sitting still made him crazy.

Wade had to control a grin as he remembered being so young he thought resting was wasting his life. He was only twenty years old, and he'd already grown out of that.

"Come on in and set a spell. Stay a few days." The old drover picked up the coffeepot.

Wade looked out at the cold fall wind. He'd much prefer to stay. It was going on evening and he'd have a cold night outside. But he could ride a few hours toward Belle's drive, and he felt rushed to get there. She'd already be two days down the trail by now.

He deliberately didn't refer to the drive being run by a woman. "I told the Tanner outfit I'd help run their herd up to Helena. They're trying to beat the winter. You know that mountain valley the Tanners live in. It's a late start, and they need to push hard and get back home before the gap snows shut for the winter. I'd better hit the trail."

Buck straightened from where he'd settled on the floor. "We could use a month's work." He tipped his head at his son and Shorty.

Roy got to his feet as if he was dying to hit the trail right now. No doubt he was.

"It'll be a hard drive because they're shorthanded. I told 'em I'd come along as quick as I could." Wade was uncomfortable hiring three men on for Belle, but by the time they rode the trail to catch her, Wade would have a good idea of what they were made of. And he'd be there to help her run 'em off if necessary. Belle'd most likely welcome them.

"I can't make promises for the Tanners. . . ."

Shorty frowned but remained silent.

"Let's do it, Pa." Roy began pulling on his buckskin coat. The boy looked like he planned to hunt Belle down himself if Wade didn't lead the way.

"It's a hard ride through mean, cold country. We'll be days catching up." Wade waited to see what the men were made of.

Buck grinned. "We'll partner with you for the ride over. If we don't get hired on, we'll just keep drifting."

Wade looked at the three men. Considering he was taking three strangers toward a pack of females. . .he knew Belle well enough to know those salty daughters of hers would be along. . . Was he turning wolves loose on a herd of lambs?

He thought of Belle, those direct eyes and scarred hands. Not all lambs, not even close.

"Saddle up. We can put a lot of miles behind us before we sleep."

❧

The Tanner girls were tough, Silas'd give 'em that.

Lindsay was the leader. He saw countless instances of the oldest girl bossing her little sisters around, and sometimes even him and Belle. For the most part, they all did as Lindsay told them because the girl was organized and uncommon smart.

When it came right down to it, Belle was the boss. Silas had noticed that the girls listened to him when he thought things should be done a certain way. But for the regular stuff where no out-of-the-ordinary decisions needed to be made—which described almost everything on a cattle drive—Lindsay was the one in charge.

Emma was the natural horsewoman—so confident in the saddle that Silas rarely quit wondering at it. The first to mount up in the morning and the last to quit the saddle come suppertime, she seemed to have limitless energy. She was also a quiet kid, not prone to much give-and-take with the rest of them. Emma reminded Silas of a lot of cattlemen he'd known in his day who worked and ate and slept and worked some more without having much to say that wasn't about the job.

Sarah was the talker. She was the one often as not who made them laugh or made Silas squirm with her straight talk. The eight-year-old could ride like an Indian, and she did her share in the saddle, often with the baby on her back. But in many ways, Sarah was like the mother. She was quick with a word of sympathy for cuts and bruises. She changed the baby's diaper more than her share. She ran circles around most chuckwagon cooks he'd known.

Belle's contribution to the order was in the way she respected her daughters. She didn't shout words of caution or advice. She expected her girls to be capable, and they were. Silas could see the proud, confident way the girls rose to their mother's expectations. And while they were at it, Belle was outworking them all.

Silas pushed himself hard. At first he thought it was to take up the slack for a bunch of womenfolk. But he soon admitted it was to keep from being the slacker of the group.

The second day, at the fire at night, Silas noticed Emma had bound her three middle fingers together with a leather thong cut off her deerskin coat. "What happened to your hand?" He sat on a fallen log with a plate of beans and beef Sarah dished up.

Emma shrugged as she got her food. "Broke my finger." She

scooped up the first bite of beans without further comment.

None of the rest of them spared the broken bone a glance.

Silas felt a spark of annoyance at the unsympathetic group.

Sarah kept stirring the beans. Lindsay was feeding the baby. Belle was still riding herd.

"Let me have a look at it."

Emma arched a blond brow at him. "Why?"

With a snort of disgust, Silas set his plate aside. "Just do it."

Emma shrugged and untied her fingers. "I checked to see if the bone was lined up proper before I strapped it down."

Silas took her hand gently. The girl was right. The middle finger was swollen but straight. Emma was patient, but she acted as if he were just putting off her getting to eat.

The next morning, Lindsay's horse bucked her off twice, while Silas had his hands full saddling his own bronco. Each time she hit the ground with a dull *thud* and a kicked-up swirl of dust. Then she got to her feet, rounded the contrary beast up, and jumped on his back again before Silas could help.

After the horse kicked its morning kinks out and settled down, Silas noticed a vivid red streak of blood running down the side of her face. He rode over. "Are you okay?"

She was attending to her horse and looked up surprised. Following the direction he was looking, she swiped the back of her leather glove over the cut, smearing blood across the whole side of her face. She glanced down at the bright red on her hand without much interest. "Cuts on the head bleed something fierce," she said matter-of-factly. "I'll be fine." She rode off without further comment.

Silas had to grind his teeth to keep from telling her to get down and let him doctor the cut.

Belle almost got gored by a longhorn steer that same day. She caught the uncooperative critter diving into the brush and woods that came most of the way up to the trail. She harried him with her nimble cow pony, dodging his flashing heels and wicked horns.

Silas was busy with his own side of the herd, but when he saw Belle tangling with that desert brown monster with the white lightning blaze on his face—the brute had given him trouble since the first day—he spurred his horse to get between Belle and certain death.

He got there just in time to see the steer wheel and charge Belle and her horse. The horse jumped out of the way so quickly it almost unseated Belle, riding with Betsy, but she hung on. The razor-sharp horns slashed within inches of Belle's left leg.

Silas snagged his rope off his pommel. He whipped out a loop and sent it flying toward the steer's head. Silas's horse skidded hard to snap the steer off its feet. Silas hit the ground and had the animal's legs hog-tied within seconds.

Silas was riding his own buckskin, and that horse was as good a hand as any of the people he'd ever worked with. Every time the steer tried to regain its feet, the buckskin backed fast enough to keep him laid flat.

"I am sick of this old he-grizzly." Silas took a quick glance at Belle, who still sat on horseback, breathing hard, her expression calm, but Silas thought he saw a tinge of fear and, probably his imagination, just a hint of gratitude.

Silas tied the blazed-face steer's head down to his foreleg with rapid twists of his pigging string and then released the string hog-tying his legs together. Silas released his lasso from the broad horns and jumped free before the spooky mossy-horn knew what had hit him. Silas stepped back into his saddle.

Hazing the beast back toward the herd with his head strapped down to his foreleg, Silas waited until he was satisfied the steer wasn't going to attack; then he turned and rode back to Belle. "We'll leave him like that till he settles in for the night. It won't hurt him, and it might gentle him some."

Belle stared after the steer. "I've seen that done a time or two, but I've never done it."

"You can't throw a steer like that."

Belle looked at him and shrugged. "Sure I can. I run a branding iron every spring, but that's mostly calves. Still, you can't run a ranch without busting cattle."

Silas couldn't seem to get his mind to twist around the sight of Belle doing something like he'd just done. Cold fear shook him at the thought of Belle wading into that mass of churning hooves and stabbing horns. "I don't believe it. You're too small to throw a steer."

"Are you calling me a liar?" Belle dropped the question into the space between them like a drawn six-gun.

Silas'd seen that level, challenging look before out West. A man's word was everything out here, where thousands of acres or whole herds of cattle might change owners on a handshake. To call a man a liar was to cause his reputation damage that might destroy his ability to make a living and follow him to his grave. Silas knew better than to call anyone a liar. And he hadn't meant that now, but judging from the golden lightning flashing out of her eyes, Belle didn't see it that way.

His Western learning kicked in. "No, I apologize for that. I haven't done much this whole trip but underestimate you, and I'm sorry. I just thought as little as you are. . ."

"How much do you weigh?" Belle asked through clenched teeth.

Silas shrugged. "Don't rightly know. A hundred and eighty, or two hundred pounds, I guess."

"And how much does that steer you just threw weigh?"

"A ton. At least."

"I'd say more like twenty-three hundred pounds."

Silas was a good judge of cattle, and he'd say that steer weighed within twenty pounds of Belle's estimate. "What about it?"

"Throwing cattle isn't about *weight*. If it was, the few pounds difference in ours wouldn't matter."

"It's more than a few pounds, Belle. You're a skinny little thing, and I—"

"It's about leverage and quickness." Belle cut him off. "And, more than anything, a good cow pony. You know your horse did most of the work there, and mine is just as good. All of my horses are well trained to work cattle. Emma can bust a steer better than I can. Lindsay just as well. This is the second year Sarah has bulldogged calves at branding time."

Belle rode her horse straight up to Silas's side. "Don't *ever* tell me what I can and cannot do."

Belle's voice was so cold it sent shivers up Silas's spine. "I'll try and watch my mouth, boss. But I'm trying to learn about a new kind of woman here. The two I almost married weren't a thing like you."

Belle's chin lowered, and the anger left her eyes. Silas knew that was the very reason he'd spoken of such foolish things. Belle was a woman after all. She'd forget about whatever was going on inside her head if she could listen to his mistakes.

She didn't ask, not out loud, but her eyes burned with curiosity.

"The first one was the tough one. I really thought I was set in life. I owned a nice spread in New Mexico. I had a house built, a good herd started, and I had a woman set to marry me. I got caught in the middle of the Lincoln County War. Ever heard of it?"

"I've heard a little. Mainly I've heard of Billy the Kid."

"I met him. I wasn't even involved with that fight. It was between two other bunches of hotheads. But when the bullets started flying, they were none too particular who got caught in the crossfire. My girl thought she saw the future and hitched her wagon to another star. I still thought I'd win her back until the day I came on a group of men on my property. I rode up to order them off."

Silas could still feel the icy chill running down his spine. "One was Billy the Kid. The way he stared at me. . .killing-mean eyes." Silas paused to swallow. He was a coward, no denying it. "I knew it wasn't a fight I could win. The Kid didn't say much. He didn't have to. The law'd broken down, and Billy and his outfit were taking whatever they wanted. The only way to stop him was to kill him, and he was a mighty hard man to kill."

Silas rubbed the back of his neck and forced himself to admit the truth. "Too hard for me." Silas looked at the ground between their cow ponies, not wanting to see what was in Belle's eyes. "They let me ride off."

He'd seen contempt before because he'd ridden to Millicent's pa's ranch and told her he was leaving the country. He'd asked her to come with him.

Contempt. She'd figured out before Silas had that he was a coward.

Millicent had turned Silas down. She'd dealt her cards into another game and she'd made what she saw as the best choice. Later Silas heard the man she'd taken up with had died in the fighting. . .so she'd backed another loser. He was well rid of her, but it still hurt. It was all part of the shame. The failure.

Belle might as well know the truth. She'd know what Millicent had known. Silas wasn't a good bet for a woman. "I quit the country. Went home and paid off my hands and fired 'em. I rode out with what supplies I could pack on a string of horses and what cash I could scrape together. I didn't even try to move my herd. I knew I wouldn't live long enough to enjoy 'em."

"Smart man."

Silas looked up, figuring she was making a joke.

She looked dead serious. Then she smiled. "Did you think I'd say you should have shot it out with Billy the Kid—backed by a pack of his friends? My life has little time for fancy dreams, Silas. You did the right thing, and you know it. You've been drifting ever since? What, two years? Three? That's when that trouble was brewing, right?"

When she put it like that, walking away from Billy the Kid sounded like an act of wisdom. The next wasn't so easy. Running from Lulamae. Belle might as well know.

"I started a new spread in the far corner of northwest New Mexico Territory and got run out of there by a woman. Not as exciting as Billy the Kid."

Belle laughed. "What happened?"

"I got caught kissing her in the stable."

Belle narrowed her eyes, and the smile faded from her pink lips.

Silas wasn't above feeling ashamed.

"And when you were caught you refused to do the right thing?"

Silas well remembered Belle had four daughters. This wasn't a woman who liked seeing young women treated wrong. "She set me up. She grabbed me and kissed me. Her pa was there, handy with his rifle, yelling about my mistreating his daughter before he could even see us, so I knew the two of 'em had it planned. He had friends right behind him, and they took his word against mine. He demanded a wedding. I guess Lulamae was ornery enough that they'd given up finding a husband for her by the regular means."

Belle shook her head. "Overpowered by a girl, huh? I feel *real* sorry for you."

"Well, don't. I've learned my lesson. If you haven't figured it out by now. . .well, I get that same message right back from you, so you understand. I'm *not* gettin' tangled up with a female. Never again. I'm drifting now because it suits me. But I like having land I can call my own. I like a nice spread, and I aim to build myself another one of these days."

"We understand each other then. That. . .that first morning.

Just a stupid, weak moment on my part. I don't have many."

Silas remembered that moment. He'd spent far too much time remembering that moment. *Weak* and *stupid* about explained it. And he knew she didn't have many. That was the honest truth.

"Let's get back to work." Belle looked at the cattle spread out in front of them. Almost trail broke, except for a few like that blazed-face steer. "The sun's moving low in the sky, and there's good grazing up ahead with plenty of water. I might let the cattle stay put for a day or two so the girls can rest."

"After only three days on the trail?" It just came blabbing out of his mouth without a thought. He'd like to let the girls rest, too. He could see that Emma had already lost weight. Lindsay had a gaunt, hard look around her eyes, and Sarah had cried when they woke her up this morning, though only until she was fully awake. Then she cut the tears off instantly and went straight to work setting up breakfast for the camp.

Before Belle could cut him off at the knees, he said, "I think they need it. The first few days on the trail are rough. The cattle are almost trail broke, so it won't be as hard from here on. And we've got that mountain pass ahead of us. We'd better rest now, because there'll be no stopping then."

When he'd first opened his stupid mouth, Belle had looked like she was ready to bite his head off, and he wanted to save his neck. Then, when he'd changed his tune about stopping, she got that soft, sad look in her eyes. The one that'd made him kiss her that first morning, and he wanted none of that either.

Well, that wasn't strictly true. He wanted it something fierce. It just wasn't going to be one of those things he let himself have. He decided maybe he was safer when she was mad.

Before he could think of some way to get her hackles up, she said, "It's so hard on them. They're game as any man, and they'd never ask for me to give them any kind of break. But I'm worried about them. And I don't know if you've noticed, but. . ." Belle stopped talking, and with practiced ease she swung the baby around to her front and looked down at the wide-eyed little girl who rode so patiently day after day. "Betsy has changed."

Silas thought of diapers. "Changed how?"

Belle ran her hand over the baby's cheek. "She doesn't cry anymore."

Silas leaned over and looked at that pretty baby, smudged with dirt and so quiet. Her huge black eyes, lined with lashes too thick for any baby, blinked up at her mama. Silas followed the baby's gaze and saw the feminine side of Belle. He saw the mother in her and wished almost violently that she didn't have to work so hard and that men hadn't done her so wrong.

"Is she sick?" Silas nudged his horse forward to stand side by side with Belle, facing opposite directions, and looked at the little one.

Betsy turned her eyes on Silas, but she didn't smile. Just watched.

Belle shook her head. "All the girls did this. They started out being these pink, perfect little babies. Then I'd carry them along with me while I did chores, and they'd get quiet and watchful. I've seen Indian babies act like this." Belle raised the little one so she could look directly into her eyes.

Betsy reached for Belle's nose, and Belle kissed the little grabbing fingers.

"I don't suppose it's bad. It just doesn't seem quite normal to me. I don't know what else to do than. . .than br–bringing them along."

Silas heard that break in her voice again.

Belle pulled Betsy into her arms and hugged her tight, burying her face in the baby's neck and rocking her gently.

"Betsy has been cared for more gently than the others were in a lot of ways, because Sarah stays in the house with her most of the time. But after only a few days, this drive has changed her."

Silas looked at Belle holding her baby, and something burned in him that almost overwhelmed every lick of sense he had. And right at that moment it was a good thing they had two horses, a thousand head of cattle, a baby, and three suspicious girls between them, or he'd have dragged Belle Tanner into the nearest town and married her without another thought just so she could spend a little time sitting in a rocking chair, tending her baby, while someone took care of her and her girls. And while he was at it, he'd make sure her roof didn't leak!

Belle hoisted Betsy into the crook of her arm and shook her head as if to clear it. "You have a knack for making me doubt myself, Silas. I don't thank you for that."

Silas sat silently, afraid of what might come out of his mouth if he spoke.

Belle turned her gaze on him. "I do thank you for saving me from that steer though." She tucked Betsy back into her sling, lifted the reins with one hand, and squeezed her knees on the sides of her horse. With a soft clucking sound she rode away.

Silas turned to look after her as she rode away, and he surely enjoyed the sight of her working that horse.

Belle Tanner might be the toughest cowpoke he'd ever partnered with. She might talk and work and even think like a man. But Belle Tanner was 100 percent, through and through, pure female, and no one who got within ten feet of her ever doubted it for a moment. He had no doubt that when Belle turned up widowed each time, men came a-runnin', and it wouldn't be any different when word got out about Anthony. The thought of droves of no-good saddle tramps trying to get their hands on Belle didn't sit well with him.

If she was going to get herself mixed up with a no-account saddle tramp, it might as well be him.

He tore his gaze away from her, and it was almost physically painful. Then he spurred his horse for the far side of the herd and worked himself hard the rest of the afternoon just to keep his mind off those hordes of worthless men. . .and the way Belle sat in a saddle.

CHAPTER 8

Resting a day was a poor excuse for an idea.

Rest was not agreeing with her. Instead, rest was giving her the energy to have her imagination running wild.

"I'll go ride a circuit." Silas bent over the basin of warm water and slid his scraped-clean plate in. Belle watched every move. What the man did to a pair of chaps was exactly why resting a day was a poor excuse for an idea.

Silas walked away from the camp, and she almost went after him. She felt her muscles bunch to rise and chase that man down right there on the mountainside.

It wasn't the first time. She'd started toward him every time she came within seeing distance of him. She stopped herself before she could do anything foolish like catch the man alone and kiss him again, but she was fighting some powerful instincts. In the end, only the girls being there kept her from chasing him.

The cattle spread out across a high valley in the foothills of the Bitterroot Mountain Range. They would swing the herd slightly east after this and scale a saddleback pass that took them on the east side of a rugged peak Belle had heard called Mount Jack. That was the worst stretch of the trail. The herd would move slow, wear itself out climbing, line up mostly single file, and trudge at the most two or three miles a day for the next week. Then they'd drop down off the peaks to an easier trek with plenty of water but poor eating for the most part, which would take weight off her steers and make them edgy and difficult to handle for the last two weeks of the drive. The herd needed a few days to fill their bellies and rest up for what was ahead, just as her daughters did.

Belle thought of Silas, out there riding in slow circles around her cattle. She thought of the way he'd worked without asking fool questions or making excuses. She knew in her heart he was a different kind of man than the ones she'd gotten tangled up with before. But she also knew that Gerald had shown no signs of being a drinker before they'd married. And William had seemed like an eager, hardworking young rancher when he thought he'd be getting Belle's pa's ranch. And Anthony. . .well, she'd been down on men by the time she agreed to marry him. She wanted to stop the crowd of suitors, and beyond that, she had expected very little. And that was exactly what she'd gotten.

So, even though she thought Silas was different, she didn't trust her judgment, having proved to be sorely lacking in that ability in the past. Belle spent a moment in silent prayer, asking God to forgive her for the life she'd provided for her girls and the sins she'd committed by marrying men who weren't decent Christians.

It was her. She knew it.

Maybe God could give her a miracle and make her smarter, but so far the miracle hadn't happened. She'd always thought she'd just had bad luck until near the end of her marriage to Anthony when the man had left her on the trail in the midst of giving birth to his child. Anthony was more than worthless; he was evil. And she'd picked him and exposed her children to him.

There was something broken inside her. It wasn't bad luck. She was a pure fool when it came to men; or worse yet, there was something in her that brought out the worst in a man. Maybe Gerald had taken to the bottle because of the way Belle acted. Maybe Anthony had been driven to other women when Belle pushed him aside and did everything herself.

Belle knew there was some truth in it. More likely though, she picked men who were weak because she was used to being in charge, and men who could be pushed around tended to be shiftless from the start. Then she'd run roughshod over them.

"Why be surprised that they ended up being exactly what I expected?" she asked no one, or maybe God. Her question drifted on the air unanswered, but Betsy, who sat on her lap, looked up and raised her pretty dark brows.

The older girls were all away from camp, so Belle smiled at her baby and kept talking. "Maybe if Gerald had needed to get the chores done, he'd have sobered up. You think so, baby? You think I should have let the cattle next thing to starve in the hopes Gerald would take charge?"

Belle's jaw clenched at the very idea. Betsy swatted her playfully on the chin, and she relaxed. "Maybe if, when William wanted to spend the few dollars my pa gave me on foolishness, I hadn't stepped in and told him how it was going to be, William would have had to grow up and do something to put food on the table."

"Mama." Betsy kicked her feet, and Belle felt almost as female holding this baby as she did looking after Silas.

"It makes sense, doesn't it?"

Betsy smiled.

The more Belle thought on it, the more she believed it. "I didn't want a man to take charge, so I got exactly what I deserved, didn't I? I've got no business complaining when my husbands turn out to be exactly like I knew they were. But that doesn't mean I want a man bossing me around, now does it?"

Belle shook her head and tickled Betsy's nose. Maybe resting a day wasn't so bad if she could spend a few minutes playing with her baby. "What it boils down to, little girl, is that I am more determined than ever to stay unmarried."

Betsy smiled and clapped her hands as if applauding Belle's good sense. Or maybe the child was playing, but Belle didn't see it that way.

Looking around to make sure no one was near enough to overhear her little conversation with the only person she dared tell, Belle leaned close and whispered, "But the way that man kissed me, Betsy darlin'"—Belle drew in a deep breath as she recalled it oh, so clearly—"well, it does make me forget some of the hard lessons I've learned about my complete lack of skill at picking husbands. It makes me want to just hunt that man right down on the range and kiss him all over again."

Saying those scandalous words—at least scandalous considering she was determined never to remarry—made Belle look up and search the mountain valley for *that man*. She saw him just as he pulled out his lariat, dabbed a loop on a yearling calf, and started dragging it out of the herd. The herd scattered a bit, but they were too tired and too busy eating to worry about one of their own being hauled away.

He backed the steer a good distance away from the others then busted it and hog-tied it.

"What's the man up to now?" Belle gave Betsy a final bounce then settled her into the carrier.

Before Belle got her horse saddled, Silas got the young longhorn in the clear, busted it, hog-tied it, and knelt on the ground by its head. Emma rode up beside him and got off, kneeling on the steer's back. Belle rode over just as they were releasing the steer. It was skinnier than most. She'd noticed it as a straggler almost from the first.

It jogged away from her when she got close. Then, after a running start, it kicked up his heels the way young cattle do in the spring.

"What was that about?" Belle asked as she pulled her horse to a halt and crossed her arms over the saddle horn.

Silas pulled himself onto his horse's back with a single smooth motion, not using the stirrup. Belle noticed that Emma mounted her horse like Silas did. Her daughter, the best horsewoman among them, was imitating Silas.

"I've been thinking that critter was doing poorly. I wanted to see him up close. I found a goiter growing in his throat and cut it out." Silas turned to Emma. "Thanks for the hand."

Emma nodded wordlessly and turned her mount toward the head of the herd.

Belle said, "Take a break, Emma. It's almost time for my watch and the noon meal is on."

"I want to check the horses first." Emma nodded at the horses. "Some of the green brokes've been harassing the cattle toward the front of the herd. I might have to hobble 'em."

"I've noticed them doing it," Silas said. "I'll go check. We'll need you rested later when your ma has to see to the baby."

Emma hesitated and studied them both for a long minute. Finally, she shrugged and headed toward camp.

When Emma was out of hearing range, Silas laughed softly. "I don't think your daughter trusts us to stand watch together."

Belle smiled. "I can't say I blame her."

"Not with your history of killin' off husbands, then turnin' around and marryin' the first man what comes along."

Belle turned angry eyes on Silas.

"Gotcha." He grinned at her.

Anger twisted into laughter, leaving Belle sputtering as he turned his horse away from her and started riding toward the front of the herd to check the riding stock.

Belle clenched her hands so tightly on the reins, her horse skittered sideways a piece. It was only through pure force of will that Belle kept herself from riding after the confounded man and kissing the daylights out of him.

She was extra careful not to share the night watch with Silas, just because she wanted so much to ride alongside him in the dark. From the first, either she or Silas was riding herd at night, never together at the campfire, never alone in the night. It was exhausting for both of them.

The daylong break was good for the girls and good for the cattle.

But it was the longest day of Belle's life.

Glowing Sun hit the ground hard. The world twisted around, made no sense. Gasping in pain at the collision, she noticed the world was black. She blinked her eyes but couldn't see. Even in the dark of night her eyes should have picked up something.

A hard jerk and something was pulled off her head.

Suddenly she realized she was on her back on the ground. Light blinded her and she blinked and squinted at the pain. Sunlight filtered through towering trees.

Then two dark heads blocked the light. Evil men.

She attacked to find her hands tied.

She screamed to find her mouth gagged.

She jumped to find her feet bound.

So she lay still, inhaling terror.

The one man she'd seen before, holding her feet. His angry eyes had followed her into unconsciousness.

The other, the one who'd cut off her breath, was shorter but otherwise like the angry man, full beard, dark hair, fur coat and hat. The shorter one reached for her with scarred, ugly hands. He lifted her up, steadying her. His grip didn't hurt. His eyes didn't glow with cruelty. He seemed a bit kinder than the other man. Of course, she'd kicked the bigger man. But in fairness, the shorter man's face bore the marks of her fingernails, so if their cruelty was over her behavior, this one had as much cause as the other.

"We're just takin' you back to yer people, miss," the shorter man said. "You've been caught by the Flathead Indians, and we're doing our duty to return you to whites."

Whites. Glowing Sun understood *whites* and *Flathead.* She'd heard that word used for her village.

She shook her head frantically, hoping they'd understand she couldn't speak this language. Maybe if they went slow. Maybe some of her white parents' tongue would return to her. So many years since she'd heard it. Even the missionary to her village spoke the tribal language. The missionary was one of their own people who had learned about God from another village.

The smaller, kinder man said, "We've put a far distance between us and your village. But we're not lettin' you loose, and we're not takin' off the gag. You don't know what's best for you, missy. So we'll keep you bound until we can turn you over to your own kind. It'll only be another day, so missing a meal won't hurt you none."

Glowing Sun had no idea what it meant. She heard "far." She heard "village."

The two men set her back on the ground so her back could lean against a tree.

When she leaned on that tree, something poked into her back, and suddenly she knew what she needed to do.

She waited until they were settled down to eat a cold supper in the fading light. The hard jerked beef made her stomach growl. Studying the area, she noted the moss on the north side of the tree, the slant of the sun, the slope of the mountain. She could see a distant peak and recognized it. She had no idea how far she'd come, but she knew where she needed to go. All she needed was a running start.

God, do not take another family from me. Help me find freedom. Help me find my way home once that freedom is mine.

She watched the men and prayed fervently to bear what pain

might be coming her way with her reckless plan.

She waited until the men were done eating and busy setting up their night camp. Then, when their attention was diverted, she grabbed the kerchief knotted so tightly over her mouth and jerked it down to her chin and screamed.

The two men whirled and dashed at her. The short one clamped his hand on her mouth as he had earlier, knocking her head back against the tree.

The other muttered. Unintelligible words growled back and forth between the two of them. Then the tall man untied her hands and twisted her arms painfully behind her back.

The man holding her mouth jerked the gag back into place. "I'd hoped we could leave you with your arms tied in front. You'd sleep better." He shook his head.

The other man took pleasure in jerking the binding tight and pulled so hard on her arms her shoulders ached.

"Hey be careful of her," the shorter man said. "We have to keep her tied, but you don't have to hurt her. She don't know no better than to run back to her tribe."

Glowing Sun cried out in pain. She could have controlled it and normally would have. It wasn't her nature to fuss over a bit of pain. But she wanted them to think she was weak and defeated. She wanted them to be confident. She wanted them to sleep deeply.

The tall man dropped her roughly so her head struck the tree behind her. Stars burst from behind her eyes, and she did a good job of acting hurt. As embarrassing as it was, she faked that she was crying, sobbing. Though it wasn't hard to fake it, because she was afraid and the ropes cut into her wrists and her stomach growled and her village was far over the next mountain.

The tall man laughed in triumph as he went back to his side of the camp, leaving space around her as if *she* were the one who smelled bad.

The other man crouched down, and she withdrew to the

extent she was able. Eyes wide, doing her best to look terrified and defeated, she whimpered a bit.

"We only mean to help you, miss. Don't worry. We'll get you back to your people." The man seemed kind, though he smelled bad enough.

She nodded just to let the man think he'd won. None of her triumph showed in her eyes. But now her hands were tied behind her back just as she'd hoped. She'd wait. Bide her time. As soon as the men had settled for the night, Glowing Sun would move her bound fingers to the hidden seam in her skirt, in the middle of her back.

And get her hands on her razor-sharp blade.

CHAPTER 9

Wade set a fast pace, and the men who came with him kept up. They rode well beyond the setting sun.

"We've got to lay up, I know." Wade turned to the men who had stayed with him so faithfully. "Let's find a spot to camp."

"We've ridden hard before," Buck said genially.

Wade found himself liking all three of these men. They shaped up to be decent, hardworking, and tough. He hoped as much could be said about him.

Shorty had a campfire going and coffee on by the time the horses were stripped of their leather and pegged out to graze.

Settling in with a cup of what was, at this point, barely warm brownish water, Wade marveled at the comfort of it in his hands. "Thanks, Shorty. I figured to make a cold camp. This is mighty nice."

Shorty grunted.

Roy got out a brush and worked on all four horses as if he couldn't quite sit still.

"Your son's a workin' man, Buck. A fine youngster." Wade wasn't that much older than Roy, but the four years seemed like twenty.

Buck smiled, as if he knew just how old Wade was. "You're in a hurry to get to this drive. Any reason?"

"I know—" Wade stumbled. He'd almost said Belle's name. He concealed a smile. No reason not to tell the truth. The men could stick or not. Probably would. But he decided to leave them to the surprise. "I'm not sure what's riding me, really." Wade studied Buck a moment. "There is no reason to feel this strange burden for them, but I feel like God Himself is pushing me to hurry." Wade wondered what this three would make of that.

Buck nodded. Shorty kept pouring coffee. Both of them acted as if it were the most natural thing in the world.

"I know they're shorthanded. I'm sure they're handling things. It's a crew that takes care of itself." Wade had seen the Tanner girls once because he'd been roaming the high country and ridden into their range. Belle kept them so secluded there were some who weren't quite sure even how many children she had. All of those girls were tough. Tougher than him by a long shot.

It occurred to Wade that this might be more of his need to rescue, as he'd felt for Cassie Dawson. The fever to protect her had calmed once he'd seen how happy Cassie was with Red. He'd never have gotten over her without God filling the awful, empty places in his life.

Now this urgency to get to Belle reminded him a little of that desperate need to rescue Cassie. The main difference being, if he implied to Belle she needed to be rescued, she'd rip his arm off and beat him to death with it. "But I'm also sure they're all pushing themselves to the limit. They need help, and I said I'd give it. I guess I'm just bent on keeping that promise. And wanting to get there before they wear themselves down to the bone."

"Good enough for me." Buck finished his coffee and a piece of jerked beef he was gnawing. He turned to Roy. "Son, hit the blankets. We'll be up riding hard before daybreak."

Roy left his fussing with the horses and came to where he'd

laid out his bedroll, collapsed on it, and was out almost instantly.

Wade finished his coffee and took Buck's advice, too.

The next morning they kept up the ground-eating lope, slowing only when the tortuous trail twisted across talus slides or was so steep Wade and the others dismounted to walk.

They'd put hours behind them before the sun rose, and as they reached the bottom of a treacherous slope, Wade saw the flickering light of sun on water and knew it was time to give the horses a rest—a brief rest. He raised his hand, signaling halt, just as a deer darted between two bushes straight ahead. He barely saw its form, but it was fawn-colored and quick. He reached for his rifle, thinking to bring grub to Belle along with helping hands.

He heard a shell snapped into a rifle behind him and knew Shorty was taking aim.

Something else moved, something bigger. Something human. "Hold up." Wade spurred his horse forward just as what he thought was a deer raced out of the underbrush.

A woman, looking back, ran straight into the side of his horse. She cried out and fell backward. White blond hair flying. Ropes dangling from her wrists.

Not far behind, two men crashed toward Wade through the trees and brush.

Wade swung himself to the ground to stand between the woman and two men on her trail. They emerged just as Wade leveled his rifle on them. The one in front skidded to a halt. The one behind nearly knocked his partner down.

Wade had two seconds to wonder if he'd have the guts to pull his trigger. Rifles cocked. Buck, Shorty, and Roy were ready, backing him.

"She's ours," the taller pursuer shouted while he gasped for breath, looking from gun to gun, all beaded on him or his saddle partner.

A barrage of words escaped from the woman who was scrambling to her feet.

Wade saw her take one running step away from him. Snaking out a hand, he caught hold of her wrist.

The girl fought his grip.

He never took his eyes off the men who were after her.

Buck came up beside him. "I've got 'em covered, Wade. See to the girl."

Wade turned to study his prisoner. She clawed at his gloved hand. A white girl—woman rather—but young. Dressed in Indian clothing. "I mean you no harm."

She moaned and crouched low, like a cornered animal. Words erupted from her lips Wade recognized as Flathead, but he didn't know enough of the language to respond.

"*Hau.*" Shorty spoke to the woman, kneeling beside her.

She didn't respond.

Wade shook his head. "That's Sioux. She won't know it."

"She might." Shorty came up beside Wade and looked at the gasping, trembling woman.

Wade could well imagine what she thought. Two men were after her, but she'd been running free. Now there were six, and she was caught. "Can you tell her we won't hurt her?"

Shorty shook his head. "I know a few words of Sioux and a little Cheyenne, but I've only been in Montana a coupl-a years. I can tell she's Flathead because of her clothes, but I don't know any of the lingo. But maybe. . . *Okiye niye?*"

"What's that?" Wade wanted the old man to get on with helping her.

"It's Sioux. Their territories overlapped years back. She might know a few words. I think it means 'help you.' Or 'help me' maybe."

"Great, she'll think we want *her* to help *us.*"

The woman made a sudden move, darting to her feet. Wade grabbed her. She lashed out with her feet and raked fingernails across his face.

Wade held up both hands to protect his face and crowded her

toward an outcropping of rock, cornering her. "We can't just leave you here. Let us help you. We won't hurt you."

A hard fist slammed into Wade's jaw. Grabbing at her flying hands, dodging her thrashing feet, doing his best not to hurt her, he wrestled with her until she jumped back, pressing against the rock.

"She's wild but she's white," one of her pursuers said. "We found her with the Indians, and we were taking her home. We weren't hurtin' her."

Wade registered the men's statement. It might be true, but it didn't mesh with the bleeding scrapes oozing from behind the leather strips dangling from each arm. They'd tied her up for her own good? There was a laugh. "Do you know where her home is?" Wade asked. "Does she have a white family waiting for her?"

"We don't know. But it stands to reason she belongs with her own kind, not a bunch of heathen savages."

Wade's jaw tightened. He'd known a few of the natives. The ones he'd met were often Christians and often gentle people. Oh, he knew there had been massacres. But there were bad seeds among all people.

The woman collapsed on the ground, wailing. Her eyes, so blue, tears drenching her face, though she seemed more fierce than sad. She was too angry, too combative. Her tears were ones of rage.

"Home? Home to your village?" Wade stood over her, feeling like a brute for making her stay when she so obviously wanted to run. He touched his cheek and pulled his fingers away bloody.

Her cry faded and her eyes locked on Wade. She pulled in a deep breath. "V–v–village? Salish village?"

Wade felt his eyes narrow. "You speak English?"

Her voice riveted everyone's attention. Only when Wade heard running footsteps did he realize they'd allowed her assailants to escape.

Roy whirled around.

"Let them go." Wade decided. "What are we gonna do with 'em?"

Her gaze slid past Wade to the men. If it was true—that they were attempting some kind of rescue—then they hadn't broken any laws. Even though any fool could see the woman wanted her village, her Indian village, plenty of whites would think she should be taken back to her own kind. Studying her, Wade could see that her clothes weren't torn and her bruises weren't serious or plentiful.

"I've heard the Flatheads called Salish." Buck stepped to his horse and slid his rifle into the saddle boot. "We'd been roaming these hills, and one day hunting I noticed an Indian village...must be two days' ride from here. They're camped along a river. Maybe if we pushed hard we could get her home before nightfall. You reckon they took her from there?"

Roy stepped closer. "B—but she's white. Doesn't she need to be with white people?"

Wade watched the woman. Her eyes shifted. She looked constantly for escape. If they let her go, could she get back to her village on foot? If her home was, as Buck thought, a long day's ride on a horse, she'd be three or four days walking it, alone in the wilderness. He dropped to both knees beside her. "Wade." He touched his chest. He pointed at Shorty, Buck, and Roy in turn, saying their names. "Salish? Flathead?" He waited.

"Salish village. Far." She stared at him, some of the terror fading from her eyes.

"Speak English?"

She shrugged then pointed at him. "Wade."

"We"—Wade circled his hands to try to include himself and the other men—"take you"—he pointed at the woman—"Salish village."

"You can't do that," Roy shouted, clenching his fists. "You can't turn her back over to them."

Wade looked from one man to another, his face stinging in the brisk morning breeze. "What do you think?"

Shorty shrugged. "She looks like she's been hurt more at the hands of white men than the Flatheads."

"The clothes, her inability to speak English, she's obviously lived with them for a long time. Some tribes take in children of whites and raise them. She'd think of them as her family." Wade watched, sure she planned to run off at the first chance. But that wasn't the only reason he watched. Despite her wild hair and bruised and dirty face, she was beautiful. Those eyes, as blue as the wide Montana sky, brimmed with tears and terror.

The vulnerability touched something deep inside him. The same kind of thing that had driven him to want to rescue Cassie. But Cassie hadn't needed rescuing. Belle would pound on him if he suggested she needed rescuing. It was Wade's own mixed-up desire to save someone. . .anyone. . .the way he wished someone would have saved him from his father. And now this woman most likely didn't need rescuing either. But it went against the grain to return a white woman to an Indian village.

She blinked and two tears escaped her shining eyes and slid down her grimy face. "Wade." She touched her own chest. "Glowing Sun."

"She spoke English." Wade looked up at Shorty. "She knows her name in English."

The man was quiet, but he was savvy. "Someone must have taught it to her. Or she maybe spoke English when she was young and a bit of it is coming back."

"That's your name?" Wade asked. "Glowing Sun?"

"Glowing Sun. Village far."

Wade's heart ached to see her cry. But the pain was almost pleasure, because she was so lovely and fragile yet ready to fight a crowd of men if it meant freedom.

"I think we need to calm her down before we take her back."

Buck came around the horse and patted his son's shoulder. "Make sure she knows she has a choice."

"She can't want to live with Indians, Pa." Roy looked frantic, as if considering saving the woman from his own father.

Wade smiled, recognizing the reflex. "We could take her with us to the Tanner drive. If we ride hard, we could get *there* tonight. Treat her gently and she might decide she doesn't want to go back with the tribe."

"Cold weather's comin' on." Shorty scratched his chin. "Her people might be ready to move to winter hunting grounds, and we'd have a tough time finding them in the middle of a Montana winter. If we don't take her back now, she might never be reunited with them."

Wade couldn't take his eyes from Glowing Sun—such a perfect name for a girl with billowed white gold hair. Her native family could hardly have named her anything else. Moonlight maybe, or Snowbird. She was filthy, her face bruised and bleeding. Even with all that, she was the most beautiful woman Wade had ever seen. Wade watched her eyes, hoping he could head off an escape as he slowly gripped her arm and pulled her to her feet.

She flinched and gasped in pain. He looked down at her battered, bleeding wrists and immediately released her, cornering her between himself and the rock. She crouched again.

Wade held a hand out in front of him, shaking his head. "Don't run, please."

She narrowed her eyes as if searching deep in her memory. "Please?"

Wade's heart lifted. She did know English, at least a little. It might come back if she'd just talk with them for a time. He nodded. "Please."

"Thank you," she said, as if the words just came. She'd been trained in good manners at one time.

Wade smiled. She frowned and jerked her head at him as if she disapproved. Of what? *His* manners maybe?

If someone said thank you, he should respond. . . . "You're welcome?"

She smiled.

Wade motioned to his horse. "Ride?"

She looked from him to the horse.

"Please?"

She jerked her chin as if in agreement. "Village." She swung up on the horse so lightly, it was almost like a moment of flight.

"Well, where are we going?" Wade held the reins tight. He wasn't fooling himself that she was content to be with them.

The two older men sighed and hesitated.

"The Tanner drive." Roy was most adamant. Too bad he knew less about this than the rest of them.

"She's gonna be mad. She thinks we're takin' her to. . .you know." Shorty looked worried and was smart enough not to say the word *village*.

"Yeah, and when she gets mad, it's something to see." Wade pulled a kerchief out of his hip pocket and dabbed at the raw wound on his face.

"Will she catch on right away?" Buck asked.

"Depends on how far she is from home. She might be lost with no idea what direction to head. But Indians are mighty savvy about the land. She could have her eye on a mountain peak or some other landmark, know she needs to head west and we're going east." Wade lifted both hands in surrender. If his kerchief had been white instead of blue, he'd have been waving the white flag of surrender. "Let's head for the Tanners for now. We can change our minds later. We've got time before winter shuts down on us."

"Sounds good." Shorty mounted up.

Buck and Roy followed suit.

"Can we make room on the packhorse for another man?" Wade looked at the woman occupying his saddle. He touched his bloody face again.

"Not without dropping most of the supplies." Shorty started down the trail.

"If she don't wanna ride double with you, you'll find out soon enough." Buck laughed and kicked his horse.

Wade produced his knife and made sure Glowing Sun saw it. Then very carefully he reached for her wrist and cut the rope dangling there.

She nodded. "Thank you."

He tore a strip off his shirt and bound her wounds. "You're welcome." He didn't know the words to warn her they were sharing a horse. Wade reached for the saddle horn and braced himself to get clawed again.

CHAPTER 10

Belle had the herd moving at first light.

By midday they were climbing steadily and the mountain pass was getting narrow. Silas rode ahead to scout the trail, and because the pass was treacherous, Belle wouldn't let anyone carry Betsy but her.

The cattle were unhappy about the steep, rugged climb, so Belle rode drag to badger the stragglers. She made Sarah give over the lead to Emma because there were talus slides in spots that might give way under a horse's hooves, and Emma would be better able to stick her saddle. The cattle walked with ever fewer abreast, and the slow-moving herd strung out over several miles.

The sun rose high in the sky, and the mountain trail was ground into a cloud of dust as the cattle churned up the earth. Belle pulled her kerchief over her mouth and nose and fixed one for Betsy, who spent most of her days lulled to sleep from the monotony of the steady rocking of the horse. A fine white dust hung in the air and coated all of them. The cattle all began to look the same under the sifting powder. Belle's eyes burned and watered, and she wiped the grit from her face wearily until she gave up and let it blanket her.

She bullied and whipped the stragglers as they balked. They were especially cantankerous at places they needed to scramble over rock slides. She saw in the cattle a desire to quit, and she knew how they felt. Still, she pressed them onward, each step an effort. Each inch gained a triumph.

Belle knew that when they got through the pass ahead that dipped low on the mountain like a saddleback, the trail dropped steeply. She watched her first cattle, over two miles further on, reach the summit ahead, skyline themselves, then drop over the lip of the mountaintop. Hours later, when Belle finally reached the top, she looked at the rugged trail going down and back up the mountain. Her stomach swooped at the sight of it. It was late afternoon already and they had to get over it before they could stop for the night.

She took a moment to ask God for strength and to thank Him that she hadn't realized what this trail looked like until now.

Far down the path, Belle saw her cattle plod through the choking dust. Here at the top, with the wind blowing unchecked, the dust had been dispersed. But she looked down that tortuous trail full of switchbacks and drop-offs into what looked like a bowl full of dust. In some places, it hung so thick Belle couldn't see the cattle. These animals were the work of nearly sixteen years of her life. Now here it was before her. Her life's work, moving slowly along, no more than three or four abreast, trailing an older steer as cattle are prone to do. She saw Emma in the lead and she saw Silas appear from over the pass far ahead, where he'd been scouting the trail.

The whole day's journey had been almost no forward progress because of the twisting trail that went around every craggy outcropping. Belle knew the next week would be filled with slow days that accomplished little.

Silas came up to Emma then turned to walk alongside her. They were so far from Belle they looked like miniatures. They walked into a thick cloud of dust and were invisible for a time. Then there must have been a place the wind would whip in because they were visible again. Emma was turned toward Silas. Belle wondered what they were talking about. Knowing Emma, Belle assumed it was work.

After a time, Silas started to drop back along the herd. Emma picked up her pace a bit, and Silas urged the cattle to do likewise, cracking a bullwhip in the air over their heads and hollering, driving them until the whole line was nearly trotting. He let them pass him until Sarah drew even with him. She walked along with the cattle, following at their new pace. Sarah started moving faster, pushing the herd, passing a few of them as she gained the higher elevations.

Next, Silas dropped back again until Lindsay, who was nearly three quarters of the way to the back, eating as much dust as Belle, rode up beside him. Belle saw Lindsay pick up a little speed and trot her horse toward the front of the line. Lindsay was halfway up the mountain when Emma reached the top. After hanging, skylined against the lowering sun for a moment, Emma dropped out of sight. Then the cattle steadily passing over, out of sight as Belle still trudged downward with a long way yet to go, soon made the top of the hills. Then later Lindsay disappeared.

Belle would be hours making her way to that peak where she could watch her girls again. She knew that Silas had told them everything they needed to know.

The day droned on, and Silas dropped closer to her, urging the herd on as he went. Belle picked up his need to hurry and pushed her stragglers a little harder.

When Silas finally came even with her, he said, behind his own kerchief, "The girls should be making camp by now. There's a passing fair spot over the hill. Not great, but a little grazing and enough water. The cattle will be tired. I think they'll be content to stand pat there for the night. But it will be full dark by the time we've pushed the rest of them over that hump."

Belle nodded. The day was getting long for her. There had been no place along the trail to so much as step off the horse and stretch her legs. She'd eaten beef jerky in the saddle, gulped tepid canteen water, and nursed her baby with the kerchief tied over Betsy's face.

"Have you fed her lately?"

Belle looked at him. His eyes were red-rimmed and bloodshot. He was coated with the same white powdered dirt she was. She couldn't make sense of his question, and she knew she must look stupid. "Fed who?"

"Betsy. Is it close to feeding time? You could drop back a piece and sit down and do it. Get out of the dirt. I can take the herd for a while. You look all in, Belle. Riding drag in this dirt is about all a man's. . .I mean. . .about all a *person's* life is worth."

Belle had a moment of wondering how they would have gotten through this drive without him. She had no doubt they'd have done it, but she knew they'd have all been breaking their backs and their hearts to survive it. "It's okay. She's just done eating. I'll finish the drag."

She thought she saw concern and maybe anger flash across Silas's face, but both impressions were gone so swiftly she might have imagined it. She was too tired to wonder anyway.

Without saying a word, he reached behind her back, and with swift movements, he unhitched the sling and took it, baby and all, away from her. He hung the carrier over his own back, double-checking with his hands to make sure Betsy was secure, then trotted his horse forward, calling over his shoulder, "I'll carry her for a while."

Before her slow reactions could overcome her surprise, Silas was out of earshot. Or at least he didn't respond when she yelled, "Give her back."

He rode slightly faster than the cattle, and he gained the high pass and vanished. The summit never seemed to draw any nearer to

Belle. He came back after a time, just as Belle was near to reaching the bottom of the trail with the long climb upward left. He didn't have Betsy.

It had been a good idea to get the baby back to camp and let the girls care for her. She'd never have asked him to do it, but she was glad he had and glad for the weight of the growing baby to be off her shoulders for these last grim hours of the day.

He rode in a steady canter down the hill on a fresh horse. The cattle were so deadened that they didn't react to the fast-moving roan. When he reached her side, he said, "Go on up. The girls need some help."

"The girls don't need my help with anything." He was just trying to take over the dusty job of bringing up the rear.

"They didn't tell me what it was. I got the impression it was. . .a. . ."

Belle saw him start to blush. She flickered her eyes open and shut to clear her vision. Silas? Blushing? The man was darkly tanned and coated with dirt, and she couldn't be sure, but she could swear his cheeks were slightly reddened with embarrassment.

"I think it's a. . .female thing. You'd better go."

Belle knew of all the lies he might tell to get her to give up the job, that would never occur to him. They really must need her. "Okay, I'd better go see what's wrong."

Silas nodded, and his eyes didn't quite make contact with hers. The embarrassment again.

Belle rode on up the winding trail, covering it in minutes instead of the hour or two Silas had left to face. The sun was just dropping over the high mountain slope on her left when she crested the hill. She came down into a heavily wooded, steeply canted area with a rippling creek at the bottom.

She saw yet another hard climb, this one narrower than today's, ahead of them. They'd face it together tomorrow.

Lindsay was giving Elizabeth a bath in the creek upstream of the milling cattle. Sarah had a campfire going and stew made from their endless supply of dried beef on to boil.

Emma was on horseback.

The girls all looked just fine.

What did that low-down man mean by "a female thing"?

Well, that was about as low as he'd ever stooped.

Silas pulled his kerchief up to protect his mouth as he thought of Belle's expression. He would have laughed if it wouldn't have made him eat a mouthful of dirt—even with his mouth covered.

It was the only thing he could think of that would have made that blasted woman move out of this dirt. He'd only thought of it because of the way he'd been brought up. He was a man who had been surrounded by dance-hall girls all his young life, and there wasn't much he hadn't learned too young and too well. And one thing he'd learned was the phrase "female thing" would gain a woman instant sympathy from the other women and set a man running in the opposite direction. In both cases, it was the perfect lie. He hadn't been able to say it without feeling like six kinds of fool, but feeling embarrassed played into his hands.

Of course now he was a liar—although a "female thing" could include cooking supper, now couldn't it?

He prayed for forgiveness and had the sense that not only did the Almighty forgive Him, but the good Lord sympathized. Maybe even laughed.

It wasn't that hard to quit thinking about his stubborn boss, considering he was half dead from exhaustion. He shooed the loafers along faster. The sun set before he was halfway up. But the worst of the slides and cliffs were behind him. The cattle could smell water now, and that picked up their speed more than all his hard riding.

By the time he topped the mountain, it was full dark. The

stars were out and the temperature had plunged like it always did in the high country. He practically stumbled when he unsaddled his horse.

Then Emma was beside him, working on the roan with a handful of grass and cutting his work in half.

"I don't know what you told Ma, but she's riding night herd right now, and I'd eat and get to sleep before she comes in. She was right prickly with us when none of us were sick."

"I made it up so she'd come into camp quicker. She'd been back there all day."

"Ma always rides drag. It's the boss's job."

"Your ma says that so you won't have to take a turn, and I agree with her when it comes to you girls. And it's no big deal for her to do it when you've just driven a dozen or so head into Helena. But it's *not* the boss's job. In a regular outfit, everyone takes turns, and I'm from a regular outfit. But I can't convince her to let me spell her. So, I made something up, and now she's mad at me again. I reckon I deserve that."

Emma looked over the back of the roan they were working on and smiled at him. Her teeth glowed white out of her dirty face. It was the first time he'd seen the girl be anything but dead serious. It occurred to him in that moment that he was really starting to like the game little girl with the outsized horse skills.

Emma said, "I reckon you do deserve it, but if she asks me again if I'm okay, I'll try and act sick if'n ya want."

Silas started laughing then and shook his head. "Better let her get after me for lying instead. Me lying she might forgive. Me getting one of her girls to lie for me, well, she'd be after my head for sure."

Emma smiled again. "I 'spect that's right."

They finished the horse in double the normal time because they worked so well together. Then they went to the camp and Sarah had a plate of food ready for Silas. He swallowed it fast then dove for his bedroll as quickly as possible to avoid getting scolded by Belle. He meant to lay awake and watch for her to see if she still looked mad, but he was asleep as soon as his head hit his saddle.

The next day was a repeat of the first, except this time Belle hoped Silas would spell her at drag. He rode up after two hours of watching her eat dust.

"My turn back here." He glared at her and braced himself for what was to come.

"You must really want to do it to make such a fool of yourself last night. Have at it." She rode away without further comment.

Silas managed to smile as she rode down into more of the same monotonous dust.

The trail twisted back and forth, up and down the mountainside like a prairie rattler, only meaner. When they crested the next ridge, they'd gone half as far as yesterday and the sun was setting on them. In the waning light from the mountaintop, Silas saw what looked like an endless series of ridges out in front of them, and he almost fell into bed, he was so exhausted from thinking about what lay ahead.

Wade's body had been too close as they'd ridden. Glowing Sun didn't like it. But he was strong and she was exhausted, and her stiff back finally relaxed against him.

She awakened as he lifted her off the horse. She struggled against him, and he quickly set her on her feet. Her knees gave out. He caught her before she sank to the ground. Then he escorted her to a log and sat beside her.

The sun had been lost behind clouds, leaving a cold, murky day that pulled at her to sleep again and confused her about their direction. She couldn't tell how long they'd traveled, but if this was the midday meal, she'd slept for hours. She hoped they'd get to her village soon.

Glowing Sun sat at the warm fire on this cold day. The men produced jerked beef and hard biscuits from their packs and shared with her until her stomach was stretched and full.

Wade opened a tin can and gave her a half of a yellow fruit. "Peaches," Wade said. He stabbed at the fruit with the same knife he'd used to open the can and extended the dripping fruit to her.

She carefully pulled it off the knife with her teeth. The juicy sweetness nearly brought tears to her eyes.

"Have some more." Wade speared another slice, holding it carefully over the can.

She reached out to steady the knife as she bit. The warmth of his hand mingled with the sweetness startled her into looking away from the treat.

Her gaze met his and was captured. The moment lingered. His hard, calloused, gentle hand remained joined with hers. She slowly took the peach, and his eyes flickered to her lips in a way that made her hand tighten on his.

At last she blinked and pulled her eyes away and spoke to the ground. "Thank you, Wade."

He touched her chin so she had to look at him again. "You're welcome, Glowing Sun."

"Wade." She puzzled the name over. "Wade in water." She arched her brows.

Wade nodded. "Wade in water." He smiled and offered her more fruit. "Peach."

"Peach." The word tickled her brain, but she couldn't remember it from before. However, she was sure she'd never forget this delicious dessert.

"Horse." Wade pointed at the buckskin they'd shared.

"Horse."

He seemed to enjoy this game of making her say his white words, so she'd play it. But the words made some sense. *Horse.* She remembered that now.

She wondered if she should tell Wild Eagle that she'd slept in another man's arms. Would he be angry? He was a warrior and possessive of her. The springtime would see them wed.

"Beef." Wade extended more of the salty, tough meat to her.

She shook her head and rubbed her stomach. "Thank you."

"No, thank you," Wade said.

Glowing Sun smiled. She remembered that, too.

They had a halting conversation over the meal, then Wade stood and began packing the scanty camp.

She did her best to help, eager to be on her way home.

Wade crouched down on the heavily traveled trail. "They've already gotten through this pass." He shook his head. "They're making good time."

Shorty came back from scouting around in the fading light of sunset. "I thought you said they needed hands."

"They do." Wade looked up from tracks that were obviously at least a day old.

"I can read sign. They've got five seasoned hands. They might need another hand or two, but not all four of us."

Wade hadn't looked that close, but he could tell the herd moved steadily, and it was obvious they were making good time. He'd also bet his hat that the seasoned hands were Belle's daughters, but he didn't mention it. He'd come to trust these men though, so he didn't worry that they'd hurt the Tanner women.

He looked up at Shorty. "I guess we can go on and check. It sounded like they were taking this herd with almost no help. That was the day before they started. I hope they did find more help. I've been worrying."

"Can we catch 'em tonight?" Roy asked, always full of energy, eager to work and push. A good trait in a boy.

Wade shook his head, looking up at Glowing Sun, sitting

perched on his horse. She watched him closely, her eyes narrow. She seemed to be listening, but Wade doubted the woman had learned enough English in an afternoon to follow their conversation.

He didn't like keeping her out overnight with four men. It wasn't proper. But nothing about this situation was normal. "I know this trail. It's a killer in the dark. Rock slides and cliffs especially on this side, going down. We've got to wait until morning."

They went back down the trail a ways until they got out of the wind and set up camp. They ate well. Wade had brought plenty with him, planning to join the drive after he'd left a winter's worth of supplies at the line shack.

Glowing Sun ate as if she were a bear storing up fat for the winter. He wondered how long those men had kept her prisoner.

He kept after her to talk English, and she'd gotten better through the afternoon. She was speaking in broken sentences and learning so fast, Wade knew she'd been familiar with the tongue in the past.

He settled into his cold, blanketless bed—Glowing Sun had his only cover. He fell asleep instantly. He woke in the wee hours of the night to find her gone. "Wake up." Wade lunged to his feet. "Glowing Sun ran off."

Shorty shook his head as he sat up. "She must have figured out we weren't taking her home."

"So we took her another day's ride farther from her village." Buck stood from his bedroll.

"And now," Roy added, "she's alone out there."

"With wolves. Both the two-legged and four-legged kind." Wade felt sick. This was his fault. And now he had to make it right.

He should just let her go with his best wishes. She was probably better equipped to take this journey than he was. But he knew God wanted more from him than just wishing her well. He couldn't live with himself not knowing if she made it to her village.

The worry for Belle rode him for some reason Wade couldn't understand. God seemed to urge him to ride quickly to the cattle drive. He paused and opened his heart and mind to the still, small voice of God.

And he had an idea.

He turned to his three saddle companions. "I'm going after her. And this time I'm taking her home. I think you three oughta go on and help handle this drive."

"You can't do that. It ain't right," Roy fretted.

"I promise to ask her, Roy. I'll keep at it until she understands. I'll give her the choice to leave the tribe."

Roy didn't speak, but his jaw hardened in obvious dissatisfaction.

Shorty shrugged and pointed down the trail they'd followed. It was the only way over this mountain. "I reckon you can catch her. And if she doesn't want any part of you, you can just tag along to make sure she gets home safe."

"It's settled then." Wade saddled up while Shorty studied Glowing Sun's tracks.

Buck explained where he'd seen the village as Wade strapped down his saddlebags.

Before he was done, Wade started to laugh out loud.

"What is it?" Roy asked. "What's so funny?"

"That little maiden we're all so worried about?"

"Yeah. . ." Roy looked down the trail. "Do you see her? Is she coming back so we can help her?"

"I doubt she's coming back, Roy."

"Why do you doubt it?"

Wade started laughing again. "Because I just noticed she's stolen half my beef jerky."

He laughed as he mounted up and struck out to help poor, helpless Glowing Sun. While he rode away, he hoped when he found her, she didn't kill him.

CHAPTER 11

Silas got to ride drag so much he was sorry he'd ever pushed for the job. He couldn't decide if Belle was punishing him or if she'd had the tiniest of female reflexes spring to life and was looking on the hardest jobs as "men's work."

No sense hoping for the second, so he decided she was punishing him. Always best to put bad motives onto the way Belle treated him.

They pushed the herd on through another long day, with Silas eating dust and squinting against dirt in his eyes. It was late in the season. The daytime was hot, but the nights were frigid, and it snowed on them once. The women cuddled up together, and Silas resented that he was rejected from their little bevy of warmth while he shivered under his blanket alone.

They lost several head of cattle that slipped on washouts along the narrow pass and fell, bawling horribly for hundreds of feet. One steer skidded across a shale slide and broke its leg.

Silas saw Belle preparing to shoot it with hands that visibly trembled. He spurred his horse toward her and shouted, "Hold up!"

She lowered her gun so willingly Silas worried about her. He also knew she wouldn't thank him for trying to take this tough job.

"Belle, let me drive him away so the girls don't have to see." Ah, he was beginning to know how to handle her. He almost patted himself on the back when her furrowed brow smoothed.

"Yes, that's a good idea. The girls." She made no word of protest.

That worried him some. She must be nearing the end of her strength. Belle argued over everything.

He came back with a haunch of beef. The fresh sizzling steaks for supper that night and again the next morning lifted all their spirits.

By the time they'd ridden through another day, the warm, encouraging meal was long forgotten. Silas hated to see how quiet and gaunt the girls were getting. When the two older ones stood side by side, their skin was as white with dust as their hair.

Silas rode ahead and found a trail that led to the best grass he'd seen in a week. He came back to find Belle holding her quiet little baby in front of her, talking to her. Probably whispering endless apologies for bringing Betsy into this bleak world of craggy points and smothering dirt.

At sunset they started coming down out of the high peaks. He worked the herd well away from Belle until Betsy was back in her sling; then he rode up. "Grass ahead. It'll make a terrible long day, but once we're there, let's hold the cattle a day and let them eat." *And let the girls rest.* Silas would say it if he had to.

"How long a day?" Belle's eyes rose to his as if it took all her energy just to lift her chin.

"I could barely see the grass through the next pass; I didn't come close to riding all the way to it. We'll be pushing them in full dark for a couple of hours. But the uphill side of the trail to get there is clear, no slides or drop-offs."

Belle nodded silently for far too long. Then she squared her shoulders and lifted her reins.

"We're going to make it, Belle." Silas wanted to give her a hug for encouragement and to thank her for being so steady.

"I know." Her eyes flashed. The first sign of spirit she'd shown, and Silas decided she needed him to pester her into having some gumption.

"You womenfolk have held up pretty well. I'm mighty proud of you."

Those words might seem like a compliment to some. To Belle they were fighting words.

She rammed her gaze into him like the tip of a bullwhip. "Well, Silas, for a man, you're holding up pretty well, too. I'm mighty proud of *you*. And may I say, surprised."

He could set her off, all the way off. She'd be scolding and yelling and maybe threatening with about one more well-chosen word from him. Instead, he laughed. "That's the spirit."

Belle's temper melted and she managed to smile. Then laugh. "We're going to make it, Silas. No doubt about it. And. . .well. . .I will say. . ."

Silas waited. Yes, she could compliment him. She could thank him. She could even say she liked him a little.

"I will say you haven't slowed us down overly." She smirked.

Silas laughed out loud and decided he might make it through this cattle drive yet.

Still smiling, Belle reined her horse aside and rode down the trail.

Betsy waved bye-bye from her place on Belle's back.

They kept the cattle moving well into the night. They had two more passes to go through before Helena. Both shorter, but also higher and more perilous. Bringing up the rear, Silas was long after the others getting to camp.

Belle was already on the first watch. Emma and Sarah were asleep, cuddled up next to Betsy on the far side of the fire.

He ate stew from a warm pot and tumbled straightaway into

bed to get a couple of hours' sleep before taking midnight watch. He knew, even as he collapsed, that just as he was trying to carry as much of the weight of this trip as possible, the womenfolk were trying to ease things for him. And for all their efforts, they were all almost dead. He knew he should insist on taking the first watch part of the time, but his eyes fell shut before he gathered the strength to stand.

The next time his eyes opened it was full daylight. He jumped up, alarmed to realize he'd slept through his shift. He immediately scanned the camp and saw all the girls sleeping soundly.

Except Belle. She'd been on the first watch last night. She couldn't have done the whole night alone. Silas was moving toward the nearest saddle horse before he'd finished stepping into his boots.

God, what happened? Where is she? His prayers were hard and desperate and laced with dread.

He rode out, afraid he'd find Belle trampled to death or thrown from her horse with her neck broken. He moved soundlessly, unwilling to wake the girls and have them go with him for fear of what they might find.

He had been riding half an hour through the wooded grazing land when he saw Belle's saddled horse standing with its head down. Silas spurred his buckskin, scattering a few standing cattle, but the stock were tired and they didn't pay him much mind beyond getting out of his way. He got through the herd and, with desperate eyes, scanned the ground around the horse.

A hundred yards away, in a notch between two trees, he saw Belle's boots sticking out. He galloped toward her, his heart pounding. As he pulled up, Belle cried out softly and sat up.

"Belle, what happened? Were you thrown?" Silas leaped off his horse and knelt by her side. He ran his hands over her arms and legs, looking for bleeding or broken bones.

Belle looked at him, her eyes dazed. He ran his hands over her head, looking for the bump that must have knocked her cold.

Suddenly she swatted his hands away. "I'm fine. I. . .I guess I fell asleep. I remember getting off my horse to sit by that rock because I was getting so saddle sore. The next thing I knew you were waking me."

She looked over Silas's shoulder and seemed to register the rest of the world. "It's morning! I slept all night?" She stood and pushed past him. "I fell asleep before midnight. I've got to check the cattle. They could have stampeded all the way back home by now. I've got to—"

"They're fine, Belle." Silas got off his knees and cut off her rising panic. He knew just how she felt. "I rode through most of them getting here. We'll check on them in a minute, but I didn't see any sign of trouble."

Belle looked at the steers scattered in the woodlands around the stream and shook her head as if to knock away the last vestiges of sleep. "I can't believe I did that. Anything could have happened. The whole herd could have been rustled. Someone could have come up to the camp and killed all of you in your sleep. The cattle could have trampled you all to death without—"

"Stop!" Silas grabbed her shoulders. "Stop making things up to panic about. None of that happened. We're fine. And we all needed the rest. I haven't slept a night through in probably twenty years. I wake up a couple of times an hour no matter where I am. I should have known something was wrong hours ago. But we got away with it, Belle. We'll start making shorter days of it and resting up a day every chance we get. The drive will take a few days longer, but it won't matter. You're smart enough and *tough* enough to know we can't go back and stay awake last night. So what's the sense of getting all twisted up about it?"

"Tough." Belle laughed. "I guess you could say I'm tough."

"A woman would have to be to live the life you've lived, survive all you've survived."

"And I've thrived with it."

"You've done a lot better than your husbands, I'd say. How'd you find your way to this rugged place anyway?"

Chuckling, Belle rubbed the sleep from her eyes. "You want to know how I ended up here, way out in the wild, living alone."

"Your husbands died. Your worthless husbands. Your girls told me too much about it that first night."

"They didn't tell you the half of it." Belle smiled. "My ranch sits in the most beautiful mountain valley God ever put on this earth. William, my first husband, claimed one hundred and sixty acres of that valley. Gerald claimed another one hundred and sixty because I nagged him until he did it."

"Gerald's the one the girls said hit—"

"I don't talk about Gerald much." Belle cut Silas off and pulled away from him, crossing her arms tight. "Makes me want to grab for my shootin' iron, but yeah, he's the one."

"I'd like to grab for my shootin' iron myself." His fingers itched with the wanting. Or maybe they itched because he missed holding on to Belle. "How many husbands are you up to now?"

"Anthony was third and last. I had to browbeat him until he claimed a hundred and sixty acres. I selected each claim, and they are sitting square on top of the richest grasslands and most reliable springs west of the Colorado River. Plus, now I've got use of thousands more acres because I've got the only water, making it useless to anyone else. All rugged mountainside, but there's feed enough to keep my cows thriving. I'd say I control around twenty thousand acres all told."

Staggered by the amount, Silas looked at the husky, lazy cattle—not as fat as when they started but a good, healthy herd. "Sure enough looks like they're thriving."

"I own three thousand head of fine longhorn cattle." Belle's arms relaxed, and she leaned against the tree she'd been sleeping beside. "I built the herd up from the fifty William and I herded into

Montana along the Boseman Trail. We came out here a couple of years after the 1862 Gold Rush. I had the bright idea all those men hunting gold'd get almighty hungry. And there stood underpriced beef in Colorado just begging to be pushed into the mountains."

"Pushed." Silas laughed. "Probably as backbreaking as this drive."

"It was tough and a lot longer, but with only fifty head it was nothing like this."

"So William wasn't so bad of a husband then?"

"None of this was his idea." Belle snorted. "It was mine and mine alone. And with all the knowledge I'd gained growing up in Texas working alongside Pa, we prospered."

"Why didn't you just stay there with your family in Texas?"

Belle frowned, clearly annoyed by the question. "For the first fifteen years of my life, Pa made do without a son. My ma wasn't well and spent most of her days ailing, so Pa let me tag after him. He shared all his know-how with me, figuring it would all be mine someday. When I was about thirteen, Ma up and died. Pa's second wife was a spoiled, vain thing that didn't know the kickin' end of a horse from the bitin' end. But she did manage to present Pa with a son. The boy was born about six months after William and I got married. We'd gone into it thinking William would step in for Pa and run his ranch. Now, with a son, William and I were just in the way."

"Your pa threw you out?" Silas had never had a pa, not one he'd known and met, but the thought of a daughter being cast aside disgusted him.

Scowling, Belle nodded. "Without a second thought. William married me thinking Pa's land was part of the deal. But with a son and heir, even though the ink had barely dried on the marriage license, Pa showed me the road. He gave me a pat on my pretty little head, two hundred and fifty dollars—called it my inheritance—and let me take my clothes."

"What about William? Couldn't he find work in Texas? Why'd he drag you to Montana of all places?"

"William never had much of a backbone, and he wasn't one to work if it could be avoided. Since I seemed to be the strong-minded one in the family, William just trailed along with whatever I decided. Well, I was mad as a rabid Texas sidewinder and out to prove I didn't need Pa to make my way. So we headed for Colorado and spent every penny of my pa's money, plus every other penny I'd saved, on cattle. Then we herded them to Montana."

"I can't believe if William was so lazy he went along. Didn't he know what working a ranch was like?"

Belle shrugged. "What he knew was he wanted to put half a continent betwixt him and the War Between the States. That was enough to keep him moving west. Once we got to Montana and filed a claim, William discovered a troublesome back—or no, that was Anthony." Belle seemed to hunt around inside her head awhile then give up. "Well, both of them were laid up for one reason or another. I had to build our cabin, and even though I did a terrible job, William didn't help. He probably knew less about building than I did. I dammed up a creek and cleared brush and built fence. In an act of spite, I registered our herd brand as the Lazy S, but William never seemed to get that."

Silas had to laugh.

"The cattle thrived. The roof leaked. Two babies were born. And then William ran afoul of Rudolph and I hauled him up to the Husband Tree and buried him."

"The Husband Tree, Belle? Shame on you." Silas rolled his eyes.

Defensively, Belle said, "We didn't exactly *name* it that. It's just. . .what it is. So we *call* it that. You're the one who asked to hear all this."

"You're right. Go on." Scrubbing his whiskered face to keep from saying more, Silas smiled behind his hands.

"A new husband joined the family. Sarah's pa. Gerald O'Rourke sat on the porch and contemplated his whiskey supply and nurtured his annoyance at all the injustices that had been done to him in his life, whilst I learned to dodge drunken fists and increased the herd by hunting down mavericks running wild in the high-up hills."

"Gerald." Silas lost any urge he had to laugh.

"Then with Gerald just barely finished twitchin' from his untimely horse ride, I had a brain spasm I'm still kicking myself for and found myself married to Anthony."

"Which all just proves you're tough. So why are you so mad at yourself for sleeping through one night? What difference does it make if we slow down covering this trail? We can rest up. A few days more won't matter."

"Yes, it will matter," Belle snapped. "For one thing, heavy snow could come at any time. It can snow year-round in these mountains, but the heavy snows haven't started yet. The first one will block these passes, and they won't open up again until spring. I'm not feeling pushed to get to Helena so much as I'm feeling pushed to get home. My herd will be food for the wolves if I'm not there to bring 'em down closer to the cabin. The pond freezes over, and I need to take the ax to it and keep it open. I can't risk being snowed out of my ranch. I can feel winter in the air. The first storm could come any day."

"I know, but that doesn't mean—"

"For another thing," Belle interrupted, "we are already stopping at every half-decent camp we find. There just aren't that many. Once we start out for the day, the place we're going to stop at is already set. We can't hold this herd on one of those dangerous mountain trails overnight, and you know it. So having shorter days isn't possible."

"Belle, we're going to be fine. We're almost—"

"I should never have tried this. I didn't realize how much the herd had increased this spring. A bunch of older cattle moved up into the highest valley. I don't check that pasture very often because it's an overnight ride, and Betsy was newborn and I just couldn't cut it. I didn't want to let the girls go alone, and I just plain didn't feel up to making the trip." She fisted her hands as if she were ready to begin punching herself for her weakness.

Silas couldn't stand it when Belle got in one of these infernal female moods. She was tough and game and made of nothing but gristle and nerve. "Belle, honey, now—"

"When that grass wore out in the late summer, I was surprised to see how many cattle were coming to the lowlands from that way. A lot of yearlings that weren't branded. I had no idea the herd had thrived so. I rode up and was shocked. I not only undercounted, I was planning on that high grass for my herd this winter. I realized I couldn't feed them. I was sloppy."

"You have ten times the courage of any man I've ever known. And then you go and pull this female stuff." Maybe if he could make her mad at him instead of herself, she'd calm down. She seemed to enjoy hollering at him.

"I cut corners."

She hadn't even reacted to his reminding her she was a female. This was serious.

"I took the easy way out, and now I'm risking my girls' lives on this trail drive and—"

"Belle, you are the toughest woman—no, no, who am I kidding—the toughest *person* I've ever known."

She jabbed him in the chest, which was a good sign. "I wasn't tough enough to check—"

"Then you go and start beating on yourself—"

"My own herd, and I'm honest enough to admit when I—"

"For not working hard enough and before I know it, I'm—"

CHAPTER 12

Kissing her.

Silas was kissing her.

Belle didn't even fight him when he pulled her into his arms. Honestly, she moved toward him the second she saw that fire in his eyes. And she didn't know how to judge such things, but she was pretty sure she got to his lips before he got to hers. Except that wasn't possible, because their lips got to each other at the same second and they stayed together with the full cooperation of both parties involved.

Silas's hands pulled her firmly against him.

Belle didn't stop him. In truth, she grabbed ahold, tight, and hung on like it could be forever. Stopping him was the furthest thing from her mind.

"Breakfast is ready, you two." Sarah did it for her. "Knock it off and come eat."

Silas staggered back.

Belle whirled around. Sarah's horse nudged Belle's shoulder. Sarah had ridden right up to them, and Belle had never noticed. Belle's knees sagged, and she had to grab the saddle horn on Sarah's horse to hold herself up.

Silas moved again, and Belle looked over her shoulder to see he'd backed away about ten yards. Their eyes met, and his were wild. He turned away and ran both hands through his hair with a motion that spoke of the depths of his frustration.

Belle knew just how he felt.

"Ma, should you be kissing a man you're not married to that-away?" Sarah's face creased into a worried frown.

Belle shook her head back and forth slowly. With complete honesty and a husky voice she didn't recognize, she said, "Absolutely not."

"Then why are you doing it, Ma? If you do it, it must be okay, 'cuz you wouldn't do anything that was bad. So—"

"Sarah?" Silas cut in, still with his back to them.

"Yeah?" She sounded vulnerable and confused.

Belle braced herself to repair the damage of whatever ridiculous excuse Silas might have for their behavior.

"Give your ma a ride back to camp. I'll catch up her horse and my own and be right in. We're giving the cattle a day to rest up." And themselves, but Silas didn't admit that out loud. "And Sarah?"

"Yeah?"

Silas turned so he could look in Sarah's eyes. "Your ma is right. We shouldn't have oughta been kissing like that." Silas sighed deeply then forged on. "That's for two people who are married, or soon to be married, and no one else. I was worried about your ma because she didn't wake me for my turn riding herd. I found her asleep out here. For a minute I was plumb scared that she'd been hurt. Then when she was okay, well, I kinda got carried away because I was so. . .relieved. And that kiss, well, it shouldn't have happened, but it did. And it was wrong of me, and it won't happen again, because we are *not* going to get married. I apologize to you and your ma."

Belle listened to his neat little explanation with growing anger. With a sharp twist of dismay, she realized that when she'd decided letting Silas kiss her was too tempting to resist, she'd also known she was accepting the idea that she'd take the leap again and get married to the confounded man. But it didn't sound like Silas was interested. She'd known plenty of men who wanted what Silas wanted but weren't interested in offering marriage. And every one of them was a low-down, dirty, stinking polecat. And she'd slapped every one of them down hard.

Listening to Silas brush aside what had passed between them with his fumbling apology was humiliating, because while he'd been playing a man's game, she'd been falling in love.

Falling in love with Silas?

No!

Belle had been down the husband road too many times. She had learned that marriage was, at its most basic, a business deal. It took two people to make a baby. It took two people to run a home. She had the babies to prove the first. And Belle had survived when the scoundrels had disproved the second. But just because her husbands hadn't come through for her didn't mean it wasn't the way it was supposed to be. People got married for sensible reasons, and if they were lucky, they'd have some affection for each other and call it love. But it wasn't *required*. It wasn't even good, especially if one had affection and the other didn't.

Belle knew without a doubt she'd never felt anything close to love for her husbands. She'd thought she cared for William, but that had died on the vine shortly after their marriage when William realized he was getting a few hundred dollars instead of a ranch.

A husband had his rights in marriage, and she'd endured it when she couldn't think of a way to take the starch out of 'em. That was part of the business of being married.

But love? *Love!* What if she'd loved her husbands and then

they'd treated her so badly? Remembering Gerald's fists, remembering the way Anthony had abandoned her to her fate when she'd gone into labor on the trail. . .the hurt was staggering and she hadn't cared a whit for either man. If she'd have loved them, it would have destroyed her.

Just listening to Silas say there would be no marriage between them was breaking her heart.

My heart will not be involved, Lord. Please protect me from love.

Her backbone stiffened. It was *not* breaking her heart. She *wouldn't* love Silas. She wouldn't love *anyone*! She'd been thinking she'd marry him, but that was another matter altogether from love. And now it looked like he thought Belle was one of those women who. . .who would be willing to be with a man. . .share passion with a man. . .because Silas's kisses were more passion that she'd ever felt with a man. And he thought they'd share such without wedding vows.

Realizing that stung badly. Tears burned Belle's eyes, but she blinked them away. "Let's go, Sarah."

Sarah studied Silas for a minute before she clucked gently to her horse and removed Belle from temptation yet again. They rode back to the camp in silence.

Silas watched after the two womenfolk until the herd swallowed them up. Then he stared sightlessly at the T Bar cattle.

Belle.

He couldn't be around her. He couldn't stay here knowing how she responded to him. He couldn't stay.

And he couldn't leave.

He thought back to Lulamae and knew now the sheer depths of the little liar's sham desire for him. She'd held him tight, and he'd believed she welcomed a kiss—until her pa came in. But compared to the way Belle melted in his arms. . .

Silas turned away from the steers and tried to gather his senses. He looked around for his horse, and at his shrill whistle, it and Belle's black gelding ambled over to meet him. He didn't mount up but instead led them along while he headed for camp on foot. He didn't want to go back and face the hen posse that might be shaking out a loop and looking for a low-hanging branch right this minute.

There'd be a new kind of Husband Tree for this crew.

More than that, he didn't want to see the confused look on Sarah's face as she asked him about men and women and whether her ma was being good or bad. Silas shook his head in disgust. He had more to think about on this trip than how warm and passionate Belle Tanner was. How warm and passionate and vulnerable and beautiful and strong and tired—

He shook his head again. He had four little girls to think about. Their welfare had to be his first priority. And taking care of Belle was important, too. But he was *not* getting married. He didn't trust women, and Belle was one of the orneriest critters he'd ever seen, even if she *was* a different sort.

Except, for the first time, he wasn't going to marry her for a different reason than the one he'd had before—that reason being a fear and disgust for the two women he'd run afoul of. No. He wasn't going to marry her because *he* was worthless. He was penniless, and he had run like a coward from two ranches. He had to make something of himself before he could tangle himself up with a woman as fine as Belle.

To go into a marriage without a way to support a wife was dishonorable. Oh, he knew he could make a place for himself at Belle's, but even if he worked the land hard, it would never be his.

The Tanner Ranch. In Divide, that's what they called it. Not a single name of one of her husbands had stuck. He could move in and claim his place and set the holding to rights and make Belle's life easier, but none of it would ever be his.

He knew as he thought it all through that he was making excuses. The idea of being sucked into Belle's all-girl household reminded him too much of the way he'd been raised, surrounded by women. It had been smothering. He'd escaped that life at the earliest possible moment, and he couldn't willingly sign up for another hitch of it.

He thought of Emma's toughness. Lindsay's quiet confidence. Sarah's homey mothering. Betsy's silent watchfulness. Sure he liked them. Not wanting to be the only rooster at a hen party didn't mean he thought there was anything wrong with the girls. As a matter of fact, he'd gladly thrash anyone who said there was anything wrong with his girls. But that didn't mean he wanted to buy into their brood.

He caught a handful of mane on his own horse and jumped onto its back. He set out to circle the herd and take stock. He was ready to face the Tanner women again, but just to be on the safe side—what with the way Lindsay handled a gun and all—he started his inspection in the direction that led him directly away from them.

Silas didn't return to camp until close to noon. The cattle were fine, munching away on a fair stand of native grass and young pine boughs.

He ran into Emma once and noticed she must have bathed in the creek, because he could see her instead of dirt. She was out doing her own inspection. She nodded to him without saying much, but normally she'd have come up and talked to him for a minute, so he wondered what had gone on back in camp.

His inspection led him near the camp, and he was debating whether to face the Tanner women or starve to death. He was having a hard time picking.

Then three riders came over the top of the draw they'd punched the cattle over yesterday.

Silas headed for camp and got there while the riders were still a half mile away, winding down the steep trail. He watched them from a distance, and although they looked like average cowpokes, he didn't trust anyone around his women.

He was swinging off his horse when he realized he thought of Belle and her girls as his. He was lucky he didn't fall all the way to the ground. He might have if there'd been time. For now, he stepped over to Belle. She'd cleaned up in the creek and was all sweet-smelling and pink along with the girls and was now busy spreading a batch of washing on bushes near their camp. This wasn't the usual batch of diapers they did every night. This was a full washing.

He grabbed Belle's arm to get her attention. "I'm going to say you're my wife. I don't want these men to think you're an unmarried woman. Let me deal with them. Go along with me."

Belle looked shocked at his suggestion. "Silas, I'm not going to—"

"Just do it." Silas talked over top of her then stepped quickly over to Lindsay who was peeling spuds along with Sarah.

Belle went on protesting, but he ignored her. "Lindsay!"

Lindsay turned to him, her eyes narrow. So she'd heard what went on between Silas and Belle this morning, too. Well, he didn't have time to talk about that now.

"I want you girls to call me Pa while these men are around."

Startled, Lindsay exchanged a look with Sarah. Then the two of them looked over their shoulders at the approaching men. They'd all noticed the strangers and were wary. But Silas's order surprised them.

"Sure, Pa." Lindsay shook her head and grinned. "That's a good idea. I've been trying to get the potatoes peeled before I went for my gun." Lindsay was a practical girl.

Silas admired that. "You too, Sarah."

"Silas," Belle scolded. "We are not going to lie to—"

"Put a few more potatoes in the pot. If they're just passing through we'll let them sit up to a meal."

Sarah giggled. "Glad to help, Pa."

Betsy was tied onto Lindsay's back. She waved her arms at Silas and said gleefully, "Papa."

Silas bit back a grin at Betsy. He'd have laughed out loud at the little imp if he hadn't been in such a hurry.

"Now, Silas. . ." Belle caught his arm.

"Wait just a second, Belle." Silas patted her arm and kept giving the girls orders. "Lindsay, ride out and tell Emma so she doesn't come busting into camp and give us away. I'm not saying there's anything wrong with these men. But it's best to keep a careful eye at first. And even if they're decent men. . .well, men are notional critters when there are beautiful women to hand. So, I want you especially to ride careful around them. Don't ever be out of my sight while they're here. I may try and hire them to help with the herd if they measure up. If they do, you'll have to keep calling me Pa until they leave."

Lindsay's chin lifted, and her eyes shone as she asked breathlessly, "You think I'm a beautiful woman?" She stuttered and shook her head and looked at the ground in embarrassment. "Or, no, you're talking about Ma."

"You're as pretty a little thing as any man has ever set eyes on," Silas said in pure disgust. "And I don't want those men thinking you don't have a pa around to fill them full of buckshot if they so much as look at you sideways! And it ain't a compliment, Lindsay. Being pretty can be a blasted nuisance. Ask your ma."

"You do." Lindsay looked back at Silas, her face glowing with pleasure. "You think I'm pretty. You think Ma's pretty, too."

Silas could have sworn Lindsay grew about two inches right there in front of him. She stood up taller. A different expression was on her face than he'd ever seen before. She squared her shoulders. "I'll find Emma and let her know what's going on." She lifted Betsy out of her carrier. "Sarah, you take Betsy."

"I've got her." Silas took the baby without thinking about it.

He was too worried about what ideas he'd just planted in Lindsay's head. "Lindsay, I won't have you making any sheep's eyes at these *hombres*. Don't go gettin' ideas."

"I won't, Pa," Lindsay said fervently. "You can count on me to behave myself." She turned and walked quickly toward the closest horse.

The men were drawing nearer, so Silas hissed after her, "I don't want you riding out any farther than where I can see you. And get Emma back to camp, too. And your name's Harden, every one of you."

Lindsay hung a bridle on the horse and jumped on it bareback. "Harden. Yes, Pa. I'll tell Emma her name. We'll both be careful. . . Pa." She kicked the horse and rode toward Emma, who was way down the hill but clearly visible.

"Hello, the camp," the men called out, pulling to a stop from a decent distance. Silas felt better knowing these men were wise in the ways of approaching a cow herd.

"Silas," Belle said quietly enough the men couldn't hear her, "I've handled men many a time. I don't need you to pretend—"

"You mind me woman"—Silas spun around and jabbed a finger right at her nose—"or I'll tan your backside right in front of these cowpokes."

Belle opened her mouth, but no words came out, which suited Silas right down to the ground.

"You want me to take the baby, Pa?" Sarah asked.

Silas hoisted Betsy up against his chest, barely noticing he held her. "She's fine. Get on with your chores."

"Yes, Pa."

"Silas—" Belle started in yapping.

Silas turned on her and saw pure spitfire in her eyes. Well, there wasn't time to palaver about it. She'd just have to do as she was told by her husband the way the good Lord intended. "If these girls call me Pa and you Ma but you say we aren't married, what kind of loose woman does that make you?"

Belle gasped.

"What are those men going to think?"

Silas closed her mouth by giving her a sound kiss. He pulled away and said in a voice that brooked no objection, "You're Belle Harden. Don't forget it no matter how many last names you've had before."

Then the men rode up and Silas turned to them with one of his arms around Belle and Betsy perched on his shoulder.

The very image of a happy family man.

CHAPTER 13

"That coffee smells mighty good, ma'am." The middle-aged man, riding between an old grizzled cowpoke and a boy, did the talking, and Silas pegged him for the leader of the group. "I'm Buck, and this is my son, Roy, and my saddle partner, Shorty."

Their gear was clean and neatly packed, and their horses looked well cared for. The men themselves looked a little rough, but riding a long trail would do that. Silas didn't like that they'd addressed his wife before asking his permission. Still, a woman was a wonderful thing, and the men were probably so fascinated by Belle that they could barely remember Silas was there.

"You're welcome to join—"

Silas dug his hand into her waist and squeezed so hard she quit talking. "Get back to the meal, woman. These men aren't here to talk no hen talk." Which was probably wrong. These men would no doubt welcome hen talk—or anything else Belle suggested— just to hear the sound of her voice.

Belle looked at him, and Silas wondered if she hadn't just left burn marks on his skin with the fire in her eyes. He grinned and eased up the grip on her waist then caressed her stomach with a little circular motion of his thumb. She looked confused for a second. Then she turned to help Sarah with the noon meal.

Obedient. Belle Tanner. . .Harden, he amended. . .was obeying him.

Silas could have wrestled a grizzly bear he felt so powerful. "And take this young'un off my hands," Silas added gruffly.

Belle turned back and took Betsy without speaking a word.

Silas wondered if it was because his behavior had left "his little woman" speechless. The thought almost made him smile. More likely she was too busy plotting his slow, painful death to talk.

Silas looked back at the men. They'd ridden closer but still waited a respectful distance, which spoke well of them. "Light and sit. No one ever walked away from the Harden campfire hungry."

He watched every move they made, conscious of how close a gun hand got to a trigger and whether he saw something behind the eyes of any of the men that made him uneasy. Silas had been down the river and back more than a time or two. He'd seen every kind of low-down trash the earth had to offer in the men who came to see his ma and her friends. He'd seen fine, hardworking, honest men who dressed in rags and smelled worse than their horses. He'd seen well-dressed, prosperous men with eyes like snakes and hearts dripping with filth. He'd ridden hard miles and dug a living out of a hard country, and he trusted his judgment when it came to sizing up a man.

The riders settled into the camp, resting against a fallen log one of the girls must have dragged in while he was busy kissing the daylights out of Belle. They introduced themselves, as did Silas sitting across from them on the other side of the fire. He never mentioned Belle's or Sarah's names.

Belle served coffee, careful to stay a healthy arm's length away from the men. Then she removed herself from the circle as quickly as possible. She was acting for all the world like a proper, demure, and obedient wife.

Silas wondered when she'd learned to fake that.

"We've been riding with Wade Sawyer." Buck held the coffee cup cradled in two hands like he needed to warm himself. Silas held his same way. So did every experienced cowhand in cold country. "He said you'd asked him to help with the drive. We were Tom Linscott's line camp, just passing through, when Sawyer delivered supplies. He said maybe you needed more hands. He didn't make any promises about hiring us. We understand that, and we'll ride on if you say the word."

Silas had no idea who Wade Sawyer was. He didn't mention that.

Belle came up beside him and actually wrung her hands a bit as if she were afraid of displeasing him, when what she was probably really thinking was she'd like to wring his neck.

Who'd'a guessed the little woman was an actress?

"Remember, I told you I saw Wade at the diner, just after you left? I told him we were shorthanded, but he had already hired on to deliver Linscott's supplies. He said he'd ride out this way if he made good time."

She had talked about asking others in town to ride herd. Maybe she'd mentioned Wade in passing. Silas couldn't be sure, but he appreciated his little woman filling in the gaps. He looked at Buck. "So why isn't he with you?"

"The strangest thing," Buck said. "There was a white woman dressed in Indian clothes running from. . ."

The men talked openly as men did who weren't on the dodge. After they'd finished their tale of Glowing Sun, Silas noticed they all said their pleases and thank yous as if it came straight from their heart when Belle poured more coffee. Silas didn't doubt that they were sincere. Coffee being poured from the soft hand of a pretty woman was mighty rare in the wilderness.

With coffee refilled, Buck went on. "We were riding out from the goldfields near Helena."

Buck eased back as if settling in for his storytelling. "The mines played out a decade ago, but dreamers still came and tried to hammer wealth out of the tightfisted ground. Us among 'em. Roy was just a boy then."

Buck wove that tale with Shorty chiming in—a man of few words, but the ones he spoke were worth hearing.

Silas liked the look of them. He wanted to tell them they were hired but decided to wait until Lindsay and Emma came back to camp. He needed to see how they acted when they saw "his girls." The boy drank his coffee quickly and asked for more before Belle offered. He kept looking at Betsy like he was hungry for the sight of a baby.

When Sarah took the baby from Belle's carrier and bounced her, Roy got up from the fire and went to stand by the womenfolk as if he were being drawn in by a magnet.

"Don't mind the boy," Buck said quietly. "He's never seen a baby before. Not up close. Maybe an Indian baby a time or two from a distance. I had a spread on the Musselshell in the foothills of the Rockies for a while, but we got driven out by the Sioux seven years ago when the boy was ten. Found my wife and two older daughters massacred and my home burned. My cattle driven off, too, all while the young'un and I were riding the range. Didn't have the belly for startin' over without my woman to make a home of it. We've been driftin' ever since. Shorty was working for me when it happened, and now we ride the trail together. It's been mostly line shacks and frontier towns for my son. We've lived a far piece away from folks out here. That baby. . .well. . .Roy wouldn't be any more fascinated if a leprechaun came sliding down a rainbow with a pot of gold."

Silas nodded, but he made sure he knew where Roy was every minute.

Lindsay and Emma rode up about the time Belle was stirring the beef stew for the last time.

Roy's blue eyes lit up, and he quit looking at the baby.

"I found lion tracks back a ways, Pa." Emma dismounted and began stripping the leather from her horse.

Something big and strong grew in Silas's heart at the sound of Emma calling him "Pa."

"I trailed him a spell, but I never caught sight of him." Emma's knowing eyes took in the men, their horses, their guns, and the look in her ma's eyes all in one sweeping glance. She must have liked what she saw, because she kept talking and working. "The tracks look a couple of days old, but this is probably his range."

"I'll take the next look around." Silas noticed Roy edging close to Lindsay as she began working with her mount. "Lion meat would surely add something to our kettle."

Belle said with a meek voice Silas had never heard her use before, "Silas, there's plenty of stew and biscuits for these folks if it's all right with you."

That big, strong feeling Emma had awakened was nothing compared to how powerful it was to hear Belle, however much she wanted to kill him, pretending to be a submissive wife. He knew enough to enjoy it while he had the chance. "My Belle's a rare cook." He didn't really know that for a fact since Sarah had done most of the cooking, but the girl had to learn it from somewhere, so it stood to reason.

"We've been eating hardtack and jerked beef, with a venison steak thrown in once in a while. I can't remember what a warm meal served by a woman tastes like," Buck said. "We'd be proud to have a meal with you."

Silas heard the respect and honest appreciation in Buck's voice and, with some misgivings based on the way Roy was looking at Lindsay, asked, "Are you boys looking for work? We've got another two weeks on this drive into Helena. I left it too late because I couldn't find hands. Now we're trying to drive on our own, and though my womenfolk are good, handy girls, all of 'em, we could surely use the help."

Shorty nodded. "Reckon I can go that way as soon as another. How many hands have you got riding herd?"

Silas was surprised Wade hadn't told them. His respect for the unknown man rose for not telling strangers about the nearly all-female crew. He also decided the reaction he got from these men would decide the near future. "This is the lot of us. My girls and I are taking this herd alone."

Shorty's eyes narrowed.

Buck leaned forward. "Just the womenfolk and you? And you've moved them through these mountain trails?"

Silas didn't answer. Buck knew full well that was a fact, because he'd just come down the trail, and no one could miss that a thousand head of cattle had passed that way.

Buck shoved his hat back and smiled. "They grow 'em tough in Montana, I'd say. Women as well as men. You should have seen that little spitfire giving Wade all he could handle."

Roy's face had now turned an alarming shade of pink, and he was staring straight at the ground as if his feet fascinated him. Every once in a while he'd take a quick glance up at Lindsay then go right back to inspecting his boots.

"Can we hire on, Pa?" He pulled off his well-worn hat and finger-combed his overly long, dark blond hair as if suddenly worried about his appearance.

Lindsay walked to her horse to rub it down.

Roy trailed a good twenty feet behind, not speaking to her and not listening to his father's answer.

Silas's eyes narrowed as he watched Roy. He clenched his hands between his splayed knees until his knuckles turned white and considered rescinding the offer of work. He looked back at Buck and made sure the man saw his displeasure.

Buck looked from his son to Silas. He leaned forward and said low, "I'll see to the boy. Don't worry none about him. He's a good 'un. Just young."

"I know what goes on in a young man's mind." Silas frowned. "It's not that I don't understand. But it's different when you're a man with pretty little girls like mine, Buck. Real different. I won't put up with a single wrong word from your boy."

Buck nodded. "I'll be right beside you if he steps out of line." Then he grinned. "But the day will come when you're gonna have to let the fellers near your girls."

Silas couldn't manage a smile, but he did nod.

"Your oldest is marryin' age, I'd say," Buck added. "And the next, well, I've known gals hitched that young, too."

Silas's stomach did a dive that almost brought him up off the ground. He didn't respond, but he wanted to grab Lindsay and drag her back home and lock her in the house. He stared hard at Roy. "It's not that I won't let 'em near. I will when the time comes a few years from now, but I'll be near, too. Standing close at hand with my shotgun."

Then Silas thought of the way Hank Tool acted when he caught Lulamae in the barn. Hank had set the whole thing up with Lulamae, not just *allowing* her to be treated in such a way but most likely instructing the poor dumb cluck to behave so. Silas was suddenly furious with Hank Tool for being so cavalier with his daughter, and only the distance of four states kept Silas from hunting the man down and thrashing him.

Buck laughed. "A man after my own heart. If you're still interested, we'd appreciate the work."

Silas leaned forward and offered the man his hand. "You're hired."

Buck leaned across the campfire and shook Silas's hand. Shorty nodded from where he sat, leaning lazily against a tree trunk. "I think we'd be willing to take the job just to eat at your campfire."

"Well, you'll do that and earn thirty a month, too. Although the job's only got two weeks left."

"Done," Buck said. "It's a pretty country, but it's a hard route you're takin'. God made most of the land stand on end instead of lyin' flat like a decent piece of land had oughta."

Silas nodded with a wry smile. "You've just come over the trail. You know what the last few days have been like. We've got one blazed-faced steer who spends all his time trying to go home."

"We rode through some of the herd. It's a good-looking bunch you got. Fat and sassy. They've been well tended. A lot of steers are mighty gaunt by the time they've been on the trail a few weeks. You must know ranching."

Careful not to crack a smile, he said deliberately to goad Belle, "Thanks. I put a lot of care into fattening them for market. I'm really pleased with the way they've stood up. We've driven them hard. We had one spell. . ."

Silas sat ignoring his obedient little Belle and taking all the credit for her hard work. He imagined her going for his throat and somehow ending up with her arms around his neck. It took all his will to pay attention to cow talk about the hills behind and the hills ahead.

Belle handed Buck and Shorty plates of food with a kind word and a demure smile then turned back to the fire and returned quickly with food for Silas. He thought she slapped it a little hard in his lap, but she didn't dump it on his head, so he silently thanked the Lord for looking out for him and ate his meal.

Roy was helping Lindsay rub down Emma's bay. He was working energetically on the off side of the horse, occasionally glancing over the animal's back at Lindsay. It occurred to Silas grudgingly that a young man who tried to impress a young lady by working hard by her side wasn't a bad sort. He also made a mental note to keep his shotgun to hand while he slept.

Silas went out to ride the circuit with all three men. He wasn't about to leave a single one of them alone with his girls. He did remember, as his thoughts ranged over how he'd defend his women, that his women could probably outrope, outride, and outshoot most of the men in Montana. It made him smile with pride to think of it.

The four men rousted strays out of the thickening brush that grew up the mountainside. They got the cattle settled in for the night, and Shorty trailed the mountain lion off a few miles into the hills and came back to report it seemed to have been on its way out of the country.

When the sun set, the night had more than the normal bite of cold, and white began sifting down out of the sky. Silas knew the heavier snow wouldn't be long in coming. He thought for the first time that if he rode back to Belle's ranch with her, and as a gentleman he would have to escort her home, he might accidentally get himself snowed in with the Tanners for the winter. The idea made Silas feel so good inside it scared him right down to his boots.

Belle and the two older girls went out after supper to stand first watch.

"I don't rightly know when I've let a woman ride herd while I warmed my toes by a fireside," Buck said with a furrowed brow. "It don't seem right."

Silas could have taken that as an insult, but he knew exactly what Buck meant. "The Lord hasn't seen fit to give me a son yet." And the thought of having a son with Belle made him so restless he could barely continue the conversation. Clearing his throat, he said, "I need the help, and the women are top hands with a horse. My Emma can hold her own with any man, and that includes me, and they love it. All of them would rather sit a horse than sew a dress. I don't know if that's the proper way to raise a girl, but we're all to ourselves most of the time, and we just go our own way. When a man comes along for the girls, well, he'll take 'em as they are or he won't get near 'em. If there's any changin' to be done, he'll be doin' it."

Shorty leaned back against his bedroll, using his saddle as

a pillow. He tilted his trail-worn Stetson over his eyes. "I'll take second watch with Roy. I'd like to get a little sleep before then if you two are done yammerin'."

Buck settled back, too. "You'd better stay in and keep watch over the girls, Silas. We'll take this first night."

Silas said cordial-like, "Appreciate it, Buck. I sleep light, so I'll ride out time to time." It was the barest of warnings, but Buck grunted his approval as he rested his head on his saddle and pulled his blanket over himself in the flicker of the campfire. No one would respect a man who didn't watch over his daughters and his herd with equal vigilance.

Silas settled into his own bedroll, thinking of the soft snow and the winter closing in and how much he enjoyed the idea of Belle giving him a son. . .or another daughter. Yes, he'd be contented with a girl all right.

Then he did his best to turn his thoughts to something else before it became impossible to sleep. He wasn't all that successful. In fact, he was as bothered as a man could be and almost went out to ride, since he wasn't sleeping anyway. But he couldn't leave.

Shorty woke Roy, and the two of them left the camp quietly. Silas heard them go and lay awake until Belle, Lindsay, and Emma all came riding in. The snow had stopped, and the night was sharply cold but not bitter. The women went straight to caring for their horses.

Silas pushed aside his blanket, stood, and walked over to Belle. He rested his hand on her elbow. "Let's step away from the campfire for a second."

Belle nodded and followed him as the girls worked their horses. Silas stayed where the sleeping girls and Lindsay and Emma working with their mounts were in their line of sight.

Silas whispered, "I just wanted to remind you that you have to show me a bit of affection from time to time to keep this idea in these men's heads that we're married."

"What?" Belle's shocked question rang out clearly enough to be heard down the whole mountainside.

Silas squeezed her elbow. "Shh. What else? A wife gives her husband a kiss now and then. You'll do it, too!"

"Silas," she began sternly, but at least she wasn't yelling, "I am not—"

Silas shut her up by kissing her, and when she melted against him, it occurred to Silas that this was the most fun he'd ever had in his life. It was the plain honest truth that he was a happy man when he was tormenting Belle Tanner. He eased his lips away from her and said with his mouth a bare inch from her ear, "I'll sleep with the men."

Belle shuddered and Silas breathed softly against her ear again to see if she'd repeat the telltale movement. She did.

"Silas," Belle said with reluctant protest, "what about the girls? They can't see us behaving in a way that's not proper. They'll think—"

"I already told them what we had to do. They understand." Silas leaned closer again and murmured, "Now think, darlin', the yarn I spun these boys is the only one we could have told. When it gets down to it, me being along on this drive with you is about as improper as anything can be."

"No, it's not. The girls are better chaperones than a fire-and-brimstone preacher backed by a convent full of nuns."

Silas grinned. "That is the honest truth. But I'm here as your husband while these men are with us. We have to make do as best we can."

"But it's all a lie, Silas. I'll spend my night praying for forgiveness for this nonsense. All you had to do was be honest."

He kissed her again because it seemed to quiet her down. "Now I've been calling you *my woman* and the girls *my girls*. I've been real careful not to say the word *wife* and *daughters*."

"You told the girls to call you Pa. Don't try and pretend that's not a lie."

He was holding a smart woman in his arms. He found it suited him. "Well, I've already asked for forgiveness, and I feel like God understands. Which means you're more stubborn than God, and why am I not surprised?"

Belle jerked her arm out of his grip, but Silas caught it and reeled her back in for one last kiss. When she'd calmed clear down to being limp in his arms, he pulled back just enough to whisper in her pretty ear, "I think we've been over here long enough." He said it all scoldinglike, as if Belle was keeping him over here just because she wanted a few minutes of privacy to smooch. "Now you go on back to camp and behave yourself."

Silas pressed his bristly cheek to her smooth one and slid his arms snug around her waist. "We have to do this, darlin'." He nodded, his face nudging her chin up and down. "It's to protect you and the girls. You can see that, can't you?" He kept nodding, kept her close, marveled at the woman smell of her.

Finally, she nodded, too.

Pulling back, he thought her eyes looked a bit dazed, and she flickered a glance at his lips that made Silas step back before he had to do any more explaining to the girls. He took her hand and led her back to the campfire where she'd sleep well away from him.

He felt a niggling of guilt for not being honest with the new hired hands, and he especially worried about letting the girls call him Pa. Was he teaching the girls sinful lessons? He opened his eyes to see snowflakes drifting down again.

Silas asked God to help him figure out his feelings for Belle and how they matched up with his feelings for women in general.

This being a father business is complicated, Lord. I don't know how You've managed it for all these years. I'd appreciate some guidance.

A breeze moved over him, and the wind carried a whisper that he knew he imagined. It whispered something like, *"If you married her, none of this would be a lie."*

That whisper cracked like a bullwhip in the air and jolted Silas wide awake. He lay there, watching it snow for two hours, his prayers mixed up with remembering the scent of Belle's hair.

When he finally drifted off, he woke up every few minutes all night long. And it had nothing to do with being suspicious of the new cowhands.

CHAPTER 14

The little minx barely left a trail. And Wade considered himself a fair hand with tracking.

Since he'd left his father's ranch, he'd spent long weeks living off the land in these very mountains. He felt close to God up here. The big sky felt wide enough to hold heaven, and the mountains would make a grand footstool as God watched over His children. Finding he could survive with the strength of his own hands gave him hope that he was a worthy man. It tore down all the mountains of self-contempt his father heaped on him with constant criticism and hard fists. This land made him believe in his own worth.

So Wade didn't expect to have trouble keeping track of Glowing Sun.

But he did.

She was easy to follow for the first day. The only trail she could take was the one they'd been on.

He pushed his horse and hoped to close the gap between them. But once he was through the toughest passages, there were choices. Scared he'd choose wrong, Wade studied the ground often until he assured himself he was still on Glowing Sun's trail.

Buck had given him detailed directions to the Flathead camp, and Wade considered several times just riding straight for it as the second day stretched to three, then four. He could go to her village, stay back from it but remain watchful, and wait for Glowing Sun. All he needed was to see her arrive safely.

His common sense told him the woman was well equipped to survive in these rugged mountains.

But if he was so sure she'd be fine, then he might as well go throw in with Belle's cattle drive and be done with the wild-goose chase. His reason for following after Glowing Sun was to protect her. Abandoning her trail didn't figure in.

He swung to the ground, checking what looked like the pad of a moccasin on a stretch of damp forest soil, when his horse reared with a wild squeal and jerked the reins out of his hands. Wade made a dive for the suddenly frantic animal and managed to swing himself up onto the buckskin. Even with Wade's hand pulling hard on the reins, the horse ran nearly a hundred yards back in the direction they'd just come. Only then did Wade manage to halt his gelding. Snorting and wheeling, the horse must have been far enough from whatever upset him because, though he fidgeted, he let Wade take charge and hold him nearly in place.

"Wade!" A woman's voice. Glowing Sun.

Wade turned, trying to locate her.

The horse stopped and perked its ears forward.

A snarling grizzly lumbered out of a clump of quaking aspens near where Wade had stood just seconds ago.

His horse whinnied and backed away.

Wade patted the horse on the neck to show his thanks. As the bear charged forward a dozen feet, baring its teeth, Wade pulled his rifle from its sling on his saddle and snapped a shell in place.

The bear skidded to a stop. The wily animal had obviously seen and heard a gun before.

"Wade! Help!" She spoke English. Granted, it was only two

words, but he'd taught her those words. He didn't look away from the roaring brute, but the direction of her voice told him Glowing Sun was in the upper branches of a tree just behind the bear. "Hang on. I'll. . .save you." Wade knew it was foolish, but he felt himself grow taller when he shouted the words. His shoulders squared, his chin lifted. Pathetic as it was, he had to grin as he sighted down the length of his rifle.

Sorry, Lord. I know I've got a problem with rescuing women. Most of 'em don't need rescuing one whit. But just maybe this one does.

The grizzly shook its head as if forbidding Wade to take a shot.

Wade waited. If the old grizz didn't want a fight, it'd have to turn tail and run.

With a furious roar. . .that's just what it did. The bear, nearly as tall in the shoulders as Wade's horse, whirled and vanished into the thickly wooded mountainside.

Wade wasn't about to go after the old monster, but he'd gotten to know Glowing Sun well enough in their time together that he reckoned if he waited too long she'd climb down from the treetops and run. Trusting his mount, Wade waited until his horse settled down before he approached.

She wasn't in the copse of aspens. He moved on into the forest, watching the treetops, until he saw her peeking out between the thinning leaves. Looking disgruntled, she sat on a branch so high she should have had a nosebleed. The tree, an oak, magnificent in its fall dressing of red leaves, nearly concealed her, but enough leaves had fallen that he could catch a glimpse.

The claw marks told their story. The grizzly had followed her up a long way, forcing her into the slender upper branches. She clung there now, hanging on to the trunk so far up that the tree bent under her weight.

When she saw him she gasped in relief. He saw her release the trunk then frantically grab it back. Even as far up as she was, Wade could see that terror had her in its grip.

"Just take one step at a time." He could see her whole body trembling.

"P–please. H–help." Her voice shook and Wade heard the tears making her voice waver. "W–Wade, help me!"

Wade didn't think the tree would hold both of them up that high, but the vulnerability in her usually strong voice forced his hand. Grimly determined to get her before she fell, he tied his horse to the tree, said a quick prayer that the grizzly had quit the country, and began climbing.

The ancient oak was as easy to scale as a staircase. It had limbs low to the ground. Probably why Glowing Sun had chosen it to escape the bear.

"Oak tree," Wade called up.

Maybe if she would talk, her panic would ease. Glowing Sun had been terrified when he'd first found her running from those men, but even then she'd been fighting mad.

How long had she been up here? Wade had set a slow pace. He couldn't guess how far ahead of him she'd gotten. It was possible she'd been treed overnight, even longer. She must be exhausted, her muscles cramped and cold.

"Oak tree," she answered, but her face was pressed to the bark, and he could barely hear her.

"I'm coming."

She risked a glance down and saw him, still with yards to go. But her eyes locked on his, and Wade saw relief. Then her gaze slid to the ground, so far below, and she turned back to the tree, her trembling arms clamped even more tightly around the trunk.

Wade felt like he was scaling a castle wall or climbing a prison tower. Very heroic. Very white-knightlike. He grinned and climbed faster. "Grizzly bear."

She looked down again and nodded wildly. "Grizzly bear." She put enough feeling in those words to fill a book.

Wade remembered his mother reading fairy tales to him when he was very young. *Rapunzel* was one of his favorites. Wade had pictured himself climbing to rescue the princess trapped in the tower. He remembered his father's unkindness to his mother, though he'd been very young when she died and wished he could have rescued her.

The reality of the bark under his hands and the maiden overhead furrowed his brow. *Did* he remember his mother? Maybe he just regarded everyone with the same cruelty his father did.

Wade shook his head and paid attention to his very own imprisoned princess. "I'm coming to save you, my little damsel in distress." He grinned at his nonsense. Glowing Sun would probably pull her knife on him and try to run away as soon as her feet hit the ground, so he might as well enjoy the moment.

Glowing Sun frowned, clearly not understanding his words. He noticed she didn't look away. Maybe if he just chattered she'd forget her long hours of terror.

"I know you must have been kidnapped from your family years ago. From your ma and pa."

Her forehead furrowed. "Ma? Pa?"

Wade moved up to the next branch. For the first time, the branch he stood on protested at holding his weight. The leaves had turned a stunning glorious red, and some fell as Wade jiggled branches. Still, he felt surrounded by God's glory in the middle of these leaves. "I'll slay the dragon for you, release you from your tower prison, and return you to your home." Wade's heart clutched as the next branch he grabbed cracked. He spread his weight. A branch under each foot and one in each hand, he hoped the combination would hold him.

God, lift me up. Bear my weight.

Wade silently prayed with every move. The Bible was full of stories like that. And he decided maybe praying aloud would be for the best.

" 'The Lord is my shepherd; I shall not want.' "

The terror faded from Glowing Sun's eyes, and she focused on Wade in a new, sharper way. She said, " 'He maketh me to lie down in green pastures: he leadeth me beside the still waters.' "

"You know that verse?"

Glowing Sun looked at him as if she were irritated.

Wade wanted to laugh. He'd interrupted her. "I'm sorry."

"I forgive you."

The girl had definitely been raised as a Christian, both before and after she'd lived with the Flatheads.

She went on. " 'He restoreth my soul: he leadeth me in the paths of right–right–ness. . .' " Faltering, she quit and scowled.

" 'Righteousness for his name's sake.' "

Her voice joined his. " 'Yea, though I walk through the valley of the shadow of death, I will fear no evil.' "

This was about the most perfect verse they could have chosen for all Glowing Sun's troubles. His, too, more'n likely.

Wade thought of his father and how deeply the old man needed God. Wade had no doubt God had led his father in the path of righteousness. But Mort Sawyer had gone his own way.

While he was distracted by thoughts of his tyrannical father, Glowing Sun went on reciting. " 'For thou art with me; thy rod and thy staff they comfort me. Thou pre–pre. . .' " She stumbled over the words.

He added his voice. " 'Thou preparest a table before me in the presence of mine enemies.' "

It occurred to Wade that if he took Glowing Sun all the way home, he'd have to face an Indian tribe, and they weren't all friendly. He might well be asking God to prepare a table in the presence of his enemies before the day was out.

" 'Thou anointest my head with oil; my cup runneth over.' "

The branch under his left hand was about double the width of a pencil. It bent but didn't break. Wade moved as quickly as possible up the ever-narrowing trunk, hoping that if he didn't leave his weight on any one branch for long, it'd hold. Each one that broke or was even cracked would add to the challenge of getting back down.

" 'Surely goodness and mercy shall follow me all the days of my life: and I will dwell in the house of the Lord for ever.'"

And with those words, Wade's fear evaporated. Yes, God's goodness and mercy followed him. Since he'd found the Lord, he'd found the courage to leave his father's house, and his life had been so much better.

It gave him courage to know that if the worst happened and he and Glowing Sun fell, then they'd dwell in the house of the Lord forever. There was nothing to fear.

Considering Wade believed himself to be a coward, that was a powerful notion to settle in his heart.

He looked away from his handhold as he drew even with Glowing Sun's feet. She stared deep into his eyes. It was clear she understood the scripture and it had calmed her. He reached his hand up for hers. She reached down and held fast. Wade nodded, and Glowing Sun lifted a trembling foot from the slender twig it was perched on. She took her first step down.

He went lower. The trunk was leaning too far in one direction, and Wade shifted his weight so he was on the opposite side from Glowing Sun. He descended a step, then another. She came along.

Wade felt the violent trembling of her hand and suspected it was as much exhaustion as fear.

"Just about ten more feet down and we'll get to the strong branches."

Glowing Sun looked at him, confused.

Wade touched their joined hands to a branch between them. "Branch."

She smiled. "Branch. Oak tree branch."

Another step, then another, one more and Wade got his foot

on a sturdy limb for the first time. He breathed a sigh of relief. He descended until that sturdy limb was under his hand instead of his foot.

Glowing Sun sighed in an almost perfect imitation of him. Did she think he'd been teaching her that as a word?

He looked over at her and smiled. "We're safe now."

True, the ground was still fifty feet away, but they *were* safe.

A bit more climbing down and Wade felt Glowing Sun recover her courage. She let go of his hand, which Wade didn't like, but they made better time and were on the ground in just a few more minutes. When she landed beside him, light on her feet, he laughed. She smiled then threw her arms around his neck and laughed with him.

He lifted her and swung her around. "My very own damsel in distress. I've finally saved someone."

Her head dropped back as he whirled her around. Her wild, blond hair whipped in the fall breeze. A fluttering of crimson leaves rained on them as he lowered her to the ground and grinned down into her sky blue eyes.

Their gaze caught.

Wade's arms tightened involuntarily.

The smile faded from Glowing Sun's face, replaced by a fascination with his lips.

Suddenly his whole life made sense. He had a future, and he could see it. . .with Glowing Sun. They'd start their own ranch. They'd have beautiful little blond daughters as wild and courageous as their mother. He'd be a father and a husband. A strong, courageous man with God fully in his life.

He leaned down to kiss her.

"Not so fast."

The voice, accompanied by the *crack* of a jacked shotgun jerked Wade's head around.

CHAPTER 15

Every time she woke, Belle remembered Silas's kiss.

It was infuriating the way he'd ordered her around. But his bossiness warmed her heart, too. No man had ever cared enough to take his place at the head of her household. She'd hated it at the same time she felt drawn to that strength.

Belle woke up in the first light of dawn and didn't know who she was anymore. She was lying with Betsy in her arms, and the little girl was wriggling. That had no doubt awakened her. She looked around and saw Sarah quietly tending the fire. In the distance, Emma was filling the coffeepot with water from the stream. Lindsay was saddling her horse with help from Roy.

Since when did Lindsay need help saddling her horse?

Belle should get up and run that young whelp off, but Betsy swatted her in the face and fussed, and Belle put off rescuing her oldest daughter—who was surely fully capable of rescuing herself—and tended her youngest.

"Mornin', Ma." Sarah smiled. "I'm gonna gather more wood."

Belle nodded and got Betsy into a dry diaper then settled in with the fallen log at her back to get the baby her breakfast. Alone for a few moments, all Belle could think about was what Silas had made her feel.

God, I want more of that. I want his attention and his strength and even his bossiness. I want a man who cares enough to want to run his own family.

As she sat there, her child in her arms, memories of Anthony and Gerald and especially William crowded her thoughts. All the times she pushed them around and they'd just take it.

"They didn't care." Belle spoke to her baby, sad for the hard life she'd brought to her child. "They didn't care one whit if I liked them or respected them or loved them. Your pa was probably the worst of the lot, and that's saying something after Gerald, but he was a low-down coyote of a man. The only decent thing he ever did in his life was to give me you, beautiful girl."

And the giving had been dreadful, and it hadn't happened at all after the first time he came home smelling of another woman's perfume.

"They weren't men. To say they were children is an insult to you and my other girls, because they work hard and respect me and love me, and I them." Belle ran her hand over Betsy's lustrous curls. No, she couldn't love Anthony, couldn't stand the man, but she did adore this pretty baby.

Would Silas make babies as lovely?

Her head filled with images of her cooking for him and jumping to do his bidding, saying, "Yes, Silas," and, "Whatever you say, Silas." And letting him lead her away into the dark from any campfire they were ever near.

"I can actually imagine doing that." Betsy stared at Belle silently. Belle needed to talk to the baby more. Sing to her. Cradle her and rock her. She could do that, at least some, if she was really married to Silas. She yearned for that, and yet that wasn't who she was. Belle had learned to trust no man to take care of her. She'd learned to please herself, and any man could follow or get out of the way. There'd always been plenty willing.

She thought of the things Silas had said to Sarah yesterday about not marrying, and it occurred to Belle that, for the first time, she might have to do something to bring a man around. She'd never had to consider enticing a man before. She'd spent most of her life trying to discourage them. She had no practice in convincing a man he should propose.

"How does a woman fetch a man to marrying her, Betsy? I've never had to do such a thing in my life." She sat there thinking how to please Silas. Wondering how to dab a loop on this one particular man. She thought of his kisses and the stern way he'd dictated to her, and she wanted him to belong to her.

And he'd told Sarah he wasn't going to marry her. He'd said it like a man who knew his own mind.

So, did she catch him by being a submissive little wife? Or did she lasso him and toss him over her saddle and drag him to a preacherman?

The sharp cold of the morning made Belle wonder if they could get home before her mountain valley became locked away from the world for the winter. There had been snow already in the heights. She could see the white peaks from where she lay. She thought of her cattle back at her ranch and the ones on this trail and the extra help they now had, and forcing her mind to practical matters, she jiggled a burp out of Betsy and got to her feet to help build up the fire.

If she fussed with her hair a little longer than usual and started to make a couple of apple pies from the dried apples they packed along, well, that didn't have anything to do with snagging Silas. She just had time for once was all.

She was pulling the last pie out of the fire and had just started mixing hotcakes when Buck rode up in the first full light of morning. "Silas says we're pulling out. Shorty rode ahead and found good grazing not too far up the trail. We'll make a short day of it. He says your girls have been pushing too hard and need the rest."

Belle offered Buck a cup of coffee and a slice of pie. The man dismounted and ground-hitched his horse. He was taking a bite of the warm pie almost before the reins hit the dirt. Buck talked pleasantly of the good condition of the cattle, which warmed Belle's heart.

He polished off the pie within a couple of minutes. Then he got up reluctantly from the fire and said, "Mighty fine eatin', ma'am. Mighty fine. Thank you."

Belle knew an admiring look when she got one, because she'd gotten hundreds of them—thousands of them—in her life. But there was nothing improper in Buck's glance. It was just a look that said, *I'd marry you in a heartbeat just for this slice of pie if it wasn't for your husband.*

Belle could have corrected him. Yet her silence wasn't a lie.

I'm sorry, God. I know we're doing wrong.

He took one last swallow of coffee. "We'll be on the trail right after we eat. Silas said to tear down the camp."

"I'll have a proper breakfast of hotcakes ready in ten minutes then have the camp stowed away in half an hour. And tell the others there's pie and coffee to go with breakfast."

Buck laughed and tipped his hat. "It'll start a stampede, but I'll tell 'em, Miz Harden."

Belle fed the hands and had the strange sensation of being left out of the hard work. She didn't mind. It felt kind of nice to have time to make a meal special and pack up the camp for everyone. But it made her nervous to turn such a huge part of her life over to someone else. Even if the girls were riding along and watching out for the Tanner interests.

They started punching the herd along by midmorning and found the going easy. The sun rose high in the sky, but it didn't drive away the sharpness of the cold like it would have earlier in the season. There were narrow trails and some spots with bad footing, but those were less frequent than before.

With the three extra hands, Sarah never even forked a horse to tend the herd but just stayed with the packhorses, seeing to Betsy. And the older girls got a long break during the day.

Silas found the water and grazing Shorty had spoken of early. They made good enough time that they could set up a camp and get a meal on with some light left in the sky.

Lindsay came riding in just a few minutes after the others, and she was alongside of Roy. The two of them seemed to be talking and smiling at each other. Belle felt a pang of dread in her stomach to think a boy had caught her little girl's interest. She had to control the urge to fetch her skillet.

There was plenty of dead wood at hand, and they built a huge, roaring fire to ward off the ever-increasing chill. Shorty had brought a haunch of bighorn sheep back from his scouting, and they broiled mutton steaks over the fire and had fresh-baked bread instead of the usual sourdough biscuits. And they ate the last of Belle's pie.

Shorty had a fine singing voice, and he started in on one song after another, finally lifting himself off the comfortable softness of the pine boughs they gathered for bedding to stand the first watch.

The days fell into a rhythm after they had cowhands. Although Belle rode out every day, she did little more than take a couple of circuits around the slowly plodding animals and go back up front to the string of pack animals. As the trip stretched out and the responsibility eased more and more from her shoulders, Belle felt herself relax more completely than she had in years. She took pleasure in cooking good meals, with lots of help from the increasingly idle girls. She relished the time she had to cuddle Betsy in her arms. She accepted Silas's strong arms around her every night and the sweet kisses he insisted were necessary for the sake of the cowhands. That didn't exactly make sense to her, especially since he often kissed her when none of the men were around. But she trusted him, so if he said a kiss or two was necessary, she went along. Then they went to their separate sides of the camp.

They had a few more days of needle-sharp peaks to scale, but with Buck, Roy, and Shorty helping, they went smoothly. Belle took on the job of scouting the trail. She rode ahead with the camp gear, chose a site, and set up early, without eating a drop of dust.

The twenty-fifth day on the trail, Belle descended a high peak well ahead of the others, with Betsy on her back and Sarah by her side, and saw the raw little town of Helena that had been named the territorial capital just recently. From their high perch, they could see many miles across the lower mountainside and the sweeping valley around the town. But it was close, so they'd be there in two days. One day if they pushed hard.

They'd made it. She'd gotten her herd to market. She'd saved her ranch. Joy caught so hard in Belle's throat she almost cried, which was too embarrassing to contemplate. Choking back the pride at making this trek successfully, she scouted out a spot to bed down the cattle for what might be their last night on the trail.

She and Sarah pushed past several likely camping sites as she longed to get her cattle as close as possible to trail's end. They finally found a lush valley so beautiful it awakened a longing in Belle to own it.

"We'll camp here." Belle looked at Sarah, and they smiled at each other.

"This is a beautiful place, Ma." Sarah looked around almost reverently.

A tumbling stream poured out of a fissure in one of the snowcapped mountain peaks that stood like sentinels around the valley. The creek cut across the lowest spot in the valley and spilled down a ledge and out of sight.

"Look up there." Belle pointed overhead. "A bald eagle." It

screamed as it soared around the cliff sides, catching updrafts and diving for what looked like pure joy.

A herd of bighorn sheep spotted them and leaped up the mountainside so gracefully that they might have been flying. Grass grew belly deep to her horse, and the woods didn't encroach onto the grass except in a few places, where they formed islands of shade around the babbling creek.

"I'd never part with my ranch. But this is as close as I've ever been tempted. I believe that if I'd seen this mountain valley first, I might have picked it for myself." She rode her horse around until she found a sheltered spot up against the mountain that would cut the icy, north wind and reflect the heat of their fire back to them when the night grew cold. She did the first stages of her setup for camp, started a rising of bread, hobbled her pack animals, and turned them loose. Then she and Sarah started back up the trail, finding Silas.

"I want to push farther tonight."

"There's no need, Belle." Silas had that gruff, bossy tone she was starting to love. "We'll be in Helena in just a couple of days."

"I found good grass."

Silas looked at the lowering sun and the ample grass along the trail where they now stood. "Belle. . ."

She smiled and rode her horse right over to him, thinking of a few times he'd persuaded her to do his bidding with a well-timed kiss. She decided to try that for herself. "Please, Silas. I've already set the camp up. It'll be hard work to go all that way and tear things down."

She leaned forward, caught the front of his shirt in a fist, and pulled him toward her. He came along so willingly she knew she had him.

By the time she was done kissing him, she'd've probably, judging by the stunned look on his face, been able to convince him to drive the herd all the way into Helena without stopping.

God forgive me, I'm wheedling just like a woman.

Belle was half horrified at herself, half elated to know she possessed such a skill. Manipulative, too, as if Silas was saving her work by driving himself into the night.

"We can go farther if it'll make things easier for you." Silas had a heavy-lidded look in his eyes and a strange, satisfied smile on his face.

But Belle was pleased, too. She wondered if she looked just like him.

There was still a bit of dusk left when the thousand head of cattle waded into the grass. She looked at Silas, and he smiled. It was a sweet moment, an intimate moment, shared by the two of them alone. Well, alone except for four children, three drovers, and one thousand cattle.

But sweet.

Chapter 16

I wonder if it's been claimed," Silas muttered.

Belle heard him and had a flash of worry. Was he thinking of leaving her? He'd been adamant to Sarah that morning about not getting married. Maybe he'd finish the drive, stake a claim, and come straight back here to live forever.

"Great location," Buck said. "A short ride to the territorial capital."

"But still wilderness," Shorty said, as if *wilderness* was the same word as *heaven*.

Belle noticed that Roy didn't join in the talk. He was sitting on his horse, alongside Lindsay, as he'd taken to doing all the time. They were apart from the group, talking quietly.

Belle marveled at her daughter's shy smiles and easy conversation with the boy. Belle knew Silas kept an eye on the two youngsters. She'd suggested it, and the serious look in Silas's eyes as he agreed wholeheartedly helped Belle put her concerns in Silas's capable hands.

Silas hadn't let the men go out riding herd with the girls for the first few days, but Belle could see that he'd eased his watchfulness after a bit, and Belle allowed it because she trusted Silas's judgment.

Lindsay and Roy put up their horses. Belle was busy bending over her coffeepot, and when she straightened, she noticed the two were gone. Curious and uncomfortable with their budding friendship, Belle headed into the wooded area near where their horses stood grazing. She wandered without a direction for a time. Then she rounded a thicket and came upon Roy kissing Lindsay.

"Roy! Lindsay!" Belle cried.

The two of them jumped apart.

Lindsay tried to say something, but her face went crimson and she brushed her hands over her skirt and hair. Finally, to get her hands to stop fidgeting, she clenched them in front of her.

"I reckon I owe you an apology, Miz Harden. I just. . .Lindsay and me. . .we were only. . ." Roy's voice faded to nothing, and he lifted his hat and pulled it forward on his head until it shaded his eyes.

"Roy, you go back to camp right now," Belle ordered.

"Miz Harden, please don't take none of this out on Lindsay." He laid his hand on Belle's daughter's shoulder, and Belle wished for her skillet. "She's a fine girl and I wouldn't shame her. Nothin' happened. We were talking and. . ."

"Roy!" Belle cut him off and crossed her arms. "I'll leave your father to talk with you. Right now I'd like a word with my daughter. Alone!"

Roy looked at Lindsay, who glanced at him then looked back at the ground. Roy started to the camp. He had to walk past Belle to get there. When he was only a few feet in front of Belle, he stopped and pushed his hat back. "Lindsay and me. . .I know we're young, ma'am, but we have decided we're gonna get hitched."

He'd have done less harm if he'd punched Belle right in the stomach. "No you are not. Now go!"

She jabbed her finger behind her.

He didn't budge.

"I'll say my piece first. If you're mad, then yell at me, not Lindsay. She's a good girl, and I haven't behaved in a dishonorable way to her." Roy looked Belle square in the eye.

Although he was young, Belle was reluctantly impressed with his desire to take whatever anger Belle might have upon himself to protect Lindsay.

"We're getting married in Helena tomorrow if we get into town early enough."

"You are not!" Belle interrupted.

Roy kept talking as if she hadn't spoken. "If not tomorrow, then the next day. I haven't talked to my pa yet, but if he's agreeable, the two of us will stake claims, along with Shorty, that would cover this whole valley. Pa and I talked about the claims some, but I didn't say a thing about Lindsay because I hadn't spoken to her yet. But now Lindsay has said she'll marry me. We'll set up our own spread here if the valley isn't claimed. If not here, then somewhere else close by. We've ridden through some likely spots."

Belle's heart pounded harder with every word. Roy was determined and Belle was terrified.

"I had just convinced her to say yes when you came upon us. That kiss is the first and the last one she'll get from me before we're married. I love Lindsay, ma'am, and I respect her too much to dishonor her."

Belle's mind unwillingly skittered to the way Silas and she had kissed. Without intention to marry. *That* had been dishonor. As their lies about being married had been. Roy's behavior was better than Belle's.

"I'll always see to her safety and happiness above my own. I promise you that."

Roy stared at Belle for a moment longer, and Belle saw clearly that he wished she'd say something so they'd have her blessing. . .

or at least her permission, however grudgingly given. Belle just couldn't do it. At last he nodded his head firmly and walked on past her without further comment.

Belle turned to Lindsay who was still fixated on the ground. Belle chided, "Lindsay."

Lindsay looked up from the ground then stared past Belle's shoulder. Belle could tell the minute Roy disappeared from sight, because Lindsay suddenly had a huge grin on her face, and with a few running steps, she crossed the distance between them and threw her arms around Belle's neck. "Oh, Ma, I never knew how it could be. I know now why you keep marrying the low-down varmints." Lindsay laughed then pulled back to arm's length to look at Belle. "Only Roy isn't no varmint. He's a good 'un. He is, isn't he?" Lindsay asked fiercely. "He will treat me right and work hard. I'm as old as you were when you got married. And I think his pa will stay with us, so it won't be the two of us alone in the world like it was with you and my pa."

"Lindsay, you're only fifteen—" Belle began somberly.

"I'm sixteen in a few months, Ma," Lindsay interjected. "You were fifteen when you married my pa. And now you have Silas." Lindsay's voice dropped to a whisper. "I haven't told Roy about him not bein' my real pa, and I won't until after you and Pa are married. Roy won't mind, but I don't want I should embarrass you none, what with all your kissing and such."

Belle was struck speechless by the way Lindsay so casually mentioned the. . .the play acting she and Silas had been doing. Silas had said he'd talked to her, but what had he really said?

"I wouldn't want to leave you with no help," Lindsay went on. "But with Pa around, you'll be okay. Aren't you happy for me, Ma? I love Roy so!" Lindsay wrapped her arms around Belle's neck again and almost strangled her with her enthusiasm. She seemed oblivious to Belle's dismay. She was walking on a cloud and couldn't believe anyone could be less than thrilled.

Well, Belle was a whole lot less. "You're too young to get married."

Lindsay laughed. "I'm young, I know. So's Roy. But we're old enough to start a life together. Roy will be tellin' his pa right now." Lindsay turned toward the camp, grabbed Belle's hand in hers, and towed her along. "I want to go stand by his side when Roy tells him, like Roy stood by me."

Belle couldn't think what to say. Hoping and praying Buck or Silas would talk some sense into the young couple, she went along.

They got to camp in time to see Buck shaking Roy's hand and laughing. Silas was standing beside the father and son, looking very serious.

Belle met his eyes as soon as she saw him and knew he was of the same opinion she was. She went straight to his side, and as soon as Buck's hearty congratulations were finished, Silas said bluntly, "Belle and I think Roy is a good boy, Buck. But how can he marry Lindsay when he doesn't have so much as a roof over his head?" Silas's curt announcement brought the festive mood to an abrupt halt.

"Now we. . .we *might* agree to Roy courting Lindsay, but we want him to have a start for the two of them before there's any wedding.

"I have an idea that might work," Silas continued. "Why doesn't Roy come on home with us? He's too young to stake a claim to any land, but he could court Lindsay proper, get to know her this winter. Buck, you and Shorty can stake a claim. In the spring, Roy can come and help you start a herd. When he's twenty-one and old enough to claim some land, he and Lindsay can get married."

"I do the work of a man right now," Roy objected. "Age is just a number you write on paper. I'll stake my claim now and prove up on it by the time I'm twenty-one. That's five years from now. We're not waiting that long. We're not waiting another week!"

"Well, son"—Silas tilted his hand low over his eyes—"maybe you don't need to wait *five* years to marry, but you could wait say. . .two years. Lindsay's only fifteen. She's not—"

"Ma was fifteen when she got married," Lindsay interrupted. "I'll be sixteen in a couple of months. And Roy is going to be a lot better for me than—"

"Lindsay!" Silas cut off Lindsay's yelling and threw her a warning look. Lindsay covered her mouth before she blurted out something about Belle having a different husband than Silas all those long years ago.

Then a gleam appeared in Lindsay's eyes that made Belle nervous. "And how old were you, Pa? You and Ma are about the same age. Ma was fifteen and you were. . .sixteen if I remember. Same age as Roy. And you had nothing or the next thing to it. Didn't you say, Ma, that Grandpa Tanner gave you two hundred dollars and the two of you set out and crossed practically the whole country? Ran fifty cattle across most of the Rockies because you'd heard of the gold strike in Helena and heard they were hungry for beef and paying prime dollar for it?"

Belle felt Silas clutch her hand tightly. She said, "We did start out that way, Lindsay. That's why we know it's hard. I'd like something better for you."

Buck added his voice to the mess. "The boy and I talked about claiming that high valley. The two of us'll do it, and Shorty will throw in and get himself another one hundred and sixty acres right next to it. We've been riding the grub line long enough. We can have a roof over our heads by snowfall, and I can make it tight and comfortable. I've got enough money to buy a few head of cattle to start up a herd, and with all of us working together, we'll be okay. Now, I know they're young. But folks marry young out here. My Caroline and I were settled young, and I think that's the best way to do it. Having Lindsay with us, well, that would make starting a home something worth doing. Silas, I'd help Roy take care of your girl. You have my word on it."

"Maybe in the spring we can—"

"I don't want to wait until spring. . .*Pa*," Lindsay said with clenched fists.

Belle heard the threat in Lindsay's voice, but she wasn't going to let her daughter threaten her into doing something Belle thought was wrong, no matter how much disgrace she brought down on her own head. Silas squeezed her hand again before Belle could angrily confess their lies. She looked sideways at him.

"Folks *do* settle young out here, Belle." Silas looked over at Lindsay and said with open longing, "I don't want to let her go. I wanted to spend more time with our girl. I'm not ready to give her up. But however much we don't like it, Roy's a good boy, and Buck and Shorty will be there to take care of her."

Lindsay's eyes filled with tears as Silas spoke. She took two uncertain steps then ran the short distance between them and threw her arms around Silas's neck. "I don't want to leave you either, Pa. I love you."

Lindsay cried into Silas's neck, and he hugged her tight. Then Lindsay let go of Silas and turned to cling to Belle.

"I love you, Ma. I don't want you to be unhappy, but my heart is telling me to go with him. You know I do the work of an adult woman. I have for years. I *am* an adult woman. And adult women get married. What I feel for Roy—it's so strong and good, I don't want to let him go, not even for the winter."

Belle looked over Lindsay's shoulder to meet Silas's eyes.

Silas seemed to have made up his mind for both of them.

Belle felt a scream gathering deep in her belly.

Wade shoved Glowing Sun behind him as he whirled around.

It was one of the men who'd held her captive. With a shotgun out and level and cocked.

A distressed moan came from Glowing Sun.

Wade didn't move his hand toward his gun. This man had the

draw on him, and not even a fast draw—which Wade wasn't—could beat a pointed shotgun.

You wouldn't be able to pull the trigger anyway, coward.

An inner voice reminded Wade he was a weakling. He'd been no different before he turned his life over to God, but the cowardice had tormented him back then because his measure of a man was whether he had the guts to kill. Now Wade found comfort in knowing he didn't have a killer instinct. He'd shoved away the knowledge of his yellow belly and mostly forgotten it.

Until now.

Now, when his ability to pull the trigger might be the difference between life and death, not for himself, but for the woman he'd just realized he loved—that taunting voice came back and reminded him he had no guts.

"Move away from the girl." The man stayed across the small clearing, well out of reach but not so far he could miss with a shotgun.

"We're going back to her village." Trying to talk sense to the man, Wade saw the viciousness in the gunman's eyes.

"I've given her the choice whether to live with her Flathead family or not, and she's chosen them." Wade knew he intended to try harder to convince her. If he'd kissed her, held her, spoken of love and marriage, would she stay in his world? If she wanted him to, would he join hers? If her tribe would allow it, Wade knew he'd go with Glowing Sun.

"That ain't no choice. She's wild. She don't have the sense to pick right. She's going with me. I want her, and she'll be mine." The greedy, hungry eyes told Wade that this man wasn't interested in rescuing Glowing Sun at all. He had terrible plans for her.

Something hardened inside of Wade…pushed out the taunting voice and brought his courage forward in a way he'd never felt. He could do it. To save Glowing Sun from the dreadful fate this man had in mind, he could pull the trigger.

Dear God, help me protect her. Help me save her.

Wade knew he would die for this. This man would get his gun fired first. But Wade would take that lead shot and still get his own gun into play. He'd give his life to protect this beautiful woman.

"Please, just go." Wade had to try reason again. "I won't let you take her."

Cruelty leeched through the man's laughter.

Wade flexed his fingers, close to his holster, but not close enough. The man raised his gun.

Wade slapped leather. A shot rang out before Wade could get his hand on his gun.

So intent on rescuing Glowing Sun, Wade fought through the expected impact. He pulled his gun and leveled it—to see the man drop to his knees.

Stunned, suddenly aware that no bullet had struck him, Wade watched the man fall, and as he dropped, Wade saw a man behind him holding a smoking pistol. The saddle partner who'd helped capture Glowing Sun to begin with.

The man slipped his six-gun into his holster and raised his hands. "Don't shoot."

Wade realized he had his gun leveled straight at the man's heart. He lowered his weapon.

"I knew he was up to no good." The man walked up to his partner and prodded him with his toe. "We split up right after you'd taken the girl back. I'd only been riding with him for a couple of weeks since we finished a cattle drive. I didn't like the way he treated the girl, but I thought it was right to take her back to her own people, so I went along."

"He wasn't here to return her to anyone." Wade felt his hand begin to tremble. He hadn't needed to take that shot, but he knew, deep in his gut, that he would have. He should have been proud of that. Instead, he felt changed, scarred, ashamed. "He wanted her for himself."

"I heard. And I'd figured it out myself. He was loco to beat all when you took her. Way too hornet mad to explain him wantin' to help her."

"Thank you. You saved my life. You saved both of us."

The other man nodded. "I'll stay to bury him. Reckon I can do that one thing for him. You go along and take the girl home."

Wade nodded then looked once more at the man who now lay still and lifeless on the ground. It was awful to kill a man. A terrible thing to carry on your soul. Wade thanked God he didn't have to do it. Knowing he would have done it was burden enough.

He prayed silently for the man who did take that shot.

Then he turned.

In time to see Glowing Sun vanish into the woods.

CHAPTER 17

Belle didn't scream. Mainly because she took one look in Lindsay's eyes and knew it would do no good.

It wasn't just determination, though there was plenty of that. In fact, more than determination, Lindsay just had a solid, settled look that said she was getting married. With or without Belle's blessing.

Belle could go along or be trampled, so the only real choice Belle had here was in how much she hurt her relationship with Lindsay.

But even that wasn't the look that stopped Belle in her tracks. Lindsay was in love. It shone out of her.

For one second, Belle remembered how she'd felt about William at the very beginning. No one could have stopped her. And William wasn't half the man Roy was. Whether Belle liked it or not, her daughter was getting married.

Silas's firm hold on Belle's hand grew tighter until he might have been the only thing holding her up. Belle gave one hard jerk of her chin, and that was all she could manage.

Lindsay laughed and threw herself into Roy's arms as joyfully as if Belle had clapped and yelled with delight at this wedding. A bright girl, Lindsay knew this was the best she was going to get from her man-hating ma.

"Let's get settled for the night so we can get into Helena in time to sell these cattle tomorrow." Silas kept hold of Belle's hand and dragged her away from the tight circle of people talking and laughing and planning.

As Belle moved, she landed her eyes on Emma.

She saw frightened eyes. And Emma never showed fear. Belle tried to tug loose of Silas, but rather than let her go, Silas let himself be dragged to Emma's side.

"What's she doing this for, Ma?" Emma let Belle slide her arm around her waist. Looking past Emma, Belle saw Sarah tending the campfire with Betsy on her back. Sarah was crying and salting the stew with her tears.

And why shouldn't they be terribly upset? Belle had spent all her years as a mother filling her girls' heads full of dire warnings about men.

"Lindsay will be okay, girls." Belle didn't believe it, but she tried to sound convincing. "Roy's a good man."

A boy. A young one at that. God, how did this happen? I'm losing my daughters. She's starting her life out as bad as I did. All my warnings and she up and marries the first man her age she's ever seen.

Emma didn't answer.

Sarah kept stirring.

Silas led them back to the campfire in the dusk. "He is a good man, Belle. I've taken his measure, and I trust him to do right by our girl."

It was no comfort. The man who wanted to hold her and kiss her but didn't want marriage earned no trust in Belle's book.

"I'll make the best of it." Belle pulled away from Silas. "And so will Lindsay. That's all a woman can do in this life."

Silas gave her a long look. Then he nodded. "That's all any of us can do, Belle." He strode toward his horse. "I'm going to ride a circuit. I'll be back in time for supper."

They drove the herd up to Helena late the next night and held them on the flatland south of town.

"Shorty and I're gonna go into town and hunt cattle buyers." Silas's voice from behind her turned Belle around.

He'd quit with his kissing nonsense ever since Lindsay and Roy had announced their engagement. Belle was too upset to miss it.

Truth was, Belle had come to think of Silas as Lindsay's pa, looking to him whenever her doubts were too much for her. His shared concern gave her strength. He quietly assured her that allowing the marriage was the only real choice. That alone kept her from screaming.

It occurred to Belle to protest Silas handling the sale of her cattle. But she trusted him. It was that simple. "Thank you. I'll get the camp set up and have supper waiting when you get back."

"We could be late."

"We'll expect you when we see you then." Belle was struck by this quiet, reasonable conversation. She couldn't remember talking with any of her husbands like this. She gave orders. They followed them or lit out to hide until mealtime. There was no relaxed discussion of plans and duties. Silas was a good man. She'd finally found one.

And he wanted no part of marriage.

Silas rode off with Shorty.

Belle watched Lindsay and Roy sharing every chore, whispering, excited.

"Let me get that." Buck came to where she was dipping water from a quiet stream. He reached for a bucket she already had filled.

"You know they're too young." Belle scooped the water without looking at the man.

Buck took the pail from her and straightened, holding both, leaving her hands free.

Why had she never been able to find a man who would work beside her?

"I know they're young. I do. But my son does a man's work every day. He's honest, with no vices. I've raised him to be a Christian, and he's taken it to heart. He'll give full weight to his marriage and keep his vows. And I've never seen him so happy. He's got a powerful love for your daughter."

Belle heard a twinge of resentment in Buck's voice. Resentment aimed at Belle because she wasn't excited about Roy marrying Lindsay. The two of them turned to watch Lindsay and Roy in the distance, chattering and smiling as they rode a circle around the herd.

"It's not about Roy." Belle looked seriously at Buck. "He's a fine young man. You know I like him. It's just. . .I married so young. The work was hard and relentless. I wanted my daughter to be a child for a little longer."

"I've been riding with you for two weeks now. Lindsay's already not a child. She works her heart out for you. I wouldn't be surprised if her life with us was easier than her life with you."

"Most likely will be." Belle sighed. "Her life with me is hard, but it's. . .safe. I love her and treat her with respect."

"I won't—"

Belle held up her hand. "I'm not insulting you, Buck. I promise I'm not. It's not you and Roy and Shorty. I'd feel this way no matter who staked a claim on my girl's heart. I can't stop this wedding, but I think I'm allowed to hurt a little having to let my girl go."

Smiling, Buck nodded as they turned together and walked toward the camp. "How about next spring, as soon as calving is done and the snow melts, I send Lindsay and Roy over for a visit. Say the first of June. They can stay for two weeks."

Belle thought of her ramshackle cabin and wondered where

they'd sleep. Maybe Silas would help her add a room. No, Silas would be gone. He'd sell these cattle and ride away. Her hurt over Lindsay multiplied by her hurt over finally caring about a man.

She was tempted to tell Buck the truth, not wanting falsehood between her and Lindsay's new family. But even that was beyond her as she watched Lindsay and Roy and ached for what lay ahead for her daughter.

Buck didn't wait for Belle to agree to the visit. He seemed to be satisfied that he'd had his say. He set down the water. "I'll go spell Emma."

Belle's other girl rode the far side of the herd. Sarah puttered around the camp, going about business as usual, talking and being herself. Belle wished herself eight years old again, without a care in the world. . .except for feeding nine people every day using scant supplies and an open fire, of course.

Emma rode in.

Belle went to her quiet, horse-crazy daughter.

Emma hadn't said much about losing her big sister. Of course, Emma was quiet in the normal course of things. But she'd been even more so today.

"We'll miss her, won't we?"

Emma kept busy stripping the leather off her horse. "I reckon we will."

"She'll be okay, you know."

Emma shrugged then looked up at Belle. "Running the Tanner Ranch took all our energy every day. How can we get by without her? Will Silas stay?"

"I don't figure that Silas will stay, no. We talked about marriage, Emma. Silas isn't interested."

Emma shook her head. "The two of you act married already. Why doesn't he want us, Ma?"

Belle didn't know what to say. She'd expected to talk about Lindsay, not Silas. But she'd known from the first that Emma and

Silas were close. Emma had opened up to him as she had to no other person. As for wringing a marriage proposal out of the man, Belle had no idea how. No man had ever *not* wanted her. "I don't know, Em. But he doesn't, and that's the end of it."

Emma's face crumpled, but she didn't cry. Belle didn't think Emma had cried since she was three years old. "I'll help get the meal." Emma walked away, her shoulders slumped, shut off from Belle and the whole world. She turned as she reached for the boiling coffeepot and stared at Lindsay and Roy for a minute before she poured herself a cup of the blazing hot brew.

Sarah hummed as she worked over a stew using the last of their jerked beef and potatoes. She mixed up sourdough biscuits and talked at Emma. Emma released Betsy from the pack on Sarah's back then fussed with her, teasing a smile out of the little one while she sipped her coffee.

Silas and Shorty didn't come back. The rest of them ate a quiet dinner, and the night sky spread over them and gleamed with a million stars. They all took to their bedrolls except Buck and Roy. Buck adamantly refused to let Emma ride a watch so close to a settlement where strangers might happen by, and he didn't believe it proper to let Roy stay in with the womenfolk alone.

Belle knew that no chaperone besides herself was necessary. She'd make such a strict watchdog Roy might not survive it.

After the men rode out, Belle heard singing wafting across the night air. The steady noise wasn't cattle drovers being whimsical, singing the cows to sleep. It covered strange night sounds apt to startle the herd. But it felt like a lullaby. Like a long-lost chance to be a child again and have her mother crooning over her, protecting her against all that was big and bad in the dark of the night.

That kind of safety had ended too soon for Belle with her mother's death. And now it was ending too soon for Lindsay.

In the sleepless night, Belle was left thinking of her father's cavalier dismissal of her when he had his long-desired son.

Thinking of William's unkindness after Belle's inheritance was lost.

Thinking of Gerald's drunkenness and his raised fists that she hadn't dodged nearly as often as she'd let on to her daughters. Too many times she'd stayed behind to give them a chance to run.

Thinking of Anthony's unfaithfulness and the way he flaunted it, shaming Belle as often and as publicly as he could.

Thinking of Silas and his strength and warmth. . .and rejection.

It wasn't fair to measure Roy with such a wretched yardstick, but it was the only one Belle had. She was giving her daughter over to a man because no other choice was forthcoming.

Belle lay on her side, stared into the crackling, glowing embers of the fire, and cried. Tears soaked into her sleeve where she rested her head on her arm. She was letting her firstborn go. With her tears, Belle came to see she'd accepted the situation. She was going to give Lindsay and Roy her blessing.

Crying silently, Belle fell asleep praying for life to be kinder to Lindsay than it had been to her.

Glowing Sun saw her chance and ran.

Her village was only miles away now. She was in territory she recognized. She was home.

But even as she dashed up a steep incline, she admitted she wasn't running from those evil men. She ran because she feared what Wade made her feel.

She had taken a direct route no horse could follow and had gone nearly a mile when the thudding of hooves sounded behind her. She didn't have to turn around to know he'd come. Wade, with his warm, kind eyes that spoke of dreams and a future, would always come.

And he'd take Glowing Sun away from the only world she understood.

Away from the man she'd promised herself to. She couldn't betray that promise, even if now the thought of marrying Wild Eagle frightened her. How could she marry him when she'd been willing—no, eager—for Wade to kiss her?

She didn't dart into the woodlands or scale the rocks. She'd been riding with Wade long enough to know he wouldn't stop until he caught her. He'd want to hold her again.

She didn't think she could say no.

Finally, as she ran alongside a trickling brook, the horse drew up beside her and she stopped. Turning, she saw Wade rein in his horse and swing down to the ground with a jingle of spurs and the creak of leather. "You're safe. That man is dead." He said it with such kindness, as if she were running for her life, not from her emotions.

Glowing Sun nodded. Much of her white language had come back to her as they'd talked. "Safe" she knew. "Dead" she knew.

Wade dropped his reins to the ground, which kept his well-trained horse in place. The animal turned its muzzle to the crystal stream and drank noisily.

Coming until they stood toe to toe, he tipped his hat back so his eyes weren't shaded and smiled down at her. "The saddle partner, the other man who held you prisoner, took care of the outlaw who got the drop on us. He's a decent man who means you no harm. He's not following us. You're safe now."

Those words meant the world to her. Except she was only safe from that man, not from Wade. Not from herself.

"Go home to Salish village." Glowing Sun nodded.

Wade shook his head. "Stay."

Glowing Sun understood that, too. "Home."

"Come home with *me*. Marry me, Glowing Sun. I love you."

She understood every word. She loved him, too. But his world frightened her. His world had killed her white family, and it threatened her Indian family every day. And she'd made promises. "No."

Wade smiled. "Yes. Please."

"Thank you." That wasn't exactly right, except in her heart the words were perfect because she was so thankful a man as fine as Wade wanted her.

Cradling her hands in his, he dropped down on one knee. Glowing Sun had no idea what that meant. She only knew it looked like begging. Such a proud man, so strong, so courageous, and she was making him beg. She felt shame and tugged on his hands.

"I love you. I know we haven't known each other long. . ." He fell silent, struggling.

Glowing Sun knew he searched for simple words that made sense to her.

"Time." He swiped at his hat and threw it to the ground beside them and his eyes gleamed with hope. "Give me time. Come back to *my* village. I've got a safe place you can stay until you. . .you're. . . uh. . .until you love me, too. My friends, the Dawsons, will let you stay there, safe. We can get to know each other better. Please just give me a chance."

He seemed so sure. And why wouldn't he be? He'd held her after he'd guided her down from the tree, felt her respond, felt her longing to kiss him. What else could a man think?

Glowing Sun pulled harder on his hands, and he stood, as if he'd do anything she asked of him, devote his life to pleasing her.

Wild Eagle wasn't a man like this. He wouldn't think of her pleasure. He was strong, harsh even, a great warrior who would give her strong sons. An Indian woman wanted that in her husband.

Not this softness, the kind eyes and sweetness and concern. Glowing Sun's heart ached to think she'd have none of this in her life.

Wade stood before her, waiting.

"I have remembered much white words." She squeezed his hands, wishing he would let go. Wishing she could want him to.

"Abby. Abigail. My white name. My family dead. Fever. I—ten. Ten summers. Salish father found me. Took me from house of death. Went to Salish village."

"They saved you." Wade smiled, listening to every word.

Had Wild Eagle ever listened to her this way?

"I have to go home. To my Salish village. I—" She fumbled for the right word. "Promised. I would keep my promises to my people." Her heart cut like a knife, each beat a stab to her chest. "No, Wade. I will not marry you. No." She had to force the next breath through the thickness of tears clogging her throat. "Thank you."

Wade shook his head as if her words made no sense.

Perhaps they didn't. Perhaps she'd spoken them wrong.

"Come home with me. Marry me. I love you."

Glowing Sun jerked her hands free, shaking her head. She took two steps backward, planning to run. He'd catch her. Maybe his arms would wrap around her. Maybe he'd kidnap her this time and force her to do the thing she wanted most—be with him.

The betrayal of Wild Eagle and her people wouldn't be her choice then. She could live with the decision if Wade made it for her.

She took another step, and joyfully, she braced to have her future decided for her. . .by Wade.

CHAPTER 18

Belle was barely aware of it when Silas came back to camp, ate quickly, and crawled into a bedroll on the far side of the fire. She should have gotten up and asked about the sale, but her head ached from her tears, and she was groggy and stupid with exhaustion.

When morning came, there was no time for sorrow or second thoughts.

Silas got twenty-five dollars a head for the cattle. Cash money. He'd ridden back to camp with twenty-five thousand dollars in his saddlebags and slept light with his shotgun close to hand.

Riders came and drove the herd away before breakfast.

Silas took charge of the morning camp. "We've got to see to the wedding then hit the trail for home before the mountain passes close up on us. Let's go into town."

"I'll see to the preacher," Belle said.

Silas doused the barely smoldering fire. "Let's meet at the Cattleman's Diner for lunch and have the wedding right afterward. We can start making tracks before the day is done."

Which mean Silas was going back with her. Or was he going as far as Lindsay's valley? Maybe he planned to stake a claim there, too.

It didn't matter. With him or not, getting back home before her valley snowed shut for the winter was still a worry.

The men planned to head for the land office and stake their claims, sixteen-year-old Roy included.

Before they rode off, Belle pulled Silas aside. "I'm planning on buying some things to help Lindsay run a household. We'll have some cattle to herd and a wagonload of goods at least."

Silas nodded as if Belle was asking him permission, when in fact she was just warning him of more work. But she liked having him in agreement. He tugged on the brim of his hat. "Good thinking. Lindsay's earned a share of the herd, so don't be tightfisted." He rode off before Belle could punch him.

Belle and the girls went to the mercantile, and Belle went on a shopping spree.

"We need to set you up for housekeeping, Lindsay. It will be my wedding present to you and Roy."

"How do you do that, Ma?"

Belle realized that Lindsay had hardly ever been to a town. For their own safety, Belle had left the girls home when she'd bought supplies. And Belle had bought only the most basic goods, living off the land for the most part. Salt, sugar, flour, little else. Smiling, Belle said, "I'll show you."

She bought a winter's worth of food for four hungry people. There would be no garden supplying them, so she bought canned vegetables and fruit. Salt pork, salted fish, slabs of bacon and ham, and anything else that caught her fancy. Then she turned to yard goods for curtains and sheets and bed ticking, heavy cloth for winter clothes and lighter fabric for summer. She also found several ready-made dresses for Lindsay, since she wouldn't be coming home to pack, and several pairs of wool pants and flannel shirts for Roy. Belle also threw in new outfits for Buck and Shorty, worried that a man might not think of such things. Needles and thread, pails and tools. She added dishes and pots and pans, including, of course, a good-sized cast-iron skillet. She threw in an extra just to be on the safe side.

The list kept growing, but Belle didn't hesitate. Nor did she restrict herself to household goods. She found a livery that sold her two teams of oxen and two big freight wagons to carry the ever-growing load.

Belle found chickens and a milk cow with a calf and a pair of suckling pigs, though they were expensive. She bought a fine Hereford bull and ten head of cows.

She'd spent nearly five thousand of her twenty-five thousand dollars before midday.

She ordered the supplies loaded then headed for the land office to buy several tracts of land. She already controlled them because of her water rights. She also owned the passes into the valley, so she could block anyone else from entering. She considered the land hers, but she wanted a clear title. Pointing to a map, she described the acres she wanted to the slender clerk.

Wire-rimmed glasses perched on his hawkish nose. His skin had a pallor that said he rarely stepped outside. "All of this is fine except for this one parcel. Someone staked a claim on it." He indicated the high valley where she'd lost track of so many cattle last spring. "I'm sorry, but that's already taken."

"But there's not water up there. I own the springs and the gap into the valley. No one can live there."

The man shrugged. "I didn't quibble with the buyer. I expect a man to know what he's claiming. Maybe once your new neighbor finds out the lay of the land, he'll sell to you."

Belle's heart pounded at the thought of some man invading her home. "Who bought it? Is he here in Helena?"

"Now, ma'am, I can't tell you any of this." The land agent lifted his nose at her. "It's not my business to go blabbing about land sales. Trouble can come of it."

Belle fought the urge to grab the smug man by his shirtfront.

She'd show him trouble. "Just give me a name. I'll ask around and see if he's still in town."

"I'll figure out what you owe for the rest of this property, though it's irregular to sell to a woman." The haughty tone grated on Belle's already-shredded temper.

Clamping her mouth shut, Belle produced the note she'd carried for years from her lawyer, giving her authority over the fund she'd created for her daughters. That authority granted her the right to buy land.

The man sniffed but let the sale go through.

As she signed the papers and handed over her money, she thought of that piece she wanted most, a high valley that stretched itself down almost to her ranch house, the one that she used for a summer range. Fear twisted Belle's stomach. She had used that valley for sixteen years.

When she produced five thousand in cash, the land agent was slightly less rude. The purchase brought her holdings to over twenty thousand acres. A lot of it was rugged and next to useless. Still, it connected her ranch into one solid block of property.

She walked out of the land office shaken from leaving it too late to get hold of the high valley. Her cattle could winter over in it, unless she got home to find a settler had moved in already, but she'd have to cull the herd sharply again next year or she'd hurt her range from overgrazing.

Whoever lived there would be a close neighbor and might dispute some of the water rights Belle owned. The titles were all clearly in her hands. But the law didn't mean much when you lived as far out as Belle. Strength held land more than a deed. She could only hope that whoever her new neighbor was, he would be friendly. With a clenched jaw, she wondered if she'd be able to keep the buyer out by refusing permission to cross through the gap. But that gap was a fair ride from home, and she couldn't guard it day and night.

With her grazing land reduced, that meant a repeat of this blasted cattle drive next year. With a catch in her throat, she realized it also meant she'd get to visit Lindsay. If Lindsay and Roy came for a visit in the spring and Belle drove past their valley later in the summer, she'd see her daughter twice this year. Only twice.

Only years of self-discipline kept Belle from crying her heart out.

Her girls quietly followed her out of the office. They'd sat waiting on a bench near the front door, out of earshot. Belle didn't share her worry with them. Emma would have to know eventually, but why burden Lindsay with these problems? She'd soon enough have her own.

"Now we'll go see about the preacher."

Lindsay giggled. Emma rolled her eyes. Sarah bounced Betsy and tickled her chin.

Everything was in order in time for lunch at the Cattleman's Diner. Lindsay was wearing a new dress, and they'd all cleaned up, though Belle refused to buy a skirt that wasn't split for riding, so she knew she probably still looked like a cowhand.

As Belle slipped into her chair, she announced, "The wedding is right after we eat. The parson will be waiting for us at the church."

Roy sat next to Lindsay, looking at her with a gleam of joy. The rest of the table was pretty quiet.

At the end of the strained meal, Belle led the way back to the preacher.

There were nine people in attendance. Ten, counting the preacher. Rather than sit down, the women lined up beside Lindsay and the men lined up beside Roy.

With the preacher, it was six men to four women. Maybe that's why Belle felt defeated. She was outnumbered.

"Dearly beloved." The pastor had a shining bald head and kind eyes. Small golden wires framed a pair of spectacles, and he held the Good Book open in his broad hands.

Lindsay and Roy exchanged smiles and clung to each other's hands.

The parson droned on a bit, and Belle looked past her daughter and the man who was tricking her into marriage to see Silas next to Roy. Just as Belle was beside Lindsay. The two of them, both against this marriage, were the worst possible choices to stand up for this marriage.

Lindsay never looked away from Roy, her face set in happy, determined lines, and Belle knew this was no accident. Lindsay could have asked Emma to stand beside her. Roy could have chosen Buck. By selecting Belle and Silas, Lindsay was forcing them to bless this union.

It was tempting to turn the little imp over her knee.

"Do you, Roy Adams, take this woman to be your lawful-wedded wife? To have and to hold from this day forward, for better or for worse, for richer, for poorer, in sickness and in health, to love and to cherish, from this day forward as long as you both shall live?"

The parson looked at Roy, who didn't so much as glance at the man of God. "I do."

Belle had to admit that none of her husbands had ever sounded as fervent as young Roy here.

"And, Lindsay Harden, do you take this man to be your lawful-wedded husband? To have and to hold from this day forward, for better or for worse, for richer, for poorer, in sickness and in health, to love and to cherish, from this day forward as long as you both shall live?"

That wasn't even Lindsay's name. Belle opened her mouth, but she caught a look from Silas and a tiny shake of his head. Well, what did it matter? Lindsay's name wasn't Harden anymore anyway. And these vows before God had the power of a lifetime commitment, if Roy could manage to stay alive.

"My real name is Lindsay Svendsen, I reckon. Ma was married to another man before my pa. Though I think of him as my father and call myself by his name. But I want to do this right." She smiled at Roy who didn't look a bit concerned. "I do." Lindsay said it loud enough to stab Belle right in the ears.

"Then before God and these witnesses. . ." The parson blessed the union, just as parsons had blessed all three of Belle's.

But Belle felt God here in this room, between her daughter and this young man. She'd never felt such from the men she'd married. Yet another sin to pile on her conscience that she hadn't insisted on a man of faith to marry.

Tears burned in her eyes as Belle watched her daughter make a better, more intelligent choice for a husband than Belle ever had.

Belle managed to hug her daughter once the vows were finished, and they all walked out of the church, Belle on Silas's arm. She realized she was leaning hard. The loaded wagons had been hitched up so they could ride straight out to Lindsay's new home.

Roy took one look and frowned. "We aren't accepting charity from you." Roy squared off in front of Silas.

Silas looked straight into Belle's eyes, and she could tell he was apologizing for Roy's assumption.

"Lindsay isn't a hired hand, Roy." Silas answered the question knowing Roy wouldn't understand his deferring to Belle. "She's been a full working partner in the Tan. . .uh. . .that is the *Harden* Ranch—"

Belle did her best to burn him to the ground with her eyes for claiming the ranch as his own. This was a bad day all around, and she needed to take that out on somebody. She decided right then it might as well be Silas.

Silas continued. "She's a partner and she's leaving the partnership. Now that might not make sense to you, but that's the way we run our place. So this is her part of the partnership paid out in supplies and livestock. It's not charity. She's fully earned this. I expect you to let her have every bit of it."

Roy held Silas's gaze.

Belle had a fight on her hands to keep from shoving between the two of them and taking charge.

In the end, without Belle sticking her nose in at all, Roy gave an uncertain jerk of his chin. "I've seen Lindsay work, and it's true." He looked at Lindsay. "You really are a partner. That's one of the things I love most about you—your strength."

Buck said, "A wedding gift is a traditional thing, son. It'll help smooth out the first months up there, make things easier for Lindsay. Take 'em for her if not for yourself."

Nodding, Roy reached out a hand to Silas. "Obliged, sir."

"Her ma is the one who figured all this out, bought it all, and helped raise up our girl to be the woman you love. Thank her."

"I've missed my ma something fierce over the years. I'm glad to be in your family, ma'am." Roy turned to Belle and, after a second of hesitation, launched himself into her arms.

Belle caught him close, her eyes wide with shock. She saw Silas suppress a smile.

It was strange holding a young man. Belle had always been determined to have daughters, and if determination could decide such a thing, she'd gotten her way. But maybe a son wouldn't have been so bad. If she could keep him from growing up to be a man.

She hugged him back mostly to get him to let go of her. Then they set out with the cows and supplies. It eased Belle's mind to know what could have been a hard beginning for Lindsay's married life would be comfortable. They'd have a good start, partially because of Belle's gifts.

Buck had bought a few head of cattle, too, not knowing of Belle's plans. They all rode out of town together, driving the horses and Lindsay's beeves ahead of them, with Buck and Shorty driving the freight wagons.

It wasn't easy to pry Lindsay loose of Roy's side, but Belle contrived to have a private talk with her daughter. Riding abreast, Belle nervously began her talk. "I want you to know what to expect of a wedding night."

"I know what goes on with a man and a woman, Ma."

"How do you know that?"

"Well, Ma, I've watched the animals mating over the years, and you and the husbands all shared the same little room we slept in. I think I know what's coming."

Belle was horrified to think her children had overheard her and her husbands. Heaven knew she'd done her best to keep the men at arm's length. Even to the extent of sleeping in a separate bed and keeping a baby with her whenever possible, the soggier the baby the better. Belle had found wet diapers to be a powerful deterrent to a man. "There may be things you. . .uh. . .don't know . . .exactly."

With a firm squaring of her shoulders, Lindsay said bravely, "All that happens is I do my best to get away." Lindsay added sadly, "Except I guess after all is said and done, no woman, nor no female animal, ever gets away, does she, Ma?"

"Lindsay," Belle said, barely able to speak past her surprise, "the thing is. . .I didn't. . .um, care overly much for any of the husbands. I think if'n you *liked* your husband, and you say you like Roy—"

"Oh, I do like him, Ma, I really do!"

"Then, well. . .you might not *want* to get away. And anyway, it's a little. . .different than animals because of. . .the hooves and such, I reckon. You just. . .you just. . .well, a man has his rights." Belle felt her neck heat up. She rested her hand on Lindsay's shoulder, and Lindsay looked up at her, her face as pink as Belle's felt.

"I've been able to teach you a lot of things in my life, Lindsay," Belle said solemnly. "But I'm not one to teach a young girl about how to love a husband. I think you already know more about that than I ever will. I think you're gonna be real happy."

"I think so, too, Ma," Lindsay said fervently.

"And if Roy is ever bad to you, well, just remember you can outshoot any man I ever knew," Belle stated firmly. "And if you can't get to your shotgun, I bought you a cast-iron skillet. So you can—"

"Belle!"

Belle and Lindsay twisted in their saddles to look behind them.

Silas had ridden up and looked outraged.

Belle wondered how much of their conversation he'd heard.

"Belle, you ride on ahead. Lindsay and I need to have a talk."

Belle exchanged a wild look with Lindsay then looked back at Silas. She might have protested if she hadn't fallen into the habit of pretending to be an obedient little wife over the last few days... and if he hadn't looked as if he were considering killing her.

Spurring her horse a ways, she looked back and saw Silas talking. He and Lindsay rode together for the better part of an hour and seemed to be having a nice conversation. Belle knew it couldn't be about a wedding night, because there just wasn't that much to know, so she decided it had something to do with the cattle they'd bought and she left them to it.

Later, she noticed Silas talking long and hard to Roy, so she was sure it was about setting up ranching. She almost went over and offered to give them her own advice, believing she was a better rancher than either of them, but she remembered her role as a submissive wife and stayed away.

CHAPTER 19

Glowing Sun took a single step to run, to force Wade's hand, to make him decide for both of them.

A loud cry broke the silence. A scream as wild and fierce as a soaring eagle. Her eyes lifted to the mountaintop and she saw her. . .future.

Wild Eagle. He rode his horse without reins or saddle, carrying a spear, painted for war.

Wade tried to push her behind him.

"No, don't touch me. He'll kill you."

Wade raised his hands away from her.

Glowing Sun moved quickly so her body blocked Wade's from the possibility of a hurling spear.

In her own tongue she called a greeting. "I'm safe. This man brought me home."

To Wade she said, "I am to marry him. This is why I say no to you." She looked over her shoulder and saw Wade's shock.

He shook his head, denying it.

"Yes, I will go with him to my village. We must never see each other again." She turned back to face the Salish man she respected but now knew she could never love. "Do not harm him, Wild Eagle. The man who took me is dead."

Wild Eagle rode up until his horse nearly knocked her back. Her warrior husband-to-be landed on the ground with the grace that had drawn her to him from the beginning. Wild Eagle poured a torrent of words over her. She'd gotten so used to the white words that it took her a moment to understand what Wild Eagle said. He spoke of anger that she'd been taken, as if his possession had been stolen. There was nothing of love or fear. He caught her around the waist and nearly threw her onto his horse. No gentleness, no kindness, no love. Without a look at Wade, as if rescuing her wasn't worthy of a single thank you, Wild Eagle vaulted up in front of her.

She thought of the way Wade had lifted her onto his horse. The way he'd sat behind her, holding her, letting her sleep in his arms.

Wild Eagle wheeled his horse and, with another war cry, charged up the mountainside he'd just descended. She'd have fallen if she hadn't known what to expect and been ready.

Glowing Sun couldn't stop from looking back.

Wade watched her, still shaking his head. His heart in his eyes.

"No!" His cry echoed across the land.

She heard it, but if Wild Eagle did, he showed no sign. Her only answer to Wade was prayer.

Please, God, let him understand.

She turned away and put her arms around her man.

The wrong man.

Because the winter sky was threatening, Belle pushed hard.

They reached the high valley by early that evening, making much faster time without a thousand cattle to prod. The freight wagons had lagged behind, but they were pulling up by the time a fire was crackling and supper was ready.

They bedded down for the night, Roy and Lindsay picking a spot well away from the rest of them, even starting their own campfire. Belle with her three remaining girls. Silas with Buck and Shorty.

The next morning, despite the urgency Belle felt to hurry home to the Tanner Ranch, she didn't for one second want to leave before Lindsay had a roof over her head.

The men were master carpenters, at least to Belle's inexpert eye. Shorty tirelessly hewed down logs. Roy and Buck dragged the logs on horseback and threw their backs into lifting, working like no men Belle had ever seen. Silas was the unquestioned boss of the job. He showed a knack for turning a stack of logs into a sturdy, tight little house.

Belle envied her daughter the nice cabin. Belle planned to spend a piece of what remained of her money hiring her own cabin repaired or maybe a whole new ranch house built, but that would have to wait until spring. She and the girls would need to spend another winter in her rickety cabin, struggling with the bitter cold. She'd chink the cracks with straw as Red Dawson had taught her, but that only slowed the wind. It didn't stop it.

She spent the whole day setting up a camp and unloading the wagons. She and the girls rode herd on the livestock and helped whenever possible with the house. Belle gave one piece of advice after another to Lindsay, always followed by the thought that maybe Lindsay knew better how to do things than Belle.

Lindsay kept working hard, but her eyes strayed to her new husband every few minutes, and sometimes Roy would be looking back at Lindsay. The two of them would stare at each other as if there were no other people alive in the world. They'd had their wedding night together, and already Belle could see that Lindsay was no longer a girl. She was a woman and might one day soon be a mother.

By nightfall the one-room cabin stood, doorless, windowless, but with a roof atop it and a big stone chimney dry enough to hold a fire. There was also a good start on a stable, enough to keep the pigs, milk cow, and calf from wandering. Lindsay and Roy slept in the house, but the rest of them stayed outside. This would be their last night in the majestic mountain valley that would be her daughter's home.

The next morning they rolled out of bed to a light sprinkling of snow. With the snow came a renewed urgency for the Tanners and Silas to move on. Belle hugged Lindsay good-bye with tears streaming down her face.

Lindsay had the serene look of a woman in love, and though her good-byes were tearful, she never wavered from her new husband's side. Silas hugged Lindsay as if she had been his child every minute of her almost sixteen years. Belle saw Silas and Lindsay whispering together and felt strangely left out even though Lindsay's good-byes to her were fervent and loving.

Just as they were leaving, Lindsay pulled her aside. "I want you to know how much I respect the sacrifices you've made for me all my life, Ma. Watching all the menfolk work so hard to build this cabin has made me realize how hard you've worked to make a home for us with no help. I'm trying to imagine what I'd do in this lonely valley with a herd of cows and a no-account husband. Building a cabin myself. Tending the herd myself. Doing everything alone with a baby on my back and another on the way." Lindsay laid her hands on Belle's arms.

Belle was shocked to realize her daughter felt sorry for her.

"I'm sorry you ended up with the husbands you did, Ma."

Belle was sorry herself.

"But I'm glad I was born, and I'm glad for my sisters."

Belle nodded. She'd always known that whatever lousy things her husbands had given her, they'd also given her the loves of her life and a reason to live and be strong.

"I think, Ma, that. . .things. . .don't have to be so hard between a man and a woman as they were for you. Silas knew things that I reckon you don't know. And he explained things to Roy so. . .well, Roy was wonderful."

Belle tried to keep up with what Lindsay was saying. What things could her daughter possibly be referring to?

"I hope someday you'll know what it's like to. . .be with. . .a man you love. And who loves you enough to be gentle with you." Lindsay hugged her tight.

Well, Belle knew she was already with a man she loved. And it hurt more than anything she'd ever known, short of saying goodbye to her daughter.

They hugged, and finally Belle let go, swiping at her tears while Lindsay turned to Roy. Belle's last sight of her daughter was Lindsay crying her eyes out and being held and comforted in the strong arms of the man she loved. Each of their two blond heads rested on the other's shoulder. Their tall, lithe frames clung to each other. It occurred to Belle that they would have beautiful children. And Lindsay would at least *think* they looked like her.

Belle's heart threatened to break. There would be other cattle drives, and the rugged mountain passes couldn't stop a determined woman who wanted to visit her daughter, but the West had a way of swallowing people up. There was a chance she'd never see her daughter again. But she also knew that the girl could have waited a long time and searched the world over and found no better husband.

It was small comfort.

The snow fell more heavily, and the Tanner-Harden party headed up the mountain pass at a sharp trot.

"We'll be home in four days if I have anything to say about it," Silas yelled from where he brought up the rear, leading the spare horses. They'd eaten all their supplies on the trip and brought very little home. Belle had put in stores for the winter before the drive started.

Heartbroken at leaving Lindsay, Belle looked back; she had Betsy on her back and trailed Sarah and then Emma, who was in the lead. She decided bickering might be just the ticket to get her gumption back.

"A hundred miles in four days? You're crazy. It took us a month to come in to Helena."

Flashing a grin at her, Silas said, "We pushed a thousand head of cattle over this trail. Reckon that slowed us down some."

"This is a mean trail, with cattle or without." Belle had made this trip in four days before, but in good weather, and it had been a hard, heartbreaking ride. She'd done it before she'd married Anthony, to find a good lawyer and write a will that favored her children and cut off her husband. It wasn't easy finding the right man for that will, because most lawyers barely recognized a woman as having legal rights. But she'd done it.

"I think four days in the snow is mighty bold talk, Pa." Emma could probably stop calling Silas Pa now. Belle didn't remind her.

"Well, men could do it. But with you womenfolk slowing me down, maybe you're right."

Emma flashed him a smile over her shoulder. "We'll see who has to hustle to keep up." She leaned low over her horse and pushed to the limit of safety and perhaps a bit beyond.

The race was on. Against men, against time, against nature.

It gave Belle something to focus on, and she needed that bad. All of 'em had their hands full keeping up with Emma.

Late that night, long after the stars were out, Silas finally let up pushing them.

They got a hot fire blazing high, the girls on one side, Silas alone on the other. It hurt Belle to think of how cold he was over there alone. There was no way she could think of to convince him he belonged with her. Remembering his certainty that they weren't going to get married, she quit her foolish daydreaming and slept.

Come morning, they were up, building the fire and starting coffee. They had a warm meal in their bellies and were on the trail hours before first light.

The next stretch of the trip was a repeat of the harrowing series of passes that had taken them five days coming across. The wind picked up through the day, and snow drifted down occasionally, especially when they'd crest a peak.

They neared the top of one of those dizzying trails, and in a wide spot, Silas rode up beside her, their horses wading in three inches of snow. "We've got to get through this whole stretch today, Belle."

"It was five days coming across." Belle hated the way she sounded—whiny. But the cold was like taking a beating. She hated that she was putting her girls through this.

"These peaks get higher with each one we cross. Look how deep the snow is already." Silas looked up at the whirling white that sifted down steadily on the higher elevations. "And this doesn't come close to a heavy snow."

Belle stiffened her backbone. "We'll make it." She pulled the front of her buckskin jacket tight at the neck to keep out the biting cold.

Nodding, Silas reached over, even as they trotted side by side, and flipped up the collar of her coat. He gave her flat-brimmed Stetson a tug as if to pull it to cover more of her head.

They exchanged a smile, and Belle wondered, maybe, if they weren't half dead from cold and exhaustion and separated by the space between two horses, with three children looking on, if he might kiss her again.

Smiling, he said, "Sure as certain we'll make it. I've never been with a tougher bunch of cowhands. I'll go tell your girls to pick up the pace."

Once they got through that stretch, it was lower, except for that one last sky-high peak they had to climb to get into her valley. The first one they'd driven the cattle up when leaving home.

The day wore on and the peaks rose and fell. The cold wore on her. They ate beef jerky in the saddle, and Belle fed Betsy and changed her diaper with almost no break in the pace. They had to stop, water the horses, and switch saddles to fresh mounts, but it was never for long, and they pushed on hard.

As the sun set, they began the long climb up the last treacherous trail they'd tackle tonight. The snow had stopped, but the wind cut and howled. Belle wanted to beg for mercy, but she clamped her mouth shut.

Silas tied the horses onto Belle's saddle. "I'm going to spell Emma—take the lead. The snow looks deep ahead. If a trail needs to be broken, especially where there are drop-offs, I want to do it."

Belle wanted to beg him to be careful, but she didn't have the energy. He passed Sarah, talked to her, coaxing a smile out of Belle's little redhead, then rode up, patted Emma on the shoulder, and passed her. Belle brought up the rear carrying Betsy. Belle saw Sarah's head nodding, but she was too stupid from exhaustion to react. Her mind wanted to yell, her heels wanted to goad her horse, but she had no strength to do it. She just sat her horse and watched in numb horror as Sarah slid sideways, falling, which was unheard of for one of her girls, short of being tossed by a bronco.

Silas glanced back, as he did constantly, and spurred his horse to Sarah's side. He caught her in time.

Belle breathed a prayer of thanks into the bitter night.

Silas's gently muttered words blew back to Belle on the cold wind. "Here, ride with me." Her heart ached as she saw the careful way he lifted the little girl onto his lap and let her sleep in his arms. He strung a rope between himself and Sarah's horse and pushed past Emma to take the lead again, all without letting up the pace. The rest of the nearly dozen horses were tied onto the back of Belle's saddle, and they plodded along in a line, one behind the other. The three riders—Silas, Emma, and Belle—struggled on up the last peak they had to face today.

Snow started sifting down when they still had a mile to go up and several miles on the other side to descend before it was safe to camp. With the slippery snow, the downhill side might be more treacherous than the switchbacks they were climbing.

Silas led the way through the deepening snow, breaking the trail. Belle constantly checked Betsy, strapped on her back, to see that she wasn't being smothered by her blanket and that she hadn't let so much as a finger slip out from under the covers. Emma rode in the middle, a quiet, intense little girl who hadn't said much since she'd hugged her big sister good-bye.

Belle sensed a world of sadness in Emma and didn't know how to get her taciturn daughter to speak of her hurt. Belle wasn't sure speaking of it was a good idea anyway. And good or bad didn't matter much, because there was no time now for talking.

Belle couldn't remember when there'd been time for anything in her life except work and more work with Emma always at her side, doing a man's share. And Lindsay. And now they'd have to do it all with one less pair of hands.

They reached the peak at last, the horses floundering in knee-deep snow that came light and blew with the sheltered wind into drifts against the side of the trail. A white world against a coal dark sky, filled with blinding snow and whipping wind, surrounded them.

When the trail was wide enough, Silas dropped back to speak a word of encouragement.

As they began the downward slope, the sure-footed horses slid often, sometimes sitting on their haunches to stop. One switchback would lead them so close to a sheer drop, Belle's legs would dangle out over thin air while the other scraped the mountain. Another would take them into the side of the mountain where the snow was deeper and the winds whipped stronger, sapping their strength with its clawing cold.

They dropped lower and the snow got deeper. For a while, Belle wasn't aware of anything beyond her horse putting one hoof in front of the other. She knew if they didn't get below the snow line soon, they'd have to get off and walk the horses, because their mounts were spent.

Then, just when Belle began to think there wasn't a place in the whole world that wasn't icy and white, they passed a sheltered spot and the snow wasn't so deep there. They moved out into a more difficult stretch again, but they could see ahead that the trail was improving. The snow slowed and stopped, and stars shone overhead. The horses seemed to sense relief ahead. Their ears pricked forward and they picked up their pace.

At last, after making more demands on the animals and the people than seemed possible, the trail widened. The going became easy enough for Silas to drop back beside Belle. "The trail clears ahead, and we can camp just as soon as I find a good spot."

Silas laid his hand on her shoulder, and feeling numb and stupid, Belle looked sideways at him in the moonlight. She realized she hadn't reacted when he'd spoken to her. Sarah was sleeping on the saddle in front of him, wrapped up as tightly as the baby on Belle's back. The sight of her daughter in his arms almost shook loose some useless tears, but she held them off.

"Emma's all in, Belle."

Their eyes met. Her throat ached from what they'd put her children through today.

"I don't think she can hang on to her horse much longer." He leaned closer, and Belle wondered if her eyes were focused, because he seemed unsure if she understood him.

She forced her head up and down. Words were beyond her.

"I can't handle both of them. I'm sorry, but you're going to have to take Sarah. We can't stop, not yet. Can you do it? Can you hold her?"

Belle didn't know where she found the strength, but she checked Betsy quickly, realizing in her exhaustion she'd forgotten she had a baby on her back. Betsy blinked her eyes owlishly up at her, and Belle could see that the little girl had weathered the storm better than the rest of them. Tucking the baby back in quickly so no heat would escape, Belle accepted Sarah into her arms.

Silas helped balance Sarah so all her weight was on the horse, not on Belle's tired arms. Sarah moaned and shifted her body around a bit, but she never woke up as she was passed between the two of them.

"Are you okay?"

Belle nodded again but didn't speak.

Silas rode forward and bent over Emma. Only when Silas reached for Emma's hands did Belle realize Emma had lashed herself to the saddle horn and now rode along in her sleep. Silas untied Emma's hands and lifted her gently into his arms. Emma was as tall as Belle, yet Silas lifted her as though she were a small child.

Belle's throat closed. Tears bit at her eyes with their salty heat. The valor of her daughter and the kindness and strength of a man they didn't even know a month ago swelled her heart. And if she wasn't in love with him already, she fell in love in that instant.

She quit fighting her fear of love and the danger to her heart. She couldn't stop her feelings anyway—so the only thing she really quit was denying them.

Belle knew now that she had loved him for a long time. Maybe it wasn't love when she'd been afraid to hire him the first moment she saw him. Maybe it wasn't love when she discussed her plans and problems with him on that long ride from Divide to her ranch. Maybe it wasn't love when she melted under his kisses. But it had been the beginning. From the first instant, love had been growing in her heart until tonight. As he worked to care for them to the limit of his strength with an unending reserve of gentleness, it had bloomed into something that would live in her forever.

She loved Silas Harden. She was his.

And he didn't want her.

They plodded along the last mile of ever-thinning snow until the white on the trail vanished as if it had never been. The going was still too steep for a camp, but once they dropped into the tree line, Belle found a reserve of strength without the wind that deepened the cold.

Silas checked over his shoulder to see if she was still with him. With the moon and stars overhead, she could see him as clear as day, even in the mottled light of the forest. She nodded, and he smiled and turned back to the winding trail. At last they reached a plateau that was level and had a water supply.

Silas rode his horse to a sheltered spot under an overhanging cliff and dismounted with Emma in his arms. He jerked his bedroll off his horse, and with a few flicks of his wrist, he had Emma settled, asleep on the ground. Belle was still trying to swing her leg over the back of her horse when Silas was at her side.

He lifted her down, and when her legs buckled, he kept one hand on Sarah and lowered Belle to the grassy floor. "Just rest," he whispered. "Let me get Sarah settled and I'll help you with Betsy." He led the horse a few steps away so a nervous movement wouldn't allow him to trample Belle.

Belle heard the exhaustion in Silas's voice and forced herself to sit up and, with clumsy fingers, lift Betsy around to the front. Betsy was wide awake when Belle uncovered her. The quiet baby made sounds of distress that reminded Belle the child hadn't eaten or had her diaper changed for hours. Belle saw to the diaper.

Silas was by her side, helping her to her feet and guiding her to a felled log to rest her back. "You feed her and put her to sleep. I'll get a fire going and see to the horses."

Belle nodded dumbly, and as soon as he stepped away, she nursed Betsy then tucked her little girl back into her blankets for the night.

She awoke briefly as Silas eased her from a sitting position to the ground. He murmured, "I'm sorry. I'm sorry I put you through this, baby. You're the bravest thing I've ever seen." It might have been a dream, but she thought he pressed his lips to the top of her head as he eased her close to the fire. And she must have been dreaming when she heard him whisper, "I love you."

Silas moved away to his lonely side of the camp, and as she dozed off, Belle wondered briefly if she'd heard it but convinced herself he was talking to Betsy. Of course he was. Betsy was a baby after all, and who wouldn't love her? But why say that when the baby was sound asleep?

She wished with everything in her heart that he would have said those words to her. And she wished she had the nerve to say them back. He deserved to know how much she loved him.

Though she was too tired and too afraid to say any of it out loud, in her dreams she told him everything in her heart.

CHAPTER 20

I love you, Silas. So much."

Silas sat up on his bedroll, stunned.

"I've never known a man as strong." Her voice slurred.

But Silas could hear every word. "You're so steady. So smart. I wish I'd married you. Not the others. Only you. Love you. Love you so much."

Narrowing his sleep-heavy eyes, he couldn't see Belle in the dim light. She was talking in her sleep, or maybe it was a stupor rather than sleep, but she'd said it. And that meant she'd thought it. And, whether she'd ever admit it or not, somewhere, some part of her had those words to share.

He was so thrilled he would have asked her to marry him right then and there—except she was fast asleep, and he was tired all the way to his bones. He forced himself to lie back down, and within seconds sleep dragged him under.

He jerked awake to see stars hanging like an explosion of diamonds high overhead. The moon was low in the sky. Dawn would begin to blot out the stars very soon.

Every muscle in his body objected and every sensible cell in his brain hollered, *No!* but he held his eyes open anyway.

God, I almost killed my girls yesterday. I'm sorry I forced them through that. But it had to be done.

He knew from the conditions last night that they'd never have gotten through today. Silas thought of how battered his girls were and how they'd bedded down for the night closer to unconscious than asleep. He thought about the glazed look in Belle's eyes as Silas added to her burden by making her carry Sarah. He remembered the heart-wrenching sight of Emma's wrists strapped to her saddle. The only reason he didn't break down and cry was because he was a man. He got mad instead.

He aimed his anger at himself mostly for staying that extra day to help Lindsay when she had three able-bodied men to see to her needs while Belle only had him and three young children to boot. But Silas had needed to be sure there was a roof over Lindsay's head. Whether or not it was smart didn't matter. He'd had it to do and he'd done it.

He spent awhile raging in his mind at Belle's worthless husbands. They were lucky to be dead and beyond his reach, or he'd have hunted them up and beaten them within an inch of their lives. Fury built in him at Belle, too. She hadn't needed to choose such a hard road for herself and her girls. She could have easily stayed in Texas, even if she didn't stand to inherit a ranch. Her pa would have made sure she got by, even with that no-account husband. And she could have just left it to the worthless bum of a husband to eke out a living while she stayed to a woman's place and cared for her children.

When he was in full mental rant at Belle, he knew it was exhaustion talking, because everything about her spoke to his heart. Every tough, courageous choice she made touched him all the way to his soul. He'd finally worked up the nerve to tell her he loved her last night, and she'd said the words back. Trouble was, he hadn't realized his feelings until they came out of his mouth.

He should have married her in Helena. Instead, he'd still been stuck in his fool notion that he didn't want any part of marriage.

Now they had trouble. Silas couldn't think of a way to marry her and still get back to the ranch ahead of the snow.

He could do it without shame now. He might have been a coward before, but no more. His days of running were over, and with Belle at his side, he'd never need to run anyway. She was tough enough to handle whatever came along.

And he had plans that would make him worthy of her. But he needed to do that work before he could present himself to Belle as a husband fit for her and the girls. Of course, Belle would go ahead and marry him most likely. She'd shown a bent for marrying all and sundry.

The right thing to do would be to take her home, climb out of that valley of hers any way possible, then come courting in the spring. But spring seemed like an eternity away. No matter how Silas worked it around in his head, he couldn't fit a trip to Divide for a preacher into their plans before the long Montana winter shut down on their heads.

Maybe once they were home, if it looked like the weather was going to hold, they might make a run for town. But they didn't dare ride away from the place and leave the girls, and they didn't dare take the whole family out and leave the herd.

Silas thought again of his girls' hard lives and got angry all over again. And that was just as well, because nothing else could have kept him awake.

Today wouldn't be so brutally hard, but it would be hard enough. They had to press on and get close enough to the pass near the Tanner Ranch to get over it the next day. They'd come twenty miles from Lindsay's valley, and that valley was nearly fifteen miles from Helena. They would ride forty miles today because the going was better, but the day had to start now, and it had to last until well after dark.

That left ten miles of clawing their way straight up and down the mountain that sheltered the Tanner Ranch at the same time it cut it off from the rest of the world. He knew that what they passed through yesterday was a sign of things to come. The gap into Belle's place would still be open, he hoped, but it was just a matter of time. There was a lower pass on the south end of the Tanner Ranch, but they'd have to ride three days around the mountain to get to it, and by then *it* might be closed off.

No, they had to make the north pass today or tomorrow or a winter storm could lock Belle away from her ranch for the whole winter. And Silas knew Belle. He knew the stuff she was made of. He knew she'd do whatever it took to get home. If it meant risking her life and the lives of her children, she'd scale that mountain on her belly in snow that'd bury Goliath and get home. The woman didn't have an ounce of backup in her. His only goal was to get her there before it came down to life and death.

Throwing back his blanket, he rolled to his knees, aching in every joint, and crawled to the fire. He stirred up the flames and had coffee going and the horses saddled before he woke his girls. They moaned and groaned, and Sarah cried and begged him to leave her alone. Silas could have let it break his heart to hear his sturdy female ranch hands whining up a storm, but he teased them and called them lazy. It didn't take long until their grit kicked in.

They were on the trail an hour before first light. As soon as the first blush of dawn brightened the sky, Silas set the pace at a ground-eating trot. They switched their saddles to fresh horses twice during the morning, never letting up the pace. The horses seemed able to trot along forever as long as they got a break from the weight of a rider.

"Silas, we've got to walk a spell," Belle yelled from behind Sarah and Emma.

Wanting to snarl at the delay, Silas knew this was for Betsy, not Belle. Belle never asked for a break for herself.

They walked along for close to half an hour, Silas careful not to look back but smiling at his unlikely cowhands.

"Let's move out," Belle hollered as soon as the little tyke was returned to her carrier.

Silas pushed on again.

They made a quick cold lunch, and Silas insisted the girls walk briskly around the little clearing he'd found so their abused muscles would loosen up some. "Let me carry Betsy for a while, Belle."

She shook her head.

Silas caught her chin. "You know how bad it got last night."

"Betsy's my responsibility."

Silas looked over at Emma and Sarah, walking along briskly, out of earshot. "Please, can you just this once mind me, woman?"

Belle's eyes flashed. "Mind you?"

Smiling, Silas said, "Nice to see you've still got some spunk."

He stole a long, deep kiss. "You'll probably end up with Sarah and Betsy both by nightfall. It'll be all I can do to handle Emma. This will help you save your strength now."

Looking bemused by the kiss, Belle said, "Okay," and handed the baby over.

Silas decided he'd remember this method for persuading the stubborn woman. It would be his pleasure to convince her to do things his way from now on.

"I'll give her back come feeding time." He took the carrier and strapped it on his own back. "Girls! Let's hit the trail."

By late afternoon, Belle had taken Betsy back for a while. Then Silas retrieved the baby during a saddle switch.

The horizon filled with the last mountain they needed to climb. Silas knew it was still far away, but he watched it loom over his head and wondered how they'd ever scared those cattle up and down this twisting trail.

Just as the sun set, they started climbing from the base of their last obstacle. Silas considered laying up to sleep right then, but he felt the lowering sky and smelled snow in the wind, and he wasn't bold enough to stop and dare the winter to swallow them up.

An hour later, no more than a quarter of the way up this massive climb, Silas saw Sarah's head bob forward. He lifted her out of her saddle over feeble protests.

As full dark came over them, they reached a level spot that would have worked for a camp. But the horses were jumpy and Silas was, too. He saw the fear in Belle as she looked over her head at the sky. Looking behind her, she saw darkness pile on top of the stars. They slowly blinked out, and the moon disappeared behind the encroaching snow clouds.

Silas dropped back and yelled over the rising wind, "We'll be riding all night, but I don't think the weather's gonna hold till morning. Let's change saddles again and try to make it to the top and over."

Even in the darkness, Silas could see the dark rings around Belle's heavy-lidded eyes. She nodded her head. "Let me take Betsy. Sarah's enough for you."

The woman was pure heart, with more guts than any man Silas ever knew. Silas dismounted, lay Sarah down, and dragged Belle off the saddle, lowering her to a sitting position. He made sure she had a firm grip on the baby; then he eased Emma off her horse. He changed the saddles, handed out some beef jerky, and got them mounted up. Emma looked about all in, but he didn't think Belle had it in her to carry Sarah as she had the night before, so he left Emma riding alone. Betsy rode on Belle's back because she'd need to feed the little girl. Silas carried Sarah in his arms. Belle was so tired she was actually just taking orders at this point. Silas decided to enjoy it as it wasn't likely to happen again.

They started the frisky mounts up the trail. The horses smelled the storm, or maybe they knew they were close to home, because they seemed to be as fresh as if they had just started the day. The lively horses roused Belle and Emma somewhat, and they fell into line behind Silas. Every few steps he checked to make sure they were still with him. As they reached the halfway point on the climb, snow began to filter down from the sky, and Silas pushed the horses harder, knowing that when the snow accumulated it would make the going slippery.

But it wasn't soft snow like they'd had on the high ground. This was heavy. And it was coming from behind them, snowing even in the lowlands. Snow could come by the foot up here rather than by the inch. Add in drifting winds, and the pass still high overhead could be closing up even now.

His mount nickered and fidgeted, sending the metal in its bridal clinking. But it was a good horse and it minded. Silas remembered a series of dead drops near the peak where they'd lost a few head of cattle who stumbled at the wrong time. He wanted to get past those before the drifts started to form.

The snow began to collect until it covered the horse's hooves with every step. They trotted on through shelter where the snow hadn't covered the trail, along wind-whipped cliffs that cut through their woolen clothing, along rock faces that rose high overhead, and caught every flake of snow, dropping it down and deepening the going.

Silas looked back steadily, worried about the womenfolk. Time to time he'd see Belle pull little Betsy off her back and tend to her. Silas knew Belle wouldn't neglect her baby, but he couldn't quite imagine how the woman managed to feed and change a baby without once getting off her horse.

The last of the stars were blotted out as the clouds moved ahead of them. The wind rose until it whined eerily among the thinning trees.

Silas looked back to see Emma tying her hands on the saddle again. Behind Emma was Belle with their horses strung out behind her.

Silas dropped back. "Give me your reins."

Emma looked up, her blue eyes vague, her lids heavy. She didn't obey him. In the normal course of things, Emma would have refused to let anyone do anything for her. But right now, Silas was sure she disobeyed simply because her head was too foggy from exhaustion to understand his request.

He unwound the reins without waiting for her to respond and guided her horse. This time he didn't carry her. He didn't think he had the strength.

As they climbed higher, the wind cut more sharply as if to punish them for daring to be abroad in this weather. Silas caught himself dozing. Scared to his boots because the sheer drop-offs that were so treacherous were just ahead, he grabbed a handful of snow off a rock and smeared it on his face. He was already so cold he barely felt it.

"Belle!" Silas looked behind him. Emma sat with her head bowed forward, almost certainly asleep. But he had her reins. He could control her horse. But Belle had to be alert.

Belle didn't respond.

"Wake up, Belle. Listen to me," Silas hollered. The trail was too narrow for him to drop back. The wind was so high his voice barely carried. "Belle Tanner, you stop lazing around and wake up and ride that horse!"

He continued shouting until Belle lifted her head. With a jerk, she looked around and realized how dangerous the trail was. Her hands tightened on the reins. "I'm awake." She shook her head. "Lazing around?"

Silas thought he heard a little spitfire in her voice. Well, if calling her lazy didn't set her off, nothing would.

"I'm paying attention, Silas."

"You'd better be, woman," Silas shouted back. He kept shouting pure nonsense, whatever his thick head could think of, about the cold and the climb and the cattle. Anything to keep himself and Belle going. Finally sure Belle and even Emma after a while were alert, he rode on, talking with them, making his voice carry above the wind.

They were tough women, and they worked as hard as he did to keep their group going, encouraging each other and pushing each other to go on, even when sometimes it didn't seem like the next step was possible.

Then suddenly, they were at the summit.

"We made it!" Silas shouted and looked back to see Emma and Belle crane their necks to see ahead in the darkness.

"We're home!" Belle smiled, pure triumph.

"Home." Emma spoke more quietly, but she squared her shoulders and looked down to realize she didn't have her reins anymore. She looked up, straight into Silas's eyes. "Thank you."

He felt more than heard those words. They filled his heart until his throat clogged with something that *could not* be tears.

Silas turned back and looked down in his arms at Sarah with her eyes open, smiling up at him. He boosted her around so she sat, looking forward, while he minded his horse. The vast canyon where Belle had held her steers before the drive was before them. There was still a long climb down to get below the snow line and another ten-mile ride to get to the cabin, but they were home. Silas felt a weight lift off his back.

After the first dangerously steep yards off the peak, the trail widened. In the heavily falling snow, Silas was able to ride back and untie the horses. He unhitched them from Belle's saddle and from each other. "Hyah!" he yelled and slapped the closest horse on the rump. These critters were almost asleep, too. Just like the people traveling with them. First they walked, speeding up on the wider trail. They passed Belle and Emma. Then they picked up speed, trotting at first, then, when Silas saw them pass the snow-clad ground far below and gain more solid footing, they broke into a gallop. They charged down the mountain. He knew they'd run until they got to the cabin. There was no longer a need to watch them.

He looked down at Sarah in his arms and chucked one gloved hand under her chin. "We made it home, Sarie."

She smiled and nodded then lay her head back against his chest and went back to sleep.

He rode on up to Belle's side. "We're almost below the storm. I don't have it in me to ride until we get home. I'll find a place and we'll camp one more night on the trail."

Belle nodded.

Sarah stirred slightly and murmured, " 'K, Pa."

Silas dropped a quick kiss on her curly red head and hugged her close as the horse dropped down out of the rugged peak.

Finally, the snow was behind them.

Belle rode up beside him. "I know where to camp."

"Lead on, darlin'."

Belle smiled at him and urged her mount ahead. Belle didn't go much farther. She picked a well-sheltered spot with an icy cold spring trickling down out of a crack in the mountain.

Silas used the last energy he possessed to get the horses picketed for fear they'd head for home with the other horses. Silas had no interest in taking a ten-mile hike in the morning. Then he built up a roaring fire to make the bitterly cold night bearable.

Belle sat feeding Betsy, both of them mostly asleep, while he did everything to prepare the camp, including finding the last of the beef jerky and urging them to eat it and drink some water.

He settled Emma and Sarah next to each other and covered them with a blanket to share their body heat. He found Belle asleep with a dozing Betsy in her arms. He woke her enough to urge her into the nest of warmth with her girls, resenting that he didn't have the right to share that warmth.

He intended to fix that—and soon.

Belle stirred awake as Silas covered her, and struggled to sit up. In a voice rusty with sleep, she said, "Silas, we're home. We made it. Thanks to you."

"We're going to be married, Belle, just as soon as I can figure out how to get us to a preacher."

"But Silas—"

"Go to sleep. Just sleep. Tomorrow we'll be home, and we'll figure everything out then." He stalked away from her, knowing he was already her husband in his heart. But they needed the vows to be said before God.

Belle murmured, "Home." From across the camp he heard her utter, "I love you."

Silas lay awake for several minutes trying to believe the other lower pass, nearer Belle's cabin, would still be open and he could risk taking her to Divide for a wedding. He knew, unless it was completely impossible, he was going to try first thing tomorrow, because he knew he had reached the day when he could no longer be near Belle Tanner and not be her husband.

Rather than having even the slightest twinge of regret at the loss of his freedom, he fell asleep excited about the future and eager to get on with it.

The wind moaned and howled, and the snow fell in the high altitudes, but they were safe. Silas and his girls had made it home.

God, help me get out of here tomorrow. Help me find a way to marry this woman now.

CHAPTER 21

Belle slept late the next morning.

The sun was already brightening the horizon in the east when her eyes flickered open. The first sight she saw was Silas, crouching by the fire, lifting a coffeepot.

They'd made it. This was her valley.

"Silas, we're home."

He looked up and smiled. His face was wind burned, his hair knotted and flattened by his Stetson, though he wasn't wearing it now. He had a week's worth of stubble on his face because he hadn't shaved since the day Lindsay had gotten married.

And he was the most wonderful thing she'd ever seen.

"We made it, didn't we, darlin'?" A dark look in his eyes reminded her of warm words she'd dreamed in the night.

"Because of you." She pressed against the ground to sit up, wondering what kind of mess she must be. It was a wonder the man didn't turn tail and run. She smiled and wondered when the last time was she'd cared about her appearance.

"Because of all of us." His eyes went past Belle's shoulders.

Nodding, she glanced to see all three of her girls, still fast asleep. And with the sun well up in the sky. Shameful. "A pretty tough bunch, huh?" She looked back at him and smiled.

He was wonderful and brave and strong. He was everything a man should be.

And she might have dreamed it, but she thought the man had asked her to marry him last night. She wondered if he'd ask again just so she could be sure. Lowering the coffeepot back onto the fire, their eyes held. "So are you going to quit wasting the day away and get going?" Belle challenged.

A smile spread wider. "So we can get married?"

Silas hadn't spent much time smiling on this cattle drive. All things considered, that was understandable. Belle hadn't done much of it herself. So now she looked at his smiling face and noticed for the first time that he had a dimple. A single dimple on the left side that for some reason fascinated her. Then she shook off her bemused state as she thought of what he'd said. Belle sat all the way up. "Silas Harden, I've had a lot of proposals in my day."

Silas said dryly, "I'll bet that's right."

"And that is the worst one I've *ever* heard, bar none."

"Is that so?" He stood and came straight for her.

Belle's eyes widened. "Now, Silas. I haven't said yes yet."

Dropping to his knees, he leaned in and kissed her hard with his whiskery face, still grinning. Then staring straight into her eyes, he asked, "Don't you think I oughta marry her, Emma?"

Belle thought that seemed like yet another strange proposal.

"I think you're gonna hafta, Pa," Emma said solemnly.

Belle looked over her shoulder and saw Sarah and Emma had joined the living. They were standing behind her, watching the man kiss the living daylights out of her. Even Betsy was awake and watching.

"We talked it over, Ma," Sarah said earnestly. "We think you and Pa oughta get married. I mean, I know we didn't want any-more husbands. Heaven knows up till now you've picked a useless lot. But we're all fond of Pa and kind of used to calling him Pa, and we talked it over with Lindsay, and she's for it. So we vote for you marryin' him."

"You talked it over with Lindsay?" *How long ago?* she wondered.

Emma said gravely, "It was unanimous."

Betsy, perched in Sarah's arms, waved wildly and bounced until Sarah almost dropped her. She yelled, "Papa! Papa!"

Sarah tilted her head in Betsy's direction and nodded ruefully. "Completely unanimous."

"Thanks." Silas smiled at the girls. "I'm mighty proud to be your pa, too. And I'm glad to hear I've won the election. Majority rules." Then he looked back at Belle. "You don't even have to vote. I *am* their pa. You heard 'em, and that's the way it is. Now, *Ma*, isn't it high time you married their pa?"

"Silas, you're not their. . .*mmmph*. . ."

When Silas quit kissing her into silence, he said, "And you hadn't oughta carry on, kissin' and such, in front of youngsters. Not with any man, but for sure not with a man you don't plan to marry. So, it's settled."

"Can I say something?" Belle snapped.

Eyeing her mouth as if prepared to silence her again, Silas said warily, "Depends."

Belle narrowed her eyes at him. "I had no intention of letting you get away without marryin' me, Silas Harden."

Then Silas laughed out loud and kissed the daylights out of her, and the girls jumped on his back, and pretty soon the whole family was within a gnat's eyelash of rolling right off the mountainside.

When the jubilee was over, Silas poured coffee all around and doused the fire. Then he started saddling horses while the women gathered bedrolls. Then he herded them all toward the horses. "We've got to get back to the ranch and get to Divide before winter closes in. I'm not spendin' the winter in the barn. And while we're there, we can get some lumber to patch up that sad excuse for a cabin."

"Silas," Belle said uncertainly. His eyes dropped to her lips again, so she thought over what she had to say with some care. "The thing is, what if we get snowed away? I can't risk leaving the herd, and I can't drag these girls over that south pass when they're so exhausted. But I dare not leave them, in case we don't get back."

Silas said shortly, "Just get in the saddle. We'll be home in four hours. . .three and a half if we push hard. And we can talk about it then. But we're going to be married if we have to ordain Emma and have her perform the ceremony."

Sarah said pertly, "*I* want to perform the ceremony. I'm more religiouser than Emma."

Emma slapped Sarah on the arm. "You're not religiouser than me. Why, I'm the most Bible-believin' person in this family by far. And I'm oldest."

"You're not oldest. Lindsay's oldest."

"Lindsay's not oldest no more, 'cuz Lindsay's not here. In a family where the ma and pa ain't married, it's the oldest child's job to do everything she can to fetch 'em both around to doing the right thing."

Belle interrupted, "Emma, you shouldn't say your ma and pa ain't married."

Emma said, "I know, I know. My ma and pa *aren't* married. I knows grammar rightly enough."

"No, it's not the *grammar*. It's saying Silas is your pa but I'm not married to him. That makes it sound like I've got a twelve-year-old child and have had. . ." Belle shut up before she dug herself in any deeper.

Emma went back to fighting with Sarah.

Silas dug a few forgotten, beat-up pieces of jerky out of one of the packs, picked the horse hair off of them, and gave them to Sarah and Emma.

The girls still bickered as the family started down the trail.

It occurred to Belle that the girls didn't fight much. The good-natured sniping seemed childish to her. Her daughters had never had much chance to be children. Maybe with Silas to carry part of the load, her girls could have a little taste of being young before they found themselves married with adult responsibilities to shoulder.

Belle thought of Lindsay and had a wave of loneliness for her oldest child. Lindsay had been forced to grow up far too soon. But on the other hand, if ever a fifteen-year-old was mature enough for marriage, Lindsay was.

Belle breathed in and out evenly until any risk of sentimental tears passed. Then she spurred her horse into a trot and passed Silas on the trail. As she went by him, she grinned. "A woman might think you're not in that all-fired of a hurry to get married, the way you're doggin' it."

He laughed. "Don't you believe it, woman." He urged his horse to a faster pace to keep up with her.

She set her horse to a ground-eating trot, and proving Silas didn't know her range as well as he thought he did, they were home in two and a half hours.

Silas told all his girls to get in the cabin and go to sleep. He'd be back before nightfall with a preacher if he had to crawl a hundred miles on his hands and knees across bitter cold snow.

Belle said, "No, I'll just go along. But I'll have to take Betsy. She'll need to eat."

Silas dragged Belle out of hearing distance of the girls. "Here's how it is, Belle. If we go together, there is a chance we won't get back and the girls could spend the winter alone. They'd probably survive it because they're good strong girls, but neither of us wants to test that. If we take the girls, there's a chance the whole family won't get back and the cattle won't survive the winter, which wipes out your years of work, and I won't let our marriage cost you so much."

Then Silas lifted Belle onto her tiptoes. "If I don't go, there is no way I can spend the winter here with you and not. . .not be. . . be with you as a husband. It would be better if I go alone, and if I can't get back, at least the snow would preserve your honor. If I *can* get back, we'll be married and I'll hustle the preacher out of here the minute the ceremony is over. You can ride out to the low pass and meet me and the parson. Figuring a six-hour ride, I should be back about midafternoon. Me going alone is the only thing that makes sense."

"But what if you get to the pass and can't get out?" Belle asked worriedly. "I love you, and I don't want you to risk your life trying to get us married."

It was all Silas could do not to drag her into his arms and kiss her, but he just didn't have the time. Instead, he tugged his hat low on his forehead. "I'll be back before nightfall with a preacher. Be waiting at the pass so we can send the poor man straightaway back to Divide. If I don't make it, I'll be in here the minute the pass opens up in the spring. Whatever it takes, however long I have to wait, I'm marrying you."

He gave her one hard kiss because he couldn't resist; then he turned his back, grabbed up a horse, saddled it, and was running it at a full gallop before he was out of the ranch yard.

She'd had a lot of men eager to marry her. Dozens. Hundreds! But none more so than Silas Harden. And for a fact, she'd never been anywhere near so eager to marry one of them.

She shooed the girls into the house and started heating water for baths. One by one she dunked her girls in the water and scrubbed a month's worth of trail dust off of them. By the time she was done, their nails were clean, their hair squeaked, and even the tips of their toes were shining. They all went to sleep with very little urging, even though it was the middle of the day.

Then Belle, knowing she had hours before the time came to leave for the south pass, rode out and inspected her herd. She rounded up the horses Silas had sent running ahead and herded them into the corral. She found the milk cow and roped her and coaxed her back to the barn so the animal would gentle down some before her baby came and she needed milking again. She found a goodly number of the chickens brooding in the barn. She moved the ones who weren't nesting back to the chicken coop so she could be sure any eggs they laid were fresh. She found enough work to do to keep her busy all afternoon and into the next week, but finally she had to turn her back on it and take her own bath and get the girls moving, because she wanted them at the wedding.

She dressed all of them, including herself, in their prettiest dresses—which weren't all that pretty, but it was all they had—and headed out. They were just starting the steep climb toward the snow line when she saw Silas coming down the hill with another man. A thrill of excitement made Belle shiver, and she tried to control the smile that kept breaking out on her face.

"You really love him, don't ya, Ma?" Emma asked with hushed pleasure.

Belle watched him come, still over a mile away on the winding path. She knew the minute he spotted her, because his horse broke into a trot. It warmed her heart till she thought it might catch on fire. She said quietly, "I think I finally got it right, girls. I think I've found a husband to be proud of and a father for the lot of you to love."

"I hope it's the other way around, Ma," Sarah said. "I want him to be a husband for you to love and a father for us to be proud of."

Belle laughed. "Maybe we can have it all."

She saw Sarah nodding with quiet satisfaction, and at the same instant, all three of them, with Betsy on Emma's back, started trotting forward.

The two parties met at an unlikely spot on the trail. There

wasn't a spot wide enough for them to dismount and stand before the preacher. And the preacher had a disgruntled, kidnapped look to him. The horses looked exhausted, and there was snow clinging to the preacher's boots.

"It's snowing in the highlands. Let's make this quick so the man can get back through the pass," Silas said.

It might not have been the shortest wedding ceremony on record, but that's only because no one kept records of such things. It had to be in contention.

The preacher was still pulling his horse to a stop when he said, "Silas Harden, do you take this woman to be your lawful-wedded wife?"

Silas grinned as he dragged his Stetson off his head, "Well, why else did I drag you all the way up here?"

"Just answer, 'I do.'" The preacher glared at him in a way that didn't strike Belle as all that holy.

"I do."

"And do you, Belle Tanner, take this man to be your lawful-wedded husband?" The preacher wheeled his horse to face Belle who was just riding up and turning her horse so she was beside Silas. She'd heard the first question put to Silas, though, so it counted.

Before she could answer, Silas reached over and grabbed her hand. "Aren't you gonna tell her to obey me? I think you oughta say it 'cuz she's a headstrong little thing."

The preacher snapped at Belle, "Are you gonna obey him?" His horse danced sideways toward the edge of a fifty-foot drop-off at the unusually testy voice coming from the peaceful, God-loving man who sat on his back.

Belle leaned across her horse and subdued the fractious mount before they lost their parson. "Not likely, unless he orders me to do something I was gonna do anyway."

The preacher looked at Silas. "I've known Belle for a while now. I could have told you that."

"But it's a promise before God, isn't it?" Silas asked in astonishment. "It's required."

Since Belle had his horse, the preacher felt safe enough to take off his broad-brimmed felt hat as was due respect for the current occasion. He tapped it impatiently on his Bible. "Now there's no sense making Belle take a vow before God that she doesn't have a ghost of a chance of keeping. It'd be a sin to my way of thinking. So, if you want her so all-fired bad—and the way you as good as stole me out of the diner in Divide tells me you do—then take her without 'obey' and shut up about it. It's all the same to me, and I'm leaving here in thirty seconds whether you're hitched or not. Now, no offense, folks, but I don't want to spend my winter with you. Do you know I've got a wife expecting a baby in January?"

"I already said I'd take her," Silas protested. "It's her vows we're speaking of now."

Belle said, "I do."

"I do what?" Silas growled. "I do take this man, or I do know about his wife having a baby?"

The preacher slapped his hat back on his head, leaned over, and wrested his reins out of Belle's hand. "Thank you kindly for holding Blackie, Belle. Much obliged. Try to keep this one alive for a while. These weddings are wearing me out." The preacher turned his horse and started up the trail. After about twenty yards, he stopped and turned around and yelled, "I almost forgot. I now pronounce you man and wife!" He wheeled his horse around and headed at a gallop for the summit.

"Will he make it? How bad is the pass?" Belle worried. "We should follow him and make sure he's all right."

"It's not bad and the snow's not real heavy. With the trail we broke, he'll be fine. Besides, his wife found out I was hauling him out of town, and she was after me with a posse before we were out of sight. We stayed ahead of her, but she'll be waiting to haul him down off the mountain if he should run into trouble. That is one tough woman!" Silas leaned across the space between his horse and Belle's. Sliding one hand firmly behind Belle's neck, he said, "You may now kiss the bride." And he did just that.

Sarah yelled, "Hurray!"

Betsy clapped her hands together and yelled, "Papa."

"High time," Emma said. "We got evening chores. Let's get back to the ranch."

Silas let go of Belle, and she touched her lips to keep the warmth in them. "Yeah," Silas said with a sparkle in his eye. "Let's go home, girls."

Belle smiled at him with a heart that felt younger and a spirit that felt lighter than it had since before her pa had given her to William. "Yes, girls, let's take the new husband and go home."

Silas laughed and kissed her again. When he was close enough that only she could hear, he said, "You're gonna forget you ever had another husband 'sides me before I'm done with you, Mrs. Harden."

"I already have," Belle said peacefully.

They all turned their horses for home, and the animals were anxious to get out of the sharp winter weather in the highlands, so they moved along willingly.

It was the happiest day of Belle's life.

CHAPTER 22

Belle was furious.

She'd been cheated. She had been done so wrong she thought she might dig up all three of her no-account husbands and beat the daylights out of whatever was left of their worthless hides.

Nestling closer to Silas as he slept, she knew, after three earlier marriages, she'd never known what went on between a man and a woman!

Silas's eye flickered open when she moved, and she forgot all about being mad. "Good morning, wife. You enjoying our honeymoon?" He'd made up a warm little bed for them in the barn and teased the girls that he was taking their ma on a honeymoon. Now they lay here, toasty warm, wrapped in blankets, wrapped in each other.

"Morning, Silas."

He pulled her closer till her cheek rested on his shoulder, close enough that when he looked into her eyes there was nothing else in the world. Then he leaned close and kissed her. No whiskers. He'd looked like a wild man when she married him. He hadn't taken a second to bathe or shave or even change into clean clothes

242

before the wedding. But he'd done all that later, after that poor excuse for a ceremony but long before the wedding night. He'd cleaned up real good.

Wrapping one strong arm around her shoulders, he pulled her still closer. "You're not ready to plant me under the Husband Tree yet, are you?" He kissed her, probably to help get the answer he wanted.

He needn't have bothered.

"Nope, I'm going to keep you above ground. I like you all warm and—" Their eyes met and her nonsense suddenly seemed unworthy. The smile melted off her face. "Don't speak of such things, Silas." She slid one hand into his overly long hair. "I want you with me for the rest of my life. I can't bear to think of that tree right now."

Moving with almost desperate speed, she flung her arms around his neck and kissed him. His arms closed around hers and held her tight. "You're not getting rid of me, Belle."

His words were interrupted by her lips. "I've survived—" He went on, in broken sentences, "A long time in this land." He tossed in words between the kissing. "I know my way around." The gleam in his eyes made her wonder if they were still talking about ranching and his long life. "You're stuck with me."

"I am, aren't I?" She thought now of the glow in Lindsay's eyes the morning after her wedding and knew that Lindsay was already more of a woman than Belle had ever been.

But that was before last night.

"This is my first real wedding night." She turned her thoughts from the others, only able to control a shudder at those memories because of where she was now and the strength and warmth of Silas's arms.

And although she was furious at her husbands, she wasn't going to dig them up after all, because she was too contented to move.

"We need to get going," Belle murmured. "The girls will have breakfast on by now. We're sleeping the day away."

"We're not sleeping, darlin'."

Which Belle had to admit was the plain truth. "But I need to check the herd. And I never did a good check on the saddle stock yesterday and—"

Silas quieted her right down. He drove every thought of work and the ranch and even her girls from her mind.

They got into breakfast late.

The girls were dressed and cooking. Sarah had outdone herself to make it a celebration. They had eggs she'd scrounged up just this morning. There were hotcakes on the grill. She'd sliced into a new side of bacon and shredded raw potatoes and onions into hash browns. They were all so starving for food that wasn't laced with the flavor of trail dust that they ate like field hands, which, when it came right down to it, was exactly what they all were.

After they were sitting over their second cups of coffee, Silas announced, "This cabin is a disaster. It needs at least one more bedroom, and I've got to patch the holes in it before the snow falls. Which one of your worthless husbands built this wreck for you, Belle honey?"

An extended silence filled the room. Sarah's eyes widened, and Belle could see she was trying to think of a way to warn Silas off dangerous ground. Emma slumped low in her chair as if she had been awaiting the first fight—and now here it came.

Belle set her coffee cup down with the sharp *click* of tin on wood. "I built it myself."

Silas looked around for a long minute. "Well, in that case, I think it's wonderful. In fact, I wouldn't change a thing."

"You wouldn't change a thing?" Belle roared. "Why, this place is falling down around our ears."

Silas grinned at her until she quit snarling. When she finally did, he started chuckling, softly at first then louder. He gasped over his laughter, "You said it. I didn't." Then he started laughing again.

Belle threw her coffee cup at him. But no one took it seriously, because it was both tin and empty. Silas just ducked and kept laughing. Before long the whole table was laughing along with him.

Silas finally managed to say, "Then I have your permission to fix a few things, Mrs. Harden?"

"Oh, Silas," Belle said ardently, "if only you would."

Silas rose from his end of the table and rounded it to pull Belle out of her chair. He took the seat she'd just vacated and dropped her right onto his lap. He kissed her with a resounding *smack*, then stood and returned her to the seat and just as easily returned to his own chair. "I'll have the frame up before nightfall or your name isn't. . . C'mon, sweetheart, this is a test. What's your name these days?"

"It's Belle Harden. *Mrs. Silas Harden*." Her heart pounded from that kiss and from how much she loved her new name. "And from this day forward, all the girls are Hardens, too." Belle nodded firmly to her girls, and they all nodded back just as confidently. No fussy legal formalities needed for the Harden clan.

Silas said with exaggerated severity, "And don't any of you ever forget it."

He got up from the table, dusting his hands as if one chore was done—naming his family. "Point me to the tools. Have you got an ax? I need to cut some trees."

Silas clamped his Stetson on his head and started for the door. He stopped suddenly. "No, the house isn't first. I need to ride out and check the cattle. We need to get them closer in, off the summer pasture, before their grazing in the highlands is buried under ten feet of snow. I need to check them over and make sure none are sick or injured, and I ought to do a tally before winter so we have some

245

idea of what to expect for calves in the spring." Silas dragged his hat off his head as he stood in front of the open door and stared across the rugged land.

"I'll get started on all of that." Belle got up from the table and went to his side. "Let me do it while you work on the house."

"It's not gonna be that way, Belle." Silas shook his head. "You are done doing a man's work around here. I'll just have to push hard with the tally and get to the cabin later. We've got two months before the weather closes in on us, maybe more."

"No!" Belle shouted.

Silas jumped and gave her a wary look. "Belle, I know what the preacher said about obeying, and I know you're not used to stepping aside when there's work to be done. That's one of the things I love most about you. And I'm not trying to give you orders. I'm just trying to begin this marriage as I mean for it to go on. I want to make your life easier."

"I didn't mean to holler at you, Silas. I'm not fighting with you over giving up my work. Believe me, I'd like nothing better than to run this house and leave most of the outdoor chores to you. The problem is, if we mean to have this house enlarged and sealed up before winter, you're going to have to hurry. We *might* have two months, but sometimes we get an early snow that surprises us. Let me keep on at the cattle chores for a few days. A week or two while you set yourself to working on the house. I can do the cattle, but I am a poor excuse for a carpenter. I guess I yelled because we don't have much time and. . ." Belle leaned so close her chin rested on his chest, and murmured so the girls couldn't hear, "I want our own room so bad."

Silas pulled his gaze away from the horizon and looked down at her. Somehow, even though he wasn't a huge man, not as tall as any of her other husbands, he made her feel small and feminine. He rested his open hand on her cheek. "You've done better here than any woman could have. Better than most *men* could have.

Don't you speak badly of yourself because the house you built with your own hands isn't good enough. Look what you've built here, and I'm not talking just about the cabin and barn. I'm talking about the sweet bunch of daughters, the herd, the money you've earned, plenty more things; all of this is yours and your girls', and it's something to be proud of. I wish. . ." Silas's chin dropped and he didn't meet her eyes. "I wish I could have brought more into this marriage, Belle. It isn't honorable for a poor man to come to a rich woman with his hands empty."

"Rich woman?" Belle had never thought of herself in such a way.

"Yes, that's exactly what you are. You have this whole spread paid for and two thousand-plus head of cattle and fifteen thousand dollars cash money in that bag you brought home. I reckon you're as rich as anyone in the state these days. I reckon I'm just another sorry excuse for a husband around here. This"—he waved his hand at the expanse of open pasture broken by clumps of trees and rocky outcroppings that spread out before them—"all this is yours. I want to contribute something more than I can right now. I'm going to add to it and put everything I have of myself in it, but it'll take time, and I. . .well, I have an idea." He looked up at her like he was almost scared.

Belle's heart turned over to see him so vulnerable.

"I'm not sure if it'll work, and I want to accomplish it before I talk about it."

"What idea, Silas?"

Silas lay his hand over hers where it rested on his chest. More than ever she wanted that new bedroom built on. The barn was going to get mighty cold before long.

"Hush now." Silas lay his finger over her lips. "I'll tell you about it when I'm ready. If I tell you now, knowing you, little woman, you'll just treat my idea like it's a cantankerous bull. You'll grab it by the horns and wrestle it right into line all on your own. For now,

I'll. . ." A shadow passed over his expression, and Belle knew he was unhappy about what he was going to say. "I'll do it your way and let you keep on with the cattle, but only for the time it takes me to get this place spruced up and get some headway on"—he hunched one shoulder and said dismissively in a way that made Belle worry that she'd somehow wounded his pride—"my idea."

His touch was so tender and his eyes so full of regret at letting her work at her cattle and having so little to contribute to their marriage that Belle wanted to take him off somewhere where they could be alone and cheer him right up.

He seemed to read her mind, because the wistfulness was gone out of his eyes. He leaned over and kissed her. "Just promise me you'll leave all the real hard labor to me. Just do your tally and keep track of any animals that need attention. I'll do the rest." With what sounded like honest regret, he added, "At first, I reckon I'm going to end up being as worthless as your other husbands, but only for a while. . . ."

"Don't you dare say that, Silas Harden. You've already done more for me than all three of those worthless old coots put together, so don't you ever lump yourself in with them again."

"Yeah, I noticed you enjoyed our. . .honeymoon." He smiled with heat in his eyes.

She slapped his shoulder. "I meant on the cattle drive."

Laughing, Silas said, "Oh, that's right. I do remember helping you out a bit during that."

"You work on the cabin, and whatever this idea is of yours, you go do it with my blessing."

Silas tucked one finger under her chin and tilted her face a bit and looked into her eyes for a long moment. Then, as if satisfied with her sincerity, he gave her a brisk nod and slapped his hat on his head. "I'll get on with chopping down some timber."

"I can help, Pa." Emma got up from the table. "I can hook a line to the logs and drag them back here."

Silas looked over at the girls, and Belle had the impression that Silas had forgotten they had an audience. She knew how he felt. Sometimes it seemed as if they were alone in the world.

"*Pa*," Silas said with quiet satisfaction. "I really like that, Emma. I'm mighty proud to have you call me that." He took two steps to where the girls had stood watching them hash out their chores and wrapped Emma and Sarah, with Betsy in Sarah's arms, in a bear hug. He even growled while he did it. He hugged them long and hard, and for just a second, with an especially big growl, he lifted all three of them off the floor. Sarah giggled.

He set them all down and said to Emma, "No, you're not helping. Those logs have a way of rolling wild on a person. I don't want you in the way. I can use your help when I'm back here, but I don't want you on that mountainside with falling trees."

Belle saw Emma's eyes shine. No man had ever told her no when she offered to work before, and no man had ever acted like her safety was more important than the strength in her back.

Belle remembered how she'd struggled with trees, bringing them down here. One of the reasons she'd built where she did was because there was a nice stand of young growth ponderosa pines at this spot and she could get the logs from where they fell to the house site.

Later she found out this area had a stream of water flowing through it in the rainy season that turned the ranch yard into a mud hole and the corral and barn into a swamp. The wind whipped into the cabin with nothing to stop it, but a couple of miles of clear sailing to pick up speed. The snow tended to blow into deep drifts all around them, and they didn't get any afternoon sun at all.

She'd had Lindsay on her back or toddling around her feet while she built it. Before she was done with the barn, she'd had Emma growing big in her belly. She'd only wanted a roof over her head, and she never thought to consider such things as spring flooding and afternoon sun when she'd begun struggling with the logs and the ornery horses and the lackadaisical William.

Thinking of Silas's gift for quick, tight construction, as he'd demonstrated on Lindsay's house, she got excited for what was to come and hadn't a single qualm about keeping up her grueling work with the cattle. She didn't have any plans to spare herself work and leave all the toughest jobs for Silas either. He didn't deserve to have every task on this ranch settled on his shoulders from the first minute.

Silas said to Emma, "For now, I hope you don't mind helping your ma with the cattle still. It won't be for long. I promise."

"No. No, Pa. I'll help her gladly. I never figured to quit anyway. I'm happier on horseback than I am in the kitchen. Even when you're done with the house, I want to keep riding herd."

"I'll always need help, I'm afraid." Then Silas looked at Sarah. "And I can't believe someone so young can turn her hand to a kitchen and take such good care of us like you do, Sarie. You're gonna not have much extra help for a while either. I didn't want it to be this way, but for now it's gotta be."

"I like being called Sarie," Sarah said with pink-tinged cheeks. "I never had a nickname before, Pa."

Silas tapped her nose with one finger. "I gotta get on with it or we'll be having snowflakes for breakfast one of these next days. Now, you all"—he tossed a glance around the room that included all of them—"quit making a man want to stay inside to spend time with his pretty girls and let me get to work!"

He flashed them a grin so handsome that Belle's heart seemed to be melting right inside her chest.

He hugged the girls again, and as he passed Belle, he grabbed her and dipped her backward over his arm and kissed away every brain cell she had in her head. He'd been gone for several minutes before any of them thought to get on with the day's work.

Belle heard herself sigh. She had it real bad. Then she smiled at the girls. "Let's get to work."

She went out to saddle up a bronco. As the horse crow hopped across the corral to work out its morning kinks, she took a moment to give thanks for Silas Harden. She'd always believed, but now she had actual living proof.

There really was a God.

CHAPTER 23

There really was a devil, too!

The pointy-horned, pitchfork-toting sidewinder had put one over on her again!

Silas Harden and his stupid *idea*! Belle was getting real sick of the fact that she hadn't seen hide nor hair of Silas since she married him. Except at mealtimes and bedtimes, of course. He was always right on time for those.

He'd fixed the house up to a point, tossing together a bedroom and patching a few of the worst cracks to cut the wind. Near as she could figure that had taken him about three days. He'd done nothing since.

Belle and Emma took a few days working the kinks out of their green-broke horses that they'd left behind while on the drive. They'd next thing to gone pure wild again with a month's neglect. Belle hoped to have them gentled by spring. She'd been a steady supplier of well-trained horses for the area ranchers. And Emma had a special gift for it. They'd make good money on this year's horse crop.

Still, it was a spine-jarring business getting into the saddle most mornings. Once the cayuse she picked out for this morning worked out its nerves, she turned to Emma. "Where's Silas?"

"He was gone when I got up." Emma shrugged. "He took the roan today and a bunch of the tools. I reckon he's working on something for the house."

"But *what* for the house? The extra room has been done for a full week."

"Now, Ma, don't go to nagging at Pa. He's been a purely good husband so far."

Belle had to admit that was the honest truth. When she thought about the way Silas had pulled them over that mountain trail with pure grit and iron will, her loved bubbled up like a spring. She'd never met a man she respected more. So, whatever he was doing, she'd trust it was for the best. "He did a good job with that spare room. I don't know much about building. Maybe he's fixing things I don't even notice. I've been gone for long hours. He could come and go ten times and I'd never notice it."

"We could ask Sarah. She's keeping Betsy in the house or around the ranch yard while she works. She'd see him during the day."

"We've got to get going this morning. I'm not going to start in nagging on this one. I promise."

Emma jerked her chin in satisfaction. "What are we workin' on today?"

Belle kicked her horse who seemed content to stretch his legs with her on his back. "That high rise. I've got a herd of longhorns that think they're mountain goats. I wanted to see how many calves are up there."

"Didn't Pa tell you to leave the herds that are hard to get to?"

"He did, but he thinks he's got a long time to work before winter comes. He's new to this area. I'm not going to sit around resting and leave everything to him while he's working so hard on the house. That ain't nice."

"No, it surely ain't. But that's a tough trail up there." Emma fell in beside Belle. "It'd like to scare any sensible cow into a dead faint, but not these critters."

The trail got narrow. Belle and Emma strung out to single file. They quit talking so they could attend to dodging pine trees trying to slap them in the face.

The two of them drove the bulk of those crazy mountain-climbing cattle down closer to the house. All of them took turns trying to go back to the highlands. But once they finally came down and found lush grass, they settled in to eating, and Belle knew they'd stay where the living was easy. Cattle and men: The only real difference was she could sell cattle off and earn real cash money.

This was one of many far-flung groups of cattle Belle needed to check. She'd been burned so badly by miscounting her herd last spring that she was afraid to be slipshod again. She'd check every square inch of her land before the snow fell or know the reason why.

Knowing Silas wouldn't like the brutally hard day she'd had, Belle kept her work to herself in front of him, and so did Emma, to keep from hurting his feelings.

Wade found a line shack far enough from the Flathead village to not be on their hunting ground. The cabin was ramshackle, ten feet by ten feet or so, with a shanty in the back big enough for his horse and nothing else.

He was drawn to Glowing Sun so powerfully that he could go no farther from her. But she'd left him. Gone off, just as Cassie Dawson had. Just as his mother had. Wade had let Cassie torment him until he'd lost his way completely, before finding his way in the end to God.

Tempted to go to Red and Cassie for advice, Wade felt God telling him it was time to stand on his own. Time to focus on his own strange longing to save a woman in need.

Sometimes he caught the slimmest memories of fairy tales his mother had read to him. And maybe he remembered his pa shouting at his ma. The ogres in those fairy tales and the monster that was his father were twisted together and added to by years of fear. The damsels in distress, the heroic white knights. . . Wade couldn't decide what of his memories were true.

Was the shouting from later years? Pa had done plenty of it. And Wade's longing for memories of his mother got mixed in. Whether it was memory or not, Wade knew it was time to stop thinking about saving someone else and find a way to save himself.

Not his soul. God had done that. But he needed wisdom to save himself from making the same mistakes over and over again. He knew he was lonely. It might be because he didn't like his own company. How better to get over that than to force himself to be alone.

This line shack would be a retreat for him. A refuge. He'd winter here, hunt for food, read his Bible, search his soul. He welcomed the coming snow that would trap him inside and keep him from the almost irresistible need to ride to Glowing Sun.

He sank onto the tattered blankets of the single narrow cot. The bed squeaked with protest under his weight, but it held.

Wade buried his face in the Bible clutched in his hands. Why would Glowing Sun choose him? He was a weakling. She'd chosen a warrior.

The strength he needed seemed beyond his grasp, at least for today, and he covered his eyes with one hand and cried.

The snow that would keep him from making a fool of himself over a woman who didn't want him couldn't come soon enough.

❧

Belle raced against the coming winter.

She rode out with Emma most days, though sometimes it

made more sense to split up.

Leaving the cabin right after breakfast, Belle usually didn't even see Silas, who was up and out before dawn. She came back to the cabin to feed Betsy, and he was never around. Some days, if the weather looked to hold decent, she'd head for the farther reaches of her land, and she'd take Betsy along and nurse her on horseback and eat jerked beef and hard biscuits and not get back to the cabin all day.

Silas would be there looking for all the world like a horse that had been rode hard and put up wet.

She was exhausted herself and not given to making idle talk with anyone. And when they were alone, talking was the furthest thing from their minds.

They'd been married for two weeks the first time she'd asked him, sitting at the dinner table, what was keeping him so busy.

Silas laid down his fork as if the food suddenly tasted bad. Then he looked at his plate as if he couldn't meet her eyes. "I'm not ready to talk about it, Belle honey. I'm keeping real busy and my...um...*idea* is going to work out fine. I won't be long at it"—he looked up, direct, bossy—"so don't start moving the herd down to the low country without me. I don't want you and Emma out on those passes and mountain slopes. Please trust me, Belle, and be patient. There's plenty of time to get everything done."

There wasn't, and she'd already moved a lot of her herd down. But she didn't correct him, because he looked so sad. She somehow felt like her question shamed him. She wished she hadn't brought it up in front of the girls. He might have been willing to tell her his idea if they'd been alone. He had that sad, sweet look in his eyes. And the way he held her that night made her feel so content she didn't care what the man did during the day.

The next morning she and Emma cleared downed branches from the spreader dam Belle had built years ago. There was no way to get the branches out except to wade in after them. Belle wore her oldest clothes.

"There's no reason I can't come in there, too, Ma. It'd go faster."

Shaking her head, Belle said, "Then Sarah would have to come out and drag the windfalls away. Someone has to do that." Belle shuddered to think of Emma in this bitter cold. "I can last for about an hour in here and that's enough. There's no reason for both of us to get soaking wet."

"Did you tell Pa you were doing this today?"

Belle shoved a long, many-limbed branch to the shore.

Emma grabbed hold and dragged it away from the edge so the first good rain wouldn't wash it back in to clog up the dam.

"I was going to, but you saw how he acted last night. What am I supposed to do? Kick up a fuss? Pester him to help me? You're the one who told me not to start in nagging."

"I know I said that. But I never figured him for a lazy man. Not after the cattle drive. And he was a rancher before. He knows what needs doing. Why isn't he helping us?"

Belle heard Emma's concern. It had more to do with frustration because Belle wouldn't let the girl wade into the bitter cold water than with being real upset at Silas.

"I don't know, honey. Why do you think?" Belle was as mystified as Emma.

"Maybe it's a husband thing. Maybe instead of marrying him you should have just kept him around as a hired man. I wonder how Lindsay is doing? You suppose she has to take care of all three of those men?" Emma shook her head and worked quietly while Belle waded out for another clump stuck against the earthen dam she'd mounted up across a spring runoff.

Belle was determined not to nag, so she bided her time. A week later, when they were alone in the tidy little room he'd erected, she'd thought the moment was right. "So, tell me about your idea, Silas. I want to know—" She broke off her question. Because what she wanted to say was, *I want to know what you're doing all day every day when you should be working this ranch.* And there was no way to say that right. So she let the question hang.

Silas smiled at her, came close, and caught her hands. "My idea is coming along great. Today I—" Silas's words cut off as he lifted her hands into his and looked down at the calluses. The glow faded from his eyes, and he ran a thumb over the roughness, as if he were personally responsible.

"Belle, the West is a hard land, and it's particularly hard on women and children. But you're the strongest woman I've ever known." He held her work-roughened hand for a long while, palm up.

He'd been going to talk. She knew that. So whatever he was doing must be all right. She imagined his clearing a pasture of felled trees or building fence, something to surprise her. But her ugly hands distracted him. She wished she could be a pampered and beautiful woman, but it wasn't in her nature.

Lifting her hand, he pressed the palm to his lips. The way she shivered from his touch made her think of being even closer, and she knew she had about five seconds to head that off.

Not that she wanted to. She just wanted to finish questioning him.

She pulled her hands away. "Don't, Silas. I want us to talk. We never spend any time really talking. What do you have planned for tomorrow, because I. . ."

His strong hands tipped her head back. "You are more than just strong. You're beautiful, too." He whispered that nonsense against her windburned cheek and acted as if he were starving hungry for her chapped lips.

"And sweet." Gently, he captured her hands again and pressed her palms against his cheeks.

"And soft where it counts." Turning from her lips, he began kissing each callus, taking a side trip back to her mouth from time to time.

"Your eyes shine like gold." He kissed each eye.

She found that she couldn't open them again after his gentle caress. "Silas," Belle whispered, trying to remember what she'd wanted to talk about.

"I love your hair down, like liquid silk in my hands." He touched her hair, her coarse, neglected hair, as if he couldn't deny himself the pleasure.

They never did go back to their talk.

And she never for a moment considered going after him with a frying pan.

After he was long gone the next day, she remembered.

She needed to move the cattle from a particularly dangerous stretch of high-up pasture, and she didn't want Emma out on the rocky ledges they'd have to traverse. She was especially worried about it because a wolf pack had moved into her mountain valley. They kept her hopping trying to track them down while she rushed ahead of the oncoming winter.

She should probably tell Silas about the troublesome wolves, but she knew he'd say, "Leave it for me." That's all he ever said. But Belle was finished listening to empty promises. Time was short. She'd hoped she could convince him to abandon his *idea* for just a day and come with her.

"I've gotta go to the north high pasture today, Em. I'll take Betsy along." She'd faced that last high ridge alone before. She'd do it again.

"Let me ride with you, Ma. Them wolves are a mean bunch this year."

"We've got to finish the haying. If you stay in and put in a long day on that and I get these cattle tallied, we're done with the worst of the fall chores. I don't like the feel of the wind. I want both of these things done today."

"But you shouldn't go so far alone."

"I've done it many times."

Emma stared at her.

Belle stared back. She could boss her children around just fine, but usually they agreed on things together. And Emma could smell snow on the wind as well as Belle.

Finally, Emma nodded. "You'll be late. But I'll be watching for you, too, Ma. We'll put in a tough day today; then things'll calm down. Who knows, maybe even Silas'll stay around once the wind starts blowing. Anthony did."

"Only 'cuz the pass was closed. Whatever Silas is up to must be somewhere inside the valley." Betsy shifted in the pack on Belle's back and cooed through her bundling.

"Are you sure?" Emma eyed the horizon, turning in all directions. "He could be riding into Divide every day."

Belle froze. She'd never considered that. Could he possibly be going in to find whiskey? "No, he's not drinking. I'd know the smell." But if he was careful, would she know? And would she know about dance-hall girls if he was careful to wash their perfume away? Anthony had done that at first.

Belle shook her head. A painful cracking feeling in her heart made her wonder for the first time if Silas might be betraying her. "Well, we'll know for sure one of these days." She briskly pulled on her gloves. "Until we do, I've got cattle to round up."

Emma nodded, her face calm, but Belle had seen that calm falter for a minute. Emma loved Silas, too. "And I've got haying to do."

The two women swung up on horseback. Belle, with Betsy, rode upland. Emma rode down. Heaven only knew where Silas rode.

Belle mused on Silas, denying he would drink or be untrue to her. But where could he be? She'd been all over the range. Then she realized she'd never gone near that high valley someone had claimed. Could Silas be doing something in that direction? She brought all the cattle down from up there before the drive and figured not to check that land again until spring.

For that matter, she'd never told Silas someone had claimed it. If he was working over there, she needed to tell him to quit. But why would he be over there? They'd been home over a month now, and she knew no further progress was being made with the house. When he watched her with those sad eyes, it didn't cut quite so deep.

She traveled up-country with her rifle on her saddle and her six-gun strapped down, because the wolves were coming in closer to the place following the herd. She'd already thinned the pack some, but there were plenty left. She'd had wolves all the years she'd been here, and although the pack this year was especially large and more aggressive than most, she didn't think much of their nonsense. She accepted a certain loss of cattle as the way things were but fought all the time to keep the losses small.

She worked a long, cold day in the rugged hills, dodging longhorns as wild and vicious as any grizzly. She'd be late getting home, but after today there would be no more long, bitter days. Only short, bitter ones with a husband who'd once again failed her. Before she headed home, she sat down in a sheltered spot to build a fire, have some coffee, and see to Betsy.

The little girl had stayed strapped on Belle's back all day with barely a sound—except for a few necessary breaks that had also required a fire. It had slowed Belle down some.

Once Betsy was settled, Belle packed her horse and swung up. She rode a mile downhill until she came to an open meadow. Only then did she realize the weather had turned sharply colder during the day. Up until now the timber had cut the force of the wind. It was already late. Because Belle had no plans to come up here again until spring, she'd stuck it out doing everything that was needed.

She rode on for hours, winding closer to home with still a long, long way to go, when the cold got to be too much. Belle chafed at the delay, but she'd known she had to see to Betsy at least one more time, and she couldn't unwrap the baby without a fire. She found an overhang, got a good fire going, and settled herself comfortably into a corner with the rock wall behind her.

And suddenly she was waking up.

She'd only awakened because Betsy started crying in the bundle of blankets nestled beside her on the ground. Belle sat forward quickly, shocked at herself for falling asleep. Her stomach lurched then dived hard, and she just barely managed to set Betsy down and crawl a few steps away before she threw up in the grass.

When she quit retching, she wiped her mouth and slowly sat back down. Alerted by a particularly loud squall from Betsy, she unwrapped her baby, just over nine months old, and put her to her breast, which Belle noticed now was tender.

Belle was no schoolgirl still in pinafores. She'd been up and down this trail before.

She held Betsy in the waning light and stroked the cheeks that were hollow and too tanned for a baby.

And Belle Harden cried.

She was going to have another one. Another precious little baby. She could already picture a little girl who looked just like Silas. A little girl who was too quiet because she was raised on horseback by a ma who didn't have time to fuss over every little whimper.

God, please let it be a girl.

That same old prayer. The one she'd spoken into so many lonely nights.

Belle remembered what it had been like when she had Emma growing in her and Lindsay strapped on her back. She'd built the cabin in that condition and rode herd for long days just like this. Surviving that year and the one after, with Lindsay a harum-scarum three-year-old and Emma at her breast, had taken every ounce of strength she had.

And these two, Betsy and the new one, would be almost that close in age. She thought of the branding time to come in the spring. She would be trying to brand these vicious, wild two-year-old bulls and heifers she'd scared out of the hills as well as the spring calves. Last spring had almost killed her. Dozens of times she'd been kicked or knocked to the ground. She accepted the rough-and-tumble ways of branding. But more than once she'd taken a hard blow to the belly because she was almost due to have Betsy and her stomach was in the way something fierce. More than one night she'd lain in bed and felt pains start then ease off, and she knew it was the brutally hard work that was pushing the baby to come before time.

Anthony had of course done none of the spring work. Claimed he had a bad back.

This spring she wouldn't be quite as close to due, but it would be bad enough. And if the baby did come, unlike Betsy who was close to ready to face the world, this baby would be too young. She stood a good chance of killing the poor little baby with her work.

God, please let it be a girl.

The fear and sorrow of that made her wish the baby away, and Belle hated herself for that. No baby deserved to come into the world with a mother who felt such awful things. She *loved* her girls. She was grateful to God for giving her every one of them, because her life would be empty without them. But she was a bad mother.

Belle admitted the real reason she cried was because she was going to give birth to another little girl who would never know a mother's time or soft hands. A little girl who was going to have to get tough, grow up hard, and quit wanting a mother's tenderness fast.

She looked down at Betsy who was nursing with her eyes wide open, staring at her sobbing mother. Betsy reached her thin, brown hand up and rested it on the swell of Belle's breast and opened and closed her hand as if to massage more milk for herself.

Belle wiped her eyes against the sleeve of her buffalo-hide coat and slid her work-roughened finger into the tiny hand.

Betsy clutched onto Belle and kicked as she nursed.

"I'm sorry I haven't been better to you, baby." With her voice breaking, Belle pulled her knees up to more completely cradle her neglected little angel and tried to sing a lullaby, stopping several times as she sorted through her mind for a song that wasn't one she sang to the cattle on the drive at night. She couldn't think of any, and that made her cry some more.

In the end, she just hummed and cried and let Betsy hold her finger. She tried to remember the last time she'd sung to her baby. And when she couldn't think of a single time, she cried all the harder.

Through her tears she thought of Silas. She thought of his charm with the girls and his gift for making her feel like a beautiful woman when she was so far from being one.

It was all lies. She knew that now. Yes, he'd worked hard beside them on the trail, and he'd been nothing short of heroic helping them get home. But now she could see that it had all been lies. He'd worked his way into her life; then he'd turned into another man who used her.

Exhausted from the early morning and the hard day and from growing a new life inside her, she slid down until she lay on the ground and curled her body around both her hungry old baby and her hungry new baby who was already making demands on her strength.

She'd known keen disappointment with all her husbands, but none had ever hurt like this. And it wasn't because he'd turned out to be lazy. It wasn't because he'd charmed the girls into loving him. They were so starved for a man to admire them that they would have fallen for anyone who spared them a single kind word. And it wasn't because he had lied, at least lied to Belle's way of thinking, because he'd let her believe he would hop out of the cart and pull along with her instead of going along for the ride like the other husbands.

It was because she loved him.

That love cut into her heart now like a dull-edged knife and carved out a piece of herself that Silas had awakened and warmed. Her love for him died along with her hope. She was going to have to go on handling the ranch just as she always had. She had been a fool, weak and stupid to want someone to carry the load. She deserved this. She had long ago learned she had to take care of herself. But now she knew, deep inside of her, she'd always clung to a tiny ray of hope that someone would come along and rescue her like she was some pathetic damsel in distress out of a fairy tale.

Well, there was no rescue coming. And she was no damsel. She was a cowpoke and a good one, and she was never going to be anything else.

Then she thought of the years ahead of her when she was going to have to be strong enough to deny Silas his husbandly rights. That had never been hard with the other husbands, but now the wonderful pleasure he'd introduced her to would have to die, too. If she didn't keep him away, there would be more babies— the ones she took such poor care of. When he'd shown her how it could be between a man and a woman, she had longed for Silas's baby. She had pictured herself with four more little girls, these girls chubby with light brown eyes and tawny brown hair streaked with gold from the sun. Silas's girls wore ruffles and were easy to make smile, and her other girls fit right in with them, learning to laugh and dress pretty and work in the house.

Now she knew that for a fool's dream. It would be impossible, because she didn't have the strength to give Silas all his babies and run this ranch, too. In that moment she hated Silas Harden. She hated him for making her love him and for teaching her about what could pass between a man and a woman and most of all for giving her hope.

MARY CONNEALY

She grieved for another neglected little baby girl.

God, please let me be strong enough to survive this new mess I've made of my life. Forgive me for marrying him. Forgive me for being such a fool.

Crooning to Betsy, Belle wished the baby could forgive her. But Betsy would never know what had been taken from her.

Wrenching tears wrung straight out of Belle's heart, until finally she slept before the slowly dying fire.

CHAPTER 24

Silas laughed out loud in the chilly night. He was done.

Well, not all the way done. But close enough he could finally share his idea with his womenfolk. Tell them what he'd been up to for the last month.

Knowing he was hours late for supper, he pushed his horse hard, but the animal was game and rested from lazing the day away while Silas worked. They made good time, and Silas imagined being the hero to his women. Hugs and kisses and all that would come his way when he finally told them about his idea.

He shouldn't have stayed so long today, but the long month of backbreaking work was worth it. He was overflowing with the pleasure of it. He knew he could never give to Belle what she'd given to him, but it was something.

It was a lot.

It was enough.

He thought about all Belle had given him. Of course there was the vast land holdings and impressive herd of cattle. But there was so much more. All of it more important than the ranch.

The girls.

"I'm a father." Silas's horse pricked up its ears when Silas spoke aloud, probably figuring his rider had lost his mind.

Grinning, Silas thought of his pretty, hardworking girls and patted his mount on the neck. "Never gave that much thought before, boy. If I had, I reckon I'd've thought of children as a heavy burden and a big responsibility. But I never figured it for the fun. I love being a pa to all those girls. I love hearin' the word *Pa* from them." He wouldn't mind having a dozen more of them. Thinking about Belle having his baby was enough to make him slap his hand on the rump of his horse and gallop every step of the way back to the cabin.

No, there was no comparison to what Belle had brought to this marriage compared to what one penniless, cowardly cowpoke brought, but he knew Belle loved him. He returned that love in full measure. It was more than any man had given her before. He wished he had more, but yes, it was enough.

He rode up to the ranch yard under a high, full moon. The cabin had its feeble glow shining out of the cracks in the front door. Except there wasn't much light showing—which meant there weren't as many cracks. That meant the cracks had all been patched. He'd told Belle he'd get to it, but she must not have trusted him to do it. Of course he had no intention of doing it, but still she should have trusted him. Frowning with irritation, he almost let his good mood slip but shoved the crankiness aside as he put his horse up and hurried to the ramshackle house to make his announcement to his girls.

Before he could get there, the door flew open, letting the meager heat out of the cabin.

Sarah called out, "Ma, is that you?"

There was something he'd never heard in his stalwart little Sarah's voice before. Fear. The cold night air whipped around him, but it was Sarah's voice that chilled him.

"No, it's Pa, Sarie. Isn't your ma in yet?" Silas increased his already-hurried stride. His pleasure evaporated. Belle should have been home hours ago.

"Her horse came in alone." Sarah's eyes were shaded by the dark, but Silas could see the furrows in her brow and hear the worry in her voice. "Emma is trying to back-trail him, but it was already almost dark when the horse showed up wearing his saddle and bridle. Emma said he came from the far north where Ma was combing those breaks for any hide-out steers today. Emma headed up there."

"Your ma was up in that steep timberland? I told her to leave that for me." Silas forgot his fear for Belle for just a second as he digested this latest bit of proof that Belle didn't want to move aside as boss and make room for him.

"I reckon she thought she was out of time, Silas." Sarah sounded matter-of-fact. She obviously didn't plan on Silas doing that work either. "Snow comes early up here."

"I know when snow comes," Silas snapped, annoyed with the way Sarah called him by his first name instead of saying, "Pa." He looked at his upset little girl more closely. Her worry for her mother was only part of what the little girl was feeling. He detected a note of. . .resignation. Like the little girl had resigned herself to something, but Silas couldn't think what. And under that, so slight he hoped he misunderstood it, he got an impression of disdain. "Follow me to the barn while I saddle a fresh horse."

Sarah trotted to keep up as he rushed toward the barn. "I should have gone with Emma, but she said I should tell you what'd happened. Emma said you might help."

Silas looked at her, not breaking his stride. "What do you mean, I *might* help? Of course I'm going to help."

Sarah shrugged. "We're used to doing for ourselves."

Silas bit back an angry retort. "How long ago did the horse show up?" Silas had been unusually late. He'd thought he'd come bursting into this tumbledown house and make his big announcement and be greeted like a conquering hero. Instead, the house held only one scared, disrespectful little girl.

"Hours. Emma's been gone for hours. She told me which way Ma rode."

"You can't go, Sarie. You need to stay here and take care of Betsy. Does she have enough to eat?" He knew the baby still nursed.

Sarah grabbed a lasso and went out of the barn to the yard where the riding stock was corralled. Over her shoulder, she said, "Betsy's with her."

"With Emma?" Silas followed her and watched Sarah disobey him and lasso a horse. He clenched his jaw but said nothing. If she wanted to come, she could come.

"No, with Ma."

Silas had been leaving earlier than Belle most mornings. He hadn't realized Belle took the baby along. "She takes Betsy with her to work the cattle?"

"Ma has to take her if she's gonna be gone over a feeding time. How else can she manage?" Sarah led her horse into the barn to where her saddle was kept.

Silas felt a twist of fear as he threw a loop over a fresh horse. Not only was his wife missing, but his baby might be in danger, too. Hopefully the horse had just broken its reins while it was tied up, but anything could happen in the wilderness. His fear bloomed into anger at Belle for putting herself in danger.

He and Sarah were saddled and on the trail in minutes. As they rode out of the yard into the cold night, Silas asked, "Do you know where she was headed exactly? Did she tell you?"

"It weren't no secret, Silas." She guided her horse in the direction she'd said Emma went.

Silas caught up and rode alongside his daughter. "Why are you calling me Silas tonight? I thought you were going to call me Pa."

"You're not my pa is all." Sarah didn't look at him. She just urged her horse a little faster and said over her shoulder, "I forgot

that for a while. And I don't like the name Sarie anymore neither."
She took a narrow trail that headed virtually straight up.

Silas couldn't ride alongside her, so he trailed behind an eight-year-old girl. The little slip of a thing was more in charge of this Tanner Ranch than he was.

As they pushed hard up a trail that was treacherous even in the light, he worried and fumed and prayed for Belle to be all right so he could yell at her until she stopped thinking she was the head of this family.

He made Sarah stop so he could check for tracks. Belle's riderless horse had left a clear trail coming home, and Emma's horse was heading out this same direction. He got on his horse, and Sarah took the lead again.

As the trail ride grew long, Silas turned his mind away from the worry gnawing away like a rat in his gut, knowing panic would do no good. His mind wandered to his news. He'd expected all his girls to be excited.

As they rode, he drew his coat more tightly around his neck against a wind that was increasingly bitter. He tried to set his hurt aside as he thought about his wife and his girls and how happy he was going to make them and how wonderful it was to be part of this family. Then a new idea popped into Silas's head. He'd grown up around women—too many women. He knew more about women than any man ever should, including very personal *female* things. He'd wished long and hard as a boy that he'd be spared the knowledge of a woman's ways. No young man wanted to learn such—but he had.

And that led him to his wife and what womanly event *hadn't* occurred with Belle in their month together. She could be expecting their child.

Silas's heart thumped hard as a quiet assurance settled on his heart as if whispered by the mouth of God. Belle was going to have his baby.

Belle, lost in this vast, cold night with a baby on her back, doing all the work of a ranch hand with no help because she was too stubborn to step aside and give him a chance. And she was carrying his child.

When he got that woman home, he was going to nail her chaps to a rocking chair and make her stay in the house! Things were going to change around here!

He didn't care who had built this place up. He was the husband, and it was the Harden Ranch, and Belle could just accept it and obey him, despite ducking the vow to obey with that infernal weak-kneed preacher.

His hands tightened on his reins and his mount sidestepped a bit until Silas brought himself, and his horse, under control. All that yelling would have to wait until he found Belle and made sure she was safe.

They had been on the trail for hours, and only fear was keeping Silas awake. Sarah wasn't speaking to him—which wasn't like her. She was a talkative little thing.

They got past the steepest part of the ride, and Silas rode up beside her. "You're sure she was going to the north timber?"

"You're a husband." Sarah didn't look at him as she pushed her horse faster. "Don't you ever talk to her? She always tells us where she's going."

Silas didn't like the way he'd been dropped back into the pack of husbands. They all talked about "the husbands" as if they were a group, not worthy of being remembered as individuals. He'd never minded that until all of a sudden he was one of them.

They were overdue for giving the horses a breather anyway, so he reached across and grabbed Sarah's reins and pulled her horse to a stop.

Sarah stared straight forward.

Silas leaned over and caught her chin and pulled it around so she faced him. "Give your horse a rest for a minute. What's going on here? Why are you angry with me?"

Sarah stared at him for a long time, and Silas began to believe he'd been speaking in some strange foreign language. "Talk to me, Sarah. If you're upset with me, say so. Don't be like this, all moody and rude. Just say what's on your mind."

Sarah opened her mouth then closed it again. She inhaled slowly then squared her shoulders. "Ma says it don't do no good to talk to husbands. She says men are all alike and there ain't no point trying to change 'em." Sarah tugged at her reins. "Let's get back to hunting for Ma. We don't have time to sit here yammering while Ma might be in trouble."

Silas didn't let her go. He'd been handling women long before this little one had made her way onto the earth, and he'd be hornswoggled if the contrary little filly would get the best of him. He knew the twisting and turning routes a woman's mind could take, and he knew if she was just a few years older, she'd say, *If you don't know what's wrong, I'm not going to tell you.*

But Sarah was still young for that. Silas thought he could handle her. "You haven't said anything to me that makes sense, Sarie. Say it plain. What did I do?"

Sarah looked at him with that disdainful expression, but Silas knew Sarah wanted to love him. He'd seen her light up too many times over little compliments or simple kindness. "Say anything that's in your head. I won't get mad and I won't punish you. I love you, and I want to know what I did to hurt you."

Sarah's gaze dropped, but Silas still had ahold of her chin so she couldn't forget he was nagging her.

"I think you do love me." She looked back at him. "And I don't reckon you've done anything to hurt me. It's just that. . . we. . .I wanted. . .I hoped you wouldn't be. . .lazy like the other husbands."

"Lazy!" Silas exclaimed, thinking of the long, hard hours he'd been working.

"I thought you'd help us some." Sarah plowed on with her explanation. "But Ma and Emma did the regular fall chores, even patching the cabin, which you said you'd do."

"I will do it." He had no intention of doing it, but that was beside the point. "Winter hasn't come yet. I had some things I needed to do first."

"Winter is here." Sarah shrugged in the bitter cold like she'd heard it all before. "It's time for everything to be done, and everything *is* done."

"What do you mean everything is done?"

"We're ready now for winter if we can just find Ma and get her home safe. It's just like last year, only last year she didn't have Betsy, so it was easier. But she said she did it all with the rest of us girls on her back, so it don't matter. Course the herd was smaller when I was a baby and she was a mite younger."

"You mean she's brought all the cattle in from the summer pastures already?" Silas asked incredulously.

"Well, sure. She has to. You know she cut and stacked the hay."

"But I told her to stop that." Silas's stomach twisted with regret. He'd made her promise him. They'd had a big fight over it and. . . Silas thought back to the night they'd had that set-to. He couldn't remember her actually promising. He'd demanded that she do it and. . .he wasn't sure, but he thought she'd given her word. He'd insisted, ordered her to wait. Then he'd kissed her and her arms had gone around his neck.

No woman as agreeable as Belle could be defying him and lying to him. "I told her I'd do it. She said she only did one small patch that filled in with snow real early. I told her to check the herd and do a tally. I didn't mean for her to round everything up. And to be ready for winter, she'd have to dredge out the ponds and do some branding. There are longhorns to bring in by herself before everything is done."

"She's not by *herself*," Sarah said with narrowed eyes. "Emma helps. And I do sometimes."

"I *told* her to leave that for me." Silas's temper snapped. "I know when winter comes up here, and I could have managed. I told her I had something important to do first, and she said she didn't mind waiting."

"You weren't going to help, Silas!" Sarah jerked her chin free of Silas's grip. "Me and Emma figured that out the day after you started disappearing in the morning and not coming back until suppertime."

"You decided I wasn't going to help over a month ago?" Silas couldn't believe it. They'd all been so nice. So loving. And they were thinking terrible things about him.

"I don't rightly think Ma *ever* expected you to pitch in."

"She didn't expect it? After the cattle drive?" Silas fought to keep his temper from cutting loose on a little girl. She wasn't who needed to hear hollering. It was Belle.

"We don't care that much. We're used to no-account husbands."

Although if Sarah wasn't careful, she might hear a cranky word or two.

"And you're a sight friendlier than Gerald who was drunk most days or Anthony who was always off somewhere and had a mean mouth towards Ma. So it don't matter none except for the amount of potatoes I have to peel."

Silas felt like Sarah had just plowed a fist into his belly, only her words packed a mighty big wallop for such a little tyke.

"We'll get over being disappointed. It's just that at first we had hopes you'd help is all. The only thing you did wrong was to get our hopes up."

They'd gotten Silas's hopes up, too. But being disappointed by women seemed to be his lot in life.

"Ma says that's just part of being a man," Sarah added. "It'd be right nice if we don't have to have any babies though, and babies seem to go with husbands. I love Betsy and all, but branding was right hard on Ma when she was almost due to have a baby." Sarah shrugged again. "It don't matter. When it happens, she'll manage. She always does."

"I don't intend to be a no-account husband." Silas thought of the baby most likely already on the way, and he thought of the hard work Belle had been doing, most of it on horseback. He thought of that nasty blazed-faced steer that had almost gored her on the trail. She'd be facing dozens of contrary longhorns out on the range. Even if she didn't get herself killed, she was going to manage to lose his child, but it didn't appear that taking care of his baby was as important as rounding up her herd.

Sarah shrugged. "Reckon no one intends to be no-account."

"I've been working real hard on something that. . .well, I wanted it to be a surprise. I'm not hiding out. Can't you tell I've been working?"

"On what?" Sarah asked.

A well of stubbornness rose up in Silas. It made him mad to have to answer to this little girl. She should just take his word for it that he was working hard and trust him. "I want to tell you when you're all together."

Sarah gave him a look like she didn't much care what his excuse was. "We've got to find Ma. We don't have time to talk right now. You do care enough about her to want her to be okay, don't you?" The way Sarah said it landed another blow. "I mean, you need her to do the chores, right?"

Had it gotten this bad that the girls didn't think he cared if they lived or died except for the work they could do? And it looked likely that they didn't much care if he lived or died either. There was still a side of the Husband Tree lacking a grave, after all.

Sarah pulled on her reins and Silas let go. He fell back in line behind her, and the two of them picked up the pace as they headed into increasingly rugged, cold timberland. Silas studied the vast, trackless woods in the night and didn't know how he could ever find the woman he loved in the midst of all this. And when he did find her, which he would or die trying, he didn't know how he was going to fix things back to the way they'd been when he first married her.

He thought of the unkind, disrespectful things Sarah had said and knew they came straight from Belle's mouth. While he'd been breaking his back trying to make things better for them, she'd been poisoning her children's minds against him.

As he rode on, he began to wonder if he did want to fix things.

CHAPTER 25

Belle woke up so groggy she thought for a while the warmth in front of her was Silas.

Reaching out her hand, she felt heat but no man. It was the fire, burned low, barely casting any heat. She was out on the trail.

She'd done it again. She'd fallen asleep. She didn't jump up because she could feel another roiling bout of nausea. She didn't have morning sickness much when she was carryin'. There just wasn't time for such nonsense.

She threw up from time to time when she was first expecting, often just leaned over so she missed her horse and cast up her food on the ground as she rode on. But she didn't count that as morning sickness because it didn't always hit in the morning. Besides, somehow morning sickness sounded like some big event that changed the pattern of your life, like needing to stay in bed of a morning until it passed. Belle didn't have a prayer of getting to do that, so why bother paying attention or naming the condition?

She rolled onto her back, cradled her sleeping baby in her arms, and stared up through the tree limbs at the stars. She could see it was really late. The girls would be worried, but they knew her days could stretch long. She'd just lay here another minute to let her stomach quit crow hopping around; then she'd grab up her horse and head home.

Silas would probably have to know what she was up to today, because heaven knew he'd be tucked up safe and warm in bed right now. She'd tell him and he'd fuss at her and tell her to leave the fall work for him. Then she'd protest that winter came early and he'd moan about his *idea* and fuss at her, then look sad that she had to work so hard. But Belle was all out of sympathy for him.

She finally felt up to moving and sat up slowly. Her head didn't start spinning and her empty stomach seemed willing to hold itself steady, so she stood and doused the last of her fire. With the fire gone, Belle realized just how cold the night had grown. It was going to be a hard ride home. She tucked Betsy in her pack, careful to make sure the baby was well bundled. Then she walked over to where she'd hitched her horse.

He wasn't there.

She leaned against the gnarled oak tree for a long minute, feeling as if the world had shifted and up was down all of a sudden. Then she looked around, trying to see another twisted-up tree that could be the one she'd picked for a hitchin' post. She looked at the sky again, and she thought of the horse she'd ridden. It was one of her best mountain horses and it was blue blazes as a cow pony. She knew as sure as she was standing here that somehow the contrary beast had broken loose and headed for the barn.

The minute she realized that, she started walking. The girls would be frantic. She had no way of knowing how long ago the horse had taken off, but it would beat her home. Emma and Sarah would assume the worst, and Emma would head for this timberland, leaving Sarah at home in case Belle showed up from an unexpected direction.

Emma was probably out on the trail hunting for her right now, afraid that the hard world had caught up with one of the Tanner women for a change—instead of a husband. Belle heard the distant howl of her wolf pack and knew it wasn't safe for her girls to be out afoot on the range.

Belle pushed hard. Knowing better than to try and run in her pointed-toed boots, she hiked along at a good pace. Every minute she got closer to the ranch was one minute less the girls would worry. The wolves howled again, and she wished for her rifle, gone along with her horse. She took off one of her work gloves, slipped her hand inside her buffalo coat, and rested her hand on the pistol at her hip. The hard, cold steel comforted her.

There was snow and ice in the air. Belle shuddered as the wind sliced at her face and neck. She knew to stay to the main path, because that's the way Emma would be coming. She thought of those baying wolves, their eerie, unearthly howls closer now than they'd been. She walked faster. She didn't want Emma to meet up with the pack alone.

She pulled Betsy around and strapped her onto her front inside her buffalo coat without breaking stride. Pushed faster by the sound of wolves, she heard a change in the tone of their howls and knew they'd picked up the scent of prey.

She hoped it wasn't Emma.

Her hand went to the sleeping bundle in her arms. She hoped it wasn't her and Betsy.

God, take care of my family tonight.

She thought of the baby she carried inside her and said a prayer for that wee little one, too.

Protect all of us, Lord, and please let this new baby be a girl.

The path wound into a particularly thick clump of trees. The branches almost reached out and grabbed her when she passed. Unmindful of her own comfort, Belle let the windswept branches whip across her face as she picked up her pace to a run.

The wolves were closer now, and a chill that had nothing to do with the weather raced up her spine. They'd found something for their supper—her.

With two babies to care for, she ran faster. She saw a lighter area ahead and knew she needed to make that so she could have a field of fire. In the woods, the wolves could be on her before she knew they were coming. She needed to find a tree to climb or a rock wall to cover her back with a good open area in front of her.

Suddenly the baying of the wolves stopped. She felt the evil in the silence. She knew they were coming.

Now.

Quiet.

Stalking her.

The heavy shroud of trees thinned, and she saw the sky for the first time in a while. There was enough light for her to see a ponderosa pine with branches low enough to grab ahold. The back of her neck prickled as she waited for the first wolf to pounce.

She sprinted for the tree. She heard the nearly soundless rush of something behind her, and she whirled and stared into wicked yellow eyes and bared fangs already airborne. Her hand was on her pistol. She fired without making a conscious decision to shoot.

The noise and the smashing bullet knocked the wolf back. Two wolves behind this one whirled back into the cover of the trees, breaking off the attack. Belle saw eyes glowing in the moonlight. Staring at her. Hungry.

She backed to the tree. Glancing behind her, she holstered her gun and caught the first branch. She swung up. The wolves came at her with a rush. She clung to the branch with her arms and legs. She had surprising speed for a woman with a baby on her chest.

One of the wolves caught her dangling buffalo robe in his teeth. The weight of the wolf almost knocked her to the ground. Belle knew it was hang on or die, and she had the grit to hang on.

Another snarling wolf caught at her coat. With frantic clumsiness she jerked at the leather belt that held her coat on and untied it. She shrugged it off, wrenching her shoulders as the wolves tried to drag it down. The wolves dropped back to the ground and attacked the robe with vicious snarls and ripping jaws.

Belle levered herself up to a sitting position and stared down at a pack of huge gray wolves, at least ten of them. She'd been thinning this pack for a month—probably already killing half a dozen. Her absence for a month because of the cattle drive had made them bold. She had ten to contend with instead of sixteen. That gave her some satisfaction.

Swinging up to a safe height, she pressed her back solidly against the tree, held tight to Betsy with her left arm, and took careful aim with her revolver. She shot two of them, including the one that looked like the leader of the pack. Betsy cried with fear at the loud noise. The wolves ran, and Belle managed to wound a third before they vanished into the woods.

"I'm sorry, baby girl." Belle bounced Betsy as she reloaded. "Don't cry, honey. I know it's loud. Mama has to get rid of these nasty old wolves so we can get home."

Betsy responded to Belle's voice, and like a good little cowpoke, she got ahold of herself.

Belle heard the beasts moving swiftly, circling her from the cover of the trees, just out of her sight. She didn't dare get down. But if she stayed here, she was leading Emma right into the middle of seven savage wolves.

Without the coat, the cold bit into her arms. Betsy, calm now, had a blanket over her, but it wasn't enough to keep her warm for long.

Belle looked down at her coat on the ground, a dead wolf carcass stretched out on top of it. Did she dare climb down for the coat?

The gunshots would warn Emma and make her ride cautiously. They would also bring her running no matter where she was, because the shots carried for miles in the high thin air.

Belle watched the woods with intense concentration, waiting for a shot. She had to thin out the pack before Emma and maybe

Sarah, too, rode into it. One foolishly bold wolf stuck his nose out of the brush. Belle shot him dead. Six to go.

They all dropped back, but Belle heard them out there, pacing, circling. She coddled poor little Betsy who was fretting again. Belle tried to identify the wolves' locations, but they moved like ghosts.

Belle began to shiver, only a little at first, but the cold crept into her muscles, and the shivers started to come from deep inside. She had a glove on her left hand. Her right-hand glove had been in the pocket of her buffalo robe. Even though it didn't fit, she put it onto her right hand. She worked the cold, stiffened fingers of her shooting hand, knowing her gun would save her, but she couldn't shoot with the glove on, so as soon as her hand felt better, she switched the glove back. She held Betsy close and used her body heat to keep the baby warm.

After long minutes, a second wolf emerged with a chilling, low growl. Belle cut down their number once again. Five left. Only five.

This time they seemed to vanish. She didn't hear a noise. She didn't even sense their presence. She doubted very much they'd run off, but maybe they'd been driven back far enough that she could get that coat.

Belle's shivering was becoming so uncontrollable that she soon wouldn't be able to handle her gun. She couldn't sit up here all night. Betsy wouldn't survive it. Her baby started to whimper and fret against Belle's chest, from cold or hunger or fright. Belle had to do something.

She slipped down a branch to see better into the woods and realized her legs barely worked. They were stiff and numb from sitting so long in the treetop. She saw nothing and heard nothing, so with considerable struggle due to numb legs and arms still with cold, Belle climbed lower, her eyes shifting between that blood-soaked buffalo coat and the surrounding forest.

She was to the point of climbing down to the ground to snatch that coat and rush back up into the tree, when suddenly three of them lunged at her from the side, leaping nearly high enough to sink their teeth into her dangling leg.

She whirled, off balance, and fell backward out of the tree. Betsy cried out as they fell. Belle fired as she fell into the raging fangs, until her gun clicked on empty chambers. Taking a second to look for where the next danger would come, she saw three more wolves dead on the ground.

Belle reached for the bullets in her cartridge belt with fingers numb and uncooperative from the cold. A blood-chilling growl sounded from just behind her. She shoved a bullet home and tried to whirl from where she lay, but her feet and legs were useless. They were as dead as if she'd dragged stumps of wood along with her. Her arms were heavy and limp. Even her brain was murky and slow-acting, and she had a strange sense of not caring what happened to her, just wanting to sleep.

Betsy squirmed and cried, and that forced Belle to face the new danger and keep fighting, for Betsy's sake if not her own. She turned and looked into the eyes of a pair of hungry wolves. She raised her gun with only one bullet.

A shot rang out and then another and a third. She blinked her eyes with aching slowness as both wolves slammed sideways with sharp whines of pain, twitching and dying.

Emma rode into the clearing with her rifle drawn and smoking.

"Thanks," Belle said, her voice trembling with cold.

Emma looked around at the pile of dead wolves. "Figured when your horse came home alone you was havin' trouble." Emma always got calm in a crisis. Of anyone she knew, Belle would rather have her second daughter at hand when there was trouble. By the utter calm she saw in Emma now, she knew her girl was scared half to death.

Belle wasn't yet ready to stand, but she saw her coat within reaching distance. She dragged her gnawed-up buffalo robe out from under the corpse of a wolf and, ignoring the soaked-in blood, pulled it on over herself and Betsy. Belle tied the coat around her clumsily and started shivering so hard she had trouble sitting upright.

Emma dismounted and led the extra horse she'd brought along over to Belle. "Let me take Betsy. It's warmer inside my coat."

Belle nodded soundlessly and opened her coat to pass the bundled-up baby over, carrier and all.

Emma hooked her sister onto her chest, inside her own heavy coat. Then she boosted her mother to her feet and, doing almost all the work herself, hoisted Belle onto the spare horse. Emma found Belle's second glove and, like she was dressing a child, put it on Belle's hand. Emma steadied Belle on the saddle, took the reins, swung up on her own mount, and headed out, leading Belle's horse.

Silas and Sarah charged out of the woods before they'd gotten out of the clearing.

Silas had his gun drawn. The minute he caught sight of them, he yelled, "I heard wolves. Where are they?"

Emma said in her too-calm voice, "Dead." She nodded her head toward the tree in the center of the clearing.

Silas turned toward the tree.

CHAPTER 26

Silas took one look at the carnage. Death and blood and violence filled the clearing.

He spurred his horse toward his shivering wife, where she sat slumped forward on her horse. "Belle! Where are you hurt? Where's Betsy?" He lifted Belle off her saddle onto his.

"I've got the baby, Silas," Emma said, using his name instead of Pa so calmly Silas wanted to shake her.

Maybe later. Now he pulled Belle's shredded, blood-soaked coat open, expecting to see her covered with bites and claw marks. He couldn't see a one.

He'd heard the wolves baying. Heard the repeated gunshots as he and Sarah had raced in the direction of the commotion.

"I'm cold." Belle pulled her coat closed and said with chattering teeth, "Give me back my coat."

He rode over to the tree, carrying Belle across his lap, and started to shiver himself. He counted until his mind couldn't take in the number. Then he looked down at Belle. Even in the moonlight he could see her skin was ashen and her lips were blue. There were streaks of blood on her face. "You're hurt. Where are you hurt?"

"No, I'm fine. Just cold."

Silas wiped the blood off her chin and held his hand up in front of her face in the moonlight clearing.

The blood was black on his hand, but she knew what it was. "Wolf blood." She shivered and shrugged. "They never got me or Betsy. We were fine, just cold because they tore my coat off."

"*Tore!*" Silas started snarling himself.

"*Your!*" He lifted Belle until she was sitting upright.

"*Coat!*" Her nose was almost pressed against his.

"*Off?*" His hands tightened on her shoulders.

"*Tore it off?*" Silas checked himself and said with suppressed violence, "Why were you out here? I *told* you to leave this for me."

His voice kept getting louder as he thought of how close she'd come to being killed. "And by yourself? You didn't even take one of the girls? You're hours late! We thought you were—" Fury clamped his throat shut.

Her pale skin and the tremors that vibrated through her kept him from shaking her until her bones rattled or her brain started working—whichever came first. He bet on the rattling bones, because he had no doubt her brain wouldn't come through for him.

"Silas, you came for me." She said it through a fog, and Silas realized she was dropping off to sleep. She wasn't falling asleep. No matter how tired a person was, no matter what they'd been through, they didn't nod off when someone was shouting right in their face. She was losing consciousness.

He felt the iciness of her skin and saw the blue tinge of her lips, and he forgot about being mad. Well, he didn't forget. He just decided he'd leave it until later.

He'd lived in the high country off and on most of his life, so he knew a hard chill getting a grip on a person could kill. He pulled off her buffalo coat, ignoring her soft cry of protest as she tried to keep it around her. He opened his own coat and his shirt, then unbuttoned hers and pressed her chest against his, separated only by his underwear and her chemise. He pulled off her gloves and tucked her hands between their bodies and shivered himself from the lifeless cold of her fingers. Then he wrapped his own sturdy sheepskin coat around both of them and wrapped Belle's buffalo robe over the top, flinching from the wetness and the smell of blood but using it anyway because Belle needed it.

His horse danced sideways at the unaccustomed activity of two riders on his back.

Emma rode up to hold the horse steady.

"We can't take her all the way home. She's too cold." He looked up at Emma who was studying Belle with a deep furrow of worry between her brows. "How's the baby?"

"Betsy's fine." Emma's hand crossed her chest to hug the completely covered baby. "Ma kept her bundled up."

Trust Belle to protect her children even in the middle of this madness.

Belle started shivering again. Silas couldn't pay attention to Belle's feet on horseback. They might be dangerously frozen by the time he got Belle home. "Scout out a sheltered spot, Emma. Get a fire started. We've got to get your ma warmed up."

Emma's eyes flickered between Silas and her ma. For one long second she hesitated, as if judging for herself if Silas really meant to help.

He kept from yelling by clamping his teeth together hard.

Finally, she turned and headed up the trail toward home with Sarah following.

Silas covered Belle more carefully then rode after his daughters.

When he caught up to Emma, she had sparked a handful of twigs into flame, and Sarah was dragging in a big dead pine branch. Silas knew they'd have a fire big enough to scare off every wolf in the Rockies before long. Emma had chosen wisely as Silas had expected. She'd built a fire a few feet out from an overhanging cliff so the wall was warmed along with the ground between the fire and the wall. The curve of the rock sheltered them from the wind, and the fire was reflected off the rock until it was warmer than the dilapidated cabin they lived in. But the perfect little niche in the rock wasn't large enough for all of them. Sarah threw the dead branch on the flames, and the flames licked and caught and spread.

"We have to find somewhere we can all squeeze in, Emma." Silas was getting worried about Belle's unresponsive state. He swung off his horse and settled Belle on the ground between the roaring fire and the overhang while Emma tied up his horse and Belle's. "No, don't hitch my horse. You keep your ma here. I'll go find somewhere big enough for all of us."

Sarah added another armful of wood.

"No, Silas. I picked this on purpose. It'll heat up fast. Sarah, Betsy, and I are fine. We can make the ride home easy. I can feed Betsy cow's milk for one night."

He'd been called Silas again. This time by his Emma, the one who seemed to love him the most deeply. They'd all turned on him. He should have known better than to try and make a place for himself in this man-hating household. Well, it wasn't the first time he'd been a fool over a woman.

Emma began dragging a dead branch toward the fire, stopping to grab two more smaller bits of kindling as she worked.

"We're wasting time talking. Get in here and start rubbing your ma's arms and legs. It'll take hours for you to ride home, and I don't want you out alone."

Silas turned his attention to Belle. It took him a second to notice that the girls ignored his orders and kept working, building the fire.

He didn't notice them again until Emma spoke. He looked over and saw her across from the now-roaring fire, sitting on her horse. "We'll head in now."

"Emma, I don't want you riding these wolf-infested hills with

Sarah and Betsy. We're all staying."

"I know this range better'n you, Silas. Having this place so close was pure good luck. There isn't anything else like it anywhere around." She stared at him suspiciously for a long moment, and Silas got the impression she was trying to decide whether to trust him with Belle's life.

Finally, Emma said, "You can see to her if you want, but if you don't want to do it, I will, and Sarah can get Betsy home."

"Of course I'll take care of her," Silas exploded. "I want to take care of all of you."

"I'm obliged for your help with Ma, Silas. I'll leave her to you then. But I reckon we girls'll be takin' care of ourselves." Emma clucked to her horse and rode down the trail with Sarah trailing after.

"Emma!" Fury almost blew the top of Silas's head off. He surged to his feet. "You get back here right now!"

Emma and Sarah, with Betsy, rode on without a backward glance. They disappeared into the woods as he stood there raging at the empty night.

It was all he could do to stop himself from snagging the mane of his horse and riding those impudent young ladies down and dragging them back. Only Belle's critical condition kept him from fetching Emma and turning her over his knee. Except he wasn't sure he had the right to hand out a spanking to Emma. Yesterday he'd thought he was their pa, and he would have said he had the rights of any father. But today everything had changed. The blazing anger turned into hurt. He *wasn't* their pa. He wasn't *anything* around this place but another one of the husbands. And even though he'd been working his heart out for these women, they didn't trust him to be different than any other man they'd known.

So, Belle kept the reins of the ranch in her hands, and Emma toiled along by her side, and Sarah kept the home fires burning, and none of them even minded much until something like tonight happened. Tonight they couldn't help blaming him. Emma, like Sarah, held him responsible for Belle being out here half frozen and in danger from wolves. It hit him hard that, whatever his excuse, it didn't matter, because they were right. It *was* his fault. He should have told them what he was up to. Fool that he was, he'd thought they trusted him. Just another mistake on his part.

He wanted to go after them. Beg them to forgive him. Beg them to love him again. But his wife was unconscious. She was in mortal danger from the vicious cold. He stared, bitterly ashamed, into the black, windswept night that sheltered treacherous trails and hungry wolves and fractious longhorns. The wilderness swallowed up his daughters.

With no choice, he turned his attention to Belle. He laid the buffalo robe on the ground for a bed then pulled Belle's outer clothes off. She needed every ounce of heat the fire and his body could produce to warm her skin and prevent frostbite. He turned her so her back was toward the fire, being careful not to get her too close to the flames. Then he rubbed her arms and legs with so much vigor that she awoke slightly and swatted at him in protest.

"Let me sleep. I'm tired." Although her eyes didn't open and in her semiconscious state her words were slurred, her attitude was cantankerous. It lifted Silas's heart to hear even that little bit of spirit.

As he massaged her arms and back, he studied her face. It was stark and white under her tan. Her lips were blue and pinched. He rubbed his hands over her strong, clever fingers, which lay lifeless in the flickering light of the fire. He turned back to her feet, which had him the most worried. It made Silas sick to think of people who'd lost toes, even a foot or leg, to frostbite. He hated to think of the horror Belle might go through if her feet were that badly frozen. He held her feet to his chest, hugging them in his arms to warm her ankles. Then, because they didn't seem to be warming, he lifted his shirt and pressed the bottoms of her feet against his bare stomach. They were frigid and set a shudder of cold through him. He held her feet, edging a few inches closer to the fire.

"Belle Harden, this is no time to turn into a weakling." As she drew heat from his body, he talked, hoping she'd respond. "I've got heat to spare, darlin', and strength. This time you're going to have to depend on me. Just like you did on that cattle drive." His belly ached as if her icy feet were absorbing the cold from his deepest core.

Her shivering came again. Her whole body was wracked with it. She began to moan through chattering teeth, and after a while she struggled against him and murmured again. "Feet hurt."

She kicked at him, but it was so feeble his heart clutched to think of her usual strength, now so reduced. He thought it was a good sign that his warmth was causing her pain. He hoped that meant her feet weren't dangerously frozen.

"Wolves!" Belle's hands flew wide, and Silas had to scramble to keep her from getting too close to the fire.

"The wolves are gone, Belle."

"Wolves!" Her arms flew up as if she were dreaming that one sprang at her right now. "No!"

"You're safe, Belle honey. The wolves are gone."

Belle clutched at her chest, the shivering wracking her body. "Betsy!" Her hands flailed at the place she kept Betsy strapped on. Then she cried out in terror.

"Betsy's fine, Belle. She's fine."

Belle twisted as if she planned to get up.

Silas kept a firm grip on her feet. "Emma has Betsy. You shot all the wolves, Belle." Silas crooned to her, afraid to let her feet go when they were so cold. The rest of her seemed to be working just fine. "You won." He reached out and caught one of her thrashing hands that had flopped on the ground too close to the fire. "You're safe." She jerked against the hold, but he wouldn't let go, afraid she'd be burned. "Your girls are safe." He thought there was some pink behind her blue-white fingernails and her hands weren't the flaccid, lifeless cold they'd been earlier.

"Stop! Gerald, stop. Please!" She kicked hard at Silas's stomach and cried out Gerald's name in a voice so laced with fear and pain Silas ground his teeth together to contain his rage at what Belle had suffered at the hands of men. Belle's words were almost begging. To think of strong, courageous Belle being reduced to begging by one of her husbands was infuriating.

"I'm here, Belle. Gerald is gone. This is Silas. I'll take care of you." To think she was mixing Silas up with Gerald was heartbreaking. He continued to talk to her, trying to pierce her muddled thinking.

"You're going to be all right. The girls are safe." Out in this cold night. Without Silas or Belle to protect them. But he was confident in his statement. They'd be fine without any help from him.

At last the tremors eased. Belle at last lay calm, her eyes closed.

Silas pulled her feet out from against his stomach and saw that the alarming white had pinked up a bit. He heaved a sigh of relief and pulled on her socks, then carefully arranged her close to the fire. Silas stretched out beside his wife on the side away from the fire to surround her with warmth. He pulled a blanket over them, one he always carried behind his saddle. He held her close, tucked his feet beneath hers, and prayed.

The shivering came again but it didn't last so long. There was more time in between the next bout. The color seeped into her cheeks, and Belle's movements became more languid. With a sigh of utter relaxation, she said, "Silas, I love you."

Some of Silas's anger at Belle for risking her life eased away when she talked to him so sweetly. It reawakened the excitement that had been buzzing through him when he'd ridden home so many hours earlier. He whispered in her ear, "I think we're going to have a baby, Belle Harden."

"I can't have a baby." Belle shook her head frantically, eyes still closed. "I can't." And she started to cry.

Something in Silas turned as cold as the Montana wind that howled outside this little niche of warmth. His wife, cuddled safe in his arms, cried over the thought of having his child.

Belle was just barely conscious. He knew she was only vaguely aware of what she was saying. Did that mean he should pay no mind to what she said? Or did it mean she had no strength for anything but the truth? Did it mean Belle was truly, deeply heartbroken to think she was carrying his child? Whether she was expecting or not, her tears meant she didn't want to be. So why had she let him make love to her? Belle was a grown woman. She knew what caused babies.

Silas knew the answer. Pleasure.

It was new to Belle. She wanted the pleasure and had found it irresistible. But she didn't want to move over and give up being boss of the *Tanner* Ranch, and she didn't want his child growing in her body.

She was using him. She'd support him and feed him, probably even dole out spending money if he asked, all so she could keep him around. But the ranch was hers alone, and his baby was a cause for tears.

Any way Silas thought of it, he came out sounding like. . .like his mother. Earning money in the upstairs of a saloon.

That's what a man got for coming to a rich woman when he had nothing to offer. He'd known it was wrong, but he'd married her anyway because he wanted her so much. And he thought love was enough. And now he had to pay the price of being a man with no honor and no pride.

He'd lost two ranches in his life by turning coward. Running away was getting to be a habit, because right now he hurt so badly from hearing her cry, he wished himself halfway across the country from Belle.

He tested her warm, supple limbs and saw that she'd fallen

into a natural sleep. He checked her toes, and even they were warm and pink in the crackling firelight. Trust Belle to tackle a pack of wolves and freezing cold and then shake it off with no damage to herself.

He wrapped her up good and snug. "You're all right now, Belle. You're going to be all right." Knowing he shouldn't, he held her close, thrilled that she was safely warm.

She wound her arms around his neck. She tilted her head to reach for his lips.

He met her searching lips and thought about the baby she was most likely expecting and never wanted to bear. He broke off the kiss.

She protested but settled back into a deep sleep.

He held her through the long night while he nurtured his anger and vanquished his love and planned how to be a man who could stand to look at himself in the mirror.

It was still dark when Belle woke the next morning.

Silas was shaking her. "We'd best be on the trail home."

She sat up and a wave of nausea lurched in her stomach.

The baby.

Silas was fully dressed. When she moved, he stood away and started quickly packing up the meager camp. She remembered everything. Crying herself to sleep. The wolves. Emma's smoking rifle. Silas.

Things were foggy after Silas had picked her up off her horse and started fussing over her and scolding her for working her ranch. Like she hadn't put up with enough already yesterday.

She'd never had a husband quite like this before. The others had complained and whined and laid low when chores were being handed .. But she'd never had one not only refuse to help but get upset when she did it herself. It was just a new twist on the same old story, but she couldn't figure out why Silas didn't just shut up and let her get on with her work.

Once her stomach settled, she thought of Betsy needing breakfast and got up to start packing the camp.

Silas had everything done except dousing the fire. "You up to the ride home?" Silas almost growled the question.

Belle had beaten back one pack of wolves only to face another this morning. "Yep." She brushed his question aside brusquely.

Beyond that, they didn't talk.

Both horses were already saddled, so they were on the trail within minutes. They had no food, and she was in a hurry to get to Betsy, so they set a brisk pace.

Her husband was obviously angry. Belle assumed it was because she'd gone and done another chore he considered his. She didn't have the strength this morning to deal with his infernal wounded pride.

They made good time in the sharp cold, and the sun wasn't fully up when they rode into the ranch yard.

Without making eye contact, Silas said with tight sarcasm, "If it's all right with you, I'll take care of the horses."

Belle looked at him through narrow eyes, disgusted at his temper. She checked the impulse to tend her own mount because she was eager to be away from his surly company. "Thank you." Tossing him the reins, she dismounted without checking to see if he caught them and headed to the house.

She got inside in time to pick Betsy up where she lay kicking in the wooden crate Belle had fashioned into a bed. She sat down and nursed her baby and fought back tears by building up the fire under her temper. She fumed and rocked and looked down at Betsy, not the youngest anymore.

Emma and Sarah slept on, even though it was well past their normal waking time. The night had been a late one.

Betsy ate and surprised Belle by falling back to sleep in her arms. Just as Belle laid her back down, the front door slammed open with so much force the rickety thing shattered into pieces and fell onto the cabin floor, letting the icy wind blast through into the cabin.

Emma surged out of her bed. Sarah sat up with a startled scream of fear. Betsy awoke with a loud cry. Belle whirled around, and her temper flared to white hot.

She stalked over to face Silas with only inches separating them, ready at last to put him in the place he needed to be. Ready to chalk him up as another mistake. So enraged, she was ready to plant him under the lone oak with the rest of the husbands without waiting for him to turn up his toes!

She'd trusted him! She'd thought she could believe in him! Well, so far he'd been a bigger disappointment than anyone she'd ever married. And in that instant, Belle decided she wasn't going to put up with it. She wasn't going to just accept this lazy, no-good polecat of a man and carry on doing everything herself while he lazed about and lived off her labor.

Silas was going to hear exactly what she thought of his no-account ways. And when she was done with him, he was going to measure up to her idea of what a husband should be or she was going to march him straight down the road. Things were going to change around here! "Silas, things are going to. . .*mmph.*"

One hard hand settled over her mouth, and the other clamped over the nape of her neck. He jerked her forward so hard it next to knocked the wind out of her.

CHAPTER 27

T hings are going to change around here!"

Silas leaned down until his nose nearly touched hers. "Do you hear me?"

Belle grabbed his wrist. His arm left her neck and wrapped around her waist as immovable as a band of iron while his other stayed firmly on her mouth. "Settle down and shut up and listen to what your husband has to say for once in your confounded, stubborn, bossy life."

Sarah snatched up the cast-iron skillet and waved it in front of her. Silas thought she looked pretty cute with the skillet in one hand and the baby in the other. Not real threatening.

"You get your hands off of my ma." Emma erupted to her feet and dove for her shotgun.

That impressed Silas more than the skillet. But, unlike when Lindsay had threatened him that first morning, now he wasn't afraid. He could handle all of these women with one hand tied behind his back. He noticed right now it was taking two hands just keeping Belle quiet, so maybe, just to be on the safe side, he wouldn't tie one up. He'd let things go on too long while he worked on his *idea*.

He'd been happily toiling away for them while thinking they loved him and trusted him. But it appeared that wasn't true. Still, he knew Emma. He knew what she was made of. Sure, she might shoot a man who hurt her ma. He'd expect her to. He wouldn't respect her if she didn't. But she wouldn't hurt him.

"Put down that gun." He kept Belle's mouth covered and kept his unshakable grip on her but his whole attention focused on Emma. "I'm not doing anything but making your hardheaded mother listen to me, and you know it."

Emma half raised the gun. She had her eyes riveted on Silas, then glanced at the hold he had on her ma and lowered the muzzle to the floor.

Silas noticed that Belle had quit fighting and squirming. He had the impression she did that because it was upsetting Emma. And just maybe his wife's heart wasn't in having him shot. Either was encouraging.

"And Sarah, you mind Betsy and set that pan aside. You are the most contrary bunch of females I have ever been near. I am going to give you *one more chance* to back up and make room for me in this family."

"Make room?" Sarah said in disgust.

Emma gave Silas a narrow-eyed look, but she didn't raise the gun again.

Good sign.

"Like you haven't been sneaking off every day while we do all the work," Emma said. "Like we wouldn't have let you help."

Belle made a garbled noise of accord with her daughter and gave a firm nod.

Betsy chose that moment to start crying. Silas supposed she could be hungry or wet or have a pin sticking in her little bottom, but he reckoned the truth was she was just female and decided to add to the commotion on principle. Silas wished he had enough hands to shut them all up.

"I don't imagine anyone in this family is interested in seeing the *house* I've been building for the last few weeks."

Dead silence met his announcement, except for the sound of the skillet hitting the floor. Betsy even reacted to the changed atmosphere in the room and stuck both hands into her mouth.

Belle quit fighting against his hold. "Eew ouse?"

Silas uncovered her mouth.

Belle repeated, "New house?"

"Yes. New house. What did you think I'd been doing ever since I got here?"

Silas thought he heard a cricket chirp in the dead silence.

"Never mind. I know what you all think of me." He tugged his Stetson low over his eyes. "But confound it, how could you not trust me better than this? I punched a thousand head of cattle over a hundred of the roughest miles God ever put on this *earth* for you women. I worked eighteen- or twenty-hour days. I hauled you *all* over two mountain passes even though it almost killed me doing it! I—I—" Silas lapsed into silence to match the rest of them and took his arm off of Belle's waist and stepped back.

Finally, he said, "How could you believe I'd—" Surprised at how hurt he was by their easy belief in his worthlessness, he fell silent. Sure, they'd known a lot of no-account men, but he'd next to broken his *heart* getting those cattle to market and building Lindsay her house and getting them all home safe. Didn't that count for anything?

At last he said the only thing he could think of. "I asked you to wait for me with all the winter chores, Belle. And I told you I had an idea I needed to work on. Why didn't you say something if you needed me? Instead, you just assumed the worst of me and did the work yourself. Do I have to prove myself to you every day for the rest of my life? Is that what I can expect from marriage to you?"

He stared at the floor for a while, trying to find in himself the pleasure he'd had at being married and being a father. It was so laced now with hurt it was as if he'd never even known these women. "Well, decide if you want to live here or with me." He stalked out.

He was halfway to the barn when Belle called after him. "New house?"

Afraid of the scalding things he wanted to say to her, Silas ignored her and kept walking.

She hollered, "Where is it?"

He turned back.

Belle stood in her tottering cabin with the door in pieces on the ground. All three girls peeked over her shoulder at him.

He looked back at them for a long time, studying his wife, wondering who she really was. He knew the hardworking rancher and the sweet, loving woman in the night, but underneath the years of disappointment and hard lessons her life had taught her was there someone else? Was there someone who could trust and love, someone who could move over enough to include him in her life and find joy in wanting his child?

The events of the past day told him no. He'd signed on for a lifetime of bouncing off the brick wall of Belle's doubts about all men. It hurt. He didn't like it, and he didn't want to live like that.

If there was a soft side to be coaxed out from under her toughness, he didn't appear to have the knack of doing the coaxing. And he'd reached the point where he didn't have much interest in doing it either. Letting him into her life and opening up to him had to be something Belle did herself.

"It's in the mouth of the high valley near the south pass. I staked a claim to it while we were in Helena. It's mine. I reckon I'm going to go live there." He turned away from her and caught up his horse. Then, without a backward glance, he rode off in the icy cold to his empty home.

All three of them looked at each other. Then they looked around the ramshackle house they lived in.

Hoofbeats faded in the distance.

Belle came out of her trance and whirled back to the door. She stared in the direction he went. "He said he had an idea. He said. . .he said I was a rich woman and it hurt his pride to come to me with nothing."

Belle turned back to the girls. "New house?"

"He claimed that valley you wanted?" Emma asked.

Sarah said wistfully, "I'd kind of like to see it."

"He said he'd do the winter chores," Emma added. "But I never believed him. Not for a minute."

Belle shook her head. It had never occurred to her either. It had never occurred to her to trust the man who had saved their lives several times over. "He worked so hard on the drive, but I just thought he was—I don't know—putting on an act, I guess. Remember how Anthony dug that well for us when he was courting me?"

Emma and Sarah nodded.

Betsy kicked her legs and said, "Papa."

"Anthony dug mighty slow though," Emma said thoughtfully. "Kept on and on about the rocks. Even then we knew he was no-account, didn't we, Ma? We just didn't expect no better."

Belle looked back out the gaping doorway. "Anthony would never have risked his life to haul us over the passes home. He'd have never put in the long days riding herd, and he didn't have an ounce of Silas's skill handling cattle and sticking his cow pony. A man doesn't get good at things like that without practice, and lazy men don't practice. How could I not know all of that after spending a month with Silas?"

"He did a right fine job on Lindsay's house," Emma remembered. "I could tell he knew what he was doing. Reckon any house he built'd be a good 'un."

Sarah said, "Do you think he'll let us live in the new house with him?"

All three of them exchanged a glance. Then they started smiling.

Belle said, "Let's go see."

The girls dressed. They all pulled on their heavy coats, tucked Betsy in the carrier, and headed for the corral.

It was nearly a two-hour ride to the south pass. Belle thought how nice it would be to live two hours closer to Divide. The trail split, one half starting up the mountain to the pass, the other winding into Silas's high valley. They had only gone a mile down that valley trail when they rounded the mouth of the canyon. There, sitting beside a spring, sat the most beautiful ranch house Belle had ever seen. It was all logs. One story high and built in a single straight line. The house was about four times the size of the one they lived in. It had a neat porch across the whole front of it, made with a split-log floor. Evenly spaced saplings formed a railing along the front.

Belle knew Silas hadn't been able to go to town for anything to make his building easier because the pass was snowed shut. There were no glass windows—only shutters pulled firmly closed without a sagging corner in sight. Three chimneys of fieldstones adorned the roof. Only the center one had smoke coming out of it. As they got nearer, she saw the leather hinges on the front door and the tight corners of the log cabin that had been hewn out by hand. She could see the wooden pegs that held the porch and doors and shutters together. It must have taken him forever to do such a lovely job on this big cabin.

She realized the stiff breeze was gone and the snow wasn't as deep as back home. Silas had chosen a spot that cut the north wind. Belle knew the little spring flowed year-round out of a fissure in the cliff close behind the house, so they'd always have fresh water.

Silas had thought of everything.

She rode closer and saw Silas's buckskin grazing in a corral behind the house. A big barn stood beside the corral. Built with the same attention to detail. The same *loving* attention to detail.

"He loves me." Belle stared at the proof. "He loves all of us."

Emma nodded. "He'd never've gone to so much trouble elsewise."

Belle's hand went to her flat stomach, and for the first time in her life she was excited and proud to be expecting a baby. She remembered her tears of yesterday with shame. With ironclad resolve, she decided then and there to be the best mother to this young'un and to the rest of her girls that the world had ever known.

God, I don't mind if it's a boy.

On that shocking thought, she spurred her horse and galloped toward the home he'd made for all of them. She went to the corral to turn her horse loose. Even matters of the heart took second place over caring for her horse.

Emma jumped down beside her and caught Belle's reins. "You'd better go try and cheer him up, Ma. We'll give you awhile to grovel."

Belle looked sharply at Emma.

Emma grinned.

Sarah piped up from behind, "Hand over Betsy, Ma. And don't be shy about crying if need be. That's supposed to soften men up something fierce."

"Where'd you hear that?" Belle asked.

Sarah took Betsy, and the three girls headed for the barn.

Over her shoulder, Emma called, "We won't come in until you come for us, Ma. If you have to be pathetic, then do it, but we don't want to watch. We need to explore the barn anyway. We may set up a camp and spend the night. Even without a fire, this barn'll be warmer than our old cabin. So take whatever time you need to convince Silas to let us live here." Her two smug daughters headed for the barn, giggling.

Belle glared after them for a minute, but it wasn't because she was upset. Her temper was all fake. The truth was she might have to grovel and cry and act pathetic, and if that's what it took, so be it! But that didn't mean it came easy to her.

It took awhile to gather the gumption to admit she was wrong on every count straight down the line. She squared her shoulders and headed for the ranch house.

As soon as she looked where she was going, she saw Silas standing on the porch at the top of the steps, leaning one shoulder against a sturdy support post with his arms folded and one ankle crossed over the other one.

She faltered a bit at the cranky look on his face that told her he wasn't going to settle for any less than an abject apology, but she had the guts to keep moving. Whatever he said, she reckoned she deserved it.

She stopped at the bottom of the steps, and her mind went completely blank. Apologizing wasn't something she did much of. "We. . .uh. . .we want to live here."

Silas just stared at her.

"With you."

He cocked his head slightly to the side but didn't speak.

Belle sighed deeply. "We. . .*I'm* sorry. I can't believe I didn't trust you after all you did for us. I. . . Even if I didn't, I should have *talked* to you. I should have *told* you what I was thinking, how upset I was."

Still nothing.

"Well, go ahead and yell at me if you want to." Belle was getting tired of being contrite. It just didn't sit well. She tried one more time. "I was wrong, and I'm sorry, and you don't have to prove yourself to me ever again. If you sit down on your tail and never lift a finger to help me again, even if we're married for fifty years, I'll never think you're lazy. I'll never doubt your word, and I'll never breathe a word of criticism."

Still no response.

"I promise that if you say you'll take care of the chores, I'll let the chickens starve and the cattle wander off and the vegetable garden dry up and die before I believe ill of you."

Silas was silent.

Anger stabbed her, but it wasn't her strongest reaction. She was afraid.

What if he never forgave her?

What if he never smiled at her and hugged the girls?

What if he didn't want to have a baby with her and he never came to her again in the night?

"All right!" She flung her arms wide. It burned. It burned bad. But she made herself say the most outrageous, impossible, stupid thing she'd ever said.

"I'll obey you!"

CHAPTER 28

Silas felt his eyebrows shoot up to his hairline.

His arms dropped from the stubborn crossed position he held them in. He stood up straight. "Really?"

Belle nodded.

"You'll let me give you orders?" He had to fight a smile of triumph.

"I said I would, didn't I?" Belle fisted her hands and propped them on her hips defiantly, but her words didn't match her movements. "I'll obey any orders you want. You're the boss of this ranch, and what you say goes."

"Well, that sounds interesting. Let me think." Silas rubbed his chin between his thumb and forefinger and stared at the sky so he wouldn't laugh out loud at the faces she was making while she was trying to be apologetic and submissive.

It was killing her.

He didn't think it was a good idea for her to realize how much he was enjoying the sight. She probably only had so much "obey" in her, and she was likely to start growling any minute.

On the other hand, he thought he had a right to a little getting

307

even with her for all the hurt she'd caused him. "What if I told you I've never cared much for that silly T Bar brand? We're changing it. I registered my own under Circle H in Helena, and starting this spring, all our calves are going to wear it. That's what I used to call my spread down in New Mexico, and it suited me."

Belle swallowed visibly, and Silas thought she was choking over his first order. "The T Bar stands for something out here. I've spent the last sixteen years building that name into—" Then she clenched her jaw shut.

Silas could see her physically trying to stop the words that wanted to escape her lips. She must have gained control of herself, because finally she said rather hoarsely, "Yes, Silas. Circle H sounds fine."

Oh, this was lining itself up to be one of the best days of his life. He wondered how much she'd take. "And I don't like the way you've been breaking the horses. There're none of 'em trained the way good cow ponies should be. I might let Emma help once they're green broke, but I don't want you taking a hand. You teach 'em bad habits it'll take me years training out of 'em."

"Silas! My horses are— I'll have you know—" Belle must've bit her tongue, because she got the words to stop spewing.

Silas tilted his head a bit sideways. He expected nothing less than her trying to do things her way and leave him out. And considering her horses were some of the finest, best-trained stock he'd ever seen, it was reasonable for her to want to help. Still, tormenting her was too good to miss.

She breathed in and out of her nose so loudly he could hear it. Then she said through her bared teeth, "I'll let you take care of that, Silas."

Silas started backing across the porch. He opened the door behind him. "Come in here, woman."

Belle hesitated, and Silas saw some of the flashing rage in her eyes ease.

Silas had the impression she was feeling guilty, like maybe she didn't think she deserved to go into such a fine house as the one he'd spent every waking moment of the last month building just for her. But he didn't give her a break, not when he was having such a good time. He crossed the threshold with her still standing on the ground, and he decided the best way to get her inside was to say, "While we're on the subject of changes, I don't like the way you dress. I'd like my woman to look a mite more like a female."

Belle surged forward up the stairs, so mad Silas thought her hair might stand on end if it weren't caught back in her braid. She stormed into the house. "You listen to me. . .*mmph.*"

Silas shut that yapping mouth right up with his lips. He swung the door shut and broke off the kiss just enough to speak. "Did I mention that I want more children with you than you've given to the other husbands?" He made sure to kiss her so deeply she couldn't respond to that.

Finally, he pulled back. "Combined."

When she was clinging to him, he kissed his way along her jawline and murmured in her pretty little ear, "I won't feel right about it if my young'uns aren't in the majority. So that's five more babies, woman."

"Five more?" Belle asked weakly. "That's nine children."

He silenced her again until she shuddered in his arms. "Did I say just five more? I meant five *boys.* However many babies it takes to get that number of *boys* is what I expect from you."

"I. . .I don't think. . .I may not be able. . . I've shown no talent for birthing boys, Silas." She was almost wailing before she was done.

He slid his hands down her back and pulled her hard up against him. "Are you disobeying me, woman?"

"Umm. . .the other girls all have your name." She was starting to sound wimpy. Like a regular female. He thought he almost had her toeing the line.

Silas kissed her again. He really didn't want to think of Belle going through the dangers of having babies many more times. Besides, he considered the girls to be, in all ways, his own, so there was no point in trying to match up the number of children. But what was the fun in admitting that?

Belle said, when he let her breathe, "I'll do whatever you want, Silas."

"Anything?" She wasn't obedient worth a hoot as a rule, but he remembered how agreeable she always got when they were alone. This sweetness would no doubt wear off. In fact, he was surprised it had lasted this long. And the only reason it had was because he was distracting her.

But obedience aside, as soon as he was done teasing her, he was going to sit her down and apologize for his own foolishness in not telling her he was building a house. Silas admitted he'd been selfish in wanting to impress her. He should have known his hardworking, self-sufficient wife would take care of her land with or without him.

Silas wasn't going to make that mistake again. He'd almost lost his precious wife last night through his own prideful behavior. From now on he'd talk everything over with Belle. But he wasn't going to start apologizing quite yet.

She let her head drop back as he nuzzled his way down her neck. Breathlessly she murmured, "Anything, if you'll just forgive me for mistrusting you. . . ."

Silas didn't know if she noticed or not, but he was acting real forgiving right now.

"And if you'll let me live with you in the beautiful house you worked so hard on."

"Where are the girls?"

"And let me love you again, Silas. Please, will you believe I love you? Please say you'll love me like you did before I was so bad."

Now Belle was begging, and as much as Silas loved it, he couldn't stand that he'd reduced his proud, strong wife to that. But he decided to listen for just a second longer because he wasn't likely ever to hear it again.

"I'll do whatever you want, including starting on those five boys. I do believe I've got a start on the first one already."

He paused in his kisses and looked into her eyes. "Really? I wondered. But you cried when you talked about having my baby."

Belle couldn't seem to pay attention. "When was that?"

"Last night in the woods. After the wolves almost got you." Silas shivered as deeply as if he was freezing to death when he thought about it. "You cried. Cried hard and said you didn't want another baby."

"I don't remember saying that, but I know I've been a bad mother to the girls. I've done wrong by 'em, every one. And I regret that more than anything in my life. I don't want to hurt another baby by not having time to love her and hug her and care for her the way she deserves."

The last fear eased itself from Silas's heart when he heard Belle's regret over a baby wasn't because of him. "I'll make sure you have time to do things the way you want with him, Belle. I know the girls have been raised different from most little girls, but I think they're perfect. I think they're the kind of women the West needs to tame it. I'm so proud of them, I'd like to bust every time I hear them call me Pa. And that makes you a wonderful mother."

"They are good girls, aren't they?"

"The very best. And remember I'll be here to make sure they don't get mixed up with any no-account husbands, so we won't have to worry about that." He kissed her again. "Speaking of the girls. . .where are they?"

"The girls promised to stay busy until I called them."

"Oh, yes. They are very good girls."

And that was the last word spoken in the Harden Ranch house for a long time.

EPILOGUE

Belle saw she'd had a boy seconds after his birth and looked at Silas with equal parts pride—at finally producing a son—and fear—at figuring out how to raise one.

"We'll just do exactly what you did with the girls, honey," Silas said.

She'd learned that the man could, on occasion, read her mind.

"They're all as tough and brave as we could ever hope our boy would be."

Tanner would need to be tough indeed to out-tough Betsy, Sarah, Emma, and Lindsay, but from the way he came into the world kicking and screaming, Belle suspected he was up to it.

One warm summer day Belle strapped her son on her back and took a ride to her old cabin. She guided her mount up that steep hill to the Husband Tree and sat to rest and have a little talk with her boy about what she expected in a man.

Tanner slept through it, but Belle had her talk with him anyway, just to get in practice raising a son. She wanted the boy to grow up remembering where his ma had come from and how little she'd had to start and how far a person could go with hard work.

Belle looked down on the pathetic cabin that she'd built with her skinned knuckles and insufficient strength so long ago.

"I can't bring myself to miss a single one of the no-account bums, including William, who I am most likely sitting on right now."

Tanner squirmed a bit in her arms but didn't wake up. "But I'm glad for what I went through, because surely only the steps I took led to the exact place I'm in right now with you and my daughters and your pa. And—sitting on William notwithstanding—it's a very good place."

Rocking Tanner gently, she marveled at the chance she now had to fuss with a baby and sing lullabies.

She saw Silas and watched as he spotted her and rode up to dismount.

"Missing your old husbands and that cabin, Belle honey?" Silas settled with his back against the Husband Tree and smiled right into Belle's light brown eyes.

"Not even one little bit." Belle leaned her shoulder against Silas's. "I'm thinking that I needed these husbands to get my girls. And if I hadn't had all girls and needed to hire cowhands, I'd have never gotten you. It worked out in the end, but could marrying these no-accounts have been part of God's plan?"

"I don't know if either of us took the direct route God had in mind, but in the end it led us both to a good place." Silas reached a work-calloused hand to cradle Tanner's head. It was covered with dark hair, and the boy had brown eyes.

Belle supposed she'd given birth to yet another child who looked just like his pa, but Belle could pretend the tyke looked like her if she wanted to.

"It's possible I needed to go through those early years to understand—or at least accept—the ways of God." Belle's words drew Silas's attention away from Tanner, and their matching brown eyes met and held.

Silas leaned forward until their lips met. "Well, however we got here, I like where we ended up real well."

They sat together talking. . .and not talking. . .for a long while.

Then Tanner woke up and kicked up a fuss.

They got up to head home.

Before she left, Belle patted the Husband Tree good-bye and good riddance.

ABOUT THE AUTHOR

MARY CONNEALY is a Christie Award finalist. She is the author of the Lassoed in Texas series, which includes *Petticoat Ranch*, *Calico Canyon*, and *Gingham Mountain*. She has also written a romantic cozy mystery trilogy, *Nosy in Nebraska*; and her novel *Golden Days* is part of the *Alaska Brides* anthology. You can find out more about Mary's upcoming books at www.maryconnealy.com and www.mconnealy.blogspot.com.

Mary lives on a Nebraska ranch with her husband, Ivan, and has four grown daughters: Joslyn (married to Matt), Wendy, Shelly (married to Aaron), and Katy. And she is the grandmother of one beautiful granddaughter, Elle.

Mary loves to hear from her readers. You may visit her at these sites: www.mconnealy.blogspot.com, www.seekerville.blogspot.com, and www.petticoatsandpistols.com. Write to her at mary@maryconnealy.com.